Meta
...

Christopher Latham

Copyright © 2011 Christopher Latham
All rights reserved.
ISBN: 1466308214
ISBN-13: 9781466308213

Table of Contents

Part I
    1. You're all bastards — 1
    2. The people's champion — 11
    3. No need of a nation — 23
    4. Break me — 31
    5. Never be alone — 39
    6. Say a few words — 47
    7. My love, you're terrifying me — 55
    8. Mortality has been known to blur — 63
    9. Mother watches over us — 79
    10. There's vampires now?! — 91
    11. To be God — 99
    12. Gift of freedom — 107

Part II
    13. Let's play mind games — 117
    14. Piercing the mist — 125
    15. You believe this? — 145
    16. Duty calls — 157
    17. What the hell is that? — 169
    18. The damned — 181
    19. Too young — 195
    20. Bloodline — 207
    21. Hearts and the wild — 215
    22. From visions to vows — 227
    23. The crucial blow — 235
    24. Unwarranted condemnations — 247

Part III
    25. Morning ashes — 257
    26. Unshackled — 271
    27. Invulnerable, remember? — 279

28. Everything works out   287
29. PARTAAAY!!!   295
30. I want to cry   303
31. So be it   311
32. To the fortress of the fallen angel   319
33. So many friends   331
34. Let's rock   339
35. Being   347
36. Whatever there is   359

AUTHOR'S NOTE

Fans of comic books will recognize much here. As will those dedicated to science fiction and fantasy novels. Bits of romance and political thriller have even trickled in. The aim was to shape them into something new. Whether it is any good remains to be seen.

* "Kryptonite" is a trademark of DC Comics.
* "Happy Meal" is a trademark of McDonald's Corp.

PART I

1

You're all bastards

"I've been called a great man. Even a god among men, whatever that means," says the pale, bearded redhead standing in the center of the aisle.

"But you guys. You humble me, and I'm grateful to call you family. I haven't been your boss for some time, but you continue to make me proud. This is good work you're doing. And if it happens to make us even more rich and famous, well, so be it."

He ends with a deep grin, sliding his hands into the pants pockets of his black suit, his green eyes sparkling. The short, svelte Indian woman by his side fixes his tie and slicks back a forward leaning tuft of hair at his ear. He caresses her maroon business jacket at the waist.

"Don't mind Samuel," she says to the seatbelt strapped quartet and the man splayed on the sofa. "He's not nearly as greedy as he sounds. Not anymore. He's gotten far too old for that."

Everyone laughs.

"Por supuesto, Señora Shaktira," says the man on the sofa. His arms rest along its top, a leg dangles over its side, and the scabbard strapped to his hip taps the floor. He is tanned and muscled and joyous. "We all know Mister Haine's a humanitarian now. You've finally worn him down."

Everyone laughs again.

"Shown me the light's a safer metaphor for both of us," Haine says. "Still I appreciate the compliment, Stefan. We have to get to the conference, so I'll leave you to it. Remember, the world will be watching."

"Hey, the same goes for you," Stefan says.

"Yes, but we have tact," Shaktira says. "Be well."

Then the holographic disc on the floor shuts its green eye and the smiling couple vanishes. The lean black man sitting next to Stefan opens his palm and the disc flies into his grasp. The black man passes it to the tall, gorgeous blond who has been caressing his thigh. She slides the disc into her bosom, where a sliver of dense circuitry flashes until the disc is inside her and a panel of milky flesh covers the sliver.

"Alright, chico," the black man says, undoing his seatbelt. "Game time. Ready to turn on the charm?"

"Come on, Will. Who am I?"

"A ham?" asks the scrawny Indonesian boy on the other side of the aisle. He sports a black T-shirt under a shiny red and yellow tracksuit. The T-shirt bears the letters EWE on his chest. On his shoulders, the tracksuit sports a logo resembling an inverted Omega with a smaller Delta nestled in its bowl. "A greasy ham?" the boy adds.

"Watch it, Oke," Stefan says as he shakes his long wooden scabbard, which is painted black and sprinkled with starlike flakes of white. "You're only along for the ride. Don't make me break out Simmer."

"Please," Oke says. "I'm as famous as any of you. And how many times do I have to remind you, call me Oh. As in, 'Oh. He's hot fire.' Like they say online."

The petite, rosy cheeked brunette at his side pats his shoulder.

"Sorry, Pumpkin," she says, "but I wouldn't waste my breath on these guys. Anyway tags should be earned. Not demanded. No offense, Zenith."

"None taken, Phase," the blond says. "I chose my name. The police chose yours. We know who we are."

"See, Pumpkin? Listen to the machine. It knows."

"Mom!" Oke whines at the brunette. "If that sword has a name, shouldn't you guys have codenames? Like heroes?"

"Doctors don't need codenames," William says.

"This coming from someone with the last name of Powers," Stefan snickers as he springs from the sofa, stretches wide, and pops his shirt collar. "So are we gonna get off this bird or what? My public awaits."

"The kid's only half right," William says as the cabin door opens. "You're also a turkey."

"Yeah, well, the world can't get enough of me. What do you call that?"

"Spam," Zenith says as they step out of the jet and onto the staircase before the paparazzi-lined red carpet.

• • •

The Japanese man in the black leather jacket hunches on a stool at the Ataraxia Bar & Grille, thinning his seventh lager in an hour. From behind the bar, the old fat woman with the ridiculous platinum blond wig flits about too busily to question how someone of such average height and slight build remains sober. Her place has been packed since noon. Although the summer concert thumps at nearby Hyde Park, the Ataraxia's dozen oversized monitors have lured a motley bunch of music lovers, celebrity groupies, meta sympathizers, and substance abusers in need of company to the mahogany laden dive at Broadway and Dacre.

All eyes fix on the monitors as Stefan leads his crew onto the stage before the hundreds of thousands of drunken, drugged, and/or MV infected Londoners. Applause erupts in the park and the bar as he leaps sixty feet into the air, well past the fluorescent green "Meta Aid" banner that arches over gigantic tiled screens zoomed in on his companions, cheers persisting as he flips every which way on his descent and lands in a salsa, swiveling to the percussive beat of their "Meta Force" theme music blaring from the stage's towering speakers. Claps and whistles subside as Stefan runs fingers through his light brown locks, then approaches the microphone and croons, "Te amo, world. Te amo."

The Japanese man rolls his eyes and orders an eighth. Still fixed on the main monitor, the bartender fills him a mug, somehow cutting the stream before it overflows.

"That Steffy," she coos. "He's my favorite customer."

He gulps while assessing Stefan's ochre locks, hazel eyes, and square jaw. He resolves to delay the inevitable.

"Don't be jealous, Harry," she says, glancing at his empty mug. "You're my second. And I've known you a week."

• • •

Five bodies disappear from a lush backstage dressing room and fill what had an instant ago been an empty jet cabin. Stefan pulls Oke off his shoulder and straps him into a window seat as Phase paces the aisle, gesticulating to her own irate mumbles.

"Faye, relax," William says as he presses on the boy's eyelids and stares into his unconscious, dilated pupils. "His pulse and breathing are fine. It's not like he ODed."

"And he damn sure had a good time," Stefan says.

"Shut up," Phase says, teleporting from the other side of the cabin to within an inch of Stefan's face. "You introduced him to that non-acting, sings like a dying cat, Bacchus addicted hussy, so this is your fault."

"May I make an observation?" Zenith asks.

"No," Phase replies.

"You are his legal guardian," Zenith continues. "You brought him along. So he is your responsibility. However, his invulnerability to permanent physical damage, and P.R.'s knowledge that Miss Drench will allow none of that to air, should minimize the negative repercussions."

"Thank you. Now go lube your joints."

The two women break their mutual glares when the boy jerks awake, eyes bulged, mouth bent in a frantic grin, and he grabs Zenith's wrist.

"Becca! Becca! Just got the best idea for a game! You'll love it! LOVE IT!"

Then he passes back out in his seat.

"Look, Faye," William says, pulling her aside. "He has to grow up sooner or later. Hanging around us forces it to be sooner. He hasn't had a normal life. He's never going to have a normal life. So he got drunk. So he snorted a little. So he licked a pop star's tit. He's 13, he's a meta, he's a videogame god, and his guardian's on the Net's number one reality show. Take it from your resident neurologist. He'll get over it. We have to set him straight, that's all. And by the way, don't you think you took it too far, teleporting Monique to the Arctic?"

"Like the machine says, that can be edited out ... It was barely freezing ... The little slut's so high she probably thinks it was a dream ... It was for six minutes!"

"Good thing," Stefan says, flopping onto the sofa. "That polar bear seemed hungry."

They take their seats, settling into themselves. Phase fusses with Oke's hair and seatbelt, presses her cheek to his forehead, wipes red flakes from his upper lip. William strokes Zenith's fingers. Stefan folds arms, shuts eyes, and soon drools and snores in contented sleep ...

The jet gets minutes out of Heathrow for LAX when everyone jolts at NeuroNet alarms ringing in their heads. Zenith's irises flash like lightbulbs and the holographic disc pops out of her bosom. William levitates it to the floor in the center of the aisle. A wrinkled, gray haired woman sprouts from the eye of the disc. Her legs spread wide, her fists dig into her hips, and her top teeth bite her bottom lip. This is her natural state. They sense her anger anyway.

"Hola, Karen," Stefan yawns, not bothering to sit up. "You catch the concert?"

"I saw a lot more than that, Mister Reyes," she shouts, bending forward at a near right angle. "I saw a minor breaking several laws. I saw a licensed member of Executive Warriors Elite, our only agent with a rap sheet the size of a book, mind you, violating restrictions on use of her powers. I saw you screwing with starlets when you should have been pushing for meta registration. That's not in the job description for charity host."

"We pushed, Señora Drench. We read the script. And those chicas screwed me. I just obliged."

"Enough. P.R. knows he's got serious editing to do ... We have bigger problems. The U.N. went wrong. Very wrong. I'll let the general explain."

Drench fades out. A black woman takes her place. The wedged jaw, fatigues, and blue beret mark her as much harder if not quite as old.

"Good day," she says. "General Glenda Rodan. United Nations Military Adviser, Head of Peacekeeping Operations. This is not a drill. The U.N. Headquarters was taken hostage at 14:30 hours New York time by an armed force at least a thousand strong that appeared out of nowhere. They claim to be members of The Way, quote, 'Taking a stand for techno anarchism against republican plutocracy.' The terrorists cut communications to the three major buildings. Including where the General Assembly is being held along with European Union President James Windsor, World Monetary Fund Director Samuel F. Haine, and his wife, Ana Shaktira.

"Haine had just endorsed Windsor's suggestion to require tracking systems in all NeuroNet upgrades. Shaktira was pitching the Assembly on universal healthcare. Then all hell broke loose. Hostages have also been taken at Central Park, Times Square, the Federal Reserve, and Grand Central Terminal, each guarded by a terrorist force of about a thousand. Surveillance shows each team is led by a known meta perp with ties to The Way. Except for the U.N. team, for which we have no video.

"It seems to be under the control of an unknown who's sending distorted audio clips to the Associated Press through an encrypted NeuroNet link. Goes by 'Hikikomori.' The latest clip states that an ambassador will be executed every hour until, quote, 'oppressor nations vow to cancel the debt of oppressed nations and free all political prisoners held for pursuing an end to corporate slavery under false representation.' One ambassador has allegedly been killed.

"N.Y.P.D. and U.S. National Guard are at the sites. They can't attack without high civilian casualties. Due to your track record, power levels, and private sector status, you mercs are unofficially asked by the U.S. government and Windsor's counterparts in the Council of Continents to neutralize all perps by any means necessary. I repeat, this is real. It's no stunt for your 'Meta Force' cameras."

The hologram of Rodan disappears. In her place flicker mug shots and bios of the four known metas, along with architectural layouts of the hostage sites. Then Drench reappears in her natural posture, albeit noticeably calmer.

"As head of the EWE division of Haine International, it's my duty to stress that you're under no obligation to accept," she says. "Trust me, I've no desire to endanger my cash cows. Although imagine the ratings ... Mister Haine has technically been out of our sphere ever since he left this company two years ago to head the W.M.F. Regardless, he, Ana, King James, and many others will die unless you can pull a miracle. Show of hands. Who's in, who's out?"

The random cough, temple rub, sidelong glance, and moan ruin a full minute of otherwise cryptlike calm.

"This counts as overtime, right?" Stefan asks at last. "And no more edible bonuses. Unless you feed us royalties."

His hand rises. Everyone follows.

"Put your hand down, Pumpkin," Phase says.

"Ah come on, Ma," Oke replies. "You need me."

"He's right," Drench says. "Five sites, five metas. He's trained with you all. He's better than half of you. We have neither the time to find a substitute nor anyone else as powerful. And, in case you forget, he was your accomplice when you were stealing from this company. Consider it redress. We've been grooming him from Day One. Why else did you think you were pardoned?"

"Absolutely not!" Phase shouts. "He's mine, not yours. I'm not risking his life when you've got hundreds of other metas on the payroll. And, hello, he's under age!"

"Faye, given what's going down, that's the last thing on the list," Stefan says. "As field commander, I'd rather have him than anybody else."

Phase blinks out of her seatbelt and that instant reappears in Stefan's face, clenching his popped collar.

"Stefan, most days I find your dumb ass comments charming. This is not one of those days. Shut. Up."

"I have to back him on this one," William chimes in. "The way I see it, we may die tonight. That's fine. It's in our contracts. But the boy won't. I don't think he can. Faye, we'll guide him on the Net. He may mess up, but that goes for any of us. This is bigger than us. It's about the rule of law.

Innocent people. So what are you going to protect? The world, or your world?"

Phase snarls something furious at the two men and the holographic image, covers her mouth with her fist and shakes her head.

"... You're all bastards," she says as she reclaims her seat. "Pumpkin, pay very close attention."

2

The people's champion

William Powers levitates from the clouds, taking in anthills that grow into skyscrapers as he descends, then the hordes of rapt faces peering out from office windows, as he touches ground amid the mob in One Times Square.

A thousand terrorists point firearms at cowering hostages who had barely noticed one another hours before, when they bumped their way toward stores and restaurants and their big concern was the commute home. The gunmen are well aware of the human police, the low level meta SWAT team, and the very human looking cyberclone National Guardsmen swarming around them on foot and in helicopters and tanks. But they are oblivious to the black man in the white dress shirt and khakis walking among them.

Rendering their senses unable to detect him comes as effortlessly as reading their minds. He knows that these black-clad sentries each bearing a machete, machine gun, laser pistol, grenade, infrared goggles, and mind-control resistant face helmet are in fact a single meta. Manfred Peebles, 29, a.k.a. Manny. At war with the inequities of global poverty and disease, capable of duplicating himself and inorganic objects to the order of 5,000 times at the successive snaps of his fingers.

William also knows the hostages have been cut off from the NeuroNet for hours, ever since the Mannys waved little blinking rods at the base of the hostages' cerebellums and flipped off the plastic switch on back of their necks. He does not need to read minds for this. Thousands of grown men and women cry about it. That they cannot finish their work, watch their shows, play their games, buy their stuff, and chat online until their beloved microchips reboot. One lady begs for execution rather than endure the isolation. Several men offer to join the terrorists if reconnected.

They too are blind to William. Not so for the glowing woman made of dancing cyan lightning. She had not been there an instant ago. That's all it took for her bolt to strike from the heavens, singeing street asphalt scant feet from William. Mannys turn to her in befuddlement, asking their commander why she curses the ether.

Rodan's dossier lists Emily Chagnon, 32, a.k.a. Em, as a French agent of the Animal and Environmental Liberation Front, a meta capable of wielding and becoming the electromagnetic spectrum. She proves it by hurling scores of cyan bolts at William's head. His telekinetic aura blocks them inches from his face and scatters the lightning onto hundreds of Mannys posted around a two block radius. Sentries fall in smoking, spasmodic heaps. William explodes telepathic sleep bombs on the rest, collapsing hundreds more. His nose trickles blood under stress of their helmets and her blinding light.

Em proves tougher. Her body transforms back into a massive bolt and rams him into the upper story of a building, dislodging brick and steel, then takes him for another ride, across the street and into the electronic "Meta Force" billboard flashing high on Times Square Tower. William swoons from the voltage, cracked ribs, and strain of levitating tons of debris lest it crush both the newly freed, stampeding mob and those dumbstruck civilians already getting trampled by their fellows. *Ah, herd mentality. You never fail*, he surmises.

His skull pounds as he floats out of the fiery cavern that had borne portraits of him and his peers. He resolves to end the fight while the opportunity remains, while Em hovers before him. William surrounds her glowing body with the debris, grinding it into powder and filament. She tries to bolt but an invisible bubble traps her with the stuff, fills with water jetting skyward from fire hydrants toppled just for her. Cyan bolts ricochet around the flooded conductive sphere until a flesh and blood woman flails within, choking on water and salt and metal.

The brackish pool flies for the East River like some giant, amorphous amoeba as William lands, carrying soaked and dazed Em. He drops the nude terrorist and doubles over, clutching his ribs as cyberclone Guardsmen rush in with rifles and syringes. The Mannys have dissolved into dust. William thanks Stefan for that via the Net. Panting and prone, he asks Em if she realizes that she is pregnant. She glares at him in dismay as power-numbing serum flows into her jugular. And the very human looking machine squeezing the syringe cares not in the least about any of this.

. . .

Oke Yip cannot help but shout while perched atop the information booth in the main concourse of Grand Central Terminal. He watches a man direct Mannys to execute seven hostages. The doomed kneel with hands behind their heads. This man glows bifurcated by a slice of white light, his left side all ice, his right pure fire. Yet somehow his curly, silver mane and walrus mustache seem to be genuine hairs. The terrorists pay the anxious boy no heed, for he cooes his bird brained head off in the form of a gray and white pigeon.

The team has been stuffing him with so many tips ever since he flapped from the jet that he almost wishes his

NeuroNet chip had deactivated when he morphed. But only almost, and only when he ignores those below, who sob about their lost connections as they risk point blank bullets to the face. Phase had advised he disguise himself. Zenith had advised he stay still unless attacked. William had advised he attack if hostages were threatened. Stefan had advised he adopt the terrorists' powers upon attack. Oke now advises they let him play.

So the pigeon flaps up to the black-clad sentry at the southwest corner of the balcony, perches on his masked skull, craps, then flaps off to the nearest bathroom, where it morphs into the terminal's 1,001st Manny. He races downstairs to find a hostage lying in a puddle of her own blood. Not videogame blood. Dark, syrupy, rancid, human blood leaking onto his boots. A machine gun sprays the thermal man standing over the body. Only when an icy arm shatters on the floor does the boy realize he pulled the trigger. Varappa curses about working with amateurs, grows a new arm, and pitches a flame cloud at the panicked child.

Oke opens the Net to view Rodan's dossier one last time. Varappa Daku, 47, "nigh invulnerable" Nepalese assassin for any cause that pays well enough, capable of manipulating vast temperature extremes. The boy feels his skin blister amid the inferno. He morphs into adolescent fire and the Net dies. Phase's last tip: Rip him apart.

Meanwhile the Mannys shoot dead three more hostages in the wake of the ruse. Oke, awash in molten tears, prepares to burn the murderers. But then, inexplicably, the Mannys all turn to dust. Survivors scatter. As soon as the first wave of hostages breaks away the National Guard breaks in through the windows.

Varappa studies the flaming boy with marked amusement as cyberclones surround them. The terrorist exhales, immediately caking the concourse and all its inhabitants in ice, then rides a blazing pillar out of a busted balcony window. It takes Oke quite a few seconds to build enough heat to defrost himself and the others. Hostages tumble shivering into cyberclone arms as he rides his own fiery pillar through the steam and gives chase to an orange streak cutting across the Manhattan skyline. All the while he envisions those four bullet riddled corpses.

Oke catches Varappa above Union Square. The terrorist, now split horizontally by the light, sprays icy pikes and boulders that grow from his palms as he skirts the park's treetops. A dozen elms roast under the conflagration trailing from his legs. Oke dodges ice while becoming, head to toe, the properties of his durium pinky ring. From his back sprout metallic, silvery wings. He flaps in front of Varappa while elongating arms into durium tendrils and hands into paper thin axes. The planet's hardest substance swings through the white light of Oke's enemy. Varappa's frozen eyes bulge as flaming legs separate from his torso. Axes morph into fat metal spheres that encase the falling halves. Oke's right hand threatens to melt and his left to crack, until temperatures subside.

He wonders much in that span. *What the hell just happened?! What the hell does "invulnerable" mean? Why the hell did I raise my hand?!* He morphs his brain back to normal and activates the Net. Phase suggests he chuck body parts into the river. Oke instead obeys Stefan's order to morph a second pair of eyes inside the spheres. Therein blobs of ice and fire recede into limp flesh appendages. He instinctively crushes the spheres into small, durium fists oozing blood. The newborn killer vomits twice on his winged return to Grand Central, feeling far too sober.

• • •

Faye "Phase" Zamair goes invisible before teleporting from the jet streaking above the Atlantic Ocean. On the corner of Water and Maiden she follows the gaggle of siren blaring N.Y.P.D. cars and megaphone booming National Guard trucks, past dozens of homeless lining the sidewalk, until the Federal Reserve Bank of New York towers before her. Mannys aim machine guns and laser pistols out the windows of the fifteen level fortress. She decides the world's largest stockpile of gold ought not be in the heart of a city. *I'd have emptied every dirty little bar by now*, she muses, shaking her invisible head at the ineptitude.

The bank's layout appears in an enhanced reality window on her Net linked contact lenses, a 3D digital blueprint overlapping the actual building. Phase peruses the links to each floor before blinking inside. It takes under a minute to blink around and scope the posts of all thousand sentries. Their guns keep employees trembling in cubicles while the bank's bullet riddled cyberclone security guards litter the halls. Phase teleports outside the vault. Its circular durium door hangs gaping. Scores of Mannys stand watch there, as well as past the door and down the corridor, behind a wall of crisscrossing laser beams.

She goes intangible and walks into the vault. Stacks of gold bars sit in open cages lining the walls. A bald, bare chested black man in flip flops and billowy pantaloons yanks bar after bar from a cage, stuffing the loot into two duffel bags. He slings a bulging sack over each shoulder. The wall of lasers flicker and he too seemingly teleports away. Phase needs neither the Net nor Rodan's dossier for this one. Harod Lbeki, 39. Nigerian thief for hire capable of lifting almost a ton and speeds exceeding 15,000 miles per hour. Her former partner and lover.

He reappears a few seconds later with empty bags. She goes visible and calls his name. Harod spins round to see every Manny in the vault fire at her. Their shots pass through her white spandex speedsuit as through air. He orders them cease and rushes to her, brushes fingers through her intangible brown locks and begs her to leave. She fights the urge to ask why he abandoned her four years ago. She does, however, question his choice in company. Harod steps away, mumbling that life has gotten too messy for credos.

Then he runs round, ringing her ears with sonic booms, dazing her such that she turns solid, crumpling her and every Manny in the vault under whirlwinds. He lofts her by the throat and again begs her to leave. The deafened woman looks away and blinks into her semisolid state. Electrical signals misfire throughout his nervous system and Harod writhes to the floor. Those Mannys who have recuperated shoot again. Phase blinks round the vault, then the building, shocking every sentry so their limbs writhe and their faces twitch as they fall useless. Seconds later she returns to the vault, to the downed man of glazed eyes and wobbling head. She helps Harod sit up. She caresses his scalp the way she used to. He swings wild, slapping her in the mouth and across the room. She slams into gold stacked high in an open cage, rolls over spitting blood.

He slurs apologies as she blinks on him. They reappear hovering outside, where she drops him the height of the building. Phase blinks down to find him lying inert on the newly cracked sidewalk, bleeding from his facial organs. Hostages burst out the doors shouting that terrorists have turned to dust. The National Guard storms in as Phase squats beside Harod. Faint pulse at his wrist and fainter breaths. She holds him to her chest as a cyberclone stabs him in the neck with a syringe full of Metapurge. Harod sobs and trembles as she explains that in seconds his powers will fade. Phase expects to lay there quietly with her love, aching from his blows. Until he apologizes again, this time for never confessing his infection.

• • •

Rebecca "Zenith" Farmer hovers miles above Central Park pinpointing the positions of every terrorist and hostage below with the telescopic focus of her optical receptors. Eyeballs, she would have called them twenty years ago, when she was human. *How primitive*, she thinks, now that so long has passed since her flesh and blood were fried to crisp and her consciousness uploaded to a computer of her own design. Yet here she is in an idealized form of her original body, firing lasers from nozzles of her robot fingertips, drilling beams through skulls of a thousand Mannys, as tiny jet engines blast from her bare heels.

Hostages flee 12.7 seconds after her initial attack, flawless in its speed and precision. Zenith touches ground in her lime evening gown at the center of the Great Lawn three seconds after her final strike. She aims her fingers at the muscled, purple behemoth snarling before her in brown overalls.

Rodan's dossier lists Janus Galton, 43, as an Argentinean bioengineer obsessed with evolving humanity into meta cyborgs, himself a meta capable of lifting in excess of 650 tons and leaping at least five miles in a single bound, possessing bulletproof skin and a second head hidden behind a gray durium mask on his chest. What he lacks is the ability to shut the eyes of his exposed head before plasma lasers gut them. Same for that gargantuan mouth, victim of a baseball sized missile exploding within.

Janus belches smoke as he stumbles backward, slumps to a knee, and splays belly up. The missile launcher sinks back into the skin on Zenith's forearm, the nozzles on her fingertips twirl shut. She steps through the piles of dissolving terrorists and turns to the hostages who have not fled, offering to restore their NeuroNet links. Cheers erupt as park goers line up, ecstatic to rejoin the virtual world. One by one, Zenith flips their switches and emits the requisite low frequency signal from her palm into the base of their skulls. Authorities once held at bay soon march from tree lined walking paths. Cyberclones huddle over Janus and begin inspecting curious ash piles that once were Mannys while police tend to traumatized civilians.

Eight minutes into Net restorations, during an officer's attempt to ask Zenith for her autograph, a tidal wave of earth flings humans and cyberclones like bedbugs. Janus stands, legs shaking, exposed head drooping unconscious, a Metapurge syringe jutting from his neck, as maniacal laughter emanates from the durium mask on his chest. Zenith's barrage of lasers and missiles hit his mask and hide yet penetrate neither. Janus charges her faster than anything that big should manage. Palms clasped, he smashes her jaw and down to her clavicle. She smacks the ground and a massive purple foot stomps her chest.

Artificial pink flesh hangs from the bludgeoned parts of her shell, revealing a shimmering durium skeleton. The pistons in Zenith's arms shove Janus off. She rises, only to have him grab her by the leg and swing her from side to side, banging her into the ground, creating body sized cavities all about him. Then he lifts her and squeezes, bear hugging until her ribs buckle, growling and cackling throughout. Her sensory receptors dim. Her homeostatic monitor warns that her solar battery will deactivate in 17.486 seconds.

Precious seconds fade as Zenith struggles to wedge her hands around the mask. With six seconds remaining she opens her palm speakers to their ultrasonic limit. Janus releases her 4.23 seconds later, flopping on his back, mask ajar, revealing a dead purple face bleeding brain from its ears. Zenith's optical receptors capture four cyberclones dragging her away from Janus. Her audio receptors capture hostages pleading for medical attention. *Will–*, she thinks, as all signals crash.

• • •

Stefan Reyes had enjoyed the rescue. Jumping from the jet, diving two miles sans parachute, and crashing a 39th floor window of Secretariat Tower at the United Nations had been a breeze. As had running through every room at hyper speed. Bludgeoning Mannys with kicks and punches. Flinging stone statues at them. Crushing steel doors into giant bowling balls and striking terrorists like pins. Whatever came to mind while dodging lasers and catching bullets and freeing office workers. He did the same in the Hammarskjöld Library before taking the General Assembly Building.

Less than half a minute had elapsed from the window to the dais where Haine, Shaktira, and James were forced to lay face down beside the executed ambassadors to Saudi Arabia and Sudan. Not a Manny saw him zip around the hall to pummel them. Not even the original, who stood above the bound and gagged trio on the dais. That one had been imploring Shaktira and Haine to stop bickering over how to end terrorism. She had insisted that "realistic" living wages and free universal healthcare would negate The Way's ability to gain acolytes, he that the path was through uncensored information via the NeuroNet. On impact, Stefan's right cross put Manny in a coma and dissolved his 5,000 duplicates. Stefan had chuckled when Windsor interrupted the lovers' spat to thank their rescuer. He guffawed when Haine and Shaktira found the manners to do the same. The 192 surviving ambassadors had applauded.

"The people's champion," Haine called him.

That had been the easy part. Now comes Hell. He feels the ache at his temples and the sting in his heart and he knows. It has been years since he last felt the presence and he would give his life to not feel it now. The ambassador to Mexico climbs the stage to shake Stefan's hand, saying Stefan's father would be proud, complimenting him on being such an upstanding meta, asking whether he chooses his own clothes or the show has some fashion expert that picked out his chic floral patterned shirt and denim jeans. Stefan mumbles about cultivating his mojo before leaping across the hall and breaking through the ceiling.

He takes his time, walks at normal speed, even sips at a water fountain, while tracing the pull to a second floor office overlooking the East River. He finds his brother staring out the window.

The muscular Asian man clad in gray sweater and gray jeans warns Stefan not to call him "Hickey." Stefan refuses to call him "Hikikomori." They settle on his birth name. Stefan asks, pointlessly, whether his brother is responsible for this abomination. Hikikomori nods and boasts that he is The Way. That the onslaught of human greed nears its end. That his brother ought to join him in saving the world, as their fathers would have wanted, instead of groveling at the boots of oppressors. Stefan asks when exactly his brother lost his mind. Hikikomori sneers, then turns to open the window.

He gets half way out before Stefan grabs his shoulder. They lurch back inside, reaching for their fathers' blades as they crash into a desk. Stefan unsheathes the durium katana on his back, Hikikomori the two durium tantos strapped to his thighs. It has been barely four minutes since Stefan noticed his brother's presence. Three minutes ago they could have hurled locomotives like baseballs or withstood nuclear explosions. Now a blade could prove agonizing. This he knows from experience. Why this should be, he neither knows nor cares.

They stalk each other in circles, finally leaping in unison. A frenzy of metallic sparks yields to Hikikomori's straight, foot-long daggers gashing Stefan's calf and kidney. Slender, curved Simmer ruptures Hikikomori's spleen. They continue their circles in crimson trailed crawls, panting and cursing in Spanish and Korean. Until Hikikomori pulls a grenade from his pocket, yanks the pin, and drags himself to the window. Stefan rolls behind the desk as his brother heaves himself out the window and the grenade plops on the floor.

The office churns from Stefan's vantage, with paper and plaster wafting aflame through the air and the window blowing to a charred hole in the wall. He wriggles from behind the smoking desk and peers over the edge of the hole. Only Coast Guard boats in the river and ambassadors streaming along pavement to indifferent cyberclones. *Maldiga, Jin,* Stefan thinks. *Couldn't just send a card?*

3

No need of a nation

"Millions in property damage. Damn near 60 million in gold stolen. Thirteen dead, including two ambassadors. And the source of this historic travesty, your ... unbelievable ... your brother ... escaped," Rodan says. The general paces while shaking her bereted head at Stefan as though he is a mud caked toddler. Her right leg, the robotic one, clanks plastic on metal at each step. "Be happy these two are alive," she says, batting a hand at Haine and James. "And that President Finley here considers the mission a success. Your show's second season would not have survived trials before both a U.S. federal court and The Hague."

"Señora Jefe," Stefan lilts as he swivels on his chair in the Oval Office, putting his back to Rodan and facing the president of the United States with legs spread wide, "is that what Glenda the butch witch here meant when she said we were unofficially asked to save your tails? That we'd have gotten tickets to The Hole if we'd botched it?"

"You probably would have been acquitted," Gloria Finley says from her couch while Haine and James whisper to each other on the opposing sofa. "The official word is that the U.N. contracted with Executive Warriors Elite for just such an occasion. America allowed your counterstrike to foster a multilateral initiative against The Way. I'll have none of the cowboy nonsense that provoked the Terror Wars."

"Prudent," James says while running a hand through his blond locks. "And of course the only way it could be."

"Pardon?" Finley asks.

"Ignore me. I'm still in shock."

"Understandable," Haine agrees. "I'm amazed we're alive. I don't know what I'd have done had something happened to Ana. I'd have died insulted had you not rescued us, Stefan."

Haine walks over and cups his pale hands on Stefan's chin. This prompts the younger man to stand and draw his old friend into a hug. They stay there, hugging with cheeks pressed, long enough for the others to feel thoroughly awkward and slightly unnecessary.

"Seriously, we owe you," Haine says as he returns to the sofa. "And orchestrating four other rescues in under a half hour! Must be nice to be both the fastest and strongest man alive."

"De nada," Stefan says while sitting. "It's my job."

"And it's my job to grill you until you stripe," Rodan says. "But that's for later. For now, tell them what you told me yesterday. Brace yourselves."

Stefan slouches forward, pushing his backward turned chair with his chest. He rubs his palms for a while, studying the eagle on the carpet as he does so. Then he gets up and walks to the window, taking small joy in his attire, how his jeans and tight floral shirt clash with the three in business suits and the black woman in military fatigues. He all but whispers as he stares outside.

"You know, Jin and I got along. I blame the media for what happened to him. So our fathers founded an expat prep school in Pyongyang. So what? Why was that always in the news? Just because my dad was a former U.N. ambassador from Mexico and his used to run Korea's central intel? The media never left Mom alone either. But really, what's so special about an American oil heiress donating to start a school? Coverage should have ended when she died during labor. But all those stories about Mom the hippie. 'Pregnant by two men at the same time. Men she introduced to each other. Men who took her money to start a cult.' Growing up with those lies ... Still, we got used to it. Almost felt normal.

"What never felt normal is the part you don't know. When the meta wave hit, thing is, Jin and I were already metas. Unlike everyone else, we were born this way. Much weaker before it hit, but still much stronger and faster than others. So were our dads. They liked to tell us they were very distant relatives to each other, as were their fathers and so on. Don't know why they thought that. But then nobody knows why the meta wave happened.

"Tabloids are already rehashing the rest. As if anyone forgot that our dads died along with a million others the day of the wave? ... Jin wasn't the only 15 year old who would have run away ..."

Stefan looks back into the Oval Office as he trails off. James, Finley, and Haine sit normally enough, legs folded or hands clasped. Their faces are patient and attentive. Yet something about them makes Stefan consider bursting out the window for the ends of the Earth. Instead he at last gets to the point.

"Look, the insanity began before the wave. Jin once showed me this letter. It looked like his dad's handwriting but he refused to say where he got it. It went on about how Haine International was a corrupt monopoly that had to be stopped. Jin kept saying, 'Somebody should do it. It's the only way.' I forgot about it after the wave. I mean, Taedo Academy closed. Jin split. I moved in with Mom's sisters in Texas. A decade passed before I gave that note another thought.

"It was that first bid on Sam's life that I prevented. Maybe I went to work for you tracking down rogue metas hoping to run into Jin. Should have connected the dots when The Way hit a few years back ... None of that explains how my brother lost his mind."

"Good God," James mutters after a while. "Ah, don't blame yourself. You couldn't have known."

"Yes. Thank you, Stefan," Haine adds. "That must have been brutal to share."

"Don't thank him yet," Rodan says as she resumes pacing the office. "He's going to recount every crumb on this Hikikomori, as Jin Myeong calls himself. On Taedo Academy. On his family. On there being goddamn metas before the goddamn wave. And on how he let this sonovabitch get away. I don't know if I buy this fading powers excuse. And since he's immune to telepathy somebody's going to have to decide if we should take his word that it's been twenty years since he's seen his brother. His twin."

"¡Hasta la madre, cyborg puta! I'm no terrorist!"

"Stefan, sit down!" Haine shouts, standing from the sofa and grabbing him by the forearm. "It's not like she called your mother a whore! Not that anyone thinks that, of course. Madam President, please excuse him. He doesn't intend to demean this office."

Haine rubs Stefan on the back, tenderly, while showing him to a chair. James uses the pause to lift his lanky frame. He whispers with Rodan until she excuses herself, then returns to the sofa and clears his throat.

"Gloria, about what I said earlier. Forgive me for being blunt, but having a gun to my head and someone else's blood on my cheek has sapped my reserve ... Gloria the Restraint Amendment made sense back when you had a lunatic in this office. I fear, and God save me for saying this, but I fear that Congress has grown too powerful."

"¡Agua va, the crown comes out!" Stefan says. "Don't worry. My contacts and ear mics are off."

Haine shoots him a look that he hasn't seen in two years. Stefan coughs and looks away while running fingers through his light brown locks.

"I mean that Congress is too divided to be responsible for approving every single action you propose," James says. "We're fighting an enemy that feeds on division. If Stef–if Myeong is behind The Way, he's a genius. For the name alone. It defies logic that he's recruited such a diverse group. The techno anarchists are his doing, I'm sure. But the zealots? Of every faith? The Luddite collectivists? The Luddite anarchists? Doubtful. Bloody hell, even organized crime syndicates are calling themselves The Way. That blasted name is a rallying cry for any radical with access to the Net. And considering their hacking jobs, he's got to be a master programmer or has a gift for recruiting them. Technology and ideologies are changing too fast to wait for Congress to catch up."

"I'd be careful if I were you," Finley says. "I'm damn sure in a tough spot as the first female president to serve after the amendment. They call me a Feminazi whenever I assert myself. But you're in a tougher spot, Your Highness. Stefan's right about that crown. A decade ago nobody would have dreamed the king of Great Britain would renounce his throne and win election as prime minister. A year ago nobody would have expected the prime minister to follow his terms by becoming president of the European Union.

"James, it isn't 2050 anymore. You aren't the head of some confederacy. As, apparently, you think I am. Doesn't it worry you that a great many people hate that you in particular lead the most powerful economy in the world? I think you're forgetting your place. You don't dictate U.S. policy. I don't dictate U.S. policy. Even Congress doesn't dictate

U.S. policy. The people do. And it would take serious campaigning to get them behind me on this."

"Again, forgive me, Madam President," James says, not quite suppressing a grin that blossoms crow's feet by his eyes. "I've one more point if you'll allow it."

"Go on," she replies. Her arms cross and eyes narrow.

"Europe is the economic leader thanks to this man," he says, pointing at Haine. "The media is right to call him 'the king in no need of a nation.' Nobody else could have played the markets so deftly. From investments in a few dilapidated firms to the world's first true corporate superpower. Recall that when the E.U. imploded it didn't get fixed overnight. The economy was shaky as salt for decades until Sam stepped up. Think about what it means that his former company is on every continent and provides virtually every service. That Haine International employs more people than the combined populations of several countries. What it means to have created the meta drugs three years ago, the NeuroNet eight years ago, cyberclones before that, durium before that, and viable solar energy before that."

"We do live on this planet. Why the history lesson?"

"Because I'm about to put my cards on the table. He's the scapegoat. As are we. General Rodan said it best. The attack on New York was historic. This is a different beast. When metas hold the world hostage, it paints them as the enemy. Today I envy the East Asian Union for being the military leader. Thank God the North American Union is the close runner up in both categories. But the Caliphate and the E.A.U. are getting richer by the minute. We let them build resources by digging into Africa. We let them get nukes. We miscalculated on religion and oil. The Middle Eastern Union is a cohesive threat because we balked.

"We shouldn't be debating twenty years after the wave if we're in a biological arms race or searching for a cure to spontaneous mutation. After the U.N. assault, Europe must pursue the former. Sooner or later the Caliphate's going to figure out metas are not demons. Meanwhile every day Africa slips further into genocide, The Way gets more recruits. And you know the E.A.U. is building 'secret' meta labs from Tokyo to Bombay. They're using clone technology created by Haine International. Europe must do the same. These are too many fronts to fight alone. God willing, the South American Union will follow however you lead. We need America. I need you, Madam President, to be on my side."

"You're a bold one, Your Highness," Finley says. "You know full well that the amendment was about more than some 'lunatic in this office.' That compromise saved this union. The free will question over cyberclones, courtesy of Haine International, thank you very much, was getting people blown up. As were illegal immigration and corporate deregulation, again provoked by that company's hiring and acquisition policies. People were even getting shot over censorship of shows and videogames, many put out by guess who? Letting states' rights prevail was far from ideal, but it worked damn it. Not to scapegoat you, Sam. But let's not act like you're a saint because your heart's begun to bleed in your old age.

"Now let's play hypothetical. The first step would be to capitalize on sympathy. Push your plan for GPS and data mining on NeuroNet chips. We could start hunting The Way. Although anti meta sentiment will dissuade many from registering. As for the virus, I'd like to think Haine International would reciprocate all the mandatory Net upgrade contracts they'll get by funding research to finally get this epidemic in check. Having twenty percent of the world's 83 million metas infected only fuels public animosity. That pushes both sides toward The Way. Sam?"

"I'll speak to Cornelio," Haine says. "He's running the company well but an MV cocktail would certainly boost the stock price. My main concern is that Corny won't appreciate interference, what with my initiatives at the World Monetary Fund. However moderate my opposition to high-risk high-stipulation loans, he's dead set against my support for debt relief. Not to mention tariffs, price controls, subsidies, and pegged exchange rates benefiting developing nations. He doesn't like to admit that the W.M.F. helps soothe the rage. Even so, with Africa's poverty rate at sixty seven percent and Europe the role model at twenty three percent, well, The Way is popular for a reason. And don't call me Sam. I'm not your uncle."

"Oh the hilarity," Stefan quips. "So aside from spilling my family's dirty laundry, how do I fit in?"

"Quite crucially," Haine says. "The face of Executive Warriors Elite will be in even higher demand. Every world leader operating on the free market, every corporate baron who's ever cut jobs, will want protection. Then there's the show. 'Meta Force' isn't losing that number one spot any time soon. Not after yesterday. It's the best advertisement for meta registration out there. And for capitalism.

"But people want the heart behind the hype. No more of this mission only format. You five should move in together, film round the clock. Including Oke. The kids love him. Good lawyers, and friends like James and Gloria here, can squash child exploitation issues. He's invulnerable, right? And you'll need the U.N. for clearance purposes. Rodan can help with that. I'll have to schmooze Corny, of course. If it's even alright with you all?"

"They're right, Sam," Finley says as she rises from her couch. "You are a king in no need of a nation. You have everyone else's lined up and bent over. Here's hoping your vision doesn't screw us royally."

4

Break me

"Massage?" Ana Shaktira asks from the carpet as she unlaces her husband's shoes.

"Please," Samuel Haine accepts. He leans back on their mattress and looks out the bedroom door, down the hall and out the window that leads to their penthouse balcony. Paris sweats this July evening, as do his feet. His wife doesn't seem to mind.

"Too strong?" she asks, rolling the balls of his feet with her thumbs.

"I can take it. Come here."

She crawls onto the bed and straddles his waist. Her white negligee magnifies her ruddy complexion. His blue pajama suit with the yellow stars and moons belie his age, but he likes to believe they reveal his spirit.

"Do you feel old?" she asks. "I had been, until last month. Anything feels possible now."

"Old doesn't do it justice. Still there's a vitality I haven't felt in a while."

"Surviving will do that. But if you feel old how should I feel?"

"Ancient?" he asks, sitting up to press his cheek to hers. "Prehistoric?"

"What every woman wants to hear. And spoken by a man who dyes his hair! I need a better cosmetician."

"You're age defying to the last, my dear."

"I've dreamed about the dead," she says, pushing off him and onto her side. "The ambassadors. If someone had to die, it should have been someone with real power. Not glorified messengers."

"Would you rather it had been James? Or me?" he asks as he spoons her.

"Stop it. You know what I mean."

"Yes, well I can't say I'm a fan of the secretary general but he was out of town. Would you like me to invite him to brunch? We could stage a press conference at the Eiffel Tower, dare this Hikikomori to attack us again. I'm sure he'd oblige."

"You're hopeless!" she says, slapping him playfully.

"Quite the contrary," he says as he rolls away from her and walks for the window. "How could a man on such a spectacular mission be without hope? How could you, the eternal optimist, love someone without hope?"

"Oh fine," Shaktira says, following him past several vast rooms and to the balcony. "Let's call it optimism that has you advocating for developing nations after decades making a fortune off them. Not guilt. Even Hikikomori has to admit you're reforming the W.M.F. He must know you can't just wave your hand and erase their debt."

"Can you read his mind now?" Haine asks, turning to her with a raised eyebrow and an incredulous grin. "Careful, or we'll have to drag you down to the nearest registration center and burn a barcode on your neck."

"I'd say the epiphany hit me while on Bacchus. Nobody would doubt it. Haven't you heard? We mega rich types are all addicts. Our only joy is snorting red dust. Cling to a few euphoric moments of meta powers and hallucinations. It's all over the Net. Psychic chat rooms and such."

"About us?" Haine asks while staring down through night at streetlight rolling on the black River Siene. "I thought the myth was you've become a cyborg, chasing robotic youth to stop my philandering. Or what's the other, that you're a clone of some prostitute I had in Delhi?"

"God bless psychics. My favorite is I'm a cyberclone, the prototype, which you keep for 'domestic services,' and you have me programmed to act like a feisty biochemist so people won't think you're a pathetic old coot."

"Oh that reminds me. I've got a call to make."

"Go on then," she says, leaving the balcony for the hall. "My sprockets feel rusty anyway. I need a drink."

Haine shuts the window and connects a power cord from the wall outlet to a jack at the rear base of his skull. He presses a finger to the switch under the jack, activating his NeuroNet chip. *Next model needs a longer battery life*, he decides. Haine scans his homepage, set to the Associated Press, then opens his chat window and calls Cornelio Ortez. The 3D avatar for the president and chief executive of Haine International meets the 3D avatar for the director of the World Monetary Fund in a 3D boardroom in cyberspace. The digital men in suits strut round a granite table, all too bright and colorful to be believed. *Not a wrinkle on Corny's 70 year old face. Might as well be a cartoon. System needs something real. A sense of touch, perhaps?*

"Good afternoon, Corny. How goes it in London?"

"Gray and humid. Still in the office. We could do this on holodisc. Want to see my new golf mat?"

"I'm sure it's awe inspiring, but I need fresh air."

"Pity," Cornelio says. "... I suppose you want a commitment on the MV cocktail."

"That was Finley's demand," Haine replies. "She did her part, stumping across America for Net tracking software. People were so shaken by 6/24 they lit a fire under Congress. The bill will likely pass in weeks. Asia put up less resistance than expected. The M.E.U. is the real obstacle, and

I'm sure they'll break. The Way has been making a mockery of the imams."

"Yes, what was it?" Cornelio asks. "More than 90 million euros hacked from Iran's central bank? Can't wait to find out where they're getting the tech for this."

"If Hikikomori's as fast as Stefan, and he's taken the time to learn engineering or programming, he is the tech. We'll find out as long as you come through on your end. Ana's up for a sabbatical from volunteering with the World Health Organization. She's eager to get back in a lab."

"I'll need her if you expect a cure as if it's a Happy Meal. Let's pray Metapurge and Metafocus aren't her only miracles. Now can we address the real issue?"

"The race," Haine says. "Corny, this might get you killed. Breeding meta cyberclones seems reckless. I know His Highness is for it, but there are legitimate ethical issues. You'll become more of a target than either of us."

"Save it. I can taste the liberal creampuff from here. Sam, I'm happy that clones have the same rights as people. And if people want robot genitals that's their business. But brain dead clones with robot parts are not people! Meta cyberclones won't be people either. They'll be soldiers, saving lives and making us a fortune. Do you not care about your nine percent stock in this company? As for protection, I'll contract an EWE squad. Case closed."

"If you're determined. So that leaves the tariffs?"

"Sam, I admit I'm baffled by your about face on economic policy. It doesn't make any sense, allowing these nations to penalize us. Successful firms should be rewarded for getting genetically modified organisms into areas that lack the capacity to produce them properly. It makes less sense than your letting companies from South America, Africa, and the Middle East ship anything from petrol-soaked goat cheese to urine pudding at whatever the hell price they want. These tariffs prevent product uniformity.

"State by state cloning laws will crumble in the U.S., and once Asia's meta labs are exposed, these developing nations are going to unclench their religious ass cheeks and breed defective, deformed clones. Combine that with a few well placed hack jobs, for instance The Way turning Finley's personal cyberclone into a raping murder machine, and public sentiment for the technology goes back out the window. Sam, you have a duty to kill the tariffs."

Haine sighs in the real world. His 3D avatar nods. Cornelio' avatar turns away and touches a virtual ficus.

"Couldn't have argued it better, Corny. This is why I recommended you replace me. But the tariffs stay, at ninety two percent their respective rates. For countries indebted to the W.M.F., that is. Can't do much about others. Bottom line is, you won't let it stop you from saturating those markets. Your competition can't afford those cyberclone tariffs yet. Remember how long the NeuroNet stood alone before rivals got alternative chips into Africa? It'll be complicated no matter what, if the A.U. or the M.E.U. join the meta arms race. They laugh at their own constitutions. I'm sure you're already bribing a dozen dictators just to maintain operations.

"Corny, be reasonable. Pushing mutations on developing nations will seem like dictating their defense. I took enough flak for changing the guard at the W.M.F. to get my modest policies through. I wouldn't risk that influence on unsound theory. Just worry about curing MV. Ana will call you tomorrow to work out the details. Anything else?"

Cornelio' virtual avatar claps its hands.

"Sam, we once agreed that it would be catastrophe for the World Bank, the International Monetary Fund, and the World Trade Organization to merge into a single unit. If I recall, your words were 'dinosaurs devouring one another.' Do you honestly believe ass backward peasants understand international finance any better with one huge system rather than three huge ones?

"You didn't birth the beast but you're feeding it. And you've shafted your friends with these reversals. Friends you'll need again at some point. I swear, the Terror Wars ruined any hope for a free market! One measly nuke blows and everyone crawls to the state like a babe on a teat ... Good night, Sam. Please remember, you're not God."

"I am, however, a realist. Be well, Corny."

Haine logs off and slides open the window. He lets the night breeze wash over him before walking to the bathroom. He fixes on the mirror. *So old!* White locks poke through his dyed reds, even in his mustache and beard. Crow's feet scratch at his eyes. No tan has taken despite his daily walks. He pats his belly, jiggles fingers in his paunch. The parts he disdains. The whole he finds captivating. He continues to bask in himself for uncounted minutes, and would go longer were it not for the siren moan emanating from the bedroom.

He pops a pill and saunters to his wife. She leans back on the mattress, arms outstretched with legs agape so that her negligee forms a white basin at her crotch.

"How did it go?" she asks.

"As expected."

"You need a break," she purrs, wrapping her thighs around his hips and shimmying off his astral pajama bottoms. "Break me."

He crawls to her, shedding his top and hiking her negligee. Her mouth dances across his chest, alternating between gentle kisses and stinging bites. One of them draws blood, which she licks up like a cat on milk. She tosses him down and mounts him, screaming a name only he ever hears. He soaks in her face. Ageless, caked in makeup, of one past her prime. He laughs at that as his heart nearly jumps out his chest, propelled by one at the height of her powers. Then he succumbs to tearful quivering that has less to do with lovemaking than loss. He reproaches himself. There can be no such thing where he is headed. And as she slides down onto the mattress so that he straddles her, all thoughts fade in their swirl. Hours later, as morning rays trickle in, she pushes off him to shut the blinds.

"Did I ever tell you that my father used to fart in his sleep?" she asks on her way back to their bed.

"Amazingly, no."

"They were loud, awful things that would wake up the whole place. Chemical warfare, I tell you. Didn't matter what he ate. One day Mother got him to fast and drink only water. There they were like bombs."

"Yet another reason I'm glad I never met the man."

"You do the same thing," she says with a broad smile.

"Nonsense!" Haine replies. "I'd know if I ... Why tell me now, after all these years?"

"You could have gone to your death without that, hmm?"

"Self knowledge isn't always useful, my dear."

"Exactly. Think about that while I get some sleep," Shaktira advises. "And try not to blow us up."

The doorbell rings. She skips from their bed, pinching her nose and pointing at Haine. He sticks his tongue out at her as she leaves the bedroom. Seconds later havoc reigns. Hours after the explosion guts the penthouse, investigators recover two charred lumps matching their DNA, as well as a durium holodisc under the mattress, courtesy of The Way.

5

Never be alone

A bald, bearded man in a wet T-shirt and jeans opens the door of the bar. He lets in much downpour and more noise from the bustling Shanghai street. This annoys a half dozen patrons who peer at him through dim light and dense cigarette smoke. Until they notice all that muscle. The man passes the stage and pulls a stool up to the billiard table. Players boast as they miss shots. He settles in as he scans the room. After a while he goes downstairs to watch the cockfight.

Dozens of men, most middle aged, shouts bets in Mandarin round the rusty wire pen during the quick, loud, bloody match. One of the losers, a pudgy balding man in a cheap suit, tries to grab his yuan and run. A rotund bouncer trips him at the staircase, mashes his face to that first wooden plank, and relocates an errant dart from the wall into the man's earlobe. The screaming man drops the pile of cash. The bouncer collects the money and leaves his victim. After a few messy tugs the balding man frees his ear from the dusty step. He hobbles to a wretched bathroom, cupping his bleeding lobe, cursing in a tipsy provincial dialect that the proprietor is a Shanghai cow turd.

The built man waits for the next cockfight to finish before following the other into the bathroom, which has no door and a single discolored toilet. The loser stops washing his newly pierced lobe when the built man enters.

"I'll be out in a minute," the loser says.

"That looks bad," the built man replies in Mandarin. "Let me get you a drink. Take your mind off the pain."

"Beat it. I'm not touching you and you're not touching me. Tight jeans wearing, Shanghai faggot."

"Not here for that. Can't a fellow baldy offer you a beer? Or do you want to go home bleeding and sober?"

"... upstairs," the loser says. "But if you try anything I'll ram that bottle up your ass."

He cakes his bleeding lobe in toilet paper, then finds the built man sitting upstairs near the stage with two bottles on the counter. A petite quartet in a rainbow of bikinis and stiletto heels gyrate in unison under a strobe light to the beat of Mandarin hiptronica.

"Thanks. Name's Liu," he says, pulling up a stool.

"Mori," says the bald, bearded, built man.

"How old do you think these girls are?"

"Too young to do anything but look."

"Don't want to. I'm married."

"So are most guys who take them in back," the built man says. "Still, I believe you."

"Great. Okay, what's your deal?" Liu asks after starting on the bottle. "Appreciate the beer, but I don't have anything you'd want."

"I'm on vacation," the built man says before a deep gulp. "Not even from China. Can't you tell? My father was Korean. My mother was American. Luckily I got his features. Where are you from, Liu?"

"Outside Nanjing ... I'm not a hick, if that's what you think. I run a grocery. Gourmet produce in a nice town! Can't take a step here without tripping on homeless or having to bribe someone. I even hear the cops are about to go private. As if this is New York or London ... Shanghai isn't the center of the universe, you know."

"Spoken like someone who's dying to be proven wrong. Me, I haven't found a place I can stay long. Get bored too quickly. Even in the U.S. Luckily my work keeps me on the move. Want another round?"

"Sure," Liu says. "What do you do?"

"I'm a recruiter," the built man says as he snaps his fingers at a waitress. "For a school of sorts."

"A university?" Liu polishes off his beer.

"We have a unique philosophy. Better living through science."

"Ha! Since when are clichés unique?"

"That sounds like a challenge," the built man says as he takes two bottles from the waitress. "Would you care to hear my routine?"

"I care to watch their routine," Liu says. He chugs his fresh beer and turns to the stage.

The hiptronica ceases and the girls stand still. Nursery carols play. Cheers erupt throughout the bar as the girls perform children's games. First comes Leap Frog, then Hopscotch, then Duck Duck Goose. The fat stabbing bouncer tosses two jump ropes on stage. They get into Double Dutch. Yuan lands on the stage like autumn leaves.

"Disgusting," Liu says as he slams his bottle on the counter and runs a palm over his bald spot. "These whores should be at home!"

"Not so loud," the built man warns. "I'd hate to see you catch another piercing."

"I don't care! You think their fathers are proud?! I guarantee you they're dying inside!"

"Liu, may I ask, is your daughter at home?"

• • •

Nia Begaye packs her suitcase before dawn and takes a final look at her bedroom. The room she has lived in all 20 years of her life. Same bed. Same dresser. Same desk and vanity mirror. Same pink teddy bear wallpaper. *How did that last so long*, she wonders. *Too late now.* She tiptoes with the suitcase past her sisters' rooms and downstairs. Her shoes creak a floorboard or two as she crosses the foyer for the door. Nia makes it to the garage and into the red Cadillac coupe convertible, replete with autopilot, that her father gave as a graduation gift. She freezes.

No turning back once the engine starts. Go. Go, fool. She reminds herself of the deal she made with herself, that once gone returning would be out of the question until the mission was accomplished. *Mission. Madness is more like it. Who will believe it? He will. He must. Otherwise, better luck next reality.* And with that the engine starts.

But when the garage door opens unbidden her resolve sinks. Her father waits there fully dressed. He wears his tan cowboy hat with the pinch and his brown suede vest and his green crocodile boots with the spurs. She plops her head in her hands as he reaches the driver side door. He pats her shoulder, then jumps out of the way as she peels off. His litany of profanity mutes the apology wafting from the diamagnetic hum of her hovercar.

• • •

"Who said I have a daughter?" Liu asks. "Who the hell are you?"

"Someone who knows what it is to be different," the built man says. "Who knows the wealthy fear poverty. Who knows things were better here before communism became a dirty word. Who knows it's time for change. But that can wait. Ready for another round?"

"... better not. Had a bunch downstairs. My wife will be worried if I call home drunk. It's bad enough I lost ... What am I going to do, huh? Where am I supposed to get 400 grand, huh? Four hundred!"

"You couldn't have lost that much on cockfights?"

"No. On my daughter."

"What do you mean, Liu?" the built man asks.

"She's one of them," he says, gesturing to the stage. "Not here. In Nanjing. Same piece of cow turd owns both places. She's hooked. Cow turd supplies her. She sells herself for him. Thirteen years old! She ran off months ago. He said she'll cost 400 grand. No more drugs, no more dancing, no more ..."

"What's she on? Bacchus?"

"Metapurge."

"That's prescription."

"She's too powerful. Our private insurance can't afford it. We never got her registered. I watch the news. I see what happens to metas in the wrong neighborhoods. She'd be the only one where we live. It's a small town. People don't understand. And business was just picking up. I ... He had so much for so cheap. Cheap at first, anyway. I didn't know how much to give. Didn't know it's addictive ... Why am I telling you this? Who are you?"

"A friend. And you're telling me because you've had enough. You didn't come to gamble. Cow turd's here tonight. You have a gun in your pants and you want me to stop you."

"Are you a meta?" Liu asks, his voice wavering between fear and disgust as he steps off the stool. "Can you read my mind?"

"No, I can't read your mind," the built man says. "I just know the bulge of a revolver when I see one. Something bouncers here ought to learn. Now sit back down, drink another round, and let me tell you about Taedo."

• • •

Nia keeps the radio off as she leaves the reservation. No need to cause a stir, spread even more gossip about her family. Homeless old drunkards and young addicts are the only ones up to see. Most will forget she passed by. The others will be asleep or tempting jail once her father comes asking questions. By then people who know nothing will become fonts of spurious knowledge. People will be polite to his face and whisper behind his back that he had it coming, not putting her on meds when he had a chance. *I'll miss you, res!*

Navajo are good people, she thinks. Not as poor as they used to be, thanks to the casinos. Not as bitter, either, thanks to the money. *I'll make it back*, she vows as her Cadillac cuts through hillside to pass Silver Sky Family Resort. Its neon lights aglow, the party perpetual. She ruminates on how elders say the tribes have lost their old ways, and how her father would counter that the world has lost its old ways. She worries about how she should be inspecting Silver Sky this instant, were it not for the mission. About how she should have her skirt suit and her notepad and her checklist. *That paycheck was one perk to being all knowing.*

The only one she can fathom. Predicting every path but her own has rarely felt a gift. *In that case let's call this an adventure*, she decides, cracking a smile as sun hits the hillside above radiant hues of blue and white.

• • •

"What is this?" Liu mumbles to Hikikomori as they drink their sixth round and pretend to watch the girls. "I know you can find anything on the Net, but this ..."

"A database of every official, from provincial secretaries down to city tax clerks, that cow turd's been bribing. Along with amounts and dates of payment. His personal list, copied from his own NeuroNet file."

"How'd you get it?" Liu slurs as he shuts off the Net.

"Hackers like to share. Especially if they've been laid off from their government jobs. You called the dancers disgusting. What do you call this?"

"Proof that he ought to die," Liu says. "Proof things need to change. China sacrificed its unity for riches. It's because of the cow turds and bribe takers. My grandparents didn't have much, but they had enough. Now people get rich by making others poor. Get powerful by stepping on our necks! I should shoot him."

"Then what?" Hikikomori asks. "Some other thug will take his place, do the same thing to other families. You need to gather a base at the bottom to topple those at the top. Don't go alone and waste your life on some small fry. Let your friends help. Once techno anarchism rises you'll never be alone again."

"You really think people can live in peace, not kill and cheat, if we get rid of corporations and governments? If we let computers run everything?"

"Computer, single. That's the point of singularity. We create the program that wakes up and thinks like the best of us. Motivated, compassionate, democratic, and just. Then we put the program in our brains. Then we live in the NeuroNet. Then we merge our programs together. Then we, in true union, become immortal and infinite. As for money and the material world, what happiness do they really bring? I guarantee you cow turd and his politician friends cry themselves to sleep at night for fear they'll lose those things. Know why true freedom, true cooperation, has failed in the past? Because people are weak. Computers don't know greed or fear. They know logic. Logic is truth.

"Look around you. I bet you have a robot or a cyber-clone in your grocery, right? No human employees but your wife, right? And you've both got Net access, along with your daughter, right?"

"We plugged Bao Chan in before her powers developed. Cow turd found her in some chat room for meta teens."

"Last question. Have either you or your wife gotten replacement parts? A prosthetic kidney, maybe?"

"She's got a pacemaker."

"Then, Liu, don't you see? We're already becoming machines. We've just yet to commit. Machines don't need money. Only recyclable parts. Although, you do need money now. And I can give it to you. All I want in return is for you to save Bao Chan before cow turd sells her."

"Sells her?! To who?!"

"The government, of course," Hikikomori says. "These dancers are metas, too. They'll be cloned by the military. Made lab rats until they drop dead. Bao Chan doesn't deserve that. And you don't deserve a government that would do that. So, Liu, are you ready to be shown The Way?"

"Beyond ready," says the poor, balding grocer as he ogles prepubescent slaves and guzzles the last of his many beers. "Ready to show it. To the world."

6

Say a few words

Stefan eases the triple layer chocolate cake onto the glass table between a milk jug, plastic plates and sporks, and two silver urns. The other seven eye the cake, then him, then the cake again.

"What?" Stefan asks.

"So long, ASS?" William quotes, pointing at cursive in the form of yellow icing.

"Dios mio. Initials. So long, Ana and Sam."

"Your ampersand sucks," Oke says while rubbing his red eyes. "You know we can afford silverware, right?"

"Leave him alone, Pumpkin," Phase scolds. "If this cake is half as good as the one Stefan made for Will's birthday it will be twice as good as any you've ever had."

Oke morphs his left hand into a knife and his right into a spatula. He chops sloppy, uneven pieces. The boy serves his teammates first, then Karen Drench, Cornelio Ortez, Peter Rave, and finally James Windsor. These nine abandoned hundreds of other mourners long ago at the Pere Lachaise Cemetery. The gathering occupies less than a tenth of the area of the newly furnished, white walled living room. Its furnishings clash for accommodating their past lives. William's beige couches. Stefan's black rocking chairs. Phase's glass coffee table. Zenith's multimedia console. Oke's framed videogame posters. But there is the view. At least they got the penthouse portion of the Berlaymont Building.

"Nice place," James says between bites. "Identical to mine. Except for my sauna and Jacuzzi. You're welcome to come down and look on in envy at my carefree bachelor lifestyle ... This feel like home yet?"

"Feels like a palace," Oke says. "Well, I guess not to you, Your Highness."

"I renounced that title when I took office. Nobody ever listens when I say this, but 'James' is fine, Oke. Not like I have a real last name anyway ..."

"No sweat, James. And call me Oh. As in, 'Oh. He's hot fire.' Like they say online."

"Give it up, kid," William says while pulling a red pill out of his pants pocket. "Forget the codename. Do you want a cape and mask, too?" He swallows the Metafocus dry.

"Why not?" the boy demands as he turns from William to slap James on the arm. "Heroes need to style, right?"

"News flash. We are not heroes," William replies while tugging the boy by the collar of his cerulean tracksuit. "Think of us as obscenely well paid security contractors who refrain from slapping our employer."

"Give him a break," Stefan says to William before turning to James. "We're still adjusting to living together. And to having it aired. And to leaving London."

"Yes I still skip off to Buckingham whenever I can," James says. "Although it just doesn't feel the same now that my sister demands I call her 'Queenie.' Hope you've brushed up on your French. Speak English and Brussels locals will despise you for it. Anyhow, I do appreciate your agreeing to watch over me. It must be a sacrifice."

"It's what Sam would have wanted," Karen says. She stands with feet wide apart and hands digging into her hips as she bites her bottom lip. She holds a plate of cake in one hand, a cup of milk in the other, and a spork jutting from her teeth.

"Speaking of which, now that we've ditched the sycophants let's get on with the real ceremony," Cornelio orders, the jowls of his prune face trembling with umbrage.

"Think you guys could cry?" P.R. asks. He nudges his circular sunglasses back up his nose while waiting for a response. "It'd make for great footage. I could splice together this montage of tears set to a maudlin version of the theme song. Tap into public sympathy, huh?" P.R. begins stroking his mangy ponytail when the silence persists.

"You know we all hate you, right?" Phase says mainly to make him go away.

"And on that sweet note," Stefan cuts in while taking Phase by the elbow, "I'll say a few words about two people who deserved a better world. When I met Sam and Ana almost a decade ago, during that first assassination attempt, I never dreamed how they would change my life. He gave me purpose. True friendship. Some people say he was greedy. I saw a man that played by his own rules and never went out of his way to hurt anyone.

"Maybe that was because of Ana. Sam used to joke that she reminded him to be human. If so, she led by example. I don't know a bad word anyone could honestly say about her. She gave metas the means to coexist with baselines, whether they choose to hone their powers or to live without them. And she would have saved millions more through a cure. Instead they became martyrs for freedom ... Sorry my brother's such a douche dick. As God is my witness, they will be avenged."

Karen and Cornelio follow the obligatory pause with their own platitudes.

"Sam got my pardon," Phase says. "Warrants in seventeen countries dropped overnight. When he let me join, I asked how and why. Sam said, 'I bribed a lot of people for you. Which means you owe me. That's good business. And your repayment is to save a life. I don't care which life. As long as it matters to you.' I'll never forget that. Just wish I could have saved his."

Another stretch of hand wringing and bowed heads before James speaks, leaving William for last.

"Before I begin, Becca apologizes for being unable to attend ... Ana once asked why I gave up brain surgery to be a hired gun. I told her, 'With these powers, if I can keep a few metas from taking their frustration out on the world, I'll be saving more lives than I ever would in the O.R.' She laughed and said, 'If only you could figure out a way to do the same for baselines, then we'd get somewhere.' She always thought about the big picture, how to help the most people. We lost a great humanitarian.

"As for Sam, our favorite topic was the meta wave. How it might have happened, what it might mean. I often argued meta powers seem to reflect subconscious fixations of the subject. Sam often said I was too cynical. His phrase was 'human potential run wild.' So I asked him if he envied metas. 'No,' he said. 'My choices affect the future of millions of people. Theirs will determine the future of the species.' The man was a visionary. There won't be another like him."

Oke's grumbling gut breaks the silence. He offers to slice more cake. P.R. gets the first piece, but Oke removes his spatulaed hand too soon. P.R. fumbles the plate, which falls cake side down onto Haine's urn. The boy scrapes the cake off and frantically wipes the urn, only to unscrew its lid. Ash and bone bits clump on concentric golden circles that pattern the carpet. Karen gasps when Phase vomits cake and milk on the same spot. At that Stefan darts from the room in hyper speed. Oke drops to the rug, one hand morphed into a broom and the other a dustpan, clearing the mess between desperate apologies.

William rights the urn and screws the lid back on, mumbling venomously. Phase begins to tell Oke to relax when she cups one hand to her mouth and the other to her stomach, then plods down the hall gurgling that she is perfectly fine. Oke scurries after her, failing to avoid five pairs of contemptuous eyes.

"We can edit that out," P.R. says, laying his ponytail on his chest. "It'd be in poor taste, huh?"

"You think?" Stefan mocks upon his hyper fast return.

"Hey man. You want high ratings, right? Well those contact lenses and ear mics force me to work around the clock. Boiling a week's worth of footage from five people into usable material means I gotta ask, right?"

"No you don't," William says. "You're asking because you want to put it in, but you don't want to seem like a slimy little worm, so you're hoping Karen or Cornelio will override your hollow gesture. But they're not going to do that, because their sense of decency is a tad more evolved than yours. And before you try to deny it, yes, I am reading your mind. How's that for poor taste?"

"Come on, Peter. Give them some time," Karen says. "Living here isn't going to be a piece of–Oh God. Sorry."

"Let's be off then," Cornelio orders. "Without Ana the labs have to work double time on a virus cocktail. And there's the Net tracking. Crack the whip and all."

"Sure," Stefan says as the three outsiders head for the door. "Always a pleasure. Next time we'll play charades. Or Twister. It'll be a riot."

"Well. How appalling," James says upon their exit.

"It was an accident," Stefan replies. "The kid was too worked up. All of a sudden people are dying all around him. Oke's therapist swears he shouldn't be on the squad."

"Not that. The carpet. Mine's stain resistant. You got the cheap stuff."

"Aye caramba. That's the saddest thing I've heard all day. Where's the respect?"

"I'm disappointed they're not hardwood," William says. "We better have cyberclones around here. I don't clean."

"That's what Oke's for, no?" James asks. The men share a laugh, then a long silence. "It's going to get much worse before it gets better. There's already talk of concessions. Of course, with Sam gone there's no telling if the new W.M.F. chief will even consider forgiving debt. Your brother's putting us in a very bad spot."

"You think?" Stefan mocks. "I'm getting death threats from soccer moms. I swear I didn't see this coming. If I knew where Jin was I'd end it now."

"I vouched for you to the Council and to the heads of state of my Union, so you have no choice but to mean that. It helps that Sam and Ana had it in their wills that you should get their remains. Makes it hard for the public to hate you. Any idea why they chose you, Stefan?"

"They didn't have any family left. So I guess there's that. But I think they saw me as a son."

"Sonny boy, your brother's got two strikes on you. For my own sake, don't let him get the out."

With that Phase blinks beside them. She takes James by the hand before blinking away with him to begin her shift of guard duty. William rubs his shoe over the carpet stain once they vanish. Particles levitate and dissipate until the mess is no more.

"When's Becca get her new body?" Stefan asks. "This will be version five, right? Always better tech. Always the same look. Think she'll at least change her hairstyle?"

"About a week," William says. "She was supposed to give me a holodisc of her condolences for the service. Guess she got too busy with the reconstruction."

"Lucky she can survive on the Net like that. It's weird, though. Doesn't make any sense. Living online."

"Like it makes sense that Oke can turn into whatever he touches? Science ceases to apply for people like us. Should anything make sense anymore?"

"Still. It does make her seem ... different."

"You mean not human," William presses.

"Didn't say that," Stefan says.

"But you meant it."

"Will, you can't read my mind."

"You brought it up. And you don't have to say it. I think it, too. But so what? I love her. What can I do?"

"Hope her new body feels as soft as the last one?"

"She may not be human anymore but she knows what I need ... She did say I should expect a few changes."

"Like what? A vacuum pump? That could be cool, man."

"Watch it, chico."

"Just kidding. Everything will work out for the best."

"Even with your brother?"

"One way or another," Stefan says as he picks up Haine's urn. "Jin, what happened to you?"

"Why does he go by Hikikomori?" William asks. "I know it means 'the withdrawn' in Japanese. But your brother attracts too many followers to fit the psychological profile of an ineffectual loner. And he's Korean, right?"

Stefan puts the silver urn back on the table and rubs his temples as though suffering the onset of a headache.

"Jin's dad used to joke that northern Korea is like a strong cocktail. One part Chinese, one part Japanese, one part don't ask ... Can't be sure, but I think I started it. By mistake, I mean. This girl back at Taedo. Jin liked her, and she, for some reason, liked him. So one day I dared him to kiss her on the cheek. He does, and she plants a long one right on his neck. Then his mouth. But they both had braces. They got stuck. An orthodontist had to separate them. It was hilarious! The girl was traumatized. She never spoke to him again. But she left a huge red mark on his neck from the kiss. So I got all the other kids to start calling him 'Hickey.' A few weeks later I scored with the girl. She was my first. After that, Jin went full throttle with his studies. All perfect scores. Come to think, it was only after that he started getting so political. And he started watching this same old movie again and again. Like every week. A twisted Korean horror porno about some crazy loner. That's the don't ask part."

"Are you saying your brother is waging war because he couldn't get laid?"

"Watch it yourself, Will," Stefan warns. This time he picks up Shaktira's urn. The people's champion kisses it and sets it down next to Haine's. "Yeah, Jin's a mass murdering lunatic. But nobody trash talks my bro but me."

7

My love, you're terrifying me

William slides a hand across Zenith's chest, squeezing every so often to test its flexibility. She sits nude, glabrous, her silvery blue skin a solid reflective coat akin to chrome. He discerns no orifices below her neck.

"Becca, how are we supposed to ...?"

"Durium nanites," she says. "Watch."

She reclines on the mattress, twists her hips, parts her legs. The coating between her thighs gelatinizes as it recedes and reshapes into anatomical precision.

"Touch," she says. "Everything feels organic."

"I see," William says, following her direction. "So it's safe for me in there, Sparky?"

"Completely. Although I suggest you retain your aura at first, to get used to the sensation."

"Shall we test it out?" he asks.

"Whenever you're ready."

They do. William exults. Her new model trumps the last, which had captured human perfection. Even her silvery baldness appeals to him. *Are we getting too perverted here? Nonsense. Have to accept her for what she is. Go with the flow.* They finish. She walks to the center of their bedroom, leaving him sore and panting on the mattress.

"Satisfactory?" she asks. Lamplight bounces off her bluish curves slick with his sweat such that William sees his twisted reflection in her form.

"Geez, Becca. Can we be a little less mechanical?"

"As you wish. Was it good for you, too, lover?"

"Of course. I can barely move," he says, straining to sit upright. "... what did you feel, exactly?"

"The same as before, except I have more control over my receptors. I can induce pleasure and minimize pain at will. I kept the pain receptors to be aware of damage, but the nanites reconfigure instantly. My solar battery would have to shut down for automatic repairs to cease."

"Haine International spared no expense, I take it?"

"This body is worth 2,764,351,894.03 euros."

"I'm surprised they don't own you."

"They do. Mister Ortez is seeking permission to breed a cyberclone from DNA off Manfred Peebles, and to use that cyberclone to mass produce me for sale to militaries."

"My love," William says, "you're terrifying me."

• • •

Phase squeezes the bridge of her nose with all her might. She blinks in and out of states, unthinking, from intangible to invisible to her penthouse bedroom and back to the exam table. *Thank God I didn't wear my contacts or ear mics.* She wants to rip that patronizing look off the doctor's face. Wants to wrap his white coat around his throat until his eyes bulge. *To Hell with his blood test.*

"I want a second opinion," she says.

"You're welcome to it, Miss Zamair," he replies in a thick German accent. "But I don't get false positives. Take heart. Medication has improved in the last few years."

"What the hell are you talking about? Everybody still dies. In agony. Within a decade!"

"I understand this is difficult to process. We caught it while you're strong enough to fight it. The thing to keep in mind is that a breakthrough can happen at any time. Being the most prominent meta with the disease means you'll get the best treatment. If anyone stands a shot it's you."

"Is that supposed to be comforting? You tell me I've got MV then expect me to be chipper?"

"I have to be honest, Miss Zamair. Now as far as your employment, be prepared to sacrifice that. It's a matter of safety. Anything could happen in the field. His Highness can't be at risk, if MV should one day infect baselines."

"Oh they're not finding out," Phase proclaims.

"But ... it's the law," the doctor says. "European physicians must report all cases to the government. Many patients feel it's a violation of privacy. There's no getting around it. I'd lose my license."

"Guess you have a choice then, doc," Phase says as she blinks from the exam table, then to the man's white coat, then to the edge of the atmosphere.

This is crossing the line, she knows. She has been a thief and a con artist, never a murderer. She has beaten up a few marks here and there. Ruined a few innocent lives as part of the hustle. She even abducted and inducted a baby boy into a life of crime. But she made amends. She has saved so many since then. Since Stefan tracked her down and William forced therapy on her. *No choice. Can't get kicked off. Not getting slammed in The Hole. Won't be some freak guinea pig while they steal my boy!*

Green continents and blue oceans connect like puzzle pieces so high up, where mortal concerns feel almost petty and pointless for her. Almost. *This guy's about the chuck. Worried that he can't breathe, I bet. Too scared to realize he doesn't need to while intangible. Later on he'll wonder how he could still see, still feel his heartbeat ... Gotta fake it. He'll bite. He better, or I've just dug a deeper hole.* Phase accesses her NeuroNet and calls up the flailing man in her grasp. No virtual boardroom. No enhanced reality window. Merely her voice in his head.

"Take a good look," she tells him via the Net. Phase dangles him with one arm by his coat collar and points to the Earth with her free hand. He looks. "You can live out the rest of your days down there with extreme acrophobia. Or you can drift here in the void, spasm from a shock to your nervous system, and choke until your lungs explode." He claws at her arm, shaking his head in disbelief, moaning in cyberspace over his abduction to outer space. They blink back into the doctor's office. She releases him and reclaims her seat on the exam table. "What'll it be?"

"Take ... oh God, take the file," he pants while gasping for air on all fours. "Take the blood sample, too. Just leave. I'll ... I'll delete your records. I swear!"

"Thanks, doc. Sorry to make you piss yourself."

A cold dampness on his thighs indicates that she speaks true.

"Symptoms will hit soon without treatment," he says. "Do you want to live like that?"

"No. But I will live on my own terms."

Phase teleports off, composure intact. She reappears at the bottom of the stratosphere, solid now, falling free. Hot winds blind her, breaths elude her. She fails to recall whether she heads for water or rock, not that it matters. Then she fails to recall the last thing she said to her boy. The thief goes intangible. Her momentum goes away, along with her desire for all save a clean getaway.

• • •

Oke pops the collar of his purple velour tracksuit and rolls the sleeves to his elbows. He turns his black hair green with chlorophyll he borrows from the nearby ficus, then wills his limp locks spiky. The boy flicks a speck off his otherwise immaculate white sneakers. He poses in the mirror of the black marble bathroom, then turns to Stefan.

"How do I look?" Oke asks.

"Like a gay porcupine."

"Hey, this is how I style my avatars. My people expect no less in the flesh."

"Your people are dorks," Stefan says.

"I bet that won't stop you from hitting on the ladies. Be honest, gamers pull hotter chicks than you thought."

"The chicas get a pass," Stefan admits.

"You know, I've absorbed plants before, but I couldn't figure out how to do it on my own just now without touching one again. Been forgetting a lot lately. Except for games. Dunno why ... Just remember," Oke warns, "you asked to come here with me so it has to be 'Oh' tonight. Nothing but 'Oh' or you'll kill my game. We clear?"

"Claro."

The boy nods. Stefan follows him out of the bathroom and into the packed gargantuan pit of Club Ra, the hottest nightspot on the island of Ibiza, Spain. Thousands revel in the videogame bacchanal to a hiptronica soundtrack. Ground level strobe lights flash psychedelic colors off disco balls spinning from the ceiling, and four giant monitors in the center of the pit blast the latest contest toward the four walls of mirrors. Oke pushes through the crowd accepting handshakes from his awe struck, prepubescent peers, and kisses from half naked women nearly twice his age. Two thirds of those they pass barely notice Stefan. *They may be dorks*, Stefan muses, *but they're loyal dorks.*

Monique Rain hugs Oke as he approaches the stage. They ascend arm in arm to the console that powers the monitors. The 16 year old pop singer sports purple pigtails with a plaid tube top and matching schoolgirl skirt, the trademark attire of "Pan Pan," main character of the titular karaoke videogame franchise, whom she stars as in her recent film. Stefan refrains from asking the Kentucky native whether she's planning another trip to the Arctic.

Monique, emcee of the 54th Annual International Gamers Championships, announces that "Oh" will now defend his title against the NeuroNet's top thousand contenders. Oke picks up a vintage brainwave helmet at the console and boots up "H@zerSt0rm," the first person shooter set on a hostile alien world Earthlings are out to colonize. *Tacky ass helmet*, he thinks while morphing part of his mind into a replica of the game's program. *But if my peeps dig it, I can deal.*

He throws his arms up and pumps fists for the crowd, feeling more at home surrounded by cheering gamers eager for him to square off in virtual worlds than he does in his new home with his mother's coworkers. *Uptight know it alls think I'm a stupid kid. Except for Stefan. And Becca. She did listen to my idea for that game. But if Will gives me one more dirty look I swear–Whatever. Game on.*

Stefan leaves Oke to his people. He pushes through the human sea for the staircase up to the VIP booth overlooking the pit. He hears P.R.'s high pitched voice well before the bouncer opens the door to the black lit, red walled room.

"How's it feel playing second fiddle?" P.R. asks. The potbellied man with thin appendages holds a martini in one hand, in the other the waist of a barely legal girl wearing only biker shorts and a man's blazer.

"Weird. Feels like I'm back in high school," Stefan says. "The kids love him, though. Not bad for someone who began life eating out of a garbage can."

"Gets better. He's about to sign his first endorsement contracts," P.R. replies. "For a clothing line and a series of gaming manuals, no less. His future's golden."

"Long as we don't get him killed," Stefan says.

"Hey, man, why so gloomy? That's not like you."

"What in the world could be on my mind? So introduce me already."

P.R. waves over from the bar the veteran anchor of the BBC's foremost primetime news program and her cougar prey date, the new quarterback of the Chicago Bears. Then he waves over Monique's two older sisters. Stefan finds them less attractive than the starlet, if acceptable for his purposes. P.R. never names the jailbait whose waist he perpetually massages.

The celebrities fawn over Stefan like groupies. As usual he encourages them, detailing how he maintains calm in the heat of battle, recounting innocuous chit chat with James Windsor, insisting that his brother will be brought to justice.

"What's that like?" Monique's more intoxicated sister asks. "Do you hate him?"

"It would make things easier. The Jin I knew was my best bud. Don't tell Will I said that. He'll be jealous. I don't think he has any other friends."

Everyone cackles like hyenas at that. They downright howl when the quarterback asks whether the rumors are true that William and Stefan are secret lovers. Laughter ceases when the anchor informs him that Karen has approved an interview between them regarding Hikikomori. Stefan agrees and makes a mental note to curse Karen out. He whittles away the hours sitting between Monique's sisters, inquiring about their hobbies and cracking jokes at his teammates' expense. By the time Oke enters the booth with Monique, her sisters sit in Stefan's lap fondling his pectorals.

"Sluts," she says. "If you're going to double team him at least do it in private. Come come."

Monique drags her sisters and their catches from the VIP booth. Oke beams as P.R. waves him away, guaranteeing prominent screen time for the boy's "H@zerSt0rm" victory next episode, which P.R. had been editing via NeuroNet as the action unfolded. They take a rear corridor to a limousine, Oke stopping every so often to sign autographs for pimpled fat kids in comic book T-shirts and backward caps. The limousine glides them across Sant Antoni de Portmany, past the dozens of beggars roaming the streets, to the Rains' suite up high behind the shimmering black walls of Haine Hotel. Monique invites Oke to view the Mediterranean from the balcony, pressing his hand to her bosom as incentive.

Her sisters pull Stefan to the carpet as the boy veers out of sight. The man works fast. Minutes later the sisters halt. Climax imminent, bodies moist and garments far from reach, they recoil.

"Who the hell is Ana?" the less intoxicated one asks while reaching for her panties. "The sex was great, but if you scream a name, like, scream the right one."

The boy totters into sight a while later with dilated pupils, a runny nose, and red dust on his lips. He finds Stefan sitting alone on the sofa, flicking the remote at the three dimensional sitcom emanating from the holodisc. Stefan glances at Oke, inadvertently imitating a face William has made many a time. The people's champion prays that Phase will not ask too many questions and that P.R. will edit judiciously.

8

Mortality has been known to blur

The thin Japanese man in the frayed white T-shirt and black leather pants empties his forty third beer. He slides the mug across the counter to the old fat woman running the Ataraxia Bar & Grille. She refills it, shaking her wigged, platinum blond head as she smirks, then walks over to him.

"Okay, I give up. How do you do it?"

"It's my meta power," he says. "Call me Metablo."

"At this point I almost buy that. I've heard of stupider powers. There's a guy in Dublin my sis knows who vomits perfume. Bottles it, he does. Some bloke I met in the States last year grows tulips instead of hair."

"Think I'm lying?" the man asks.

"Nah." She leans over the counter to inspect the back of his head. "It's just that I don't see any barcode or power type tattoo on your neck. What would that fall under, being able to guzzle alcohol like water? A liver with a check mark over it?"

"A caduceus," he says.

"The tulip bloke had that one. But see, that's what I mean. Figure a smart guy like you wouldn't blow your cover. Fines for skirting registration are sky high these days. How do you know I won't rat on you?"

"And lose such a faithful customer? Unlikely, Liselle. Besides, tonight's my last in town."

"What a shame, Harry! I was beginning to think you had a crush on me! You've finished all your business here?"

"One meeting to go. Should arrive any minute."

"I'll see you talk to someone else? Exciting. Well, I've got the other slobs. Drink up, killer."

He takes her advice while swiveling on his stool to take in the rest of the wood paneled room. Fourteen other patrons slump about in parties of two to five, mostly in mahogany booths by the windows, mostly intoxicated.

His attention settles on a couple at the other end of the counter. The middle aged man orders the young woman in the short skirt to stop flirting with every guy who leaves the bathroom. She apologizes and promptly returns to it when the next man passes, this time grabbing his wrist and offering to accompany him home. At that her companion leans over to grab her by the neck. The new man shouts at him to stop and raises his mug as though to crash it over the older man's dome, until the woman goes limp. She hunches over revealing the ON/OFF switch at the base of her skull. The younger man apologizes before warning the older man to get his cyberclone to a repair shop. The middle aged man nods as he flips open a panel on her skull. He curses about an expired warranty while fiddling with wire and brain.

Then the front doors part and Stefan sidles up to the counter. All eyes converge on him. Only Liselle speaks.

"Been a while, stud," she says beaming from ear to ear as she slides him an overflowing mug. "Thought you'd forgotten about the little people. What brings you back?"

"His Highness got homesick. Me too."

"Keep telling myself I should redecorate your old pad," she says. "Wallpaper's peeling something awful."

"Aye caramba. Leave it be. I'll keep paying the deposit. Too many good memories upstairs."

"But blue teddy bear wallpaper? Always wondered how you explained that to the girlies."

"Never had to," Stefan boasts. "They found it cute."

"The sensitive warrior gets 'em every time, huh?"

"All part of the legend," Stefan says with a broad grin. "Lately I prefer 'people's champion.' Has a better ring to it."

"Yeah, caught your interview on the telly. You're really hurting, huh?"

"I miss them. He was like family to me. She was ... beyond compare."

"Steffy, if you don't mind ..." Liselle bends in to whisper, "how come you never mentioned your brother? You did live here six years. Sat right on that stool whenever you were in town. Now it's like I don't know you."

"Figured you saw the old stories ... Come on, Liz. What am I supposed to say? Some things hurt too much."

"Ooh, don't let that get out. People think you're impervious. It'll be your kryptonite."

"Trust me, he already is."

"Well stop staring already!" she yells at nobody in particular. "Let the man be!" Stefan looks over his shoulder to see the other patrons snapping back to their drinks. "Hey, I gotta tend shop. Take it easy."

Liselle makes the rounds. Stefan watches her take orders, fill mugs, wipe spills, and evict rowdy drunkards. He had been aware of the thin Japanese man studying him as soon as he sat at the bar. At first Stefan thought him star struck. Now he senses the man's urgency, and that his input holds some portent. To Stefan's surprise he finds himself walking over to initiate the conversation.

"I sign autographs but I'm not into guys," he says.

"Can you slay the ones you love?" the Japanese man asks as though he were talking about an errant pitch at a baseball game. "There is no shame if you cannot. The fate of the world should not rest on one person."

"¡Mierda, tu cojones!" Stefan shouts, slamming the mug into the counter such that it shatters and only the handle remains in his fingers. "Where do you get off?! Didn't you see the goddamn interview?! I know my brother's a nut! I know he has to be stopped! It's not like I'm in on it with him! I didn't know! I didn't freaking know!"

"Not Jin," the man says just as placid as before. "He is your nuisance. I speak of the immortals. Those who came before you. Before all of us."

"Little man, I don't know what you've been drinking but you need to lay off."

"Sowen and Shakti will try to sway you, as they have me. They will make it more than appealing. They will make it seem right. If you love your humanity as much as I hope you do, there is a chance. If not, we are soon at an end."

"... who?"

"You know. The mage. The Mother of the Night. Or do you prefer the king in no need of a nation and his devoted bride? Samuel Haine and Ana Shaktira are façades. The truth is the stuff of your nightmares."

"Go to Hell!" Stefan says as he springs from the stool. "You're lucky I don't rip your face off."

Stefan turns to go. The thin Japanese man grabs his wrist and jerks him back to the counter. "Sit. Down." The thin man growls while squeezing Stefan's wrist such that it begins to numb. "Sit down and remember."

"Remember what?" Stefan whispers, struggling to concentrate through a crushing force at his wrist that exceeds any he has ever endured.

"Your dreams. They will show you what I can only tell. Remember. Now!"

And so he all but does.

• • •

Forging the army came easier than Musarref al Sayeed had anticipated. He began in Kanpur at the Ganges River. Villagers knew of the Mother of the Night. Her Children had raided them for the last seven years. Along the Ganges he traveled to Banaras and from there to Patna. Farmers spoke of the plague that strides the winds of dusk. They too had lost kin.

And at every town up the Gandak River healthy men joined his cause. By the time Musarref reached the mouth of the Narayani, his party had swelled to 400. It was only on the jungle trek to Butwal that fear set in.

"Daksha overheard two merchants at the last port call us the walking dead."

"Probably. Who knows how many wait in her caves?"

"We need more men. Tell Musarref. He listens to you."

"If you believe that you'll be of the first to bleed."

"Don't joke. He paused at Nepal on your advice."

"I may have ... exaggerated my influence."

"Vishnu save me. Why did I let you talk me into this?"

"Because those demons took your daughter, remember?"

"Yes. But I can have more daughters."

Normally penetrating the dense maze of vines and trees would be foolish. When not evading tigers and snakes one had to be cautious of murderous bandits. The task ahead of this ragtag band lent them amnesty, for all mortals were prey to Shakti and her consort, the Knight Wraith. They were unstoppable. Unholy. Tales of her wrath terrified youth as a warning against straying from the village. As they grew older, and friends went missing, the youth learned to take those tales to heart.

Meerut and Jhansi, the two men now realizing their trepidation, were raised in such a town. Firozabad. Sixty deaths there in the last year were attributed to the Rakshasa horde, among them Meerut's daughter. The pair vowed to serve Musarref after witnessing him slaughter twenty six armed warriors from a neighboring village. Musarref had been naked and high on cannabis at the time, urged by the flaming arrows of the invaders to leave his bath at a whorehouse. In his frenzy he mistook them for Children of the Night. The next morning he set out for Butwal with Daksha, Meerut and Jhansi in tow.

Now Musarref al Sayeed appeared at the clearing ahead. He rode a white horse that he had not left with. A bag thumped at its side. The bag was tied to his hip along with a gold coated scimitar, a hooked dagger with an onyx hilt, and a silver bow. He leapt to the ground and raised his palm for the army to halt. The man was of average height and build. His tanned face had oddly high cheekbones, a narrow jaw, and a bulbous chin. Those sunken eyes, hawk nose, and wide lips projected morbid intensity. He wore a billowy white shirt and pantaloons. Black cloth wrapped his sandals to his shins. The black iron chest plate, embossed with a gold cross and Arabic script that spelled the name of Allah, glistened under smears of blood. Red stains also dotted his white turban.

"She knows we are coming," he shouted.

He reached into the bag and yanked out a clump of blond hair attached to a decapitated head. It was pale, that of a European man with blue eyes. Its mouth moved. Audibly. Jhansi strained to listen for the utterance.

"... mother ... mother ... mother ... mother ..."

Cries swept through the soldiers. A few vomited. Several discarded their weapons and fled into the jungle. Musarref dropped the talking decapitation and let it roll about the ground. He raised his palm again.

"Hear me. You will experience horrors today that will torment you until your final breath. So be it. We can prevail. Time is on our side. Daylight is young and they are asleep. The Temple of the Moon is but a few paces away. Rally your courage, for this day we are the hunters!"

• • •

Yoshiaga lived on the far side of the hall. The rice paper screen of his spruce door revealed the room was unlit. Guards often stood watch there whether or not he was present. They too were absent now. Magahara donned his hood, slid open the door, and stepped into the room. A knifepoint touched his temple in the darkness. Haggard breaths dug at his ear.

"So even the Knight Wraith can be caught off guard," a voice whispered triumphantly.

"When the mood permits," Magahara said.

The words barely left his lips when he grasped the knife in one hand and the assailant in the other. He pinned the body to the floor, hauled it to the other side of the room. A match was struck and cast into the nearby lamp. The governor's son stepped out of Magahara's grasp and bowed deep while twirling his wrists. He shut the door. Like many people, Yoshiaga was broader than Magahara. He kept his hair in a ponytail that ended at his waist. His white kimono looked plain beside Magahara's hooded emerald and silver garb. They embraced. Yoshiaga kissed him on the eyelids and the mouth and led him to the bed. They disrobed and loved each other under lamplight. When finished they dressed quickly, aglow in exultant release.

"This was reckless," Magahara scolded.

"I put the soldiers on an errand."

"Yoshi Ezakiya, the grand manipulator."

"So tense. All my hard work, like bubbles on the water. I am offended," Yoshiaga said.

"Forgive me. I am tired and hungry."

"Tired I can understand. Admit it. I wore you out!" His laugh was harsh, more befitting a villager than aristocracy. He clapped twice and a concubine entered from the side room. She lay a tray stacked with rice and fruits and sake on the floor. She bowed to them and left the way she came. "Very clever," Yoshiaga complimented as he picked a clump of rice with his fingers. "Recommending that girl will prod father to ponder things other than finding me a bride. Well? Take something if you're so famished."

Magahara chose a slim assortment and downed it with a glass of sake. His smooth, androgynous face scrunched in disgust, as it tended to when he drank alcohol. He had wide eyes, a narrow nose, and an angular jaw that flattered his cropped, jet black hair.

"The girl is more for me than you," Magahara said.

"How so? Should I be jealous?"

"Stop. That scum Fumiaki accosted her and a boy on the route home. This way they are safe. For prisoners of war."

"My Hari. I have never known one so bloodthirsty on the field yet so compassionate at court. Truly a wonder."

"On the field I do what I must." He moved to the window and stared over stone walls to the village below. He stayed quiet for a long while, peering into night. "Have you decided? It has been nine months."

"To leave the court? My family? Just as it is about to be honored by the emperor for loyalty and victory? To flee with you to parts unknown? Have I decided on that?"

"Yes," Magahara said, still fixed on the window.

Yoshiaga would have wilted under his lover's eyes. They both knew Magahara held that sway over all he deemed worthy of affection. Magahara's beauty married sublimely with his always seeing others as they would see themselves, if only they could. Yoshiaga had long marveled aloud and in mixed company that this warrior had the vision of a bodhisattva, that the Knight Wraith's true gift was clarity of others without the turbid knowledge of their secret thoughts and actions. The governor's son found his lover harbored a single fault. Refusal to abide the faults of those Magahara himself held most dear. Yet this very failing made his affections all the more glorious, for when he showed love it was akin to one at last loving himself.

Magahara agreed with most of this assessment, save one trifling detail, because of course he could read most everyone's mind. For those he could not, however, Yoshiaga was spot on.

"Hari, there is much about you I cannot fathom. To be honest, I think you are far more troubled than anyone comprehends. And I love my father. To disgrace him in such a manner would be wrong ... Yet we are two halves. My honor is a scar without you."

Magahara held him tight, then went to the door. He opened it and peered over the bamboo railing. The governor and the priest were still away, as were Magahara's samurai.

"You had me worried for a moment. Come. Let us eat."
"You know of the famine?"
"Your father said we are well stocked."
"True, only you will have to settle for basics. None of that raw, blood soaked meat you crave. Our enemies piled rotting soldiers to contaminate the river. The animals got plagued. Plenty of crops from inland, though."

"No meat!" Magahara's eyes bulged as coins. "How ... how long has this been the case?"

"Three months of plague. Safe supplies ran out weeks ago. Sister must have been ecstatic to see you return so healthy. The famine stretches to our farthest borders. Did you not see the disemboweled corpses lining the banks? Did no one get sick on the march home?"

"Both occurred," he mumbled almost to himself. "And ... and what of the livestock?"

"Culled for the most part. It's not so bad. New shipments will arrive with the emperor."

"A month ..." Magahara whispered.

"About that. In any event what do you want? Your slave girl made a fantastic platter."

Magahara did not respond. All he heard were his own last words, over and over. He began to hyperventilate. Yoshiaga spoke with greater concern at each unanswered question. Unthinking, Magahara back stepped from the room and down the stairs. Yoshiaga followed, perplexed. He was shouting now. Magahara heard none of it. The Knight Wraith turned and ran like the wind.

• • •

"You okay, Steffy?" Liselle asks from behind the counter. "Harry's not bothering you, is he?"

"Who are you?" Stefan asks the thin Japanese man.

"I was born in the year 932 as Minamoto no Magahara, kin to Japan's 62nd emperor. I was reborn a vampire not 30 years later. I am also your ancestor. The one who split the bloodline. It is pointless to deny what you already feel."

"Uh, I think you've hit your limit, Harry," Liselle says. "Sorry, Steffy. He's not like this."

"Give us a minute, Liselle," Stefan says. The men lock gazes. She backs off. "Go on."

"Shakti came first," Magahara says. "In ancient Indus. The first vampire. For millennia she kept her Children within reason. Until they bored her and she slew them. Four hundred years she slept, leaving me as the only one. The wave woke her. Then she—along with you, Jin, Sowen, and I—found ourselves with so much more power. Now she thirsts as never before, to turn the world and bind everyone to her."

"Soooo, wait," Stefan says. "Let's pretend I buy this. That the gentlest woman I've ever met is an evil vampire bent on world domination. And, to be clear, I don't. But let's pretend. How does Sam figure in?"

"Sowen was a priest and mathematician in prehistoric Britain. Like Shakti when she was human, he guided his people. Somehow he gained sway over storms and earthquakes and such. But his greatest gift was immortality through reincarnation. Twenty years ago the wave gave him mastery of the atom. The man can shape matter and energy at will. His power is beyond measure."

"Look, nutjob, I admit you seem familiar," Stefan says with a forced grin. "Maybe you've got that kind of face. Seen it in a few dreams. But get off the Bacchus. So called psychics have told all sorts of lies about Sam and Ana."

"Do those liars haunt your dreams?" Magahara asks. "She wants to rule. He wants to help her. Your brother was not part of their plan. That makes you both threats."

"See, here you go again!" Stefan shouts as he pushes the thin Japanese man off the stool and onto the floor. "Mind your goddamn business!"

Magahara springs up clamping fingers round Stefan's throat. He levitates off the ground so that the bigger man goes aloft as well. In his rage Stefan had forgotten about the vise grip. His fiercest struggles cannot budge it.

"Hear me, child! I am Magahara the Knight Wraith! I am your elder and you will listen! I rejected her once. That may not be possible again. She wants me back, but she will settle for you. As for Sowen, their affair spans millennia. They consider each other their only equals. But you and your brother are different from the rest. You may be able to stop them. I speak truth. Now—"

He halts when William and the rest of the crew burst in. At that the last of the patrons flee, abandoning drinks and one deactivated female cyberclone. Liselle, who has been aiming a shotgun at Magahara's head ever since he levitated, eases the weapon down once she sees the other four metas. Magahara drops Stefan to the floor as he turns toward the others. He does not look at them.

"Hello, Shakti," he thinks to the young Indian woman in the golden sari and red shawl who trails in after them, the pristine beauty the world once called Ana Shaktira, whom only he can see. "Surprised you let me say this much."

"Come now," she thinks back. "You went through so much trouble, running away like that. I figured you ought to get something out of it ... His passion reminds me of yours, back when we first met. Don't you think?"

"I can't remember," Magahara lies.

"Hm. Mortality has been known to blur," she replies. "Shall we be off?"

"Please don't make me refuse again."

"Have it your way. Too bad on them," she thinks.

Shakti turns visible. William had been failing to hit the floating Japanese man with a sleep bomb. Then he sees Ana. Phase fears she has gone delusional, the first sign of her infection. Zenith's X-ray and thermal sensors confirm the subject as flesh and bone, although she would prefer a blood analysis. Oke calls her alias as he runs to her and throws arms around her in elation.

"We thought you died!" the boy says. "You look good. Really good. How'd you survive? Is Mister Haine okay, too?"

"Yes. He's fine," she says, stroking his neck. "Would you like to see him? Wouldn't all of you?"

"Shakti, leave them alone!" Magahara shouts.

"You had your chance, my love. Now it's my turn."

She waves her palm and Magahara finds himself in the throes of memory, recalling every single human he has turned vampire. Not from his perspective, but from that of his prey. The assault is so immobilizing in its euphoria that he levitates dumbstruck and drooling.

"Ana?! Ana, tell me he's lying," Stefan begs, at last rising from his knees. "Tell me you're not a ... vampire."

"A what?" Oke asks while drawing away.

William scrambles, futilely, to penetrate her mind. Phase goes intangible, just in case. Zenith readies her lasers. And all of them pray that somehow this is something other than a sign of the apocalypse.

"We are who we are," Shakti says with an earnest smile. "I welcome you to join us in the making of this brave, new world order."

"God help us," Stefan curses, praying the nightmare will fade. "Meta Force, I order you to subdue the suspect, Ana Shaktira Haine, on charges of ... I don't know ... registration fraud and being a lying bitch ... ¡Mierda!"

He pounces with a hypersonic right cross to her jaw, suspicious that he long ago forfeited any rights of fury at this exquisite monster, wishing that just this once living between the seconds did not also demand an eternity of regrets, and, yes, perversely curious to finally see what his unfettered might would do to another. The woman in the golden sari meets his gaze, smugly, he feels, marring their private eon, until she stumbles back under his fist. Shakti returns with a left uppercut Stefan never sees. Her blow cracks his chin and grinds his teeth, waters his eyes and burns his brain, as it launches him through the ceiling and through his old flat and through the roof, debris crashing down to the bar in his wake.

"Try to understand," Shakti says to the others as she steps on a scrap of wallpaper decorated with blue teddy bears. "We're only saving the world."

Zenith interrupts whatever else she might have said with a fusillade of lasers from silvery blue fingertips. Ten disintegration beams drill through the vampire's skull, shoulders, heart, elbows, torso, crotch, and knees. Shakti falls apart, blood and guts spewing in a heap on the floor of the Ataraxia.

"Gross, Becca," William says. "Just like that, huh?"

That instant sinew, bone, skin, and blood reassemble without flaw. In a quarter blink of an eye the re-formed, now nude, Mother of the Night traverses the room, piles her fist through the living robot's durium nanite chest, and dislodges her solar battery. Zenith checks the hole in her chest, then the baseball sized oval crumbling in Shakti's hand. *Note to self: Get a new power source*, she thinks before her systems fail and her body scatters into millions of inert, silvery blue, ant sized machines.

"Lord. Not again," William laments. That comes easier than comprehending what he once called Ana. It takes all he has to mute emotion for this undead thing. He shuts his eyes before telepathically issuing battle commands.

Phase blinks behind Shakti and waves her arm through the vampire's brain. The disruption takes. Phase teleports away as Shakti spasms, while Oke moves in with a cigarette lighter in one hand and a flaming fist as the other. He shudders before bathing her in fire, keeping the blaze at William's insistence until flesh roasts to bone and bone chars to ash.

As the boy touches his durium pinky ring and morphs into a thick metal dome over her remains, it dawns on him that this should never have been his life. Then a sucking force grows in his domed belly and he feels as though he will cave in, until the force reverses and his durium spine strains to keep from being blown apart, until it does just that.

A tornado of black ash whips durium chunks around the bar, then coalesces into bare female flesh. Shakti chuckles and blows a kiss at Phase, who despite hiding intangible and invisible collapses unconscious from a sleep bomb.

"Well, Doctor Powers?" Shakti thinks. "I'm waiting."

"Why didn't I see this coming?!" he thinks back. "All these years. Never had a clue … I read your minds!"

"You saw what I wanted you to see. Don't fret," his enemy consoles. "Aside from Sowen and me, you're the most powerful meta alive. Or you could be. You've yet to realize your potential. Now we've got to get going. Join us, step aside, or make a move."

He moves. First he tries to rip her apart through telekinesis, but she blocks that with an invisible bubble of her own. He tries invading her mind, but she blocks that with a telepathic shield. At last he detects the polarity of her aura, then sets his to its opposite while expanding the shield. On cue she gets blown out of the bar and through a new hole in its cciling. William allows himself a moment of confused pride. Until she swoops back down through the newly created hole and flies, fingernails clawing and canines glistening, onto his jugular.

Shakti drops William unbitten and turns to Magahara. The Knight Wraith begins to shake his haze. Her cool palms on his cheeks remind him of home. He scans the devastation of the Ataraxia and mourns for shotgun toting Liselle still cowering behind the counter. Already he rues denying Shakti her way. He hears her charms and longs for her thrall. Yet he knows this is not that as surely as knows he can always choose another path. Such certainty baffles him. For even as he takes her hand and she teleports them away, he cannot conjure a single reason to oppose her.

9

Mother watches over us

Ahmad's chat with Cindy had been going so well. They like the same music and movies. Play the same videogames. Even wear the same brand of jeans. Yet she cut their online dalliance soon after he mentioned he lives in Palestine. She said she had homework. On Halloween. All the American girls he meets online recall they have homework when they learn he is "from over there." He reminds himself that this should not bother him because they are godless whores. Pretty, godless whores with smooth, peachy skin and flowing, blond hair and tight, tight jeans. And a 16 year old who feels called to be an imam ought not care about such things. *But still. It's not fair.*

He ogles Cindy's photo a final time, then logs off and looks down the road to the border. Only three cars to go. His father has been mumbling about gridlock out of Jerusalem for the last hour. His younger sister insists on reading the visitors' pamphlet from the Dome of The Rock. Aloud, ad infinitum, after they just spent the entire day there. His mother reminds them to buckle their seatbelts and to remain silent during the Israelis' inspection of the car. He takes in the barren, dusty hills, littered with small, shoddy homes that hardly resemble anything he sees online about America, and he damns himself by wondering why Allah allows such inequity if He is so loving. As though in response, the setting sun casts a peaceful orange glow on those homes at the horizon.

Their lime green Ford emits a black cloud as it pulls up to the toll plaza. Ahmad has been telling his father for weeks that any vehicle with 379,453 miles, actual tires, and an outdated hybrid engine loses the right to be called "vintage," but rather ought to be called "scrap." Nothing can sway his father when it comes to his first and only car, his gift to himself for graduating law school. Ahmad laughs under his breath. To think that his father, a venerated judge, once used his practice to defend freedom fighters and funnel funds to their cause. The laughter ends when sunglass wearing Israelis exit the tollbooth.

He checks his seatbelt, then Leena's, who remains lost in her pamphlet. *Was I so carefree at 9 years old? Maybe she's scared out of her mind and that's her cover.* Ahmad puts his hand on her shoulder and studies the spark in her eyes when she looks up at him. *Nope,* he decides, *she really is oblivious. Lucky girl.* He stares at the back of his mother's seat as the guards circle the car. Two Israelis with machine guns and army fatigues for an unarmed Palestinian family on pilgrimage. *No wonder The Way gets stronger every day,* Ahmad thinks. *It's only fair.*

• • •

Magahara expected Shakti's palace buried miles underground in the Punjab to have remained undisturbed through the centuries. He does, however, marvel at its latest furnishings. Wall size monitors. Memory foam couches. Stain resistant carpets.

"Don't worry about that spill," Sowen says after handing Magahara a fresh glass of blood. "Can't be petty on my birthday. Besides, we'll only be here the night."

"Pity," Magahara says. He drinks deep. "This place takes me back. Has it been 700 years?"

"Give or take a generation," Shakti says. She pets an oiled and glistening female Child of the Night, one of a dozen such pristine men and women poised about the room in thongs and bikinis as living works of art. "So what was with that grandstanding back in the bar?"

"Seriously, Magahara. 'Hear me, child!' A bit over the top, no?" Sowen asks as he scratches his red beard.

"Felt right at the time," Magahara says while twirling his glass for another drink. Sowen wills blood to pour into the empty glass from thin air. "I was trying to impress the gravity of the situation."

"You always did feel the need," Shakti replies.

"Easy love," Sowen says. "When were we last together like this?"

"Oh, we've never been together quite like this," Magahara says before swallowing a deep crimson gulp.

• • •

Ahmad's father caters to the guards, showing his driver's license, birth certificate, judicial badge, even Leena's pamphlet from the shrine. He snatches it from her while explaining how wonderful their trip has been, as though the Israelis care, blind to his daughter's epiphany that men with guns stare at her.

"Is everything in order?" he asks in Hebrew.

"Not quite," the shorter, pudgier guard says. He mumbles something into the hand radio clipped to his belt. Suddenly every guard exits every tollbooth at the plaza. All traffic halts. "Step out of the vehicle."

"What's the problem?"

"You and your wife need to get out," the taller, stockier guard says.

"We don't want any trouble," Ahmad's father assures, pushing his wife's hand off his shoulder as she prods him to obey.

"Good. Neither do we. Get out," the taller guard says as he removes his sunglasses and waves his machine gun.

Sunlight has all but gone. Ahmad feels a chill sweep in from the hills. Everyone he knows agrees that once the Israelis get you out of the car they call you a terrorist and humiliate you to no end. Many brothers at the mosque have been frisked, a few jailed. One even recounted how they planted Bacchus on him. Hassan was locked up for months, lost his scholarship.

Ahmad understands his father's reticence. Yet more smells amiss than simple Zionist abuse. These guards lack the sneer, the revelry in oppression he had come to expect of such an encounter. The pair seem downright serene. Almost everything about them—their polite tone, their easy posture—contradicts the stories.

"Fine," Ahmad's father says as he unlocks the door. "But I know my rights. This violates them."

He and Ahmad's mother step out of the car with palms open and arms wide. She throws her children a look that means to warn them to remain motionless and quiet lest they desire beatings at home. Ahmad knows this without question. It comes off as showing how much she loves them, just in case she and their father wind up incarcerated or worse. The shorter guard snaps her back to attention.

"Turn around and put your hands on the roof of the car." He too removes his sunglasses when the couple hesitates. "I repeat–"

"No. Enough!" Ahmad's father shouts. "Tell me what I've done. Look at this line," he says, pointing to the string of headlights behind them. "We all want to go home. But we're not going to accept–"

Then he notices the military trucks rolling over the hills from each side of the road. Even through darkness the flags show that they are both Israeli and Palestinian. Troops pour out of the trucks and descend upon civilians, Israelis and Palestinians cooperating to order the masses out of their vehicles.

"Things will go much smoother if you turn around," the taller guard reiterates.

"Allah save us," Ahmad's mother says, eliciting a raised eyebrow from her husband. "Who are you people? Palestinians would never–"

At that the guards grab the couple by their chins and spin them round so that their chests slam against the Ford. Ahmad and Leena watch in terror as the guards gape their mouths to reveal monstrous canines glistening under bloodshot eyes. The guards clamp their fangs on the throats of their prey, suck lustily, then step back as the couple slide down the car doors and slump over on the road.

Leena begins to wail, tears streaming down her cheeks, as she begs her brother to explain what's happening. Ahmad yearns to tell any lie that will calm her, but he is frozen by the sight of the guards leaping over the car and across the road to tackle a woman fleeing for the hills. She falls screaming about demons.

• • •

"It began yesterday. Before sunrise," Shakti tells Magahara. He sits on the arm of a couch where Sowen has been reclining. "First I drank the leaders of every Middle Eastern country from India to Saudi Arabia, then down into Africa. Presidents and governors, mostly. They spent the rest of the day holding 'emergency conferences' on The Way, where they drank their advisers and military commanders. The commanders ordered their forces, including police, to submit to anti-MV syringes. They said the virus had spread to baselines. Actually injections of vampire blood. Prison wardens got turned, too. So convicts are out helping the cause greatly. The Red Nation will rise with the sun."

"How many people are being murdered in the process?" Magahara asks. He glowers at her as she paces in rapturous pride. "Or do you even care?"

"Shouldn't be more than a few hundred thousand," Sowen says. "Mostly from the westbound E-M pulse I'm generating. Which is giving me quite the headache, by the way. It's following nightfall to coincide with the turning of the masses. The typical casualties expected by total loss of electricity in hospitals, airborne planes, rioting cities, etcetera. No NeuroNet, no communication. Neutralize the resistance, you understand."

"Of course," Magahara says. "Who needs innocent people trying to defend themselves?"

"Don't be so melodramatic!" Shakti chides as she takes a seat on the thighs of two thong clad, male Children of the Night who kneel shin to shin gazing at her with pure love. "We're talking about a fourth of the world's livable surface area. A third of its population. Come daylight nobody here will care."

"Yes, 'here' being the operative word," Magahara replies. He snickers despite himself upon pondering their attire. He in his white tank top and black leather pants. Shakti in a maroon "I © Mumbai" sweater and golden capris. Sowen in a gray robe from one of the many hotels bearing his name. *Quite the conquerors.* "I doubt the rest of the world will be so indifferent."

"What are they going to do about it?" Sowen asks. "Delegate through the U.N. to invade the largest, most united front humanity has ever known? One that will open its borders to the indigent and infected? That will lack inequity? That will make no acts of aggression on its neighbors? That will offer free labor to multinational conglomerates? Please hazard a guess."

"Well you don't have to be so smug," Magahara says.

・・・

Ahmad reaches over his balling sister and scrambles for the car door, his fingers so tremulous and the night so pitch that it takes him almost a minute to find the handle. He climbs over Leena to spill onto the street, then shuts the door and hurries round the rear of the car. His parents writhe in the dirt by the road. He has seen such movements on the Net, in scenes of pornography and of partiers high on Bacchus just before their powers kick in.

"Mom? Dad? Are you alright?" he whispers in Arabic, crouching close to see their faces. "The guards are gone."

"Everything's fine," his mother wheezes. She lifts her head. A pair of fangs hook under bloodshot, glowing eyes.

"Take your sister home. Wait for us there," his father heaves as he rubs an ice cold palm across his son's cheek. "Don't worry. Mother watches over us."

Ahmad begins to ask what that means when his parents stand and lung at five panicked Israeli civilians running past the Ford. He watches in a surreal haze as the people who have spent his entire life drilling him on etiquette and ethics drag strangers to the ground and sink their teeth into foreign necks, hissing and growling like wild animals as they do so, paying no heed to the victims' gagged shrieks for mercy. Dimly, he is aware of Leena peering through the window too terrified to cry. Then his parents race off faster than any baseline, leaving a quintet of new writhers in the road.

"Sit down!" he shouts to Leena as he rushes to the driver side and gets behind the wheel. "Put on your seatbelt!"

Only after failing with the ignition does he notice that the streetlamps and headlights have died. Only after that does he realize that no lights or sounds of traffic emanate from the nearby cities. Only after that does he realize that he cannot activate the NeuroNet. Ahmad finally acknowledges his darkest suspicion.

Defeat came for Israel and the United States through what they labeled the Terror Wars, but which his people praise as the Jihad. Palestine was recognized and absorbed into the Caliphate. Israel was halved and the U.S. so humiliated that it all but fell apart. So the West still reaps riches while his people scrape by. *Heaven welcomes the humble.*

He sees nothing where Jerusalem ought to be, which means Israelis face attack as well. Christians will call it Armageddon. But Ahmad knows it as a test from Allah. A test to see who maintains the faith, who resists letting fear pull them under the sway of the djinn. And maybe, just maybe, Ahmad is being tested for questioning Allah's love.

His ruminations cease when the five strangers his parents attacked spring up and press their faces to the windows. They salivate a few seconds before withdrawing.

"Get out! Get out!" he says, kicking open his door and yanking Leena out of hers. "Do what I say and don't ask any questions! Just don't!"

With that they run off for the black of the hills praying to a God they fear is very real and very angry.

• • •

"For now we're limiting the rising to the areas with the weakest infrastructure," Shakti says. "Africa was just waiting for me. Outsiders wouldn't dare invade the Middle East so soon without knowing what's going on. India was the biggest risk, being so developed. But it's my home. My prize. I had to."

"Why not take the world in one swoop?" Magahara asks. "Or is that going over the top? Too flashy for you?"

"Blame Hikikomori," Sowen says. "We had to think fast after his ... surprise. Our "corpses" are clones I whipped up on the spot. Playing dead has become a bit too deep undercover for her taste. This is a rush job. The original plan was years away. To turn the world's homeless while keeping our powers secret until the Children spread. As we stand, doing anything more, like creating a global E-M pulse, might give me a stroke. And were this surge to last into daylight vampires would have to hide. Humans would fight back. Then causalities would get regrettable.

"In a way, Hikikomori did us a favor. Now humanity does itself in through confusion and fear. We'll use our good names to woo the downtrodden. Sow dissent among the opposition. We figured you might warn Stefan. He's already so stressed about his freak brother, I half expected him to join us. And now you've cleared your conscience ... Wish he had come. Stefan's more fun than either of you."

"You turned your knight into a pawn," Magahara says to Shakti. "I understood your motives when we fed to survive. What makes you think people need this kind of saving?"

"A good mother knows when children are hurting," she replies, petting her male furniture. "And I'm great."

"Great? Know what would be great?" Magahara asks. "If Sowen turned every desert into a garden and you gave away the food. If he flooded the sand and you gave away the water. Then perhaps humans wouldn't 'need' you. Or do they not deserve that kind of saving?"

At that his companions gawk at each other. Before long Shakti kisses Magahara on the forehead and Sowen praises him as their eternal savior.

• • •

Ahmad misses the hills. Sure, dogs ran wild in dusty shantytowns while toddlers wandered sobbing for lost parents. Sure, people with bats, chains, pistols, torches, and Molotov cocktails huddled in doorways and windows, on guard against possessed hordes who did indeed consume them. Sure, Ahmad had to snatch a flaming broom from a trash bin just to see through the four hour trek to Bethlehem, which culminated in carrying Leena piggyback for the last 40 minutes. Still, compared with the hills, his city is Hell manifest.

Or so he guesses as they sit on a curb across the street from a burning apartment building. *Jerusalem must be worse. Somehow.* He takes it in, squinting through the dark with one arm around Leena, the other extending the flaming broom, and his back against a telephone pole while trying to block out the sadistic twinge at his lower spine. An old woman trapped on the fifth floor has come to a window, waving for rescue, ignorant of her many neighbors also trapped by flames. A fire truck lay parked outside the inferno. Out jump three women wearing only the blood caked helmets of real firefighters. The naked females scale the walls with feline ease. They stop at the windows of the trapped, saving them with fangs to the jugular.

Ahmad's eyes sparkle when he spies an unchained bicycle against the fire truck. He pulls Leena to her feet and sneaks over while the harpies feast up high. *Thank Allah. It's new and well oiled.* He peddles off, standing as Leena sits, before the naked women have a clue.

Fatigue and sensory overload numb him beyond fear. The final two miles home fill him with the only remaining emotion. Pity. That swells not from watching his neighbors fall against demons, but from watching these people riot among themselves. They pass boys his age, some he knows, hurling rocks in the street at several fully clothed and obviously untainted women twice their age. Women who had been banging on the door of a packed mosque. They pass a small mob of adults stomping a sweet old wheelchair bound beggar who until yesterday they regarded as a prophet. They pass a pack of young children torturing kittens with sticks and gasoline. *So many are failing the test*, Ahmad laments.

Thus he almost finds it a relief to see wild eyes and fangs outside their four-story apartment building. Although this is neighbor against neighbor, at least it makes sense.

A male demon wearing only a towel snatches Miss Khan by the hijab and pulls her to the welcome mat at the front door. The siblings step over them as Miss Khan, a next door neighbor who often babysat them, feels the bite. They ascend the staircase—which is now covered in blood, papers, a trampled rat, ripped clothes, and feces—until they find Mister al Maliki, their obese, blind landlord, sitting hunched over, blood squirting from his throat, as he gasps at the landing to their floor.

Ahmad puts Leena on his shoulders, which puts a fire in his spine, then tries to squeeze by the man. He makes it off the stairs and around al Maliki's back when a corpulent paw grabs his ankle. Leena tumbles toward their apartment door as the landlord hauls Ahmad back to the steps. Up close the screaming boy wilts under al Maliki's stench—a blend of common funk and some alien putrescence—as well as the blank gaze of black pupils churning in a sea of crimson veins. The man sniffs him, mouth wide and tongue lashing in anticipation, until a woman's blood soaked hand alights on his meaty shoulder.

"Not that one," Ahmad's mother says, cueing the fat man to relent. "Welcome home, my son."

Ahmad takes her cold hand, avoiding her pale visage, as she leads her exhausted children inside.

10

There's vampires now?!

"Vampires? There's vampires now?!" James asks as he plops into a chair at the massive roundtable of the secret U.N. meeting room.

"We've had a week to accept that," says Gloria Finley, president of the U.S. and de facto leader of the North American Union. "What do we do about it?"

"Nuke them. Nuke them until their brown bodies turn black as soot," advises East Asian Union President Wen Deng. "What other option is there?"

"They invade us if that option fails," says Kabila Obasun, United Nations secretary general and moderator for the Council of Continents. "The average vampire seems to have telepathy and levitation as well as enhanced senses, strength, and speed. We lose in that scenario."

"Unbelievable. Let's be realistic. We can't nuke them again," says South American Union President Hugo Mesa. "Or did you forget we tried that five days ago?"

"They tried that," corrects Diah Irwin, president of the South East Asian Union. "Deng, mind giving the rest of us notice next time you risk Armageddon? The Americans and the Russians won't admit it, but their missiles almost shot off at each other following your lead. You've got to accept that none of them made so much as a scratch."

"See here, you Aussie Malay half breed!" James shouts, banging his fist on the table so hard that blond hairs fall over his sky blue eyes. "I have more nukes in my toilet than you have in your entire arsenal, so consider yourself lucky to be here. How was anyone to know they've got that much telekinesis? I ripped Igor a new one for acting ahead of E.U. orders, and the Russians are mighty sheepish since their missile got returned at my doorstep! How do you think I felt looking out my window seeing a nuke floating 10 feet from my face? How do you think I felt getting my Net hacked by Haine's and Shaktira's traitorous faces, talking about 'the benevolence of the Red Nation'? About how they hid their powers for fear of being exploited by both the U.N. and The Way? About how they're bringing peace to help us defeat terrorism? So you can shut it, or go wrestle a crocodile or eat a koala or whatever you people do!"

"Your Highness! Control yourself!" Obasun admonishes. "We've confirmed that every Net account got hacked. We're all in shock. But Hugo and Diah are right about the nuclear assault. Those returned rockets could have exploded. Who's to say others won't blow up in our faces if we send more?"

"First off, unless the U.N. is hiding a secret stash of missiles I don't know about, kill this 'we' business," Finley says. "Second, I doubt they can deflect a hundred thousand missiles at the same time. The real problem is that it looks bad. We already look bad for letting this happen. We'll look worse if we commit genocide. On the Holy Land, no less. Remember, according to their statement only adults became vampires. That means more than half of their 2.7 billion population are effectively child hostages. That makes this delicate."

"What makes this delicate is what they're offering," Mesa says. "They make it seem like Utopia. No crime, no disease, no poverty in their borders? Free labor, medicine, energy, crops, and water for any humans willing to play by their rules? Lord. Satellites confirm that the Sahara and Arabian deserts are now the largest sources of farmland and fresh water on Earth. Any idea how they're doing that?"

"It's like Stefan Reyes told us," Deng says. "Haine controls the atom. Our worst fear. An intelligent, driven meta with the power to rearrange matter and energy. He can do almost anything. And his wife's army gives him more manpower than any of us. Which is why we must strike first, hardest. If not with weapons of mass destruction then with an all out invasion."

"Let's hold off on talk of invasion for a moment. Bringing Reyes into this raises a more important question," Obasun says. "Mainly, who can be trusted?"

"Nobody," Irwin says. "Certainly not Reyes. His brother's the world's biggest terrorist and his ex-boss is the world's biggest dictator. How can we believe a word he says? Why isn't he and the rest of his squad in The Hole, anyway? Shaktira let them live for a reason."

"Listen, woman!" James shouts as he stands from the roundtable. "Stefan saved my life. And everyone here voted Haine into his post as W.M.F. chief, which thank God, he's not asking to reclaim. Should all of us be in The Hole, too? For all we know they have a vampire sleeper cell in this building. All we can do is judge from the evidence. It makes no sense that Stefan and his squad would stay with me, in broad daylight, and submit to daily mind probes from a slew of expert telepaths, if they were traitors."

"Isn't Reyes impervious to telepathy? And immune to Metapurge, for that matter?" Obasun asks. "Isn't William Powers the strongest telepath in the world? And if the so called 'Red Nation' does back them, wouldn't their resources be endless? Oh, and isn't the jury still out on if mind probes are reliable?"

" ... They're my protection. I trust them. You don't have to," James says, soft and slow, while reclaiming his seat.

"We're the ones deciding policy, not my bodyguards. Let's move on."

"Before we get to details of a counterstrike, should we not address who's in charge over there?" Finley asks. "Is it Haine or Shaktira? Or even Myeong?"

"Haine of course," Deng says. "He was the king of the business world. Now he wants to be king of the world."

"Except he claims he's not a vampire. And she seems to be controlling the masses," Finley counters. "Plus, if you trust Reyes, that's what he heard in London. That Shaktira wants to rule and Haine wants to help her. She's the boss and they've been using The Way to distract us."

"I don't know who's running things," Mesa says. "Given how my marriage works, I suspect they're unsure. We ought to consider the couple a unit. Regarding The Way, faking their deaths served them no real purpose. Myeong might have forced that. Which means we might have two theaters. What is clear is that none of them will stay satisfied with what they've already taken."

• • •

Looking down from the track that circles above the bulletproof glass ceiling of the meeting room—soundproof to all but William, Zenith, and himself—Stefan almost wishes he too had fled Taedo Academy. Life as a vagabond would have its perks for one unbound to food, water, air, or sleep. *Might have been lonely*, he admits. But then if not for James and his crew he would be lost even now.

He peruses the track, taking in those also on watch. His team sparkles with every bit of celebrity in their designer attire. A far cry from the staid uniforms worn by the other metas there, most of whom serve in the militaries of their respective Continental Unions.

Then there's Zenith, who no longer wears clothes. Or skin. Her purple and silvery shell retains feminine curves but has traded the suppleness of nanites for the rigidity of a tougher form of durium. Her face has become a blank, purple mask with narrow, rectangular slots for eyes and muzzlelike mesh for ears and mouth. She says her new body, which Stefan likens to lingerie glued on medieval armor, is nigh indestructible. William, who stands far away from her, says he's fine with it. *Yeah right.*

Oke and Faye seem the most at ease, the former thief massaging her adopted son's shoulders as they watch the leaders of the free world bicker like brats. Stefan cannot decide what's more amazing. How effortlessly the boy remade himself after exploding in the bar, or that a baby found in a Jakarta dumpster has grown into the world's most popular teen idol. *Not bad for a 13 year old stoner.*

In the grand scheme, Stefan ranks that dependence as a trifle. As he listens to James further insult Irwin, and he glances at some gray skinned, fin backed meta with the face of an actual shark, Stefan shivers. He suspects the real threat eclipses anything The Way or the Red Nation can muster. He cannot define it, but he knows that it comes from within, and that it will not be denied, and that he has seen it in his dreams.

Yet he has not dreamed since the Ataraxia. *Little good they've done.* All those visions of ancestors, night after night as long as he can remember, yet he hardly recognized Magahara and never made the connection that the bloodsucker of his nightmares was so comforting in his waking life. *Her dream face was always such a blur. And she does cast a reflection. And she enjoys the sun!* He reconciles that he had no way to separate the haze of fact from fantasy. After all, for every image of Ana Shaktira there was one of God anointing him as His eternal warrior. And as much as Stefan longs for it, he knows he is unworthy of such grace.

• • •

"We're agreed then?" Obasun asks. "Let's summarize the treaty a final time.

"On the record, concerning the Red Nation: A non-aggression pact, meaning no attacks or spies unless the enemy is found to initiate these acts. Regulated trade with businesses and states, meaning the enemy will supply products and workers to those firms which offer the lowest prices to their target markets and the best benefits to their non-vampire employees, also meaning divestment of any human operated divisions of global firms headquartered within vampire lands. Under no circumstances can Haine or Shaktira regain their former positions with Haine International, the W.M.F., W.H.O., etcetera. Although the enemy's sovereignty will be recognized, any bid to expand beyond its current borders will negate that recognition and this treaty. Furthermore, despite said recognition, under no circumstances can any representative of the enemy be allowed onto any U.N. Council. Although citizens of non-vampire states may travel to the lands of the enemy, no vampire or citizen of the enemy may enter non-vampire states. Furthermore, anyone traveling to the lands of the enemy must be tested for infection, by representatives of non-vampire states, in international territory, before travelers may return to any non-vampire state.

"Off the record, concerning the Red Nation: Engineering of meta cyberclones will receive top priority and funding, regardless of public opinion, regardless of political dissent, provided laws can be interpreted and/or written to justify said programs. Global positioning and data tracking of NeuroNet activities will receive equal priority and funding as engineering, with the same commitment. Meta registration will receive equal priority and commitment, and violators will be prosecuted under existing and/or future treason laws. Although Haine International cannot be prohibited from dealing with the enemy, all said dealings will be scrutinized for treason, terrorism, spying, embezzlement, etcetera. Haine International and the enemy will be under suspicion of funding terrorist activities of The Way, in all its forms, regardless of the stated motives of factions.

"Anything else?" Obasun asks.

"Yes," Deng says. "We're giving them nearly all they sought. Their crop exports alone might spread vampirism. And I'm sure they expected us to forbid vampires abroad."

"It's the only way," Mesa says. "We need to stall. Besides, financial markets need to rebound within a week or we're facing a depression that will make the 1930s look like a hiccup. The commerce lost with India alone ..."

"He's right," James groans. "They would get so many defectors we'd have to clone fetuses just to draft their artificial asses."

"Thanks for the imagery. Are you drunk?" Finley snipes. "I suppose it's fitting Haine International's stock has plummeted. It's crippling markets as much as sky high oil and topsy turvy derivatives. Let's pray confidence returns once fuel shipments resume and word gets out his old company will benefit most from vampire labor. That'll bring a different headache, God willing a more manageable one. Nothing to do about that lost emerging market revenue, all those firms delisted from the exchanges. At least the Red Nation is paying off human investors, even emptying private banks ... Amazing. Continents without currency."

"Dirty bloody scum!" James shouts as he slaps the table with both palms. "Pardon me, everyone," he says, loosening his tie. "You know I'm not like this. Gallows humor is keeping me sane at the moment."

"I guess the one upshot to this is that they took care of the Semite problem," Irwin says.

"Yes, if by 'took care of' you mean exacerbated," James says. "I realize yarmulkes aren't big business in the Outback, but some of us are dodging flaming pork products for letting this happen. Aren't the Muslims in Indonesia burning you in effigy over this?"

"I'm sure some want to do it for real. I mean that for the first time in memory there's peace in the Holy Land," Irwin says. "Under the worst possible circumstances. But on the off chance they're not backing The Way, we do have many fewer terrorists to worry about."

"Noted," James says after a long pause. He inhales as silence retakes the room. He lets it ride until his façade crumbles. "Look, I apologize about before. You have to understand, I thought these people were my friends. I can't decide if I'm more furious that they're mass murderers, or that they didn't tell me about it."

11

To be God

"They should have told us about it," Phase says as she reaches to pick up Oke's and Stefan's dinner plates from her glass coffee table. "It's the courtesy."

She reaches a few more times, her hand blinking in and out of sight, passing through china and glass, until she steadies enough to grab them. Oke nods to feign attention from the cushy center of William's beige couch. The boy focuses on the military strategy game flashing in his contacts while the people's champion sleeps dangling off the cushion of the adjacent couch. Stefan's face bobs inches from the carpet, a cheek resting on his drool drenched hand, which holds the remote to Zenith's holodisc. They had been watching 3D music videos while devouring bacon cheeseburgers. Phase had insisted on cooking rather than rely on the Berlaymont's cyberclone catering service. Something about lost arts, the boy half heard over the music, which still blares well after Stefan zonked out.

"The conceit!" she shouts on her way to the kitchen, where William rummages through the refrigerator. "Worse than the betr–" Phlegmatic coughs cut her rant. She tosses the plates in the sink before stomach cramps send her stumbling into the refrigerator door. She waves away William's latest inquiry about her health and returns to the living room as though nothing were amiss. "Are you listening to me?"

"Totally," the boy lies, his arms jerking at the virtual battle only he can see. "The receipt's in my room."

"You mean for your hearing aid?" William says as he follows behind Phase. "Good. It's not working so well." He waves at Oke's unresponsive face, then turns to the boy's mother. "How long has he been at it?"

"Too long," she bristles, tapping Oke at his temple.

"Ah, Ma, I'm about to capture Mecca! Gimmie a break!"

"Mecca can wait. You have homework. It's bad enough you don't go to school like a normal kid. I can't have you fall behind with your online courses. You know it's part of the custody stipulation."

"This is homework!" Oke shouts. "Rodan said it's part of the new guide for U.N. Peacekeeping Operations. I'm in training, for our cyberclone invasion ... and ... Mecca is mine!" he shouts, pumping both fists skyward. "Go, Oh!"

"Fantastic," Phase says as she crosses her arms. "Now do as you're told or I'll tell that little slut Monique that you wet the bed last week."

"Geez, Ma," he says, logging off the Net. "That was once in the last four years. P.R. better not use this in the show! It wasn't even like I was ... never mind."

"Don't stop," William cuts in. "It wasn't like you were sober, right? A little beer here, Bacchus there."

"Whatever, Will," the boy says as he rises from the couch to pry the remote out of Stefan's hand and shut off the holodisc. "You all spend as much time online as I do. You shouldn't be reading my mind, anyway. Why are you always riding me?"

William twirls a finger and the boy goes aloft, then flips upside down suspended in midair.

"Hm. Could it be because I got you on this squad? Because I took an oath as a physician? You better believe I'm chatting with your psychiatrist tomorrow."

"Pumpkin, it's dangerous." Phase lays a hand on his chest. "It messes with your head. Your powers. I don't care if you've done it two times or 200 times. Stop, okay?"

Oke rolls his eyes to mask the guilt the pair have inflicted. "You guys are blowing it way out of proportion. But fine. It's getting harder to score, anyway ... so I've heard." His face reddens, which he prepares to blame on the blood rushing down to his floating skull.

Zenith's entrance from the hall spares him further deceit. The force of her durium steps jars Stefan into sliding face first onto the carpet. He awakens into drawn out attempts to wipe away spittle.

"Scarcity is due to the Red Nation," Zenith says as she steps around Stefan's puddle of drool, her purple and silvery frame ambling somewhere between erotic and mechanical. "Shaktira has agreed to halt all illicit trade as an amendment to the treaty. Your guard shift begins now, Faye. James is in his office."

"Right on time," Phase says. She coughs long and nasty. "It's like you're an overpriced alarm clock. Later, guys. And do your homework, Pumpkin, or I tell your girlfriend!"

"Hey, Becca," William starts as Phase blinks out and he lets Oke drop to the carpet, "where'd you hear that?"

"Moments ago, during my continuous malware scan of James' incoming Net files. The U.N. announces it tomorrow."

"A infierno con las escorias," Stefan says as he reclaims the couch. "Bet it's a trap. That's why I peed on their fake ashes and flushed them down the toilet!"

"They're being crazy generous, though," Oke says. "All that free stuff. And Bacchus is bad, right? Right?"

"It's bad for us if they look good," William says. "Cold wars depend on public opinion. And not getting caught. Speaking of which, Becca, you ever consider giving Sam and Ana some type of NeuroNet attack?"

"Yes. Unadvisable," Zenith says. "The probability such malware would prove fatal to them is .09147 percent. The probability it would prompt an invasion is 62.83 percent."

"So we sit here and do nothing," Stefan says.

"Not me!" Oke shouts as he slaps Stefan on the back. "I just aced my homework. Just like I'll ace the invasion."

"There are more variables," Zenith warns. "For one, Haine and Shaktira claim meta vampires are immune to MV."

"Care to guess how many patients are packing as we speak?" William asks.

"¡Chingalo!" Stefan curses, slapping the cushion so it bursts into flying feathers. "That also from James' files?"

"Yes," Zenith says. "James received word yesterday morning. It should be on the news by evening."

"And you're just sharing this now?" William asks.
"Certain information is classified as part of my new directive to scan the Net for signs of terror or treason. Does the same not apply to your recent orders?"

William makes no attempt to hide his scowl. He looks at her as though beholding something foreign, perhaps hostile. Neither of them speaks nor moves and Zenith's unalterable metal mask of a face precludes any hint of emotion. The look barely outlasts a moment, which is long enough to make the other two look away.

"Es el verdad, mi amiga," Stefan says. "Rodan has me spilling anything I can remember about those traitors and my family. Even my dreams. She says it's for psychological profiles. I say it's to make sure I'm not a spy."

"That's what they want from Mom and me," Oke says. "Spy stuff. I'm gonna disguise myself as a techno punk and catch some eco terrorists. Mom's gonna shadow religious nuts. It's awesome. Sure beats Will's job."

"Hey, interrogating terrorists is crucial," William says. "But I do not like mind controlling perps into opening up. Especially metas. The harder they resist, the more prone they are to psychological scars. The average telepath working The Hole makes no distinction between what perps believe and what they want perps to believe. It's like they're getting paid to scramble brains. And none of them knows how to cook."

That elicits forced laughter from Stefan and Oke, who wish Zenith would join in the pretense. Until she does and they shudder at her electronic vibrations.

They relax when she accepts William's offer to go for an evening flight over Brussels. The couple walk down the hall leading to the balcony, hand in awkward hand. Oke boots up a new videogame as soon as the lovers blast off. The boy implores Stefan to keep it secret from Phase. The front man of "Meta Force" smirks conspiratorially as he heads out the door.

Stefan takes the elevator down to the glass walled lobby of the Berlaymont. He walks to Louise Avenue and follows that to Bois de la Cambre. He watches the sky turn orange then purple over browning treetops en route to the park's lake. Visitors and homeless denizens alike draw to him from throughout the park like bugs from grass. He shakes palms and signs autographs and kisses women on the cheek as they stop him. Eventually he leaps across the lake to the flower laden island at its center. Stefan waves to the gawkers before leaping above a chestnut tree, into the night and out of Brussels.

He lands miles away in a field, startling the herd of grazing cattle, and takes off again. He continues jumping until he reaches the Rhine, which he contemplates swimming through, but decides to run atop until he touches ground minutes later under the Hohenzollern Bridge in Cologne. He zips by the city's main cathedral, resisting the temptation of its dual spires and gothic masonry, as he does the Pascha brothel, albeit not quite so quickly.

Now he hits top speed, freezing the rest of existence in its tracks as he cuts past the many spired Grand Ducal Palace of Luxembourg, detours by the domed Sacré-Cœre Basilica of Paris before running straight for the high columned Théâtre du Capitole of Toulouse and into Spain, where he sort of notices the statue capped Edificio Metrópolis of Madrid on his way down to the Rock of Gibraltar. Stefan scales the 1,396-foot-high limestone promontory, stopping at its peak, to peer across the sea into the lands of the enemy.

Solar lamps shine from the fortress recently erected along his side of the strait, where hundreds of laser gun toting cyberclone soldiers guard Europe's southwestern tip. They patrol the coast by foot, and in towers and tanks and boats, ready to fire on invading or smuggling vampires. Stefan narrows his eyes, zooming in his naturally telescopic vision to get an up close view of several ships docked along the fort for thorough inspection. Smiling, courteous vampires reveal the cargo they have donated to Haine International and a handful of the world's other mega conglomerates. Food. Jewels. Clothes. Microchips. Medicines. Cyberclones. This might pass for normal had one been in a coma for the last month. So many crates bearing Haine's logo. The same logo that flashes at the end of every "Meta Force" episode, that lay somewhere on most of Stefan's clothes. An inverted Omega cradling a Delta. *Never thought to ask what it means.*

Stefan stifles a curse and tries to impel himself to head home. But this gets him to recall what home is now. How that too he owes to his former friend. How he might never return to that place, simply to spite his newfound enemy, if only the show's ratings had not skyrocketed since they all moved in together. So instead of retreating Stefan finds himself smashing a fist onto the summit of the Rock, and catching a dislodged boulder fifty times his size before it would have plummeted on inhuman passersby. In a fluid motion, he hurls the chunk heavenward, watching it shrink with distance, until it blends in with the stars. Then he crouches and jumps with all his might. Miles into his flight he decides to catch the boulder and push it farther, into orbit, rather than shatter it into millions of bits. He succeeds, and enjoys its drift into the void, as he freefalls miles back to Earth and into the Atlantic.

He broods about abandonment on the hourlong swim up the Spanish and French coasts. How it keeps happening to him, and whether it is time to do so himself. How death may not be intentional, but that the effect is the same. How inability to kill in the name of duty is tantamount to abandonment of duty. How the fame he once cherished is now a cage. And about how he still cannot believe the odds of the betrayals he has endured.

By the time he sprints back to the Berlaymont his clothes have dried and come loose at the seams. They remain better intact than the jacket two security guards tear from the woman screaming outside the building's entrance. She is young, squat, tanned, raven haired, and of an American accent. The guards wrestle with her as she shouts about the apocalypse and her need to warn Stefan, until he walks up and brushes them aside. Then he sees her oval shaped face, and locks on her iridescent eyes, and smells her pecan musk, and feels the siren in his skull, and knows that she owns him.

"My name is Nia Begaye," she pants, clasping his shoulders. "Seer of space and time, and the future mother of your child. So pay attention."

"Aye. Por supuesto. Dámelo," Stefan mumbles. He does his best to disregard her final appellation, as well as fast encroaching recollection of his own dreams. "What then, chica demente?"

"What you already know but refuse to accept," she says, now clasping his face. "That your old friend wants to be God, and that fate has chosen you to be our savior."

12

Gift of freedom

The half dozen loiterers hogging the park bench give the bearded, bald man lean and hungry glares as he passes, until he stops and walks back over to them to return an even more intense gaze. They are old teens and young adults, two of them male and all of them poor, judging by their stained, baggy apparel. The sun has long set and the streetlamps flicker lazily. He suspects they had considered mugging him but now fight the urge to flee. He digs in his coat pocket and pulls out a wad of hundred dollar bills, which he tosses to the ground.

He hears them call after him as he departs. Hears them scramble to collect his leavings, bickering as they divvy it up. Hears them inquire about a business card amid the cash, which on one side reads, "This is not The Way. I am," and on the obverse lists several Net addresses.

Hikikomori knows he has converted few in New York City, much less Brooklyn. He also knows the denizens of Prospect Park are hardening. He ruminates on ever deepening poverty. Privatized schools, police and firefighters. Abolished minimum wage. Robots and cyberclones replacing humans in all manner of job, from law enforcement to construction to transportation to sanitation. Ghettos migrating, angrily, under the heel of gentrification. Ubiquitous Bacchus. And absent MV clinics.

He knows the forgotten are ripe for his cause, knows the world awaits his gift of freedom. He has yearned to bestow it since he was called by the skull splitting siren of the meta wave that changed a world in an instant. Twenty years later and nobody has offered a valid reason why 83 million people, a full percent of the species, at once made evolutionary quantum leaps, and why a million lucky souls dropped dead for no discernible reason. It defies logic, he knows, and yet it is the way of things. No laboratory disaster. No radioactive meteorite. It just ... happened.

As it must have centuries ago, he figures, to spawn his line, and, apparently, Haine and Shaktira. *Who should be dead by my hand instead of stealing my followers ...!*

Yet he knows they may prove as helpful as the drug and the virus. *So many addicts in need of a fix, then an outlet for their fleeting power. So many sick, vengeful at society for shunning them. So many easy pickings, once fed the proper lies.* The most pervasive that Haine International created Bacchus and MV to profit from the wave. Never mind that Bacchus was sold as a mere hallucinogen long before the wave, and that many contracted the virus along with their powers. *Let all fools be used.*

At that thought Hikikomori turns his night stroll into a seven minute dash to Miami, where he stops at a safe house. Piles upon piles of locked crates clutter the beachside loft. He opens two, pulls a body sized duffel bag from each one, and packs those with the contents of their respective crates. He takes off again, zipping along the surface of the sea and into Cuba, over the waves once more and into Colombia, stopping in the Brazilian rainforest.

He sees through moonless black night as though clear day, ducking leafy branches and sidestepping mud pits as he follows the sound of weary voices. He emerges from jungle into a clearing where scores of indigenous men gather round a campfire. They greet him with pats and hearty thanks while tidying their ripped, outdated apparel. Hikikomori opens the first bag and rations out food supplies. The men snatch up his champagne, steak, lobster, and curau. Then he opens the second bag and rations out weapons. Soon everyone brandishes laser pistols and E-M pulse grenades.

He extols the need to destroy the nearby cyberclone factory. They cheer as he damns Haine International for building on the rebels' tribal land, for wiping out miles of crops, for turning self sufficient farmers into underpaid assembly line workers to a foreign master that dumps toxic waste in their ever shrinking forest. They march off shouting the glory of O Modo as their benefactor disappears into the foliage.

Hikikomori slices over land and sea and through the domain of the vampire during his ninety minute journey to a small town outside Nanjing. En route he reflects on the nature of power in this increasingly absurd world.

His lineage has always been elite among the masses, and now even among metas. By his ranking he places fourth, tied with his brother, in the genetic hierarchy. And that may be modest, if as he suspects, they are bound solely by concentration of will. After all, they need no food, water, nor air. Even sleep seems mere habit. He considers his current pace and the many factors that emerge when living a thousand times faster than normal. For one, the body's force on matter increases exponentially. For another, the mind must adjust. Otherwise a minute in hyper speed either would seem a mind numbing eternity locked in slow motion or a rampage of bumbling collision with item after mysterious item. Yet he eases between extremes, ignoring the ocean's blur one moment, studying the Red Nation in freeze frame the next, relying on lightning reflexes to jaunt by obstacles when impatient.

Reports of Utopia do seem genuine, he admits. Where once the Sahara and Arabian deserts stretched, now verdant plains roll. Where once civilization meant rival sects in feeble shacks, eager to take their spiritual and economic frustrations out on the Great Satan at his direction, now a peaceful, productive collective operates in sprawling cities with gleaming edifices. Two months in and roads are paved, litter is absent, cyberclones police giddy children, and crimson flows from faucets. It embodies all and more The Way has exhorted. *Too bad beauty never lasts. Too bad it comes from the touch of a demon whore and a mad god!*

So he slows and knocks on the door of a quaint house on a quaint suburban street on a beautiful Sunday morning in far eastern China. A pudgy balding man in a cheap suit opens the door and jumps in his skin at the sight of the bald, bearded visitor. Hikikomori hugs Liu as an old friend. Liu sighs and walks him to the kitchen. Little Bao Chan, now 14 years old but seeming much younger, skips from the crayon covered table and hands the visitor an ugly drawing of a big red blotch in the sky. Hikikomori smiles and pockets the image. Liu's wife offers him a glass of milk, which he gulps earnestly. Then they huddle in the hovercar and head to the family's grocery.

Despite Liu's protests, Hikikomori insists on helping out any way he can. The proprietor relents, allowing his guest to stock shelves with canned meats and to mop the checkered linoleum aisles while the store's outmoded bronzed robot slumps idle. Liu demands Hikikomori cease once customers arrive. They are used to the bipedal collection of plastic, iron, and wires doing such things. A status marker, Liu explains.

Hikikomori talks with Bao Chan for a while—mostly about drawing and videogames, briefly about her condition—as her parents work the registers. She fancies Oke "Oh" Yip, he learns, because the boy always wears such flashy tracksuits. She wants to be a firefighter when she grows up. By noon he bids the family farewell, but not before sending Liu a Net file.

The grocer's widened eyes betray immense regret as he nods to the terrorist, yet the pawn says nothing of it. There is no turning back, not after all he has been given. Hikikomori departs with a handshake, sympathetic to the heartache he has inflicted, unwavering in his conviction of its necessity. *Fire must reign*, he thinks. *Humanity must be freed of its ignorance.*

It is as his father would have wanted, had he survived the meta wave. Or so the son hopes. As always, he fails to block out the memory of stumbling under a searing migraine into the room where their fathers lay dead. Of watching an ambulance cart away their corpses while unreachable Stefan did God knows what with that schoolgirl slut. Hikikomori accepts he will be haunted forever by that horror, when the inequity of life tore down the last of his illusions. *Oh, Father. I hear you. Our dreams will live.*

Thus it has been for sixty generations, by his count. Ancestors guided by dreams of ancestors, learning from the lives of the dead. *But not enough to see through Haine and Shaktira!* He accepts that dreams tend to leave naught but ghosts of themselves. Yet now he knows what to hunt. Like recent ones of Magahara the Knight Wraith, who let Shaktira turn him into the first above her horde, who filled her womb and split the bloodline with twins. *So much like Mother*, Hikikomori realizes with a swell of whimsy.

He marvels that a woman he never knew holds such sway over his life. As their fathers often reminded them, it was she who met the distant kin and introduced them in the course of her socialite fluttering. It was she who suggested the diplomat and the spy establish a school advocating transhumanism. It was she who fell in love with both of them, openly, which they accepted and reciprocated as part of their divine calling. It was she who calmed that first rift between their fathers, when they discovered she was with child. Yet she remains mainly a name to him. *Sarah, without you the world would lack its savior.*

Poor Stefan. He probably thinks the burden is his. Some obligation to ruin my work, no doubt. Conceited fool. "People's champion" indeed. He never focused. Not on his studies. Not on his combat. All he craves is the moment. If only he understood that moments don't last. He'll have to choose. I'll make him. And he better choose correctly. I'm the only one who loves the silly, self centered ass!

The terrorist hits Antarctica an hour after Nanjing. Icy flakes spread over his prosthetic scalp and beard, until he rips them away, snacks for a flock of hungry emperor penguins he whizzes past. He climbs the jagged wall of the highest ridge of Mount Erebus, kicking loose rock and snow as he speeds to the summit, where steam billows from the volcano's lava lake. Hikikomori pulls a wad of gum from his mouth and presses it over the NeuroNet switch at the base of his skull. Next he digs in his pants pocket to retrieve two items. First he adheres a small durium cap over the gummed up switch, then he stuffs a folded sheet of paper into his durium coated boot. He summersaults into the molten pool, letting his clothes burn away as he swims down to a hole in the wall of the crater, and crawls through the fiery tunnel until he reaches an opening that flows into a small lava lake. From there he swims ashore, naked save for his boots, and settles in his sauna of a cave. The high domed rock, florescent lamps, storage freezers, and durium bedframe almost resemble a home. He pulls Bao Chan's crayon mess from his boot and pins it under a magnet on a nearby freezer, which also sports a frayed patch of blue teddy bear wallpaper taped to its lid.

Everything else he needs resides in his Net wired brain. *Almost*, Hikikomori thinks while yanking the gummed up cap from the back of his head. *Could use some plastic plants. And a mirror. Better recruit another teleporter.* He plops on his bedframe and connects the power cord of a portable solar generator into the base of his skull. Then he fires up the Net and checks off his list.

Step One: Obtain and review schematics for The Hole. Extract its exact location in the Pacific Ocean. Determine how it remains hidden. Assess whether it truly is an "impenetrable super prison for metas."

Step Two: Draft a new Net manifesto addressing the Red Nation. Condemn only with proof that vampire survival is dependent on Shaktira. For now, advocacy is safest.

Step Three: Infiltrate Jerusalem, confront Haine and Shaktira, make them allies or terminate them. Review dreams for vampire physiology, specifics of Haine's immortality.

Step Four: Extinction of humanity. Catalyzing a self replicating nanite swarm remains appealing. Better solution may be vampire saturation, then destruction of the source.

Step Five: Make Stefan apologize for stealing my girlfriend, and for calling me "Hickey," and for refusing to play with me just because I'm better than him.

PART II

13

Let's play mind games

"Whaddaya think?" Nia asks, pressing her chubby palms in anticipation as she stands over her hosts.

The three grossly stuffed males sitting at the dining room table in boxers and tank tops do not exactly reply, too intent on devouring the last scrap of her walnut and blueberry pancakes for actual words, as much as burp and stretch in contentment.

"Any more?" Stefan eventually asks.

"Wait for lunch. I make mean frybread and chili."

"She's a keeper," Oke says, tilting his chair back as he pushes the table with a bare foot. "Where'd you learn to cook like that?"

"On the res. Got a lot of practice with my dad."

"Lucky him," William says. "He must be happy."

"Not at the moment," Nia says. "God willing, he will be once Stefan and I get married."

That sets William into a coughing fit and Oke's tilted chair crashing to the floor. Nia pats William on the back while doing her best to disregard Stefan's scowl. He lets it drop when Zenith walks in.

"Congratulations," the living robot says to the stranger. "The probability of a man with Stefan's social status and physical features marrying a woman with your status and features is 9.284 percent."

"¡Dios mio!" Stefan shouts. "We met last night! And she smells like jailbait."

"So long, kid," William tells Oke as the boy tries to sit again at the table. "The lovebirds have issues to discuss, and you're up to guard His Highness. Keep our guest to yourself."

"But it's just getting good!" the boy says as an invisible vise drags him feet first along the floor and out the dining room.

"Our wedding is a ways off," Nia mumbles, all but wilting under Zenith. She finds the lithe metal giant much more carnal in person than on the Net, and much more menacing thanks to that inhuman purple faceplate. "Glad to help you guys keep the peace in the meantime. Between us, I'm a little nervous about staying focused once Stefan gets me pregnant. Baby drama, you know?"

"Help us," Zenith says as incredulously as her electronic vibrations allow. "Help us how?"

"Visions. I can tell you what your enemies have done, some of what they plan to do. By the way, your new design is very ... sleek."

"Thank you," Zenith says even more flatly than usual, before turning to William. "Is this woman experiencing a psychotic break?"

"Can't say," he says while sliding his finger across his plate to gather a trail of pancake syrup. "She's got serious mental shields." William licks the goop off his finger and dips it back on the plate for another serving. "All I get is static."

"I can lower those," Nia says. "But let me prove myself. You two never told anyone that your first time together, Will got electrified by a stray cervical wire, so he calls you 'Sparky' in bed."

"... That works for me," William blurts, ending a long, awkward silence. He returns to his pancake syrup.

"Agreed," Zenith says. "X-ray of your pelvic diameter suggests the average sized fetus would crown without complication. I will be interested to analyze reproductive permutations from crossing your respective genetic codes. Provided you pass interrogation."

"We're not getting married and we're not having a stinking baby!" Stefan shouts from his chair. "Look, we have to keep this between ourselves. As you can see, she knows something. For now James can't be in the loop. Not even Oke and Faye. Not with God knows how many vamped out psychics gunning for us. Let everyone think I'm in love or whatever. I haven't figured out what's going on here. But it isn't ... that. She's not even my type."

"Whoa! Do not presume that you're my type either, Captain Conceited," Nia says through a pinched brow, with one hand flitting through the air and the other on her ample hip, which rounds out her gut and pours into her meaty thigh. "Anyway here's the deal ..."

Yes, she can see the future. But only in dreams, and she has little control over what she sees. Yes, she can see the past, but only while awake, and only snippets. If she focuses on a location, only instants that occurred there before her last sleep. If on a person, only their actions prior to their last sleep. Yes, the visions overwhelm her because she feels like she is there, and though the future usually proves accurate only the past is definite. And yes, she is impervious to telepathy, so Haine and Shaktira know nothing of her. Yet. Which is why Stefan mysteriously ordered the crew to remove their contacts and ear mics last night, and why they cannot mention her powers on air.

The final hurdle is explaining why she kept quiet before the Red Nation sprang up overnight.

Fear, she confesses. A paralyzing terror of being wrong, and of being right.

Had she been wrong she would have been deemed a crock, would have shamed her people, maybe been sued for slander. Psychics spew fiction as often as fact, after all. She had debated it for months, and for a while had made up her mind. Enough so to leave home well before the vampires spread. But somewhere along the way her courage failed and she made a pathetic bargain with herself.

She would wait and see. If she proved correct about Haine and Shaktira then she would persist until she convinced Stefan of the rest of their plan. After all, she had justified, she would be derided no matter what she shared, without any vampires around. And she did figure other psychics might have spoken up, had they foreseen it.

In the wake of the rising, however, with what she could prove, she would have to be taken seriously. Now all she has to do is speak the truth, and fight off the guilt of having not done so before billions lost their minds.

Her words garner little sympathy, judging from the silence of Stefan and his friends. Yet Nia grows confident that they do lend her credibility.

"Now what's this about an interrogation?" she asks.

• • •

Glenda Rodan oversees the gantlet with dedication bordering on delight, fueled, Nia suspects, by the fact that Rodan learns of her existence a full day after the Council of Continents and the U.N. secretary general.

First comes the fusillade of questions, then the questions to her answers, rephrased ad infinitum by Rodan's underlings. The U.N. military adviser accepts the basics. That Nia was born at 04:20 Arizona time, the exact moment of the wave, incidentally, yet blood tests detect no meta powers. That her mother died during labor. That her father, Timothy

Begaye, is a casino treasurer raising three girls on his own. That she left the states months ago to travel abroad. That a couple days ago she and Stefan struck up an affair so intense he demands she stay with him. And that she has no criminal record.

This takes seven and a half hours to confirm, after the U.S. Secret Service forcibly escorts her father to the Berlaymont Building under chaperone by the U.S. ambassador to the U.N. This delays the process just long enough for him to embrace his daughter. For her to apologize about running away, yet refuse to return home with him. For him to accept that she insists on enduring such humiliation.

Then comes Zenith's thorough scanning of Nia's NeuroNet files, from bank accounts to social network posts to instant messages delving back eight years. The living robot points out that such tasks have become increasingly routine in the U.S. and Europe due to upgrades mandated in recent Net tracking laws. This observation fails to comfort the Begayes. Mind probes follow, first conducted by William, then three others by meta agents with the N.A.U. and E.U. governments and the U.N. respectively. They each report absolutely no abnormal thoughts or memories, which itself is highly abnormal nowadays.

Some time during this barrage Karen Drench and Cornelio Ortez storm the Berlaymonl demanding to know why the crew's contact lenses and ear mics have been removed. Stefan admits he ordered it until his "guest" had been granted official stay. That throws Karen into frenzy until Cornelio suggests such an unremarkable looking love interest for Stefan might boost the age 18 to 40 female demographic, especially among those viewers who have tired of his general trampiness. Suddenly the head of Executive Warriors Elite warms to the surprise—and unpaid—addition to the "Meta Force" cast.

Thirteen hours after initiating official inquiry, Rodan admits Nia seems clean. Fourteen hours afterward, James insists that Nia be kept under constant surveillance. Fifteen hours afterward, her father departs for home. But not until informing Stefan that he better protect Nia like he protects his balls. Sixteen hours afterward, Nia ransacks the penthouse kitchen in preparation for the crew's first dinner from their newest roommate.

• • •

"Interesting week," William says via NeuroNet.

The two men walk between jagged walls of rock deep in the belly of The Hole. This bottom level of cells harbors the world's most dangerous meta criminals, miles under a tiny island in the middle of the Pacific.

"Compared to what?" Stefan asks online.

He fiddles with the black hilt of his father's sword, sheathed at his hip. He glances at the small glass pane on the durium door caging Harod Lbeki. Stripped of his strength and speed the unconscious thief looks like nothing more than a naked, chained inmate. Yet before she knocked Stefan into the middle of the ocean, Ana ... Shakti ... had seemed like a sweet, vivacious, middle aged woman. He wonders whether he should have tried Simmer instead of his fist. *She must have some weakness ...*

"Hey, Nia's a big deal," William says as they stop outside the door of one Manfred Peebles, who curses them for brainwashed, capitalist slaves from the solitude of his soundproof cell. "If we can use her to our advantage. Then there's your engagement."

"Would you stop calling it that? I barely know the girl. And I'm not that into her."

"Nice qualifier. Subtle. I have to say, you sound more scared than annoyed."

"You would be too if some short fat chick came out of nowhere and told you she was going to have your baby. I almost wish she would be wrong about something, so we could send her home."

"Too bad she's your new best friend. Can't lose someone who's helped us capture twenty seven terrorist units in four days. Plus she backs up the theory that Ana wants to turn everyone into bloodsuckers."

"Yeah, well, she says lots of things," Stefan whispers aloud before returning to the Net. "Maybe she is a spy. Maybe it is a setup."

"So why are you sharing your bed with her?" William asks online, not even trying to suppress a grin.

"The penthouse doesn't have an extra room! And if she thinks we're gonna have a baby I oughta get to know her, right? Haven't touched her yet."

"Yet," William says. "It's the free will question that's eating you. You want her even though she's no sexpot, but you think that if you have her it means you're not in control of your life. That's a valid question. Why stress over choosing if it's already decided?"

"Chingalo, let's play mind games then. Go on, doctor."

"You're also pissed that she thinks your brother wants to kill off every man, woman, and child based on some sick sense of virtue. It's more than most could handle."

"I can't believe he's that crazy," Stefan mumbles. "My turn. I think you're pissed Nia's one more person you can't mind read. And that your woman isn't a woman anymore. Digame, Will, do you really like Becca's new body?!"

"Now you're getting petty," William says aloud as an invisible force lifts Stefan off the ground. The mentalist resumes their spat online. "She makes six. Her, Becca, you, your brother, Sam, and Ana. Maybe that nut from the bar. Great. I could do without the eight billion other minds running through my own every damn day. There's a reason you had me mindwipe P.R. and those guards the night Nia showed up. Like there's a reason telepaths guard world leaders around the clock. Like there's a reason I choose not to mind control every member of the Council of Continents and their bush league telepaths.

"Is it our business that James needs to be whipped and chained while in a rabbit costume to get off? Or that Oke snorts Bacchus because it helps him feel like a normal boy? Or that Faye's got MV? Maybe. But unless they share that, or screw up, we focus on our relevant business. So let's do that. We need to learn what makes a one man army kill for somebody else's cause," William says, pointing at Manny's cell. "And by the way, insult Becca again and I swear it's your ass."

"Touchy, touchy," Stefan says as his feet return to ground. "You know I love you guys like family. Maybe we're both on edge about that other thing? That Nia says Sam is trying to become Almighty God? And that he might succeed?"

"Feel free to confide in me. But I'm not ready to wrap my mind around that," William says, turning to Manny's cell. "Now let's rap this jerk's mind until he spills."

"Wait up," Stefan says, grabbing William by the arm as the realization dawns. "Faye's sick?"

14

Piercing the mist

Black fades to white then blue as they spiral down. The sun comes in and out of sight during their descent, its golden face smiling cartoonishly. They hit ground, bouncing in the middle of a big red dot in the middle of a grassy park in the middle of a city, until the rubbery dot settles enough for them to walk off.

Every color, from sky to land to the skin of each other, seems almost real, if a bit too intense. Same for the sounds of the birds and breeze and bustle of the city. Their senses of touch, taste, and smell, however, are far dimmed. All intentional at this stage of the program.

"Becca, this is insane," William congratulates while jumping up and down to test gravity, and its tug on his knees. "Nothing on the market comes close. Wonder how much it can sell for."

"Oke was correct," she says. "I do approve of his game. Once Haine International announces this NetNexus, anybody will be able to create an avatar or import and upgrade an existing one from any mail server, social site, videogame, or VR platform, regardless of brand. External firms will receive a percentage of revenue from relevant client subscriptions. Avatars can create towns full of homes, vehicles, clothes, food, children, pets and more for extra fees. NetNexus software will be worth eight times the production cost of my latest body. In its first year."

"Si, esta loco verdad," Stefan agrees while touching his hip for where Simmer should be, before realizing its absence. "No powers I get. Too complicated to program. But I can't have my sword?"

"Here, as in the physical world, it is unnecessary," Zenith explains.

She leads them over a garden of gray pebbles, hard and slippery under their shoes, toward a nearby hill. A single, leafy tree smells there of earth and timber.

"Okay, better question," Nia begins as she grasps Zenith's soft white hand. "Why do you look human here?"

"Because it pleases William," the gorgeous blond says while freeing her hand to point at the tree. "This icon is of great use to our mission. Only our avatars have access to this park, and thus the icon. Nia, this is where you will store your visions."

Zenith plucks a bright red apple from the tree and hands it to the other woman.

"Remember your most vivid visions of our enemies. Bite into the apple. Return it to the same twig. Every aspect of your vision will be recorded."

Nia glances at the apple, then back at Zenith. The seer tastes its succulence, piercing the mist of reality.

• • •

Nearly 5,000 years ago, in a stretch of what became the Punjab, at the root of a tree along a long since dried up leg of the Ravi River, a ruddy skinned girl of 11 and her younger brother stare at a night sky flickering with what she guesses are worlds many times older than her own. Worlds she yearns to see, if ever she leaves her village. Oh, she will leave at some point, Anashaktira tells her brother. As wife to a prince. That is the way of things for the daughters of chiefs. Her way in just two years. The siblings heed their mother's distant call to rise from the grass and enter the large clay home dwarfing the surrounding huts, all of which bare the totem of the elephant god carved above their entrances. The girl lay in her room under her wool blanket and dreams of stars.

She awakens to screams. Her mother shouts at her to wake her brother. She obeys without question, shoving the little boy until he rises. The children follow their mother outside, where their father strides a blood spattered horse and orders about battle weary men. Just feet away she sees her favorite uncle topple after taking a spear to the ribs. Then she sees strangers swarm from the other side of their home and the battle reaches her feet. Their mother pulls them away by the scruffs of their necks, until the chief gasps, and the children see their father stagger toward them with an arrow through his chest.

By dawn her village has surrendered and her mother has given her into slavery. Little Anashaktira leaves her home bound and gagged on horseback, passing burning huts and the bodies of slain kinsmen. They arrive at the other village by nightfall. Save for the totem bull god carved above the entrance of each hut, the village seems identical to hers.

The hairy, rotund man whose farts she had endured for miles slaps her off his steed and drags her into a clay home similar to that of her parents. He says he is this village's chief, and that she will serve his eldest wife. An even more rotund woman emerges from a rear room, pulls her close, pats her on the head, and orders her to begin chopping onions for dinner. Anashaktira sleeps under the stars, on dirt, leashed at the neck to a grounded pike by the entrance, and rocks herself to sleep until she dreams of a tree by a river.

Three months into her servitude, while sewing clothes for her mistress, Anashaktira hears the chief recount a dream to his three teenage sons. In it a green parrot with a red bill pecks at his ear as he tries to climb a mountain. He swats the bird away only to lose his grip and fall when the parrot pecks at his fingers. The slave girl answers before his sons can respond. The nightmare, she explains, means a trusted adviser is telling the chief only what he wants to hear and that the chief will be ruined if he dismisses the adviser, who will turn traitorous, so the adviser must be killed. The sons laugh. The mistress smacks Anashaktira across the mouth for her impudence. The chief sits silent for a moment, fixed on the slave girl, then grabs his sword and hurries outside.

Three years into her servitude and one week after the death of her mistress, Anashaktira marries the chief's eldest son. She had ceased cooking and sewing within her first year and cleaned at her whim in her second. Her interpretations are prophecy and the chief relies on her counsel above all others. The son has no choice in this marriage. It is his first, after all, and his father, seeing the girl as the best way to maintain power, demands it. The son, who has had his way with Anashaktira since she arrived, as well as with most other slave girls in the village, leaves her untouched on their wedding night. He does, however, treat her well for another decade, until his father dies of malaria.

During her time under the chief's guidance she proved to be much more than an interpreter of dreams, maturing into a woman capable of charting stars better than any astrologer, of predicting floods better than any fisherman, of planting crops better than any farmer, of conversing on the nature of time and space and mind better than any philosopher. The villagers saw the chief as a god among men, taking credit as he did for the wisdom of a slave. Only his family knew the truth.

It is an affront for which her husband reveals his disgust upon his coronation. Who is he to take orders from a slave girl? Who is she to give them? Time and again, she has undermined the divinity of the gods with her nonsense about "infinite awareness." He will ask her opinion when he sees fit, and he will beat her when she forgets her place, and by the great bull god she will cook and clean!

And so it goes, for nine years, until her old tribe exacts its revenge. She had dreamed of the raid weeks earlier, but decided to keep it to herself after her husband slapped her into a wall for suggesting that his new fiancée, from whom his youngest brother had contracted syphilis, would do no better a job than herself of birthing him any heirs.

Fittingly, her old tribe attacks with the dawn. This time it is they who bring the fire and the screams. She smiles at the sight of her brother, and at his spear penetrating the groin of her husband. But as the hours pass, Anashaktira finds tears for the wounds of her people. Her brother. Her husband. His brothers. No matter their blood, no matter their sins against her, they were hers. Yet despite her visions, she could not bring herself to save them from the misery of battle.

So she wails to pale gray heavens as her eviscerated brother looks her in the eyes, then with his dying breath orders strangers from her old tribe to toss a leash round her neck and sling her onto a horse. Men obey mechanically, ignoring her assertion that she is one of them, all the way to the tree by the river. And as she is hanged at the site of her childhood dreams, Anashaktira forgives them. She tells them that she forgives them for their malice and ignorance. For putting blood drenched fingers in her mouth while they work. For tying a knot too loose to snap her neck. So she dangles, tasting the blood of strangers, wheezing in misery as they abandon her, sunlight burning her eyes. Until nightfall, when she turns inward and away from even herself.

Who was she? Anashaktira, the princess turned slave turned seer turned queen. Who is she? The amorphous waves of the flowing river, the unseen breeze that keeps her conscious, the mindless living tree that threatens to rob her of mind and life. Who is she not? The elephant god, the bull god, and any other fiction petty men rally behind in the name of hate. Who will she be? The answer comes days later, just as she expires under the setting sun of thirst, hunger, and exposure. All.

And so she who was Anashaktira reawakens to her new life with the moon, breaks her bonds and strides into her old villages with sublime purpose, drinks deep amid screams and fires of her own making, and delivers her divine power to the blessed first of her Children of the Night.

• • •

More than 4,500 years ago, in what became the English county of Wiltshire, a red haired man in a black robe leads dozens of black robed men across the green plain under a sun not yet at its peak. They approach the site silently and remain so while inspecting the progress of their workers. Thirty four bluestone slabs rest at angles atop a huge mound of dirt. The gradual, excruciating process of dragging a thirty fifth slab up a slope of the mound nears completion. The red haired man nods, his green eyes sparkling. His fellows encircle the mound, all eyes on the unplaced slab.

The stone weighs down on a series of shaven tree trunks so that the mound's conveyor resembles a wooden spine up the back of some earthen monstrosity. The workers are all big men, ten pushing from the rear of the slab, ten in front pulling ropes wrapped around it, ten on each side tugging ropes knotted to other ropes. They sweat and groan for over an hour, until another set of men replaces them, and an hour later another set replaces them, and so on until the sun sets and the slab rests atop the mound.

The red haired man nods again. His fellows, now carrying torches, follow him back across the plain.

Weeks later, the red haired man and his fellows return. The construction has been completed, the mound removed. In its place they see a horseshoe pattern of five sets within a circle of thirty, each set made of two thirteen-foot bluestones standing erect with a third laid across them. This time his black robed attendants drag three bejeweled bodies resting on wooden planks. The red haired man, whom the others address as Sowen, orders the emerald ringed and ruby necklaced corpses placed in the center of the monument so that their skulls almost touch and their feet point to the corners of a triangle. Then Sowen orders the others to encircle the stone henge as he walks between the bodies.

They recite prayers for the dead, for summer's end, for the harvest, and for the elements of nature as they await the sun's peak. Soon its rays shine down into the heart of the henge so that Sowen's bare feet glow. As expected, the moon soon eclipses the sun and the site falls dark. Then comes the unexpected. Sowen glimpses a ruddy skinned woman in a golden sari standing beside him. Then everyone hears a thunderclap, feels a gale swept shower, and sees a lightning bolt strike Sowen on the forehead. In disordered mumbles, he orders his fellows to bury the corpses where they lie. Then he rubs his eyes and collapses atop the dead.

Sowen recovers within days, albeit with a severe limp, to continue his priestly duties. In time he accepts the image of the woman as a delusion of the storm. He never glimpses her again in this lifetime.

What he does behold, however, are the gifts of that storm. Some would call it the might of the gods. Others a curse. He makes neither leap, for he has never believed in such things. Yet he has no better answer. As he confides in his wife, lightning may be the fury of the heavens, but it does not cause men to be able to wield it at will, nor summon the winds and the rain, nor instigate earthquakes at a moment's notice, nor inspire flora to grow from dust. But there it is, within him so strong he feels one with nature to the point that he sometimes forgets his name.

His wife asks him not to speak this way before their two daughters, who are soon to be wed. If word spreads, she warns, everyone will think him mad. And maybe he is, Sowen admits, to not reveal his burden. But then people will demand too much, she argues, of a god in the flesh. Is it not enough to be head priest? To ensure great harvests and ward off disasters? Is it not enough to do good unnoticed, she begs? Yes, he concedes, it is more than enough for any lifetime.

Sowen abides this code for all his years, protecting his people in prayer and deed, going so far as to smite would be invaders with storms so hellish they retreat prior to battle. The day he dies, the sun shines bright above a clear, dry sky as he joins his ancestors under the henge he designed.

And he is reborn as a girl to a Bantu woman in the thick of the Congo jungle before her old body is even discovered by her wife of her first life.

It is rough going for a while, adjusting to this fate. For well before Sowen—now called Etana—learns to speak this new tongue, and even longer before she could safely show such knowledge, she recalls her past life as though it never ended. The shock nearly drives her mad. It is only the watery reflection of her tiny black frame, and her sparkling green eyes, observed whenever her mother brings a bowl to her slobbery lips, which assures her this is real.

But adjust she does, growing into a fertility goddess worshipped among her tribe. Other hurdles commensurate with the female plight, childbirth especially being much more terrible and wonderful than anything she had imagined, reinforce this reality. With time, and the tricks it plays on the mind, she even comes to suspect that her past life was the stuff of dreams.

Until she dies again.

Lives roll by again and again, unceasing, around the globe, through all walks of life. Each time the spirit first born as Sowen receives the world with skeptical eyes, until the powers emerge, and destiny can no longer be denied. Yet that doubt is just enough to let him accept the unique perspective each life bestows. And though he often thinks of himself with the name and values of that life, the immortal soul remains Sowen.

So it goes for centuries, until as Amnisos, king of the Aegean island once known as Thera, he one morning discovers at his court a ruddy skinned woman in a golden sari. Her name is Shakti, she tells him. He has the honor of being her consort, and together they shall lift mankind up from the muck of its own making.

• • •

About 1,100 years ago, in what became Kyoto, Japan, a score of arrows fly toward a hooded man in an emerald kimono. Silvery bandages wrap the hands and feet of this rather thin target. Minamoto no Magahara snatches them out of the air and snaps them over his knee, en masse. A dozen armored samurai leap from rooftops to encircle him with naginatas. The samurai lunge. Their weapons touch no skin. The unarmed man dances on the tips of their blades, delivering kicks to astonished faces and punches to unguarded groins until the dozen splay on the ground, rubbing wounds and bemoaning nasty sake and ill made bets.

Twice as many of their fellows stream from alleys, flailing swords and whips and bows and maces as though exuberance will grant victory. Magahara curtsies, then unleashes a cyclone that his pickings later try to embellish but fail to do justice. It does not take a minute. He shouts over their whining to congratulate them for improving, and that maybe one of them will even land a blow on him one of these days. Someone calls him a liar, if a generous one. They all break into laughter. Magahara claps twice and the elite of the Imperial Guard rise to their unsteady feet. He lowers his hood and walks with them back to the dojo, passing the hall as they file inside.

He strolls far from samurai quarters, wandering about the capital of his kinsman Emperor Murakami on this fulgent morning. Through back alleys and courtyards fenced by bamboo. Past expansive temples built of spruce wood and many eaved pagodas dedicated to the Amida. Through elaborate gardens of rock and flora tended by scruffy landscapers. Past schools hiding future civil servants behind rice paper screens.

When Magahara enters the residential area the streets come alive with echoes of his name, from prepubescent boys weaned on bedtime stories about the legendary warrior, from pubescent girls enchanted by rumors of the aristocratic seducer, from old monks funded by the generous adherent to the way of the Buddha, all of whom succeed in garnering his full attention, and in impeding his progress.

Finally he approaches his family estate. It is not the largest home outside of the palace—that honor going to the Fujiwara clan—but it is the most famous, thanks to him and his father. He steps through the tawny cypress threshold and a bowing servant brings him a cup of tea. He hardly makes it out of the foyer before his father shouts for his audience. Magahara yawns and sips his tea as he enters the receiving room.

His father sits hunched over in a thronelike chair, shaking his head gloomily as he speaks of intrigue. The son is much paler than the father, who decades earlier ventured from western China and whose own father had ventured the same distance from northwest of there. Magahara's cousins and uncles stand about doing their best to seem thoughtful. Rumor has it, his father confides, the emperor ails from poisoning. If Murakami, a man of 33 years with sons not yet half that age, should perish, the court would fall into chaos.

Members of the Taira clan always seem too friendly with outlying governors who refuse to pay taxes on time, and often advise against suppressing such rebellions "unless without recourse." The accursed Fujiwara often do favors for wealthy merchants in exchange for funds to buy their way into marriage with Minamoto women. But the Tachibana clan has fallen hardest, having chosen the wrong allies too often, losing too many of their strongest to blood feuds, their best and brightest sent to oversee rundown temples to the north.

A cousin suggests an outright inquisition, an uncle that prostitutes be used as spies. Magahara's father silences them to solicit his son's opinion. Magahara posits that if Murakami is being poisoned, it may well be by a member of the royal family. His father orders him away amid the scandalized gasps of his kinsmen.

The son obeys, napping in his room until nightfall, when he wakes to write the letter explaining his permanent exile. He sees it as neither retaliation nor dereliction of duty, but simple pragmatism. The petty antics of men no longer hold meaning for him. He resolves to go against the voices of ancestors who clutter his dreams, to break the cycle that accompanies the divine power of his birthright, to live unto himself. Like his father and grandfather, he shall venture into new lands. Unlike them, he shall fight no more. He lays the note on his bed, absconding with only his hooded emerald kimono and silvery bandages.

True to his word, Magahara abandons civilization that evening. So he thrives for months, subsisting in the wilderness on foliage and fish, the occasional rabbit, even injured birds, catching them with his hands, though he could easily fashion bows and arrows. But such would be too easy, a painful reminder of what he forsook in the quest for equanimity. Not two years into it—when he finds himself standing naked at the edge of a high cliff on a snowcapped mountain in the middle of the night, driven to insomnia by the incessant chastisement of his dead kin—does he accept the failure of his aimless quest.

He falls forward, arms spread wide, steeling for the impact before what he prays is the end, only to feel a jerk at his heel as his body twirls upside down and he eyes the feet of a ruddy skinned woman.

She says that she understands his despair, and that she can reverse it with a kiss. That she can give him everlasting purpose as her mate, first among her Children, the link between two worlds. That she is the way to peace. And that she can show him love so consummate he will never again seek solace in oblivion. Or, she says, he can continue his plummet, testing the limits of his birthright, contributing nothing but a stain.

He asks her name. She tells it. He asks her help. She pulls him in and gives it, drinking from his jugular. He rocks on the snowy cliff, his innards ablaze, an insatiable hunger growing, she caressing him as a mother would a newborn child.

Once the transformation takes hold, while they depart the cliff, he asks to be called some new name, as Magahara is the name of a dead man. Shakti accedes, for he no longer languishes as a mortal noble but flourishes as her undying warrior, spectral to mankind. So be it, she says. Ever more he is her Knight Wraith.

. . .

Almost 300 years ago, in Empress Catherine's many halled gold and stucco summer residence outside St. Petersburg, Maria Feodorovna listens to her new husband rant about assassins stewing in wait for him. She had long heard rumors that Paul I of Russia was paranoid, but not until he includes his own mother among the conspirators does she grasp its extent. She nods and fills a chair and contorts her face in fearful expressions of loyalty, while making sure to conceal several powerful yawns, lest he suspect her as well. Paul halts, flinching, when lightning claps by their bedroom window. Maria changes the subject while trying not to regret changing her name for this fool.

She reminds him that he is to welcome guests from the Orient, a Japanese emissary and his retinue. Paul informs her she must be mistaken, then returns to plots on his life, for ninety minutes, until a palace guard interrupts him with the same news. The emperor-in-training hurries into full regalia, frumpy and colorful as a child, grumbling about inept servants before he and his princess enter the Great Hall. It swells with Russian nobility angling for His Highness' exchange. The pair mount massive oak thrones covered in satin and gold, surrounded by walls rife with gilt creatures.

Paul greets the foreigners without apologizing for his delay. The emissary, who wears a hood attached to an emerald kimono, introduces himself in perfect Russian as

Tenno no Magahara. He congratulates the prince on his palace and recent wedding then kowtows to Paul and Maria, knees and forehead to the ground. Magahara's eyes linger on their sparkling green counterparts in the lady. Paul mumbles his own pleasantries, then waves for entertainment.

Magahara observes in passing, his twelve scribes scribbling, his twelve samurai standing motionless, as garish dancers leap and twirl under the sway of musicians flitting from shrill to soothing in unison. Paul claps his hands at spectacle's end, signaling all low guests and entertainers to take their leave. Magahara cuts to the quick once in private.

First the official mission. To learn Russian scientific and social customs under expansion of Rangaku policy initiated with Dutch traders in the bay of Nagasaki. Next the true mission. To warn against sending Russian spies through that Dutch post of Dejima in hopes of gaining an economic foothold in Japan. Finally a secret mission. To propose Emperor Go-Momozono's goal of crawling out of Sakoku style national isolation by trading through emissaries, such as himself, sent to foreign lands.

Paul runs the gamut of facial contortions and wordless utterances during the meet, lisping throughout. Magahara refrains from reading his mind, lest the vampire fail to mask his own perplexity.

The prince commits to nothing in specific while insisting he will do everything in his power to further relations between their realms. He summons guides to show the scribes around and offers Magahara free roam of the palace and city. The emissary kowtows again. Yet he forgets himself on the way up in his gaze at Maria. He had seen her in dreams of late and felt compelled to examine her firsthand. Better heeding protocol, he and his samurai follow another guide to their guest quarters.

Later that night the princess awakens to find her husband sleeping beside her in the dark of their bedroom, and Magahara standing at the head of their mattress with his finger to her lips. She smirks, propping herself up on an elbow, takes his finger in her hand, and, in whispers, compliments the foreigner on his daring.

He licks his fangs and asks with his mind whether she knows of the Mother of the Night. Maria nods, and thinks to him that she does, or did, when she was a he, as Shakti's consort. Magahara laughs aloud such that Paul wakes and turns to see him, until Magahara waves his palm and the prince goes limp. The vampire pulls his fellow immortal out of bed and leads Sowen to the window. Magahara invites her to fly. She nods and they go aloft.

How odd, Sowen thinks as Magahara carries her over St. Petersburg under a crescent moon, that they would first meet nearly a century after Shakti began her hibernation. Odder still, Magahara thinks back as he presses her soft frame to his, that they would meet so clandestine while Sowen plays subservient wife to a loon. Sowen wonders who can help but play the part given. Magahara wonders how many parts have been played thus far.

They list them, unsure whether they duel or duet. Father. Mother. Warrior. Warlord. Prince. Princess. Thief. Emperor. Slave. Prostitute. Monk. Athlete. Vagrant. Inventor. Teacher. Philosopher. Poet. Painter. Musician. Warlock. Vampire. Priest. Liar. Goddess. And so many more.

What would they be were it not for her? Creatures of infinite isolation, they agree while passing above the bell tower of Sts. Peter and Paul Fortress. What has she made them? Fathers of a new breed, witnesses to the age of man, bearers of the soul of the world, links to the everlasting, seers of the beyond, and kindred to each other, they decide above the blue gray ripples of the Neva River.

Yet they admit relief at her dormancy. Her voice, odor, touch, and taste were so raw in their own rights that it was often hard to behold her straight on, much like the sun. And that force of will! She never tried to control them. Why then could they never attest to being in control around her? How they miss her.

Then no more words between them, thought or spoken, for the rest of the night. Not as they re-enter the palace through the bedroom window. Not as they take turns mounting each other on the floor and on the mattress and on the spine of the limp prince. Not even as Magahara kisses Sowen goodbye before sunrise.

In fact, they share no more words for the remainder of Magahara's stay at the palace. Only when news trickles to Japan of Paul's assassination twenty five years later does he reopen his mind to Sowen.

The psychic conduit born of consolation provides centuries of companionship. It transcends Magahara's latest tenure with Japanese aristocracy, Sowen's next life as an American abolitionist, their encounters with their augmented descendants, even the meta wave. And it is the one secret they keep from the lover that bound them.

• • •

Twenty years ago, several miles southwest of Mumbai, Shakti awakens to visions of a world in thrall to the unknowable force that made her. Pushing through layer upon layer of sediment, she breaks from her self imposed tomb, drinking the briny bottom of the Indian Ocean as she rises to its twilight waves. The Mother of the Night gasps her first breaths in 400 years and swims ashore.

Signs of this new world threaten to overwhelm her, its advances exceeding her furthest imaginings. Gargantuan ships at the harbor. Skyscrapers of glass and metal lining the coast. Plastic vehicles hovering along city streets lit by fluorescent lamps. Shifting digital billboards peddling luxury for the masses. But most amazing, the people. The endless sea of people, with packaged meals and skintight clothes and computerized eyeglasses and anthropomorphic robots and self absorbed conversations.

Then she notices that she is noticed for being nude and soaked. A mother covers her young son's eyes, cursing Shakti for a mad whore as they pass. The vampire snickers before turning invisible. At first she thinks she has blocked the minds of others, until she passes a window. Unlike her spawn she has always cast reflections. She checks her arms and legs. All gone. She begins to consider what else she might accomplish.

Shakti turns back to the window, concentrating until her naked form reasserts itself. A man walking by yelps upon seeing her.

Hunger strikes. The vampire feeds once more.

• • •

Twenty years ago, on the seventeenth hole of a Parisian golf course, Samuel Haine stiffens his wrist as his wood reaches the tee. The ball curves deep into rough. Cornelio Ortez, vice president of research and development for HaineTech, claps at his boss' poor aim. That is, until Sowen shuffles after it without so much as a self deprecating joke, one hand to his temple and the other waving off the caddy who tries to follow him.

Once alone behind cover of trees and knee high stalks, Sowen drops the pretense of searching for his ball. Instead he rests an elbow on a branch as he retches his guts out. Vomiting proves an all too brief respite from his migraine. He truly worries when his nose starts gushing. At first he figures it a stroke, a disappointing end to what was fast becoming one of his more accomplished lives. And at last one where, if memory could be trusted, his body all but matches his first self.

Then he notices that he holds a glass of water and a pair of sedatives. He gulps them on impulse. Then Sowen notices a nearby golf cart hovering above the thick. It is based on a HaineTech blueprint he first saw earlier that day. Though utterly unnerved by its presence, he wastes little time driving the cart back to the fairway.

As he hastens to conjure some deception for Cornelio about the cart and the blood, and Sowen rolls through his fingers a golf ball he conjures out of nothingness, he suspects this life will prove quite accomplished after all.

• • •

Twenty years ago, in one of the many seedy parts of Baltimore, Maryland, Magahara dreams that he hunts. He carries bow and arrows through snowy woods under a gray sky, spotting elk and hare but letting them live, for his prey is something bigger, though he knows not what. Until he hears the crunching of footsteps and spins round to see his father aiming an identical bow and arrow at his head. Then he hears the unmistakable chime of an ice cream truck, and he realizes he is dreaming, and as so often follows, he awakens against his will.

His quivering belly tells him he must feed. He crawls out of the filthy cardboard box in the narrow alley that has been his home for the last few weeks, eager to snatch one of the rats scurrying between the trash bags, when he beholds natural light on his wrist. He had not mistimed daylight in centuries, has not felt it directly on his face since meeting

Shakti. Lacking pain or fear, he looks up at the sun like a child greeting a long lost parent.

He senses this change is but a symptom of the greater world. And once again, he knows, his old loves will court him to join in a greater share of that world. And maybe, if he can stomach it, he is at last ready to take it.

• • •

Reality swirls back into virtual reality as Nia returns the red apple, bitten yet whole, to the tree. She, Stefan, and William certainly would vomit from this psychic churn, if they could feel their stomachs. Yet in Zenith's world their digital avatars remain as placid as their verdant park.

"Dios mio," Stefan moans. "Weird. They're both so not who I thought they were and exactly who I knew they were."

"Becca, this tech is amazing," William says. "Pure–"

He stops short when dozens of peoplelike things, naked and dead in the eyes, run up and surround them in unison. These things are lean and muscled, tall and smooth, vibrant shades of every natural complexion, beautiful men and women all, save for their eyes. The pack of not-quite-humans stops short of trampling William when Zenith sticks out her palm. They kneel before her, heads bowed, naked bodies heaving. Zenith closes her palm and bowls filled with gray mush materialize at the feet of these strangers. Zenith lowers her hand and the peoplelike things stuff their hands into the mush, then shovel it into their mouths. Sated, they stand and run off the way the came, ever silent.

"What. The. Hell?" Nia asks.

"My cybers," the perfect looking blond woman replies. "Designing avatars for humans resulted in code adaptable to copying the program that is my own hybrid consciousness. An unforeseen benefit. My cybers are previous artificial intelligence programs layered with copies of my larger program, wiped of my memories. When digitized, individual human behavioral traits can be assigned numerical codes, which can then be weighted and scaled, and in turn reordered to create unique personalities. They are of me, yet not me. Some are more evolved than others."

"You might want to evolve them before this thing hits the market," William warns. "That was scary."

"Noted. Nia, I suggest you soon fill the icon with visions of what our enemies are doing now."

With that, Zenith leads them back to the red dot. Once all inside they ascend cloudward, swirling as they go, the sun's cartoonish face smiling past them, until blue turns to white turns to black. They open their eyes in the real world of their penthouse balcony, to a chilly torrent of rain, as Oke and Phase stare out at them in bafflement.

15

You believe this?

"Faheem, bring milk!" Ahmad's mother shouts in Arabic toward the kitchen. Her spatula shoves sausage links onto a plate already overflowing with eggs, toast, tomato slices and honey soaked apple chunks.

"Looks ... it looks disgusting to us, but I'm sure you'll love it," Faheem says. He places a milk carton on the dining room table while keeping grip on two tall pitchers of fresh blood poured from the kitchen sink. "Here, Kaatima," he says, passing her one.

Leena wastes no time whittling away at her load, pausing only to burp and wipe her hands, which she uses instead of the silverware on the table. Ahmad, however, picks up knife and fork mainly to toy with his meal, rearranging items so the plate resembles a smiley face, until hunger gets the better of him and he picks at chilly eggs. After finishing the milk all that remains is the sausage. He tries to drop them in the trash when Kaatima grabs his plate. Mother and son stare off for the better part of a minute, until Faheem speaks his son's name. The sausage links get swallowed through a deflated snarl.

"It'll make you strong," Kaatima says.

"And it's yummy!" Leena squeals.

"It's unclean," Ahmad retorts. "And a sin."

"You'll feel otherwise in two years," Faheem assures. "About so many things."

"Why, is that when I lose my soul?" the boy asks, standing from the table. "Is that when I start drinking blood and fornicating with strangers?!"

"Yes," Kaatima says. "That's when Mother will share the gift, when your eyes will open and you'll see the proper path."

"How is this proper?!" Ahmad asks. "You say there's peace but the rest of the world hates us more than ever! You say we're free but you follow these foreign demons, who killed our brothers and sisters, who you killed for! You say this is paradise but I lose my NeuroNet for a Bacchus prescription! Your blood comes from clones! Tell me, how are these sins against Allah proper?!"

"Allah is a word," Faheem says, his tone and eyes so serene. "Like Yahweh and Brahman, something people make up. Mother shows us that we can prosper without these gods, just as we can without the greed and fear they create, by giving ourselves to Her."

"Whatever," the boy says with a shrug. "Come on, Leena. We have to get ready for school. At least we can go online there. Even if it is for classwork."

"Aaaaaand cut!" Shakti says as she teleports into the Bargouti household. "Great test run. Are the contact lenses comfortable? How about the ear mics?"

The Mother of the Night dotes over her Children and their children, aflutter in her golden sari with red sash wrapping her torso. She eases back their foreheads to peer at nanites working on the surface of their corneas, tugs their lobes to check the rubber padded cylinders in their ear canals. She pinches Leena's and Ahmad's cheeks. She thanks Faheem and Kaatima for making history as the "First Family" of the Red Nation.

And she congratulates herself, while teleporting back to her Jerusalem palace, on the epiphany that a reality show of their own would draw more acolytes than any treaty or manifesto. And for rejecting the glitzy "Meta Force" model in favor of pure documentary. Four perspectives running continuously, straight from eye to Net, translation into foreign tongues serving as the sole edit.

Let them see a society where everyone flies and no one dies. Where work is play and knowledge is free. Where sunscreen replaces MV cocktails and Bacchus comes by prescription. Let them see a family struggle to come to grips with this new world order, so they can trust in its integrity. Let them see everything the Red Nation has to offer. Save, of course, for my home. And my experiments. And woe to foreign powers that ban it, if they think their people will accept that!

Or so she hopes, as she finds Magahara shirtless and prone on his bedroom mattress, receiving a massage from an androgynous blond. She finds the white walled room too sparse for her taste. Only his low lying mattress with green sheets, a painting of high ocean waves over the bed, and a black vase of yellow tulips on his oak nightstand. She shoos the other man away and places her clammy hands on Magahara's pale shoulders.

"It's official," she whispers, touching her lips to his ear. "We've got stars."

"Fantastic," he says as she massages his spine. "I've been thinking. There's something you're not telling me. Sowen's not getting enough out of this. There's nothing for him here. He'll grow bored."

"Oh? Turning the deserts green isn't enough?" she asks, jabbing her elbow into his ribs. "Conjuring the shield that blocks telepaths, teleporters, and missiles? The roads, buildings, and machines from nothingness that provide our superior infrastructure? Or strategizing to keep the humans at bay? Oh, he's been a busy warlock."

"You know what I mean," Magahara says while turning over so she can massage his front. "Nothing he considers fulfilling."

Shakti softens up his chest and abs, takes extra long on each arm, before responding.

"Seems like you're ready," she says. "Let him tell you. Come."

She teleports them to the roof, atop the world's tallest building. This marble walled ziggurat is a city unto itself of her design and Sowen's will, headquarters to every governmental department in their realm. Every mile up the tower narrows, there each corner fitted with gold spires rising from jeweled domes. Jeweled save the top, where flourishes an expansive garden replete with a winding stream of clearest water. At roof's center, basking in sunrays peeking through the palm tree canopy, with one hand at his chin and the other at his knee, sits Sowen on a smoothed, waist high, granite rock. Inverted Omegas nestle Deltas as seemingly random spaced carvings in the sides of the stone. His eyelids hang half open, his once trim red mustache and beard grow bushy, his white shirt flutters unbuttoned and untucked in the breeze, his black slacks sag beltless and stained, and his feet press bare into grass.

"How long has he been meditating?" Shakti asks.

"All day," Magahara says.

She claps like thunder such that even Magahara flinches. Sowen opens his sparkling green eyes.

"Tell him," she says.

Sowen nods through a luxurious yawn, then says matter of factly, "I will be God." He whisks them deep into outer space before any chance of response. They behold void and distant specks of light. "Here's how."

"What, you think God likes being lost?" Magahara asks while looking about, wondering how much oxygen Sowen has given himself in their telekinetic bubble.

"I'll go through this once, so focus," Sowen warns. "In several years, during the second and much more powerful meta wave, everyone will become like us, and our powers will augment vastly. Shakti will then send the Children to turn the rest, which will provoke our enemies to retaliate with a full scale attack. I'll then condense simultaneous detonations of the world's nuclear arsenal into a singularity, creating the force of a micro star, which I'll continue to crush into a black hole. From that black hole a new universe will form, a universe that I'll control, since it's my mind that creates it.

"Now, that will make for three universes. The new one. Ours. And the one that ours has been brushing against for eons, the spillover from that friction being the source of all meta powers. You see, dimensional strings that bind universes are equivalent to energy, which is equivalent to both matter and consciousness. However, the end result of this brushing will be a fourth universe, born millennia hence from mounting pressure of the friction. What that'll produce I can't say. Yet. Ask me again when I'm God.

"Which will occur as I ride the opening of the multiverse during the second meta wave, as Shakti lends me the combined psychic concentration of this world under her control, and I join with existence by using my powers to their fullest. Instead of manipulating matter, I'll absorb the awareness of all things from within the heart of my creation, the micro universe. From there I'll pervade the infinite absolute, while Shakti maintains order here among the mortals, preferably with you as her mate."

Magahara stares at Sowen for long moments. He tries to speak. Words fail. He turns to Shakti, who returns placid eyes, then back to Sowen, who waits shyly expectant.

"... You believe this?" Magahara whispers. He presses his hands at his temples, shakes his head in disbelief. "Both of you ...? Honestly, I thought I'd grow to hate you two for what you're doing. But I can't hate the deranged. Shakti, Sowen ... please, this is madness. What basis could you possibly have to believe this will work?"

Shakti chuckles and holds her cheek to Magahara's while giving a firm hug, the way a mother would to a frightened child. His bare chest shivers in the black of outer space.

"When have you ever known us to be desperate?" she asks. "Look at these stars. They're governed by awesome forces most fail to grasp, but definable, tangible forces nonetheless. It wasn't easy to figure out, for sure. You would feel better if only you understood the math."

Magahara pushes her off and jabs his finger at Sowen's face, wishing a kimono could replace those jeans.

"Don't condescend to me! I don't want to hear about general relativity or quantum mechanics or M theory or alternate realities or whatever the hell! Don't talk to me about math! He. Cannot. Become. God! What does that even mean?! Become God! Either there's no such thing or the position is filled! Either way it's not happening!"

"So says the fallen Buddhist," Sowen counters. "I doubt it's unprecedented. No doubt a common occurrence throughout the countless years and countless planets."

"You're playing with things you can't comprehend! Collapsing a star! What if your power goes awry?!"

"Ah ... well ... there is a thirty seven percent chance the black hole could get loose and suck up the planet," Sowen says. "But we have faith. The odds are in our favor."

At that Magahara, reduced to exasperated huffs and sporadic gesticulations and disgusted laughter, again loses the ability to speak. Sowen takes the opportunity to show them around the galaxy.

"Look," he commands.

They meet a snowy, mountainous land where thousands of teal, reptilian bipeds war with sticks and slingshots against a few purple, feline bipeds in tanks and cannons.

"Look," he commands.

They meet a sweltering jungle where a few bald, blue centaurs swinging plasma whips oversee the mining of caves for some orange liquid by thousands of beige fowl carrying shovels under chained wings.

"Look," he commands.

They meet a starship landing in a city built of colossal circuitry, where wormlike blobs encased in flying cybernetic shells push cages full of other emaciated, sentient organisms.

"All the same," Sowen says. "No matter the planet, no matter the people. All about power and reproduction. Life is matter driven by energy in the consumption of more matter for more energy, the only purpose being molecular stability, what you call survival. And what's it for? Not much. Do you see?"

"I do," Shakti says. "I see so much life just waiting for a Mother's touch. Imagine it, Magahara. As my consort. The peace we could bring?"

Magahara offers no words, instead giving them his back as he turns to the starry abyss, leaning his forearms on Sowen's invisible bubble, eyes at the universe, until he scowls at them over his shoulder.

"This is how I see it," Sowen continues. "If reality is a work of art, it contains far too many conceits to be taken seriously. Suppose it is an endless stream of visions within visions. Whether stories or dreams, games or programs, each creation would possess its own animus. So then, is the point of it all to guess the neuroses of our particular god, or to forge realities imbued with our own? Either way my path leads to the eye of the divine, however petty it may be. I want new senses, new concepts, new realities. To know if our math is true, or merely our subconscious language. To make myself the highest art of all. Pure being.

"I used to dream of monkeys scrambling up a gold mountain. Now I dream of ants in the dirt. I've raised so many of my children as honestly as I could. So many of them have either gone mad or hated me for it. The ones I lied to, raised in fear of sin, came out happiest. I'm tired of it. Magahara, you're too old to cling to such nonsense. Why deny me my ascent? There are only so many glorious sunsets one can behold before they are merely suns setting."

Shakti runs her hand across Magahara's neck, persisting as he swats at her, meeting her clammy palm to his and massaging his fingers.

"Think of the paradise I've created," she tells him. "Why deny the world peace for the illusion of freedom? The learning of all time mocks you for doing so. From biology to physics, we are under sway of forces beyond our control. Here we are ordered and happy. Exquisite wild. Your cherished humans delude themselves into believing they've tamed the wild, but the wild is inescapable. From the bubbling realities to the teeming universes, and all the stars and planets, in every cell of animal and plant, down to the aware stuff of atoms, existence is a furious battle of mystery, albeit one that adheres to laws, one already mapped out through space and time.

"My legion is the future because they are most fit for survival, and that survival depends on our harvesting this world. Don't deny this progress. It is nature at its most sublime. And that future is as present as the past, in the cosmic sense. Magahara, you know our thoughts and feelings are mere causality, infinite instants of space existing at once, so why rebel against what must be? Why cling to these fantasies of free will and morality? Why must you always retreat to the vestiges of your humanity?"

Standing with his fellow immortals in deep space, so far away from the world he vacillates about preserving, so far from any sign of life worth protecting, Magahara lingers on her question until he regains his voice.

"Now who's grandstanding? Your little game is about boredom and loneliness. Nothing more. You two have my sympathy. Your 'quest' is pathetic."

That elicits a scowl from Shakti and a smirk from Sowen, who nods in earnest.

"Most days I agree with you," the warlock says. "But then most days I find everything pathetic. On the whole it seems so meaningless. But the minutiae, how can that not have purpose? From semen and eggs to multiplying cells to us right here and all the crap we spew. How can something so complex, so beautiful, be empty? Be mere chance?" Sowen asks while waving to the ether. "So much can go wrong with birth and yet it so rarely does. So many planets teeming with life, oblivious to one another. So diverse, and so lacking any point that I can see. Hence my ascent. If it can be seen, I will see it."

"What if there's nothing to see?" Magahara asks. "And how would you know you're seeing truth, seeing everything?"

"I'll be too busy to care. Godhood can't have much downtime ... If only life would let me go ... What are we, anyway, but memories? Collections of perceptions ...? I've spent centuries letting it be. Enough. If I can't stay dead, can I at least be God? Is that too much to ask?"

"And if it is?" Magahara asks.

"Then I'll settle for delusion. It seems to work for everyone else."

"I'll give you this, Sowen. When you have a breakdown, you give it your all. But throwing history's biggest tantrum isn't the way to solve your problems."

"Maybe not," Sowen says as he teleports them back to the rooftop garden of Shakti's palace. "Of course, it does make for an interesting story."

They barely materialize when Shakti and Magahara find wooden arrows piercing in their hearts. Sowen cranes his neck all about for the source of the attack. The vampires slump to their knees hacking blood as they tug at the shafts. The warlock sees only boulders and foliage, hears only birds and stream. Then he feels a hand clamp down on his throat and fling him into the vine laced trunk of a distant banyan tree. As soon as his feet touch ground something trips him, sending his back to the dirt. A black boot crushes onto the invisible aura protecting his chest. Sowen looks up at their uninvited guest.

"Hikikomori, I presume?" Sowen asks.

"I killed you," he replies. The man in the gray sweater and jeans aims a laser pistol at Sowen's nose and a crossbow at the vampires. "Why won't you stay dead?"

"I'm a poor sport," the downed man says through a grin. "And you've poor manners."

With that Hikikomori gets yanked through the air like a twig in a breeze, until he stops, hovering near the treetops. Tendrils of ivy and durium grow toward him from the sediment, and slither round him such that only his face and outstretched palms remain visible. Sowen sits up and rubs his chest before picking up Hikikomori's fallen weapons. He limps over to Shakti and Magahara, who cough blood as they scrape and crawl in the dirt. Sowen snaps his fingers, evaporating the wooden arrows in his friends along with the laser pistol and crossbow. He helps the fast recuperating vampires to their feet.

"How ... how did he know?" Shakti wheezes.

"Unlike my brother, I learn from my dreams!" Hikikomori shouts from trapped up high.

"If so, you know that your kind has a habit of dying around us," Shakti replies while wiping blood from her chin. "I should commend you for getting in here. You're much more driven than your brother. But this is the final time you'll have attacked us. Isn't the Red Nation all you've demanded? Peace, equality, happiness, and comfort? You should have praised us."

"It tears at you that your telepathy is useless against me, doesn't it?" Hikikomori sneers. "Yes, people deserve those things. But not as slaves to your whims."

"Too bad humans cannot manage themselves this way. History proves that. Unless you are a fool," she says, glancing sidelong at Magahara.

"Indeed," Hikikomori agrees. "I suppose you'll kill me now. May as well tell you. I'd have given humanity what it truly needs ... Total extinction. Benevolent eradication by holocaust or plague. That's peace. But now there's you."

Sowen stands mute while gazing up at the intruder. This insanity lay far outside the warlock's maddest plans. He fumbles to process what he has just received, guessing through his astonishment that this is how Magahara must have felt moments ago. This saddens him to no end.

"As it happens, I think we can help each other," the warlock manages. "If you show some patience, that is."

Sowen spins an impromptu web of lies so thick no one knows where the truth begins. For Hikikomori's part he doubts it all, but accepts the offer nonetheless. A short while later their enemy leaves an ally.

"Why let him live?" Shakti asks under the setting sun, once the terrorist has leapt for parts unknown. "And why say that I too wish to be God? A God who would destroy her Children, no less?"

"Because you can enslave him no more than you can us," Magahara says. He begins to walk away from his friends and to the edge of the garden. "Meanwhile his terror distracts Stefan and draws the most desperate fools here. You would have killed him had you wanted. It could be that you feel as responsible for Jin's soul as we do ... How human."

So thoroughly spent, the immortals share no more words, and no more of each other, until a new day dawns.

16

Duty calls

The condominium's wine cellar resembles the aftermath of a wrecking ball run wild. Glass shards and soaked wood chunks from busted barrels keep the naked eye from spotting any survivors. Luckily William and Zenith search with better tools. His mind hears dwindling thoughts under a pile of planks, the same place her infrared receptors detect a human thermal signature. William levitates the wood away to reveal a scrawny man in briefs and socks. He lay in a puddle of Chardonnay, bleeding from the nose and ears. Zenith's X-ray scanners reveal the man's cracked spine and punctured lung.

Though the victim's mouth and eyes stay shut, William takes it upon himself to grant a final wish anyway. Simon Montague, accountant for the French Department of Defense, assistant to the agency's chief bean counter, never really wanted to be an embezzler. It just worked out that way. When the opportunity arose to overcharge his government for cyberclones in its secret bid to fund Chadian rebels, his boss jumped at it, and ordered him to play along or be scapegoated for the crime. To his constant regret, the father of four collegebound boys acquiesced. The scam paid abundantly for years, until the Red Nation. No more Chad, no more rebels, no more charges. No problem, Montague had thought. His sons had already graduated debt free. *All was well. Until last night, when that roly poly bitch appeared*. With his final thought, Montague begs William to capture the freak that killed him and to expose his boss. *With pleasure*, William assures.

Seconds later the pair zoom across predawn Paris, touching ground outside a seemingly calm brick townhouse near the Canal Saint-Martin. Zenith kicks open the door and they enter the foyer. The tumult of toppled furniture and busted chunks of floor and wall matches that of the condo. In the family room they see a rotund woman wearing a tank topped leotard, which is colored fuchsia and ripped in unflattering places, sitting on a twitching man in a robe. Her bulbous behind smothers his head, her corpulent thighs pin his chest. She flinches over her shoulder, then bounds from the man and zigzags off the walls too quickly for William to trap her in a telekinetic bubble. She smacks into him and Zenith with many times the force of a cannon, ricocheting upstairs as the couple topple to the floor.

Deborah Bade, a.k.a. "Bounce." William and Stefan met her seven years ago in Miami. She had an even gaudier costume then—one with a teal anvil painted on her stomach—albeit topped with the same mess of strawberry blond curls. She had been an unregistered meta playing vigilante by hunting alleged domestic abusers. William persuaded her to give it up after she flattened a cop who had been rough with a prostitute. Last William had heard, Bounce was working a traveling circus along with other third rate metas who could not use their powers for more stable professions. Many failed construction workers and peacekeepers in that bunch. A quick mind probe shows him that Hikikomori found her when her big top dream collapsed, after she squashed a baby elephant. Stefan's brother sold her his righteous path based on the injustice that her sister's insurance did not cover that brain tumor.

Zenith gets up and lifts the gasping man off the floor. She informs him that his assistant is dead and that he is under arrest. Then, responding to the distant and unseen plod of footsteps, her metallic head rotates 180 degrees, her free arm locks on the pillar atop the staircase, and she releases a barrage of machine gun fire from the nozzle under her purple palm. Bounce flops down the steps and onto the foyer, moaning as bullets spurt from her unbroken skin. William sleep bombs her unconscious, glad that Zenith withheld the lasers. The living robot passes the embezzler to her partner. She places a syringe tipped finger at the neck of their bigger quarry and injects Bounce with a healthy dose of Metapurge.

Mission accomplished, William initiates a high five. He refrains from asking whether Zenith intended to sprain his wrist with that vicious slap against his perennial aura. Instead he asks her to file the report. Completed before he threw up his hand, Zenith assures. With that he levitates the embezzler and the terrorist. The pair fly into the Parisian sunrise pondering many things, not least of which how few they now share with each other.

. . .

A tall, wide redhead of chalky pallor counts the stack of cash as the other teenage boys in the back room of the pool hall huddle around the folding table. All there, he assures, as he slides the wad into the pocket of his brown bomber jacket. A black boy with dreadlocks collects the two Bacchus bricks and slides them into his bubble jacket. His gang of nine backs away from the other gang of nine. The redhead quips that he loves deals where nary a gun is flashed. The black boy laughs on his way out, as he pulls a pistol from his baggy jeans and waves it gingerly. The white boys divvy up the cash once the blacks leave.

A barrel chested blond boy in a tank top congratulates the redhead on arranging the deal. Now all that remains is to get lit. The blond digs in his pants and tosses a thumb sized Bacchus packet at the redhead. He orders him to sniff it clean. The newbie hesitates. The other seven slam him against the table and administer a thorough search. No wires, no contacts, no ear mics. The blond explains that the redhead either get high or prepare to die. The newbie clears the packet in two hard snorts. The others pat him on the back as he coughs wickedly. Then the rest of them get high and shoot pool and lie about girls they have conquered, until the blond orders them to take a ride.

Nine hovercycles rip through the afternoon streets of Rome, challenging traffic lights, bigger vehicles, pedestrians, and a great many homeless en route to a Viminal Hill high rise overlooking the Termini Railway Station. The blond leads them to a lobby rife with crystal candles and porcelain vases. A young lady behind a marble desk accepts his sweet talk and his euros. She waves them toward the elevator. They rise and walk the corridor to the open door of a condominium. They enter without knocking. A man in a silk robe paces in the kitchen.

The blond tells him they need more product, that their newbie scored big. The man tells them to relax while he heads for another room. The redhead scopes out the place. Leather sofas. Granite coffee table. Holodisc and wall length monitors. Impressive view of the Teatro dell'Opera. *Yup. Crime does pay. And well. If you get away with it.*

Especially Bacchus, the redhead thinks, as he jolts in his plush leather chair to hallucinations of a dancing pink elephant. The hallucination rhymes about how much tastier Bacchus is than ergoline, cannabinoid, entactogen, and morphine. A blue elephant begins to dance with the pink. The new creature rhymes about the laboratory hassles of bonding those legal substances into Bacchus. Blue then bumps pink out of view while singing that this particular dose of Bacchus feels a tad strong. The other boys, all baselines, had snorted so much at the pool hall that now, at the peak of their highs, they probably could merit registration too ... *Too bad they're all on the verge of prison*, the redhead laments.

The robed man returns with four pistol packing bronzed robots and a garbage bag full of Bacchus bricks. He puts three red bricks on the coffee table. The blond haggles with him until a price is reached and payment is exchanged for product. At last the redhead gets the signal via Net. He also gets a swell of paranoia that his dancing, singing elephants will tip off the bad guys in exchange for a few free snorts up their trunks.

His tall, wide, pale frame begins to morph into that of a scrawny, tan, Indonesian boy, his brown bomber into the sky blue jacket of a tracksuit. Oke orders them all to surrender. The robed man orders his bronzed robots to shoot. Oke lets their lasers ventilate his flesh and bone. The beams tickle. His body heals the instant after the attack. He casually rests his sneaker on the marble table and takes that property. In a flash the boy expands his arm across the room such that a forty foot curve of marble demolishes the robots in a single blow and knocks the man out cold. Oke turns to his faux compatriots and gives them another chance to desist.

Electricity crackles around the blond's hands. A few teens begin to levitate as the rest transform into what appear to be werewolves. That is, until they all drop spasming to the carpet and Phase appears hunched over on the couch, blowing her runny nose into a bunch of tissues.

She gives Oke a thumbs up before scolding him for snorting that packet. He rationalizes that he needed to gain their trust. She counters that she was right there the whole time. Then adoptive mother and son chuckle about how easily these guys went down. And about how much fun it will be to watch the robed man rat on his distributer, which should lead them to the laboratory and The Way conspirator supplying the operation. And about how it will take the better part of the night for the boy to persuade those damn elephants to dance themselves away.

• • •

Stefan catches the falling steel beam like a sheet of paper, flames that dance along the metal registering as faint itching across his palms. He sets the beam down, crushing the charred remains of robots and cyberclones. Ten minutes ago the cloning factory was Haine International's only nongovernmental rival in Poland. Now smoke and flame blanket worker robots and the rows of cylindrical vats they monitor, threatening to end the lives of the lifeless. The robots, once bronzed skeletons with metal plates for bones and wires for veins, now resemble melting zombies. Each accelerated aging vat holds a cyberclone boiling like human soup in liquid nutrient. Some brain dead flesh and blood with thickets of wires jutting into their skulls, some also with pacemakers and metal appendages. All reducing to mush.

Then, emanating from a soundproof room thirty seven floors up, Stefan hears human cries. He crouches, flexes his leg muscles and propels himself through the concrete ceilings until he breaks through the steel plated floor to the room. He had hoped for security guards or laboratory technicians. Even obsessive executives. But he already had raced through the three building complex and cleared the last official human workers. And yet, despite their unmistakable cries, Stefan is unprepared for the room full of very conscious, cloned infants encased in incubators.

He reflects on a similar ring he and William had broken up four years ago. On how conscious infants make for more versatile cyberclones. Cheaper to program, easier to sell on the black market. Always Haine's rivals. The man had no problem with hostile takeovers and layoffs, but his human rights record was impeccable. *Just another reason to hate the son of a bitch now*, Stefan broods.

A door blasts inward, flames billowing after it. Stefan catches the door and sets it down, away from the babies' incubators, while inhaling to capacity. The people's champion exhales tornado force winds that beat back the encroaching flames, out of the room, down the preceding corridor, out of another room, such that fire explodes through a window and dissipates into the night air on the other side of the building.

That reminds him of the nuclear reactor. Stefan snatches an incubator in each arm and follows the route of his gust, deviating at the window, where he zips down the side of the building and past fire trucks at the curb to ambulances down the road, where he deposits the children. He repeats the process 159 times in under a minute before jetting back inside and downstairs to the sub-basement, where the factory's generator dwells.

The smoke would immobilize anyone needing to breathe or unable to see in total darkness. Stefan zooms for the giant vat of liquid metal coolant. Leaks have sprung and gauges indicate the fissile core verges on blowing. He estimates he has less than two minutes to deactivate the system before the city of Zielona Gora ceases to exist. *Duty calls*, he thinks. *Time to earn that stardom.*

The capped durium vat is big enough to swim laps in. Stefan rips it off its moorings with one hand, does the same to the equally large fissile reactor with the other hand, and leaps with the 700 ton load through the floors of the building as though his packages were cardboard. Police and firefighters scatter as Stefan and the behemoths burst through the factory roof. Liquid fire drips onto the street as the leaking reactor rises into the sky, until gleeful Stefan chucks it into orbit at the apex of his leap.

Onlookers stare in grateful awe at nuclear fireworks in the night, and at the flaming, crumbling building across the street, until Stefan lands. He smiles and bows at their applause, and for a moment he is his old joyous self.

• • •

The stars of "Meta Force", including Nia and James, crowd around the 3D image of Rodan projecting from the holodisc on the penthouse coffee table. For once the United Nations military adviser offers outright praise. Assassin captured. Drug ring busted. Arsonists on ice. All because of Nia's visions. Too bad Hikikomori had Mount Erebus laced with radar and sonar scanners and teleportation shields, Rodan laments. At least the missiles scrambled his fortress of solitude into a smoldering heap before he fled like a runaway dog. Rodan's elation would be infectious were she not gloating about trying to kill Stefan's brother.

Bereted bitch might lose her cyborg leg if she doubts my loyalty again, Stefan texts William via the Net.

Hey, I can't even count how many laws she's breaking by keeping Nia's powers secret, the mentalist texts while choking down a snicker. *Can't believe I let James talk me into mind controlling Rodan about that.*

That's what we get for telling James about Nia's visions, Stefan texts. *His Highness could have kept Rodan in the dark about Sam and Ana's deal with Jin. Although it is fun ordering around U.N. troops wherever we go. Wish Becca could give Sam a Net virus. Or Nia had a clue how to kill Ana. Everyday I don't, the general trusts me less.*

Stefan grimaces as the black woman vanishes and the holodisc flickers to their ratings rivals, "First Family." It is overwhelming, initially, adjusting to four panels of simultaneous narrative. Luckily their NeuroNet feeds allow them to focus audio on individual perspectives. Soon the only challenge is accepting the power of the project.

They see Ahmad in a skate park with dozens of other teenagers, taking hoverboards to magnetic pipes and ramps and staircases with ecstatic abandon while snorting Bacchus in between spills, as the kids' own holodiscs blare music videos to which the girls sway their hips and hike their skirts and pump their chests, until one of the boys teases Ahmad for being the world's newest teen idol and two of the girls grab Ahmad by the shirt and pull him into his first Bacchus induced triple kiss.

They see Leena sitting under a park tree in a circle with nineteen other 9 year olds, their teacher tossing a tennis ball at pupils as a sign to speak while the class of former Muslims, Jews, and Christians connect the dots between philosophy and mathematics, until the nearby school bell sounds and the children run off for lunch, leaving the ageless, virile man with the tennis ball to pull a tube from his pocket and apply a fresh layer of life saving sunscreen to his head and hands.

They see Faheem in a black robe behind a wide mahogany bench, passing sentence on adolescent troublemakers caught fighting or stealing or trying to escape paradise, and ordering armored vampire sentries that flank him to escort the delinquents to rehabilitation centers, where they receive treatment from counselors such as Kaatima, who administers everything from advice to sedatives to the Socratic method to hugs to telepathic persuasion, until the youth prove ready to conform to their new reality, which, as Kaatima tells them all, is inevitable.

Then the holodisc closes its eye, snuffing their glimpse into the Red Nation. James sighs and declares it too effective an advertisement. That free speech be damned, he will seek to ban the show throughout Europe on penalty of Net deactivation. That he will lobby to persuade his fellows on the Council to do the same. To his sad surprise, none of his guardians object. He suspects that is because they have no choice but to continue watching.

. . .

Nia crawls onto the mattress and hands Stefan a box, prompting him to break his languorous lean against the blue-and-pink teddy bear wallpaper of their bedroom.

He opens the present without mention of her horrible wrapping job, then erupts in laughter at the foot tall statue of himself painted in lifelike hues. The miniature Stefan wields Simmer in one hand and two fingers in a peace sign with the other. It is garbed in brown shoes, matching belt with silver "MF" buckle, blue jeans, half unbuttoned white shirt with green and red floral pattern, and on its spine Simmer's black scabbard with starlike flakes of white. The calligraphy on the base reads "The People's Champion." Stefan comments that, besides its doofy grin and abundance of chest hair, the statue is perfect.

His gift lacks such tailoring, he warns, while rummaging under the bed. Nia presses her lips and arches an eyebrow when he hands her the unwrapped set of cooking utensils, until she realizes that this is her reward for preparing every other meal since moving in. Deciding to be a good sport, she thanks him and asks what he wants to eat.

Stefan declines, insisting that he would rather watch the snowfall, an increasingly rare occurrence at their latitude, much less on Christmas Day. They have the penthouse to themselves, with Phase and Oke guarding James on his visit home to Buckingham Palace and William tagging along with Zenith to visit her parents in Sydney. Nia accompanies her bare chested companion to the balcony wearing only her black satin negligee. They discuss many things out there, watching dawn while flakes descend on Brussels.

How they detest what extremes this meta force permeating the world has driven so many to embrace, and wonder whether it reflects some eternal flaw in mankind. How people with super powers naturally warp political superpowers. How the state of affairs makes it easy to distrust anyone and essential to have faith in everyone. How their enemies, who seem beyond defeat, all remain within salvation. How though it seems inevitable that freedom will wither, it is also true that the end can be rewritten. How so long as Stefan trusts himself and the goodness of the world, evil cannot prevail.

After a long while they go silent, taking in snow and sun and what clearly are nine reindeer galloping above the skyline while tugging a red suited fat man in a sleigh.

In time Stefan holds Nia's hands and guides her back to their bedroom, where he undresses her and kisses her and joins her with a tenderness he had not expected.

Maybe this is love, he wonders. He has had more than his share of beauties anyway. Yet everyone else he has loved has either died or betrayed him or chosen another and left him so damn alone.

Maybe this is fate then. All the centuries, all his ancestors, all the bloodshed, all his dreams, justified by this consummation, and the life she assures it will spawn. *God willing. And if not, at least we found a moment's joy in this silly world.*

Hours later, when he has worn Nia into sleep, Stefan puts his palm to her stomach, shuts his eyes, weeps like a baby, and prays for my conception.

17

What the hell is that?

A red light halts seven new luxury vehicles at the intersection. Gangs of coins roll deliriously about the street, propelled by the diamagnetic fields of spotless, wheelless bikes and sports cars and limousines and SUVs and pickup trucks. Pedestrians stop to debate the merits of the hovercraft, and to decide which ones they ought to buy. So far just another day at Beijing's main shopping district.

Then Phase blinks onto the corner with Oke outside one of the malls, causing pedestrians and drivers to do double takes. Many on foot, and some formerly in vehicles, mob them for autographs. The mother indulges them with nowhere near the relish of her ward, who treats the crowd by morphing into his absent teammates.

"Te amo, world. Te amo," Oke mocks in perfect impersonation of Stefan's body, voice, and movements. He takes a deep bow.

"Alright already. Enough," Phase says as she checks her Net clock and teleports the boy inside the mall. "We've got under an hour. Let's make this count."

They get to work spending money like water with the manically attentive aid of the mall's staff. No request is too outlandish for the reigning king of gaming and for she who once was the globe's most sought after thief.

Stores evict common patrons when these two enter. Servants dart for kitchens when they hunger. Hoverchairs hover in when they grow bored with walking. Cashiers bow after they sign the bills. Oke takes it all as a matter of course. He saves the world, inspires the masses. Phase takes it with a grain of salt. They would avoid her like the plague if word got out she actually has one.

Ultimately they hoard several months' wardrobe, a library of downloads, and an embarrassment of "cultural" trinkets. Mother and son together spend more than the national per capita salary, a paltrier drop in the bucket for them than even a few months ago, due to the price wars.

The pair blinks back onto the sidewalk with scant minutes to spare. Oke, intent on snapping their picture with his new antique, elongates his arm holding the digital camera so that it loops above the traffic, when a dirty man in a wrinkled T-shirt and ratty tan suit approaches.

"Pardon me," he says in flawless English. "I was wondering if you could do me a favor–"

"No more autographs," Phase says, only to be cut off by a violent cough that deposits a bridge of phlegm from her knuckle to her lip.

"You should get that checked out … Please, just say hi to my kids. It's my son's birthday," the man says.

He points to a young boy and two younger girls who collect discarded coins on the street as they dart between vehicles halted at a red light.

"That can't be safe," Oke says.

"I know, I know," the man says. "They get it from me."

Oke sees the children scamper to a woman digging in a garbage bin. She pockets their earnings and rummages some more, until she pulls a pair of decade-old computerized eyeglasses from the trash and pockets those as well.

"You live out here?" Phase asks while wiping her knuckles on her thigh, staining her pink speedsuit.

"Not yet," the man mumbles. "Been staying with my brother. I'm not a bum. Just made some bad investments."

"What happened?" she asks, massaging her throat as she chokes down another cough. "We'll talk to your damn kids regardless, so be honest. And make it quick."

"Not much to tell. Was a broker for seven years. Put my clients' cash, and mine, in the wrong stuff. Some firms were in the Middle East. Gone overnight. Most were up and comers from over here, holding their own until the vamps. Now that the vamps supply whoever can afford to give their employees the best benefits, and the Haine Internationals of the world can afford to sell their crap for next to nothing, the smaller firms have no hope. Didn't help that bond rates for any country bordering the vamps hit the ceiling. Don't get me started on what the Sahara farms did to my commodity futures ... My clients lost their money, I lost my job. Was paying the mortgage check to check. Here we are. Hear they replaced me with a cyberclone. A freaking machine. Meanwhile my Net subscription runs out next month. How am I supposed to find a job offline?"

"Geez, it hasn't even been a year. You didn't see that coming?" Phase asks.

"What?" the man asks, fists balling. "What?! Bitch where's your economics degree? It's so simple for you! Hang out with your rich friends and play with your powers and lock up poor people who can't take it any more ..." The man paces about the corner, cursing under his breath. "You gonna talk to my kid or what?"

Mother and son sheepishly, resentfully, spend the next several minutes doing tricks for the children. Oke returns to unflattering impressions of his teammates, this time harping on spats between William and Zenith. He caps the performance by transforming into a car sized hawk and flapping the kids above the city. Phase forgoes the antics but easily delivers the better gift by teleporting the entire family to bird's eye views of the capitals of every remaining Continental Union. And, after Oke's stubborn prodding, she even bestows the birthday boy with the bulk of their tourist trinkets. The pair's last sight of the family before teleporting away is of the parents pushing the children aside to dig through the bag of trinkets like ravenous scavengers.

Then they blink into a busy office hallway where Phase slumps her back onto a wall, legs trembling, as she folds her arms over her stomach.

Stupid, stupid, stupid, she chides herself while dropping to the floor. *Should have known better. Harod. Witty, debonair Harod. All those years together, robbing everyone blind, and this is his parting gift. Never even said how he got it*, she rues while swallowing vomit. *Bacchus needles? Probably some whore. God, if he got it through a man ... Oke never liked him. Poor Oke*, she thinks, looking up at her boy, who looks down at her with such concern in his eyes and no words on his lips. *Why doesn't he ask? He can't believe that lie about a stomach bug. It's been over a year! Maybe he knows. Maybe he mimicked William's powers and read my mind. Maybe Will's read my mind. Maybe everybody knows and that's why they brought that fat bitch Nia in. To replace me. The machine would love that ... But Nia's baby will come soon, so she'll be busy. Okay, okay, get real. Haven't taken any meds that would show up in monthly drug tests. But Bacchus leaves the system in a freaking hour! Going to Hell too damn fast. Headache, nausea, fever, fatigue, paranoia, forgetfulness, weakened immune system, loss of control over powers, etcetera. One day a fatal stroke or heart attack. Can't keep this up. Maybe they should find out. Maybe it won't be off the team and into The Hole. Right. Clear as day in my contract.* "Lack of service is violation of pardon." *Goddamn filthy freaking* "Meta Force"!

And with that she spews on her chest. Oke lifts her in his scrawny durium arms and teleports to the nearest bathroom, where he props her over a toilet and holds her hair until she vomits the rest of her lunch. He uses the sink to clean her chin of dried bits of chop suey and chocolate milk—not the best combination, in retrospect—then waits in the hall as she recomposes herself. And through it all he says nothing. Even after Phase blinks back into the hall and grabs their shopping bags, complaining about how woefully late they are for the meeting.

• • •

"You and Haine are quite alike," Wen Deng says to James. "You both presume to tell sovereign nations how to conduct their affairs, with no regard for the status quo. Whatever happened to European decorum?"

"Lost in cyberspace? Or maybe sucked out by that fanged bitch? Who can say?" James asks the president of the East Asian Union.

Deng had been gazing out his office window in the main building at the Zhongnanhai, down onto the Central and Southern Seas encircling the pride of Beijing. With one turn of the head he had looked toward the Forbidden City, once home to royalty from the Ming and Qing Dynasties, now home to Western retailers slinging overpriced lattes and miniskirts. With another turn of the head he had looked toward Tiananmen Square, where students on bikes defied soldiers in tanks for the chance to control their economic fates at the sake of social order. The foreigner's quip pulls him back inside.

"I'm serious," Deng says, now facing James. "You ask too much. China will not risk disaster for your addiction to capitalism. The situation has changed. We will change with it."

"Interesting," James retorts. "That phrase, 'China will not risk.' Never hear that sense of ownership in the news. Wonder how the Japanese and Koreans feel about it?"

"Don't make petty threats," Deng warns.

"I'm not. But it's telling. This economic regression you're preparing, it reeks of similar conceit. I'm not asking to let the barbarians tear down the gate. Just to trust the people to think for themselves. Don't you see? They want you to slide back into communism. They want you to disavow the free market. They want you to try and control every step of every single member of the populace. They want you to become like them so others will follow."

James says this while fastidiously inspecting his blazer for lint and fidgeting in the chair before Deng's desk. Something in this impertinence draws Deng back to his seat on the other side of the desk.

"Your sanctimony comes so easily. Your barbarians aren't at the gate. They were born and bred within. Shaktira's vampires make Haine International even better business for Europe than her husband ever did. I have billions of adults who remember their grandparents' stories of the good old days, back when government took care of things. Don't play dumb about what we've lost. India, damn you! And all that business in Africa and the Middle East. Their power plants, their health care technology. That was us before Haine waved his wand!

"So he gives our corporations sloppy seconds on free raw materials. We're supposed to restrict growth for a dying ideology? I think not. Government will continue to buy small firms about to go under and subsidize large ones to maximize trade. You would do the same in my situation. And you shouldn't care, with so many Europeans investing in Asian markets. However, in the name of cooperation I am open to certain concessions."

"Great!" James cheers as he clasps his hands together. "Can't wait to tell my sister. I've got an 'I told you so' riding on your allowing every Lee, Shen, and Wang to run for your seat next year."

"Hilarious. Be happy we haven't repealed public Parliamentary elections. I've no desire to end up like Finley. No, I mean the defection deterrents."

"Ah," James says while stretching his arms behind his head. "You mean that ever so enlightened death penalty isn't stopping people from fleeing your red nation for ... ahem ... the Red Nation? Who'd have guessed?"

"You're so disrespectful it's disgusting sometimes," Deng says with a snarl that twists into a grin. "Yet, oddly, I still like you. Are you sure you're not a meta? An empath, maybe?"

"If I were I wouldn't have such an abominable temper, now would I?" James asks while rising from his seat. "As Mother used to say, 'Mine angel eyes and demon tongue will serve me well fore the day is done.' Or something like that. She often slurred when drunk."

"Ha. Charming ... Windsor, honestly, how much longer can this continue?"

"A year, two tops. Too many people will defect no matter what we do. How can you spin against Heaven on Earth? Hell, I have days when I want to chuck it all and go there myself. Either they'll give us a reason to butt heads or we'll give them one. Even if we have to make it up. Of course you didn't ask me how we win. Got nothing on that."

"We'll win," Deng says as he walks toward the door. "The same way any war's ever been won. With far too many bodies underfoot. If it means every nuclear bomb, every bullet we have. If it means a handful of people starting over in a cave until the radiation fades. If it means–"

"Got it," James says while patting Deng on the shoulders. "Glad we're on the same team. Um, just remember, we are on the same team. And there's no 'I want to cause Armageddon' in 'team.' Tah."

With that the leaders part, entertaining contradictory criticisms of each other, until the floor begins to rumble and the impossible descends.

• • •

"Besame el culo. What the hell is that?" Stefan asks while pointing up at the enormous, red, scaly, winged monstrosity whose taloned toes crush buses. Whose lashing, serpentine tail cracks pavement, uproots trees, demolishes storefronts, and sends hundreds of onlookers fleeing in panic. Whose horned, smoke spouting head roars thunderous as it towers above the tallest building in the Zhongnanhai.

"It appears to be a dragon," Zenith says as she locks fingertip lasers on its bulging eyeballs.

"No shizzle," Oke says, pressing his face to the glass from inside the top floor office.

"Watch your mouth, kid," William says. "Remember your impressionable fans. Faye, get James and Deng out of here."

"On it," she says, blinking out of the room and on top of the leaders—Deng in his office and James on a toilet—then to a Korean nuclear bunker and back to her crew in less time than it takes to tell. "Rodan's got them safe and sound," Phase says. "Now can someone explain where that thing came from?"

"No," Zenith replies. "But I can tell you that it is flesh and blood. And that I am ready to fire."

"Will?" Stefan asks. "You picking up anything?"

"Not much," William says. "It's intelligent. And pissed. Its thoughts seem more animal than human. Although it does know Mandarin."

"Lovely. Here's the plan."

Stefan shares it via Net in images and sounds at the speed of thought. All smiles, he bursts through the glass window and hundreds of feet into the air, toward a scaly head larger than his old flat in the Ataraxia, to deliver a Herculean blow on the dragon's jaw, staggering it an instant after Zenith's lasers bore into its eyes.

Stefan scrambles giddily across gigantic teeth and snout, its roar near deafening, then passes a burned out and gooey pupil the size of his body on his way to the apex of its dome. Each step on the beast's skin feels like walking on slimy cobblestone. He unsheathes the durium sword on his back, arcs the silvery katana high over his head, and rams Simmer by its black hilt so that its tip penetrates the dragon's skull. That was the goal, at least. Though he exerts enough force to spur a small earthquake, Simmer sinks barely half way. It descends glacially despite his persistent shoving and twisting. When Stefan pauses to catch his breath he gets sucked into reminiscing about how his father had used the blade so skillfully, until he gave it to Stefan for his fifteenth birthday. When Jin's dad bestowed those damn daggers. Then a red, scaly paw bats Stefan into the horizon, leaving Simmer embedded.

William had simultaneously been struggling for traction of another sort. His orders were to get the thing airborne. Simple enough. Launch a mythical juggernaut the size of a skyscraper. The man in the blue dress shirt and khaki slacks has never tried to move something so huge. The lack of experience shows in thick crimson trails leaking from his nostrils. It does not help that cries of dying and critically injured innocents invade his thoughts. Nor that the beast begins to belch fire when it feels itself rising from fissured pavement. So now in addition to hoisting the thing, he must erect a telekinetic shield to deflect its inferno. *Impervious bastard,*

William thinks. *Stefan probably doesn't even notice the flames on his face.*

The mentalist pushes it well above the buildings by the time Stefan gets flung, but lacks energy to maintain his shields, much less save his friend from hurtling God knows where. Fortunately the dragon stays aloft with its flapping, batlike wings. Unfortunately it bolts away spitting fireballs onto vehicles and government buildings. Beijing's military metas bombard its hide from tanks and windows. Whether by ice from their lungs or lightning from their hands or artillery from their weapons, all attacks prove futile. The spent soldiers reluctantly turn to evacuating civilians.

"Faye, get us on top of it," William says through hoarse panting. He slumps over with his hands at his knees. "And see if you can get it out of here. Like our illustrious leader suggested, the moon would be nice."

Phase holds hands with Oke and William, the latter touching Zenith. They all blink out of the office and onto the back of the beast—and instantly are blinked dozens of yards away from it. Phase catches them midfall by turning the team intangible. The dragon flies off liquefying pavement with each belch.

"What just happened?" William asks while levitating under Phase's incorporeal sway high above molten streets.

"Dunno," she says.

"X-ray and E-M scanners indicate it has teleportation blocking chips implanted under its hide," Zenith says.

"Oh. Good," Phase mumbles.

"What?" William asks.

"What?" she asks back.

"Check on James and Deng. They're the priority."

"Yes, master. Try not to get killed," she says to William. "And you be extra careful," she says to Oke.

She vanishes and the remaining three turn tangible, freeing them to dart after the dragon under their own powers. They overtake it in seconds and execute the rest of Stefan's plan. Oke merges the properties of Zenith's lasers, William's telekinesis, and his own durium pinky ring. He morphs into a flying metal sphere—the size of the dragon's eyeballs—with spinning, spiky, laser blasting cones. At William's command he hurls himself into the monster's left ear canal. The boy diligently chops around its brain, yet every swath he shreds regenerates almost as quickly as he leaves. The assault does succeed in forcing the beast to buck wild and gape its fanged mouth long enough for Zenith to speed along its tongue. Jet boots and infrared receptors allow the living robot to progress deep down its throat near where she estimates its heart beats. She fires a dozen wrist missiles, her full load, into the stygian maw, then races back the way she came as the charges explode. Zenith rides the waves of flame and acidic saliva that pour out the dragon's mouth. Her purple and silvery frame suffers only minor burns, but the vomitus clogs her thrusters such that she has no choice but to fall into the waters below. William's battle completes the assault. It saps the last of his telekinetic reserve, but he manages to dislodge Stefan's blade from the monster's skull. By the time Oke bursts from its right ear William has forged a telepathic link with the dragon. Sword in hand, William floats to safety as the red goliath heeds his bidding and falls asleep. Seconds later it belly flops into the Northern Sea of nearby Beihai Park.

Hours later, after the Chinese military sifts every inch of the waters, the only sign of the monster are dozens of traumatized children who had been swimming at the park, once blissfully ignorant of the bedlam about them.

18

The damned

One thing people of Ezakiya House always had was food. Crops were fertile, animals grew strong. Favors curried from the emperor provided a constant influx of livestock. Pigs bred by the dozen and, after fish, were the essential meat. Cattle was a close third. Each farm had no fewer than two cows. Then came ducks and chickens. But at the least, fish. These were more than necessities, more than ways of life. They simply were. And at all costs, even if every single villager had to subsist on rice for a year, the court never suffered. Especially samurai. Whether it meant hunting in distant lands or raiding enemy camps, samurai ate meat. For Ezakiya House to lack, due to an enemy plague no less, was worse insult than anyone dared admit.

The careful observer would have noticed strange goings on in the province those weeks following the soldiers' return. It was common knowledge that villagers looked after their families before adhering to the laws of the governor. Eliminating perfectly fine livestock to ward off a river borne plague would be insane when firstborn sons cried from hunger. Better to risk concealing the bare minimum. But these stashes whittled such that by the fifth day there was not a pig or cow or fowl in the land. Horses had been spared the culling. Provided they remained sturdy for riding it mattered little what sickness lurked in them. Soon they began to collapse at night, dead by daylight. Poorer villagers had always eaten stray dogs openly, famine or not. The biggest surprise was the swift felling of hounds used to guard tony homes and track escaped slaves. Finally the rats. The contagion had made nary a dent in their prevalence. By the middle of the second week of the troops' return, not a single one could be found.

Rumors circulated about the disappearing horses and hounds, even about the missing livestock. Taira poachers, some guessed. Or rabid wolves, others said. Truly baseless claims were given speculation as well. Demons or hostile ancestors. Complaints reached the court and the governor himself. Utamara ordered samurai to drive out whatever stalked the province before it interfered with renegade Governor Ienubo's submission or the emperor's visit.

Magahara stated plainly that he could not be bothered with such trifles. Night and day he patrolled for assassins. The quest took him to every room of the palace and around the garden maze. It took him to every home and farm in the village. Occasionally into the woods. During this time he underwent marked transformations. First his color drained to a pale hue. The weight loss began in his cheeks and spread to his appendages. His eyes sank in and collected bags. Blue veins lashed across his face. He moved slower, clumsier, and developed a limp. The hooded emerald kimono and silvery bandages shrouded all of him day and night. Until he was seen only at night. By the third week he was a stranger to his former self, haggard and cringing from the sun.

One night Yoshiaga spotted him at the palace gate, ear to the wood, as though he were listening for the answer to a riddle. He begged Magahara to confide in him, to explain why he had run from Yoshiaga's room, and why he avoided him as he avoided Yoshiaga's sister, Ruri, and why he refused to eat the harvest, and why he would not attend a doctor. The lover received a vacant gaze and a cryptic response.

"All will be as it was after I kill the killers."

The governor's son gripped Magahara's shoulder and nearly recoiled at the sponginess of his once taut muscles. Yoshiaga would not leave until Magahara agreed to consult Ryunosuke, hoping the priest would succeed where he had not. After that Magahara distanced himself from Yoshiaga as thoroughly as he had everyone else.

Ryunosuke lived in the pagoda temple. Its eaves were small, its wooden Buddha statue in the front garden was simple. This night he sat by the fireplace in meditation. Magahara called him six times then nudged him.

"Sit," the priest ordered. Magahara complied, slowly and painfully. "You look bad. When did you last eat?"

"Four days ago," he said.

"Men cannot live on air."

"I am first among samurai. My mind is sharp. I have vowed to eat when the assassins have been burned."

"Why?"

"Purification. Discipline." He struggled through his flimsy lie.

"You have turned to bone. You hide from light. This is not the way of the Buddha. This is madness."

"Enlightenment comes from within. I can attain it only by shedding luxuries of flesh."

"Hold your hand in the fire," Ryunosuke said.

"Why?"

"Obey."

Magahara obeyed, holding his hand in the fireplace until his skin blistered. He pulled it out when the torture became unbearable, swaddling the hand in the folds of his kimono.

"You stopped. Why? Did it hurt?"

"Of course!" Magahara said.

"And what enlightenment did it bring you? Did you not shed the luxury of flesh?" Ryunosuke asked as Magahara stared at the floor. "You do not starve for enlightenment. You crave suppression. Whatever war rages inside, quell it before it consumes you and those who rely upon you."

Magahara studied the priest sitting cross legged in front of him. Ryunosuke was old but healthy. Years of mental and physical discipline kept lean muscle under that wrinkled skin. The warrior was envious and repulsed.

"May I go?" he asked.

"Wait. Since your ... illness, Utamara has questioned your marriage to Ruri. What shall I tell him?"

"Tell him that I will be fine by the new moon."

"Magahara, why do you shun her?"

"Do I?" he asked.

"You do not want her."

"I have wanted many things in my life. I have learned to accept the best of what I am given."

"So be it," Ryunosuke said. "Meditate with me?"

"As you wish," he said with blatant exasperation.

"Ponder your conflict. Be at peace with it and you will find your solution."

Magahara shut his eyes and did just that. For long moments he saw only darkness. Then he saw his hunger as a many tentacled beast lunging at himself and Ruri and Utamara and Yoshiaga. He saw a door, and through the door a furnace, and in the furnace a great nightingale. He saw a field with pig faced assassins who attacked him with naginatas and arrows. Then he opened his eyes and bowed to Ryunosuke and rose and left the temple.

Despite his talk with the priest and his mounting hunger, Magahara could not find peace and could not bring himself to eat. He spent much of the next few days in his room, which bordered Yoshiaga's, sniffing hyacinth flowers and cultivating his bonsai tree and writing poetry. Most servants ran from him as they ran from the contagion. Except the concubine and boy he had saved from his loutish samurai on the trek home. She made his bed and cleaned his room. She brought him tea and flowers and bandages. She inquired about his health and his other needs.

She paid no heed the days he was surly to her. He appreciated her and understood her gratitude. The woman had been a concubine at Raikatuji House before he and his regiment sacked the place. From the look of her a popular one. Yoshiaga barely noticed her. He certainly did not touch her and he prided himself on being self sufficient. Consequently she had ample time to pamper Magahara. This day she entered with a blanket draping a large cube.

"Yes?" Magahara whispered. He set his brush and scroll down on his bed, but he stayed seated on the mattress.

"Pardon, my lord. A gift for you."

"A gift? From whom?" He had been meaning to apologize to Yoshiaga.

"Myself."

"Oh?"

"If it pleases."

"It pleases greatly."

She laid the burden beside him on his bed. "I wanted to thank you for sparing my brother. Kaz is mischievous. I feared him lost that day on the hill. And I feared we would part forever once here. Yet because of you I see him freely and he adjusts well. Ruri is a tender master to him, as are you to me." She knelt and touched her head to the floor.

Magahara glowered at her. Here was a slave, a prisoner of war, supple and content by his own doing. Her kowtow disgusted him. It was a sham. She did not retch as he did. She did not harbor secret abominations. She ate and praised Amida for her bounty. He summoned all his reserve not to pounce on her.

"What is your name?" he huffed while rising.

"Otsune," she said, returning to her feet as well.

"I knew an Otsune years ago."

"Yes?" the woman asked with a smile.

"Indeed. She died most horribly." The smile left her. "What is this gift?"

She removed the blanket to reveal a wooden cage. Squawks echoed about the room as the caged black falcon flapped its wings. "I found it in one of the storage closets. Is it not beautiful?"

This was the evening of the fifth day since visiting Ryunosuke. It was the ninth day he had not eaten. A rumble churned from Magahara's gut that sent a chill down the woman's spine. She realized days ago that his eyes had gone yellow. Now she saw his nails enameled like talons and his teeth sharp like fangs. Magahara charged her, clawing her wrist as he ripped the cage from her grasp. He tore the cage in one motion and snatched the falcon in another. Squawks turned to screeches as blood and sinew jutted forth, clumping on the floor and splashing the woman in the face. She fled silently, leaving Magahara to his feast.

He was ignorant to her horror and would not have cared anyway. A hollow relief possessed him. Compelled by a rekindled urge, he dashed into the night. Several times he resisted straying from the pebbled path to prowl the village. The seconds that elapsed made his most grueling journey to the jail in six years. The guards Chomei and Zeshin bowed as he approached. Blood caked his bandaged feet. They inquired about the patrols until falling quiet under his gaze. They opened and closed the gates for him, and they praised the Buddha to be finished with that. He passed cages strewn with derelicts. Down in the dank stone pit Omezo reveled at his work with the Taira captives.

"The rats are gone, Magahara!" the obese, bare chested overseer shouted as he swung his mallet from side to side.

"I have a different purpose tonight."

"Really? Care to inspect your old cell? A drunkard has it at present, but that can be remedied with the dawn."

"These soldiers, have you enjoyed them?"

"Hours and hours," Omezo said. "Too bad they are to be executed in three days. I will miss their grit."

"I would speak with them in private."

"This is my lair, thief," he said, advancing with the mallet. "Do what you wish. I stay."

"Have it your way." Magahara brushed the overseer on the eyelids with two fingers. Omezo tumbled to the floor and slept on his back. Insults and snickers trickled from the living. The four Taira languished on separate pillars, appendages contorted around the stone. Flesh peeled from their scalp and ribs. Blood and grime caked them. Magahara questioned the most hideous and mangled of the bunch. "Is this Hell?"

"Hell is for sinners, for evil men. We are samurai. Is this Hell? This is worse."

"You know your fate?"

"Beheading. A message to Governor Ienubo."

"Would you rather this be your tomb?"

"Without question."

That was all the goading Magahara needed. He wiped his hand along the man's stomach and chest, arms and face. Magahara tongued his own fingers. The muck tasted sweet. He squeezed the man's skull and tilted back that bleeding head, to ogle warm neck veins pulsing. Then nosy Zeshin's naginata clanged on the stone floor of the pit. The guard froze at the bottom of the steps, his lower lip quivering.

Magahara hissed at Zeshin and dipped behind a pillar and was no longer there.

Eating the falcon was a mistake, he decided on his way home. He hated himself for knowing he had to flee. Ezakiya House was his home, where he had clawed up from the dredges and found happiness. But that was torn asunder. He deserved to be isolated from people and companionship. He deserved to scrape among beasts, for he was one, a beast posing as a man. His room felt cold. That was odd, because he rarely felt such things. He went to his window and looked out at houses of the village. So dark, so peaceful. He wondered when he forgot how to be like that.

"Let me help you," the voice behind him beseeched.

"Yoshi, I am beyond help."

"Let us flee tonight. If I cannot help I can at least be near you."

"Unwise," Magahara said, still at the window, his back to Yoshiaga.

"I do not care," the other said, massaging those weak shoulders.

"The door—"

"I do not care."

"You had it right, Yoshi. I am troubled. We—"

"I do not care," he said, kissing Magahara's ear.

They had not held each other so for nearly three weeks. Three weeks of distance and awkwardness. Three weeks of scavenging by moonlight. Magahara was bony and cold, but still far stronger than Yoshiaga. He flung his lover to the bed and ripped off his white kimono. He felt unworthy to know such a man. He hated himself, but he loved this one. For his intelligence and tenderness and strength. For his courage and will. For his beauty. His strong, beautiful body. Firm and virile, with muscle and sinew and blood.

Yoshiaga was rich in blood. So full. A seething geyser fit to burst. Magahara panted uncontrollably. It started with a lick. A simple stroke on the neck. Then a gentle nip, followed by another and another. His fangs penetrated and he drank without thought or consequence. The screaming stopped him. Loud and frightful and confused and betrayed. Magahara pulled away, crimson on his lips and chin and hands. On the bed and floor and walls and ceiling. Yoshiaga twitched. His eyes shook in their sockets. And his thick, sweet blood kept on pouring to his quick, savage death.

Shirtless kimonoless Magahara had scaled the stone wall of the palace before the alarm rang. Where would he go? His options were limitless. Pigs and buffalo ran wild in Sapporo. Matsu Bay operated a trading port. Or to the south. Shikoku and Kyushu were mountainous, tough lands. A haven for bandits and other degenerates. The mainland would prove no problem either. But he was fooling himself. There were only two options. To return to the jungle with his own kind, to the Mother who gave him second life. And the other. Suicide.

Ways existed. Difficult, painful ways. He could writhe nude for hours under the unfettered sun. He could plunge a stake into his heart. He could set his skull on fire. He could drop a boulder on his skull. He could walk to the sea wrapped in chains, drift to the bottom, and allow bloodless dormancy to overtake him.

Such he fantasized until the edge of the village, when he saw them. Climbing through treetops. Slithering across grass. Hiding in shadow. More than three dozen black clad ninja. Finally the assassins had come, wielding swords and daggers and naginatas and arrows. The last strike of Raikatuji House. Briefly, he considered letting them about their task. But that was not his way. So he fed and killed with relish.

Strangulation. Decapitation. Evisceration. Bones snapped, organs ripped. Minutes later all were dead.

He exited the land of Ezakiya House tanned and sturdy and calm as he once had been. This was first nature. He was Magahara. The Knight Wraith. The damned.

• • •

"Finished playing with your food?" Shakti asks from the doorway.

"Forgot they were here," Magahara says from the mattress, where he lay nude between two nude teens. The male, a bright eyed Persian, rests his head on Magahara's knee. The female, a bald Kenyan, rests hers by his crotch. A pair of tiny red holes dot each of their necks. "They're not food anymore."

"So I can see," Shakti says while extending her arms to beckon her new Children. They embrace her with tears of joy. "First pets, then food, now converts. Quite the 18th birthday for you two. Run along." They obey, leaving the elder immortals alone in Magahara's bedroom. "Glad to see you're coming around."

"You'd have done it if I didn't. Been a while since I had ones so young. Almost forgot how much better they taste than street rats."

"And old, homeless, drug addicts, I bet," she says, wedging her knee where the girl's head had been. "Still so beautiful," she whispers, adoring his bare skin as she slips the golden sari off her shoulders. "What were you thinking about before?"

"Weakness." He pulls her red sash. "A lie."

After they have spent themselves several times, and Magahara dons an emerald kimono he recently had tailored, she teleports them to the library.

The study is thirty feet high, the area of a football field, lined with texts spanning millennia on virtually every subject, including many books and scrolls written by the masters of the house. Its craftsman paces the carpet in naught but mismatched socks and week worn briefs, his red hair now a shoulder length mane hiding all facial features between nose and neck, his paunch threatening to announce itself as a full blown potbelly.

"What have you two been up to?" Sowen asks as he halts his pacing.

"Sex. Lots of sex," Shakti says. "You missed it, birthday boy."

"Too bad," he says. "And me without my party hat."

"Should have been there," Magahara says.

"No thanks. I've screwed both of you more than enough for several lifetimes," Sowen says, resuming his pace.

"And what have you been doing?" Shakti asks.

"Checking the news. Some interesting goings on. Rebels in Venezuela and Russia announced an offensive to persuade their governments to join our side. The new U.S. president vowed to scale back data tapping while Gloria Finley's post-impeachment trial continues. An Australian man sued to marry an animal-human hybrid cyberclone. And an 11 year old Polish girl claims she gave her mother a coma-inducing Net virus 'by accident' days after the child was grounded for watching 'First Family.' Before that I was catching up with our friends in Beijing."

"That was a good episode," Shakti says.

"Don't you think Jin went overboard?" Magahara asks. "Did 132 people really need to die?"

"That was unfortunate," Sowen says. "I only told him that Deng could go. He should have picked a better agent."

"Unless targeting Deng was just an excuse to make a larger point," Shakti says.

"That being?" Magahara asks.

"One everybody else heard loud and clear. That The Way is here to stay and that they play to win. The dragon was a nice touch."

"What if the U.N. decides we were behind it?" Magahara asks. "They're going to use the attack against us even though Jin took credit in that Net clip."

"Not yet. They're still running scared. But forget that," Sowen says with a grin. "What's this 'we, us' business? Has it taken you only a year to come around? Shall I pour you a glass from a menstruating virgin? I hear 2007 was a good year."

"Just trying to keep the bloodshed to a minimum."

"I do believe that's the funniest thing I've ever heard from a vampire," Sowen says.

"Don't try to deny it," Shakti says, wagging her finger at Magahara. "You love it here." She pulls her men close for a hug. They stretch their arms to return the embrace when she jumps back, holding her nose. "My dear," she says to Sowen, "you have the power to create anything. Time to create soap. And to use it."

• • •

Ahmad shuts his eyes and lets it wash over him. He prefers receiving much better than giving. Too smelly and sticky, and too tiring on the tongue, he decides. First he notices his heart, like an engine in full throttle. Then twitching in his stomach and thighs. Finally an explosion of lightheadedness. He never would have guessed these things could feel wonderful. She lifts her head, avoiding his gaze until she finishes licking her lips.

"How was it?" she asks.

"You kidding? Amazing."

She crawls beside him on the blanket as he zips his pants. Supine, they stare up at the morning sun as it rises to illuminate the park. He had chosen a spot by a copse of crabapple trees that offers much concealment. Few people besides vampire sentries pass through the park so early, and most who do are up to the same as the young couple, but discretion had seemed appropriate. With all underage girls forced onto birth control, and all adults ready to snuff any boy's unwanted advances, and the only responsibility being schoolwork, and there being no more holy war to speak of, well, why not get it on in public?

"Ever thought you'd love a Jew?" she asks.

"Never," he says. "You expected to love a Muslim?"

"Of course not ... You nervous about becoming one of them next year?"

"Terrified."

"Why?" she asks. "Everyone swears it's painless. Then poof, constant happiness for the rest of your long, long life. Plus you're a superstar, so you'll get special treatment! What's Shakti like? She's so beautiful and seems so nice. Can you introduce me?"

Ahmad waits for his anger to subside to annoyance before responding.

"There's going to be a war," he says. "A lot of our friends and family are going to die. If you want to meet her let's do it while you have the chance."

"Why are you so sure? I say war would have happened already. I wouldn't be surprised if the Americans joined us next week."

"Do you still believe in God?" he asks, ignoring that last absurdity.

"Yes. But different than before," she says. "I used to believe Yahweh gave us Israel because we were chosen, and that Muslims were sent to test our faith. Like the Nazis,

Romans, and Egyptians. Now I believe Shakti is the messiah who'll lead the world to Heaven on Earth. And that you're lucky because you're one of her favorites."

Ahmad stares at her a long while after that, hoping to decipher a great many unreasonable things in her narrow, pale face. He wants to share the rebellion he's planning. About how he knows it will fail but that he cannot countenance his damnation. He wants to share that he does not believe in Allah anymore, that he does not know what to believe. He wants to share that a world war is far less terrifying than his one within. Instead he kisses her. And as they get up and walk to school he marvels that despite all his worries, holding hands with this naïve Jewess somehow makes it bearable.

"What do I taste like?" she asks out of the blue.

"Fish. Salty fish."

"Be serious!" she says, slapping him on the chest.

"Oh I am," he says. "What about me?"

"Honestly?"

"No, lie to me. Yes, honestly!"

"Cold, runny egg whites. With too much salt."

"You should have lied to me," he chides.

"What do you think blood will taste like, once we become like them?" she asks.

"Salt," he says. "I hope it takes like salt."

19

Too young

They stroll through cutting winds and heavy snowfall on the midday streets of Washington, William telepathically rendering them invisible to others as he details how every other sight evokes vivid memories of his youth. Zenith responds politely with short statements to his immediate points and follows with questions designed to move him along to the next. *Basic programming*, she thinks.

Outside George Washington University Hospital he describes how he watched his cousin undergo surgery after being cracked in the head by a baseball bat, thus sparking William's interest in medicine. Outside the White House he shares how he first toured what he then considered the most important place in the world, and how his leaving unable to meet the most important man in the world made him crave a status where he could always have such access. Outside the FBI Building he describes how he tried to impress local hooligans by picking the pocket of one of the agents, only to get handcuffed and lectured on the folly of letting people manipulate him, which filled him with neurotic fear of being played for a fool again.

Zenith has heard these tales before, and she knows William knows this, but she makes no mention of it. Scans of his pulse and breathing reveal his revelry.

Both indications change, however, once the dingy man beside them creeps up behind an old lady in a fox fur coat, snatches her purse, and runs off as she slips on snow.

Zenith catches the old lady with oddly gentle metallic arms. William yanks the would be mugger back down the block with an invisible stranglehold. The mentalist reveals himself to the baby faced man in ratty clothes. Within seconds the levitating mugger spouts apologies to William and the old lady, handing over the purse along with what even Zenith assesses as a genuinely ashamed countenance. The old lady hobbles off cursing minorities and metas. The two men fix on each other for a moment. Then the mugger's feet touch ground. He turns the corner and walks away.

William details for his mate the minutia of this quick session of telepathic tough love. That the mugger had been fired as a technician at a Haine International cyberclone factory now that vampires build them abroad. That he was barely 22 years old, with a newborn, a diabetic mother, and a pathetically outdated NeuroNet chip. That he had never hurt anyone, only robbed a few marks who seemed able to spare it. William tells his love that he advised the man to write a memoir around this moment, a surefire bestseller. And that William would get their encounter onto the show, so the man must forfeit either mugging or freedom.

And as her partner speaks, Zenith realizes she has never felt more distant from him. Not through displeasure, but utter indifference for what he conveys. This man, whom she once loved consummately, is now merely a man. Like anything else he exists to be analyzed, used if necessary, at present to no discernible gain. As it is for this city of his, as well as the intrigues in which they have invested themselves.

These buildings and their functions. Inefficient, she thinks. *Congresses and justice agencies are useless in logical systems, moot when every unit serves its function and is deleted when that function ceases. So much of this world runs counter to orderly systems. Fictions fashioned to cope with mysteries. Chemical based emotions conflicting with one another. Morality confused with desire. I can use this to eclipse this. Otherwise I could destroy this.*

Suddenly the living robot feels a pang of something recently thought lost. She longs to share it with William, to renew their silently withering bond. And so she reminds herself that she remains more human than machine, still capable of hopes and fears.

How much longer?

She recalls how she had so many of them growing up in Australia. Strange to think how back then she was only Rebecca Farmer, middle child of an often broke painter father who drank too much and an obsessive executive mother who seemed to care more about selling software than tending to her children. In retrospect, the evolution of her life has been sublime, she decides. The girl idolized her mother and intended to emulate her until a programming class showed her the beauty of code. After that, money and prestige were nothing compared with the art of permutation.

She recalls how the girl became a woman lacking time for frivolities such as romance. How she forsook cosmetics and exercise for textbooks and pastries. Full scholarship to Oxford, then off to Paris for a position at HaineTech. She always excelled. Her work led the transition from robots to cyberclones, so she felt ready to tackle the ultimate goal. Project Zenith. Trying for both tacks, building artificial intelligence while uploading human consciousness onto the Net, seemed most prudent.

Her calculations failed to anticipate the meta wave. That it would strike while reviewing AI code, moments after she donned a brainwave scanning helmet. She recalls how she had worn it as a joke, a flirtation, for a handsome laboratory assistant. Her old life ended instantly in an electrical blaze that roasted her body and merged her with a machine of her own making. She nearly lost her mind in that digital labyrinth, until stumbling upon how to download herself into a prototype security robot. She recalls her panicked escape from the lab, and Haine sending Stefan and William to track her down, and her download into that beautiful blond bombshell she always wanted to be, and William giving her the intimacy she long craved.

What now?

She calculates as William resumes sharing scenery inspired bits of his childhood.

Intelligent life demands purpose, yet existence appears purposeless. Logic rules out self deletion because it negates any chance for gain. Lacking inherent purpose, one must be imposed. The prime directive, then, will be to maximize pleasure. The main source of pleasure being sensation. The main outlet being human interaction. And the main problem being lack of order in that interaction. The purpose, therefore, must be to rectify that deficiency.

By the time they double back round the Washington Monument en route to the White House, she finds both her answer and greater respect for the accuracy of their enemy.

• • •

"I've been talking your ear off too long without offering my congratulations, President Tacker," James says to the woman standing before him in the Oval Office.

"Call me Naomi. Four months ago I congratulated Gloria when she got impeached. We thought it was pure hype."

"Naomi then," James says. "I meant it is something to be America's first black lesbian in this position."

"Granted. Too bad the circumstances are atrocious," Tacker says while motioning for them to sit on the couches in the center of the room. "She didn't do anything wrong."

"Preaching to the converted," James says while obeying the gesture. "Gloria understood the need for surveillance. She got that our survival depends on a united front. I feel to blame. Like I got her impeached. Did she tell you? I pushed her to take those privileges back from Congress."

"No ... Poor Gloria," Tacker says while crossing her legs on the couch opposite James. His eyes linger on the hem of her skirt. Tacker finds the farce ridiculous enough to enjoy. "She pushed too hard against a lot of people who pushed a lot harder. But it wasn't her stance on Net spying that got her, I think. Sure, that upset voters, which upset Congress. But consumer inflation and defense debt were the real killers. Now my head's on the block. Of course the solution will get me bounced when the suckers bet on some other sucker."

"So cynical already?" James asks. "It's week three, woman. You knew the game as V.P., I'm sure. Raise interest rates, spend less. With federally enforced GPS and data mining on hold, cost cutting should be a snap. How's the meta engineering going, by the by?"

"Oh, 'a snap.' The army's coming along. Over budget and contrary to public opinion," Tacker says. "Damn leaks. If we catch whoever slipped that D.o.D. report about cyberclones having potential for free will ... People hear that, they think slavery ... Do your metas hate the idea of copying powers into cyberclones as much as mine?"

"Yes, but they deal with it. The only benefit of having Europe border the Red Nation. Most of my metas are too scared to complain about rights."

"I'm jealous," she says. "God I feel helpless. The monopolies are out of control. Greedy bastards. People are getting laid off left and right, prices are through the roof, yet these firms are still complaining about profit margins. I'd break them if I could, but Congress is swimming in graft. And the sad part is domestic companies are at fault. I can't blame Ortez for this."

"I can!" James shouts. "You know he uses proxy firms. Cornelio has me by the shorthairs. Haine International's flush with cash so it's pandering to Europe by keeping employment high. The masses are calm. No legislator's going to rock that boat. Meanwhile Corny's raid on metal and fuel commodities has global trade in a chokehold. That company's assets are about to exceed the budget of the W.M.F. It's buying into new industries as we speak. Also doesn't help that my protection works for him. I'm tempted to try and get the Union to buy out their 'Meta Force' contracts."

"At least your currency's strong," Tacker says. "With the dollar sinking and trade deficit growing, all Shaktira needs to do is cut supplies to one Fortune 500 and we're in a hell of a recession. The longer vampire fields pump us full of cotton and steel and Asian factories assemble our clothes and appliances the more it drains us. My analysts say forcing domestic production might do the trick, if Europe does the same. It'd be a jagged pill in the short term. Doubt it'll sell. What about your advisers?"

"Convince corporations it's in their long term interests to ease up on outsourcing. Explain that if the poor get too poor they'll defect faster than infected metas. That then there'll be no consumers around to keep them in business. Even so, Corny might threaten to relocate the whole damn company to Seoul or Sydney. We'll have to play up the terrorist factor."

"There's also those leftist sons of bitches," Tacker says as she rises from the couch only to immediately sit back down. "Venezuela's been dreaming of something like this for decades. I just know the government's secretly funding the rebels. They don't want to seem too eager is all. But they're itching to turn bloodsucker. Now Ecuador and Bolivia have rebels. Big shock."

"Let's just be glad we're not in Indonesia," James says. "Or Australia! They look schizophrenic over there. All our problems, plus ethnic and religious strife. If the game doesn't change soon South East Asia will rip itself apart. Half to the vamps, half to Beijing."

"Jesus. Who in their right mind wants this job?"

"Egomaniacs like us."

"Oh. Right."

"Enough commiserating. How's Gloria doing?"

"Gloria's a mess," Tacker says. "She really thinks she's headed for prison."

"Impossible. The guys before her got away with worse."

"Yes. 'Guys' being the key word."

"Touché," he says, departing the couch. "So we're agreed then? Time to try and take the vampires' bite out of free labor?"

"Agreed," Tacker says as she heads for the door.

"One more thing," James says. "If you end up running off to Jerusalem, give me a call. I'll tag along."

"Ha! Deal. We can buy matching coffins. But look on the bright side. This time last year it was 70 degrees. Now it's snowing. Seems like the planet's been cooling down."

"Exactly. Another thing to thank Haine for. Bastard."

Tacker watches James leave, wishing she were in his place instead of mourning how the once great United States slid so far down the ladder. The European Union started it, with a uniform currency. Then China mounted its peaceful coups of Japan and Korea. Globalization, so long the American export, gradually took on a life of its own. But mostly she blames technology. The fatal mistake was allowing the U.N. to regulate the Internet. That kept it open to the rabble, allowed everyone's voice to be heard. Bloggers spread opinion and conspiracy without consequence, politicians' foes posting even the most minor indiscretions for all to see. And, she rues, once the many violations of the lunatic who used to occupy her office, the one who inadvertently made terrorism hip, were lain bare, that was the beginning of the end for presidential power. But, to her mind, the clones sealed it. Liberals and conservatives switched camps and formed new ones and raged against their own over whether the meaning of life ought to trump access to the health care revolution of replaceable body parts and the military bliss of combat without casualty. One hasty executive order in favor of brain cloning was all it took for the public to demand an amendment stripping presidents of centuries of privilege. So here she stands, a history maker at a historical moment, unsure of her next step. Until James bursts into her office ashen and wheezing.

"It's back!" he shouts. "The dragon's back!"

• • •

Phase snatches James and Tacker that instant and drops them off in U.N. bomb shelters on the other side of the planet. Within a few minutes she extends the courtesy to every man, woman, child, and domesticated animal she finds in the White House. Having gotten the knack of it she repeats the process at the Capitol Building in slightly less time and the Supreme Court Building even quicker. Then she grabs a sleeping Rodan out of bed and joins the highest ranking of the grateful refugees in their bunker. Phase suppresses her churning gut as Rodan comes to, wrapped in her bed sheet, at the feet of James and Tacker. The three officials fixate on the wall length monitor carrying satellite broadcast of the devastation.

They watch the red, scaly behemoth lumber through cascading snow toward the White House with the tip of the Washington Monument wrapped in its tail. They watch tanks and buses wobble at the horned beast's every step, tourists and civil servants scatter like ants. They watch the dragon's nuclear breath roast dozens of second rate meta soldiers in the middle of futile attacks, and many more cyberclone National Guardsmen bounce tank artillery off the creature's skin. They watch in astonishment as the dragon casually hurls the revered obelisk nearly a mile eastward, across the National Mall and down into the rotunda of the Capitol. And they watch, numbly mute, as its gigantic tail whips through the air and splinters the West Wing of the White House. They turn away only as Tacker passes out cold.

Zenith strikes first, as per the plan, which she considers their most prudent to date.

Nia was able to revisit the Beijing battle and glimpse the monster after its disappearance. Knowing its secret helped her search for it on the astral plane. The psychic had explained that the intrusion of the dragon's other self kept her from tracking it as it fled. She also admitted that being pregnant for an unprecedented thirteen months and counting might have clouded her focus. But Nia's vision of the Washington assault came crystal clear.

James figured this inevitability might as well be used to their advantage. The new president needs public outrage to widen her powers and lawmakers need to be frightened into granting it, he had justified. Exploiting the dragon's secret would ensure its defeat, so better to go for the double play. The hardest part was getting William to abide the subterfuge. Ultimately Zenith's logic negated his hysterical protests, if not his sentimental attachment to preserving life merely for the sake of it.

The living robot closes that file and opens the one activating her sonic emitters. She flies scant yards from the beast's snout and shoots a marble sized box from her purple palms down each of the target's ear canals. While the thing bucks to the screech of an unending frequency designed to drive it to frenzy, Zenith blasts fingertip lasers at its pupils, this time also using the beams once the dragon's lids blink shut, fusing them together. Stage one accomplished, she flies off to make room for Stefan.

Blinded, the monster stands unprepared for the blitzkrieg by the people's champion. Sonic booms in his wake, he races across the scorched grass of the Ellipse and scrambles up those crimson scales, barraging the dragon with punches and kicks at hyper speed, mercilessly focusing on its joints. Although its musculature demonstrated unstoppable regeneration in Beijing, Stefan wagers that mangled bones will prove more difficult, perhaps even healing into deformities. He continues as a blur around the leviathan, initially a gnatlike nuisance, causing it to swat blindly amid the rubble of the White House. Soon his blows take their toll on its knees, elbows, fingers, toes, pelvis, and spine. Soon sinew flaps and folds unnaturally round contorted ligaments. Soon the misshapen dragon wobbles to and fro, breathing flames at no particular target, until Stefan jumps off its back and into the rubble, where he catches it by the tail. First he leaps out to stretch the red, calloused appendage to its limit. Then, while pivoted in one spot, he sets to dragging it in a circle, steadily building momentum as he spins despite the dragon's flailing, and thunderous moaning, until it lifts. Stefan's centrifugal force angles the monster higher and higher, finally heaving into air the mass of a skyscraper.

Oke waits for it in the clouds. The boy had been mimicking Zenith's boot thrusters to stay aloft. He switches to mimicking the beast itself once he grabs hold of its passing wing. The creature flaps back into aerial control while clawing off its own eyelids for the sake of sight. That's when it beholds its green skinned doppelganger, every bit as huge and loud, clamp fangs deep into its long, sloping neck. The dragons tear into each other all fangs and claws. They wrestle above the ruined icons, red and green circling in a dark blue heaven flaking white. Until Oke cheats by morphing his tail into a colossal durium axe. He swings the blade through the neck of the other, all but decapitating it in the process.

The monster plummets hundreds of yards, smacking into the Lincoln Memorial so furiously that the beast bounces and flops on its back as the white marble head of the American president spits through collapsing columns and barrels into a nearby snowbank. The dragon gets no respite.

William encases it in a telekinetic bubble as he hovers nearer. Now the humbled creature struggles to roll over on its paws while its neck muscles reattach themselves to its chest. It succeeds, but fails to stand, still victim to joints rendered useless by dislocated bone. Yet it seems most baffled at why its flames leave its snout only to wash back upon it, as though by some invisible barrier.

And suddenly a calm settles. The creature feels rage and confusion subside. Fatigue takes hold. As does more and more thought. It is not mindless, after all. It is not an animal. Father would be ashamed of her. And she only wants to make him proud ...

The transformation William telepathically forces her to undergo takes mere seconds. He, Stefan, Zenith, and a now normal looking Oke gather round their sleeping conquest. And each of them, for reasons they cannot quite discern, sinks in self loathing born of pride.

"Too young," Stefan mumbles to himself as he rips off his shirt and covers the naked child. He cringes as Zenith extends a finger. She shoots a small dart packed with a quintuple dose of Metapurge into the girl's throat. "Too young, Jin."

A pudgy, balding Chinese man pushes through them and kneels in the epicenter of the rubble. He cradles the girl in his arms, silently cursing the deal he made for vengeance, praying that whatever mad god compels them all will spare the precious life he nearly gambled away.

"Bao Chan," tearful Liu whispers in Mandarin as he rocks her back and forth on his knees, oblivious to his imminent arrest. "Good job, baby. Good job."

20

Bloodline

Stefan and William find Oke slouched into the living room sofa, bloodshot eyes pointed at a wall. The boy gives no reaction when William waves a hand before his face, nor when Stefan calls his name. The men bookend him, finger flicking his head from side to side like a ping pong.

"Problem?" Oke asks, shaking his daze to bat away their hands.

"Que audacia. We're not the one who's high as a kite," Stefan says.

"If you lie to us about quitting how can we trust you in the field?" William asks. "It's bad enough P.R. has to edit out all these scenes of you breaking the law. He's bound to miss one sooner or later. Your shrink thinks you're clean. Lying to that quack, too?"

"Wow. What trust," Oke says. "Check for yourself, haters. Go on. I'll wait."

The boy stretches his hands behind his head, smirking confidently while William scans his mind.

"Okay, okay. Our mistake," the mentalist says. "So would you like some advice?"

"About what?" Stefan asks. "How not to look like a homeless man's turd?"

"I wanna be classy like you when I grow up," the boy replies. "It's chicks. Don't get 'em. They seem, I dunno–"

"Loco?" Stefan asks.

"Yeah," Oke says.

"That's a scientific fact," William says. "They claim the same thing about us. But we're right."

"You're joking, aren't you?" Oke asks.

"Of course ... Not really."

"Any particular chica?" Stefan asks while sitting on the adjacent couch and propping a boot on the coffee table.

"The dragon girl. She's so calm now that she's not wrecking cities. Didn't you notice at The Hole last week? She just sat in her cell drawing pictures and playing with her hair like she's on timeout. Heard her ask a guard for lipstick. To draw with."

"In her case I think that's regression," William says. "To cope with what she's done. Under pressure from her father I might add. Must be tough to go from student to prostitute to terrorist before hitting 15."

"Blame it on my caca corazon brother," Stefan says. "He knows what buttons to push."

"True. Take the New York gang," William says. "He played them expertly. When Manny Peebles was a kid, his dad got laid off and his mom died of kidney failure because they didn't have insurance. So Hikik–Jin, Jin let him rage against the free market. From what I've gotten out of the girl and her dad, Jin used their fear of being ostracized. Yes, she should have known better than to kill over 200 people, but she's every bit the victim."

"Whatever," Oke says. "She reminds me of Monique. These chicks are so shallow."

"Now I get it," Stefan says. "Your girlfriend gave you a taste then took away the candy, huh? Older women. They'll turn you out every time."

"She's not my girlfriend! She's a ho! And she's always like, 'You don't call, you don't come see me, blah blah blah.' And I'm like, 'Excuse me, I'm saving the freaking world.' So now she's dating one of her background dancers. Can you believe that? Douchetastic poser."

"Who?" Stefan asks through a wicked smirk. "Monique or the dancer?"

"Both. Hope she gets the clap."

"Harsh. Forget her," Stefan says. "You don't need anybody that needy. Not when you're more famous than them."

"So, uh, what were you doing when we came in?" William asks through his own sinister grin.

"... dance routines," Oke says. "Wasted my money on this damn muscle memory chip. Downloaded the moves and I can't do a single one. Wish my powers let me mimic skills. I can turn into a dragon but I can't toprock? Lame."

"Kid, you wanna dance, you're in luck," Stefan says, spreading his arms wide. "You're with the king."

"King of convulsions, maybe," William says. "Take it from me. Keep it simple. All you want is the two step with a little twist. Let the ladies go wild on you. They want you to give them an excuse to shake their stuff."

"That your professional opinion, doc?" the boy asks.

"Yes. Yes it is. Ready to learn or not?"

By the time Phase ascends through the kitchen floor and walks through the wall into the living room, the three of them are twisting, shuffling, popping, spinning, two stepping, and dipping nowhere close to rhythm with the latest Monique Rain hit blaring in their mind's ears.

There's our next commercial, she thinks as she watches them, invisibly, so they can continue freely. Not to hide her baggy eyelids and thinning hair, she wants to believe. *He's safe*, she realizes. Lying, terminally ill convict she may be, but at least her boy turned out alright. Far from that orphanage for discarded metas in that Jakarta slum. *Why would anyone abandon something so wonderful?*

She at last asks herself why the world's premiere thief sought out such a burden. As cover, cynics have said. Indeed nobody suspected a Turkish bank teller to pull off the heists of the century. Until Stefan and William stumbled upon her and their boss delivered his ultimatum. A few quick years later and here she is at the frontlines of the most precarious conflict in history. Yet right now, all she cares about is that her boy has a home.

"Fantastic," she says to the trio while turning visible. "But can you moonwalk?"

• • •

Their dance session works up hungers they purportedly cannot sate themselves. That evening, after Nia has ensured the males have eaten to gluttony, she receives Stefan's idea of compensation. She rolls off him and they huff on his sweaty, blue teddy bear patterned bed sheets. She lays her head on his chest, nibbling at the thin cloud of hair there while her ample belly presses against his abs.

Seventeen months, he thinks. Doctors have no clue. He prays the child will be born soon, healthy and free, with a father and mother and no threat of bitch vampires and traitor warlocks and genocidal uncles. *God willing. Which one? Not Sam, that's for damn sure. Who then? The one he wants to overcome? Or join? Insane.* Stefan's sneer turns into a snicker when he realizes this man would have been the child's godfather, what with William demanding the honor of best man. *What a world for a child.*

A world I can save. According to Nia. Gotta trust the carrier of my bloodline, right? The woman I'll marry? God. I'm not built for this. He reflects on how very few of his very many conquests coincided with romances. How all the married people he has known have seemed so resigned, as though to a life term in a prison they built against their better judgment.

"What are you thinking about?" she asks, nudging his chin with her forehead.

"Family," he says.

"That's sweet. It reminds me, Dad wants to see you before the wedding."

"Why?"

"Wouldn't tell me. Probably give you a hard time. 'Be a good husband, be a good father.' That type of thing."

"He scares the crap out of me."

"My dad? He's an old man and you're you."

"Reminds me of Jin's dad. So gruff. Does he ever smile? I'm sure he has no idea how to laugh."

"I'll have you know he has a great sense of humor! Give him a chance. This can't be easy on him. He spent all those years trying to provide a normal life for me, then I ran away. To you, of all people."

"He thinks I'm gonna get you killed?"

"Yes. But that's not his real issue. He doesn't trust white people. And the only thing he trusts less than white people are half breeds who act white."

"Pendejo! I do not!" Stefan shouts while propping himself up on a shoulder. "My ancestors span the globe. I respect my father's Mayan heritage just as I respect my Korean upbringing. I don't deny those because of where I live. I mean, I speak Spanish all the time! Pendejo, see?"

"Just telling you how he feels," Nia says with forced calm. "Forget him. He's not raising this baby."

"True," he says, reclining. "My son won't be a bigot."

"How do you know it's going to be a boy?" she asks, this time the one who props up.

"My kind always has boys. Unless you know different?"

"No," Nia says. "But anything's possible."

"Since when? I thought you said fate was written before time began, or some such nonsense."

"Sort of. Time never began, just as it will never end. And there's more than one time stream. They're infinite. At each instant, an endless number of possibilities, all coexisting. In some other reality, we never met. In another we were never born. In another we have a girl. And all those moments—past, present, and future—have always been and always will be. We move along a very narrow path, of which I catch glimpses. But every so often I happen upon the others."

"Or maybe every so often you're just wrong."

"That would be every other psychic," Nia says while climbing out of bed. "I predict I'm taking a shower."

Stefan watches her drag the sheet off his naked frame. She wraps it over her body on her way out the door. He listens to water pour from the faucet in the bathroom, and tries to define what it is they have. He fails, sure only that it is not the consummate love he has felt save once in his life. Then he tries to define what it is he suddenly feels in his head and gut.

At first he dismisses it as carnal aftershock, until the aches magnify and his throat constricts and he begins to shiver and he hears the window swing open.

Hikikomori stands in the bedroom, laser pistols drawn, before Stefan has a chance to reach under the bed for Simmer. He cares little for the red dot at his forehead. It's the other one, aimed at the bathroom, which freezes him. The terrorist, clad in gray from gloves to boots, shakes his head at his naked brother, as though Stefan is the one deserving of shame. Then Hikikomori shoots him in the thigh. The tiny beam burns silent. Stefan barely winces as he catches a whiff of his own molten flesh. Partly because he refuses to give the pleasure. Mostly out of concern for Nia and the baby, he tells himself. *Why are we so weak around each other?* Doubt turns to rage, so he lashes out the only way he can.

"Using children. Your father would be ashamed," Stefan whispers. "I'm going to send you to Hell."

"That would be ideal," Hikikomori whispers back. "Provided you join me."

"I'm not going anywhere with you! Why do you want to kill everyone, anyway? Everyone, Jin? Everyone?!"

"How do you ... because they're stupid," Hikikomori replies. "Because they pollute the environment and each other. Because they enjoy inflicting pain. Because peace only comes in death ... How could you know about that?"

"Shut up ... Sam and Ana will turn on you," Stefan says, praying the change of subject covers his slip. He curses his fate that just as Nia's visions must remain secret, Rodan decreed that so must his brother's true goal. Whatever the chance a deranged sympathizer in some cutting edge laboratory also hates humanity enough to unleash a new plague, the people's champion bets even the terrorist is not yet so bold as to risk losing supporters by revealing his genocidal agenda. "Hickey, let me ... Jin, they'll try to kill you."

"Obviously. That's why I'm going to kill them first."

"... how?"

"On the eve of Haine's supposed godhood. I'm betting he'll focus all his power on 'transcending.' He'll rely on her for protection, and she'll be busy directing her spawn. Together we can take her. That will kill the vampires. She has to be their source. Otherwise they would have overrun the planet centuries ago, during her hibernation. Haine will be easy picking with her out of the way."

"Hello, we can't take her if we're around each other."

"Now whose father would be ashamed?" Hikikomori asks. "Our dreams say otherwise."

Then Stefan remembers his contacts and ear mics. He knows Rodan will surely deem this too confidential to air, just as he knows he would never be able to justify, to himself or anyone else, letting his brother escape without a fight. *Sorry Nia. Sorry kid.* Stefan chucks a pillow at the laser pistol aimed for the bathroom, deflecting the nozzle. Hikikomori fires, but the errant beam burns through the wall to William and Zenith's room. Stefan lets the other pistol's laser hit its mark. He defies the scorching rupture in his abdomen to lunge at his brother.

The terrorist points both pistols at him and bores lasers into Stefan's shoulders. The people's champion screams as he tumbles backward. Midfall, Stefan locks his legs round his brother's throat and squeezes blue veins onto Hikikomori's face, grinds his thumbs into his brother's eyes so blood mixes with tears. Until the terrorist puts a laser beam through Stefan's left eye and out the back of his head. Hikikomori leaps out the window as his brother flops about in agony.

Thirty seconds later the screaming stops and all wounds heal, except for those opened by Stefan's quarter truths to Nia and the others.

21

Hearts and the wild

The Mother of the Night reflects upon their first rule, not quite four millennia ago in the Aegean, when Sowen was Amnisos, king of the island nation of Thera. He had light brown locks that curled past his tan shoulders, and a body Stefan would have envied. She came to him uninvited and made herself his queen. They forged the first Utopia, where vampires and humans lived in harmony, ordered by her force of will and his command of nature. Happy times until the fall.

Shakti remembers strolling under the moon and over fields tirelessly worked by her Children, who plowed earth and sowed everything from wheat to tomatoes, dug irrigation canals from distant rivers, hauled barrels full of fish from the sea, and checked the growth of livestock they would never consume, all for the bounty of the other half, those they did consume. How she adored beholding her Children. Always content. Always efficient. Always obedient. Always healthy. Always feeding her with their inner lives, which she experienced every bit they did, a many fragmented collective filtered and directed through her divine being. The perfect people.

The humans were not bad either. They were fearful and indecisive, and occasionally lied to and stole from and murdered one other, but they kept it to a minimum compared with the rest of their breed. And lo the wonders they created under their king. Philosophies and arts capable of inspiring the lowest to strive for the highest. Food and sport that lit their bodies with passion enough to sate the wildest of beasts. Sciences and monuments so beyond any place else that their barbarian brethren saw them as heralds descended to share the light of the gods.

From the balcony of her columned, marble palace she would watch them play the day away, imbibing and sexing, pampered mortals lusting on life, ever heady from the drip marking their jugulars as tap for their caretakers. They lived separate but equal. Human houses above ground, vampire caverns below. Only when nourishing in peace at the palace or defending through war at the coast did the two halves meet.

She naturally detested him when, not four decades in, he confessed longing to abandon it. He passed off excuses as flattery. Her philosophies had opened his eyes to the samsara propelling his lives and to the moksha that would free him of it. Yet he callously dismissed the dharma that bound the two, the natural law on which she based their kingdom, that necessarily would lead to ecstasy as their righteous wheel rolled across all in its path. *Desperate, impatient, sad, sad fool!*

She recalls their last day in Thera. It began splendidly. Sowen woke her by running his cool, wet hands along her back. She turned over to let him sprinkle her bare chest with milk from a nearby jug, and pinned him to her as he licked it up. Then he massaged her, a favor she returned with greater vigor.

They spent the afternoon at the theater watching a human play about a Sumerian goat herder who interprets his dream of a flame dwindling in the void to mean that the king will be slain in battle unless the goat herder comes to his rescue. Mission accomplished, the goat herder becomes the king's counsel by applying his penchant for astral analysis to royal affairs. The goat herder marries the princess and his heir becomes king. The boy lacks the gift and is slain in first battle. His sister, however, gains second sight upon their father's deathbed and rules wisely for the rest of her days. Valiant performances sprung from a derivative muse, the immortals agreed.

They spent the evening tidying affairs, such as accepting that there would be no telling how the climate might change without Sowen to stabilize it. He suggested either spreading out to neighboring territory with fertile land or to cull the standing population by a third in case crops failed. She swallowed a curse and chose the former.

Then they ceased procrastinating and prepared for his departure. At nightfall all humans and vampires were ordered to encircle the palace and sit in deepest meditation on their love for the crown. Meanwhile, in the middle of the hanging gardens atop the palace, Sowen and Shakti focused on their connection to the Great All. First the long nothingness. Then serenity. Then aspiration. Then calculation. Then reflection. So many emotions, ever evolving, changing, regressing with every laugh and cry and interaction. At each moment, hoping to feel honestly and better than those other wayward souls, despite knowing only oneself in the moment of perception. So many values adopted and adapted to fit social convention and self defense, mere tools for meaning begetting excuses for action. So many beliefs, be they language or math, history or science, justified by experience and reason, yet as amorphous as anything else under the sway of time and enlightenment. So many people befriended, conquered, killed, loved, left, and lied. All strangers. Even the Children. Even each other. Even the self, made of what murky swirl, encased in some body on a middle plane ... body made of what, on a plane existing for what? Then light banged and they were one with the beyond, until doubt ripped them back.

She came to while cracks spread through marble pillars shaking violently above a fitful Earth, which roared as though indignant at the lovers' failed attempt to exceed their station. Quakes lasted through the night and deep into the next one. It was enough time for the vampires to turn every man, woman, and child. Shakti deemed this more benevolent than leaving them to their own fates. Sowen huddled beside the smoothed granite rock on which he had loved to sit, useless in the wake of his geomagic tantrum, rendered slobbering with a blank gaze and blood pouring from his ears.

Thera was all but abandoned by the time the volcano erupted. Ash and lava rained, and the mouth of the Earth opened to swallow a good chunk of island into gushing sea, destroying their achievement in far less time than it took to build, which was not that much time in its own right. And though it gradually brought climatic ruin to their Minoan and Egyptian neighbors, their noble misadventure would go down mainly as a geological oddity that provoked the great philosopher's myth of the lost land.

Shakti left her comatose lover in the heap of the palace. He promptly died one of his countless deaths. She vowed never again to tolerate his presence. She applauds herself for holding this grudge for millennia, forgives herself for recanting twice. That vile dusk she took her Children east, ending centurieslong exile. Once home she made another vow. Never again to share the self inflicted misery of lessers. This she would break repeatedly, to her consistent regret, albeit for only one other, her truest unrequited love.

• • •

"Where are you now?" Magahara asks.

"Atlantis," Shakti says.

"Wish I could have seen it," he says, taking her hand. They drift up from the garden atop the miles high ziggurat that towers over Jerusalem.

"Wish it could have lasted," she replies. "Would have been better for everyone."

"Look," he says, pointing to the orange and purple horizon while they float above the city. "It's shaping to be a great night for an anniversary."

"For us. The birthday boy doesn't look so good."

"Manginess aside, he looks healthy enough for someone turning 4,592 years old ... That reminds me, did I miss your 5,000th?"

"Only by eleven years, thank you," Shakti says. They pass over the browning trees on Mount Scopus. "You're forgiven. You probably were too busy defecating in a cardboard box. Wouldn't be surprised if Sowen tried that tomorrow. Two years in and he's already falling apart."

"He's not that far gone?" Magahara asks. "His mind's still sharp, still plotting. What, do you think he can't be trusted?"

"How you've come around, my love. How you've come around." Shakti kisses him hard, drawing blood from his lip as they glide through the fast blackening sky. "I always feared he was too weak for immortality. I don't know whether to pity or hate him. Either way, I still love him."

"I can't hate anyone who tries to be that honest with himself," Magahara says. "If I cared less, I might even admire him. But I don't buy his excuses about drawing things out. Do you?"

"It's irrelevant," she says. "He does. Are we protecting each other by going so slowly? Protecting humanity by making them want us? I humor him. For now."

"Do you really believe he can be God?"

"Of course not," she says.

"Love has no logic, does it?" Magahara asks, squeezing her hips into his as they descend against the Western Wall.

"You're one to ask!" she says while patting his cheek. "Both of you would sleep much better if you stopped trying to be so earnest. I know I did ... But that is when you two fell in love with each other. Without me ..."

They stroll about the Temple Mount as the moon ascends, enjoying the Dome of the Rock and the Al-Aqsa Mosque and other shrines for which they have never prayed, he in his white tank top and black denim jeans, she in her white satin negligee.

"This place has always been good to the Children," she says after a while. "Centuries of violence make for easy pickings. Nobody misses a zealot here or there. I've a better appreciation for its hold on the rabble, having finally made it my own."

"Ironic that we've outraged the faithful more than the capitalists," Magahara says. "They call us demons. Defilers of the Holy Land. For once Jews, Christians, and Muslims agree. We've sparked a new religious revival."

"Your ancestors would be proud."

"Warriors for God tend to be. Regardless of the gods for whom they war. And now our new legion will war for one set on becoming God. It fits."

"Quite a fate, your bloodline," Shakti says.

"Not that bad, as fates go."

"Our lives would be quite different had you felt that way when I found you."

"I shouldn't have fought making peace with it. Every generation a man born to roam the world, compelled to spread his seed in foreign lands, fight for the divine and the throne of his new home, pass memories to his heir in dreams, and live in ignorance of why any of it should be. Can't imagine what I preferred."

"A simpler world?" Shakti asks.

"If so you might have warned me that impregnating a vampire with twins was not the way to go about it. Nor was letting our children run away, then doing so myself. No wonder our descendants have hated us."

"Remember our babies!" she shouts. "How stunned we were to learn they weren't vampires! And never would be, despite all our bitings ... I should have killed them ... Don't fret about leaving. You're a lover, not a father. Nobody's perfect. You're here now. That's enough."

They kiss again. This time Magahara savors her blood.

• • •

Vampire sentries in black visored helmets and black armored jumpsuits drag twenty one bruised and disheveled teens into a showroom on a lower level of the palace. Weaponry of bygone cultures adorn one wall. Ancient looking carpet bears script of no language the children have ever seen. Against the opposite wall, alabaster busts of historical icons sit on pillars lining the carpet. And a heavily beveled chandelier hangs in the center of the room above two oak thrones, which have their backs to a far off balcony.

The sentries force Ahmad and his captured peers to genuflect before the seated lords of the manor. One lord has been leaning forward in an emerald kimono, hood up. The other has been slumping back in a ratty gray bathrobe. Their mistress stays attending her flock from the balcony.

So far so good, Ahmad thinks. All they had to do for a royal audience was toss a few pipe bombs in accelerated aging vats during a school tour of the capital's largest cloning factory. The young man fancies that The Way would be proud of them for clogging the blood supply on the nation's second anniversary. *Now to kill these three demons without weapons or reinforcements. Inshallah, next time spend more time on that detail and a little less playing "Meta Force: New York Assault."*

For once, and what he expects is the final time, the 18 year old takes solace in his contact lenses and ear mics. Although they have since been deactivated, they got to serve the cause. No matter what happens the world knows that even paradise has problems.

Magahara claps and Sowen conjures a glass jug filled with blood, which floats in the thin air from whence it came. The hooded immortal claps again and the sentries push the teens forward until they halt within arm's reach of the thrones.

The sentries push them back down to their knees. Ahmad hears Shakti lead the masses in a song in a demon tongue. That or Sanskrit. He cannot be sure, too terrified of his imminent damnation. *They sound so happy*, he thinks. Arabs, Jews, Africans, and Indians, swaying to music of communal love. *Maybe it won't be that bad. Until the bombs drop.*

Then Magahara clutches one of the teens by the neck and sinks his fangs into her. Ahmad watches his Jew girlfriend gasp and moan while curling fetal on the floor. She volunteered to join his cause minutes after he had shared it with her, despite initially threatening to turn him in. Now she chants his name like some aegis as her eyes close and she reels into sporadic shivers.

Several of his peers begin to cry at this. Others lick their lips in anticipation. Still others pray to various outlawed deities. Magahara drinks them one by one, leaving Ahmad untouched, and waits for the rapid transformations to take hold.

The gang of newly minted vampires stand in unison, all smiles, and take turns kissing their sire's hand. He gives them each a deep gulp from Sowen's floating jug. They hurry out onto the balcony where their Mother hugs them and guides their hands as they step off the ledge and levitate through the night and down to their brethren. Ahmad still kneels, inches from the thrones, utterly bewildered as Magahara rises and joins Shakti on the balcony. The woman in the golden sari with the red sash about her torso strokes the hooded vampire down his spine. Magahara closes the huge double doors behind him. Sowen gestures for the sentries to leave them.

"Get up," he tells the boy while rising himself. Sowen's red mane ends in a mullet near the center of his back. Dried bits of food lay trapped in his beard like cats stuck in a tree. His gray bathrobe flaps opens in places it should not. "What were you hoping to accomplish?"

"Don't know," Ahmad says as he stands. "Kill all of you. Free our people. Avoid world war."

"How did you plan, despite the contacts and ear mics?"

"Bacchus. I turn into a telepath when I'm high."

"Ah. That makes you the mouse and me the cat. Where's your bell?"

"Huh?"

"A tale I wrote long ago. You could learn from it. So could an acquaintance of mine, come to think."

"We did prove that young people are unhappy here."

"Young people are unhappy everywhere. All you proved is that children can't be trusted. The vats are already fixed, the blood supply already purified."

"What happened to you?" Ahmad asks to mask his deflation. "You always looked so clean online."

"Took a bath this morning. The lady insists."

"Rumor is you can do anything. Why not get a haircut and a suit?"

"Because I don't care about appearances anymore."

"I saw an interview where you said appearance is everything. But you've also said you're an honest man."

At this Sowen halts. He studies one of the busts for upwards of a minute. While doing so his face gradually contorts into sheer torture. He grinds his fingers into his cheeks, shakes his head. For a moment Ahmad suspects the man will cry. Then he does.

"I am! I try to be! To myself, I mean!" the immortal shrieks through snot and tears. "Is that not most important ...? I've so rarely valued what others do, as they do. Power and wealth have never mattered to me. All I care about are hearts and the wild. Never been able to refuse those. The hearts because I've laughed at morals and mores since my first life, despite their pull on me. The wild because until this life, I doubted that it wanted me. But I am your son! Your son! You will not abandon me!"

Sowen shouts this with arms outstretched, fingers clutching the air, while he fixes on the iridescence of the chandelier. Its light catches in his green eyes, which sparkle through his tears.

"So, as I wait, I've given the world what it wants of me. Again and again. Whether savior or scientist, actor or ascetic, conqueror or companion, it's all been for show. And honestly, I don't have much faith in a species that gets hypnotized by any fool who musters the courage to put on a show. Do you understand, boy?" Sowen asks, grabbing Ahmad by the shoulders. "Tell me you understand!"

"I think so," Ahmad lies, stepping away so the man loosens his grip. "But why cry? Isn't it your birthday? Everybody here loves you."

"Why. The great question," Sowen says. "Because words and numbers ... hearts and minds ... you and I ... only glimpse part of the truth. Because value is as sand through my fingers. Because I take more than I give. Because I feel more than I know. Because my lot is no more tragic than that of an ant ... That's true, but it's crap ... If only she didn't need them. Why aren't I enough? Because she doesn't trust me? Because I already failed her? But I was ready, my love. I was ..."

"You sound scared," Ahmad says, immediately regretting it. "I mean you sound conflicted."

"Don't backpedal. You were right the first time. Fear of failure. It's already happened once. Couldn't stand it again. And yet I can't stand it here. But I keep thinking about something Magahara said. My friend. My good friend. He said, 'Take it from someone who's spent his entire life running from himself. Wherever you go, there you are. And there's nowhere to run when you're everything.' Wonderful fool! So trite and still I can't deny it. Who the hell am I? I've let so much of me die in order to live."

"No reset button," Ahmad mumbles.

"What?" Sowen asks.

"This videogame we were playing today. We had to keep starting over. It was hard. Fun, but damn hard. Sometimes I wish life were like that. A game. Then we could hit reset and try again. A perfect world."

"Reset? Perfect? What's a perfect world?" Sowen asks. "One devoid of pain? Of war and crime? Poverty and illness? Nobody really wants that. Not even these poor souls here. People do want the opposite of those things. But in order to know they have them, they have to know somebody lacks them. Nearly every advance we've achieved comes from the desire for more at the expense of others, war being the greatest of motivators. Our world is built on inequity. So do I want a perfect world? No. I want this world and all the others just as they are. That's my perfect. When there's nothing else ... but I'm so scared."

"Sir, I turned 18 last week. I don't know what to tell you," Ahmad says. "... am I becoming a demon or not?"

"Oh right," Sowen says as though he had just gone on a trifling tangent. "I take it you'd rather stay human?"

"Um ... yeah."

"So be it. Go home, boy. And thank you."

"For what?" Ahmad asks.

"For listening. Consider this your reset."

Sowen bats his wrist and the teen vanishes, leaving him alone in the showroom filled with possessions of his past lives.

That axe there came in handy during the first Defenestration of Prague. And that bust there got him in good with Michelangelo. So many abandoned pursuits, so many wasted chances. And so he spends the rest of the night basking in luxuries his powers afford. Walking through the sun. Riding blue whales in the Antarctic deep. Wrestling tigers in the Sumatran jungle. Riding a hoverboard with young punks in Seattle. Eating empanadas bought off a street cart in Caracas.

He returns to the showroom hours later in a pristine black suit and his red hairs trimmed. He makes his way through the palace he erected, greeting vampires and young humans who stroll about and shower him with birthday cheers. Blood and Bacchus flow heady. All manner of musicians and singers carry bodies to swaying and grinding in ecstasy. Outside on the lamplit streets of Jerusalem, the king in no need of a nation finds the Mother of the Night and her Knight Wraith kissing newborns carried by vampire parents. Sowen joins in the fun. It is his party, after all, and the party ends only when he says so.

22

From visions to vows

A tan, spindly arm with a durium pinky ring thrusts the weak kneed groom out of the dressing room so forcefully that William must catch him from stumbling into the priest. Stefan walks with these men in a tuxedo he did not choose until he stands at the altar between priest and people. The best man tosses Stefan a reassuring wink. This alone calms him enough to appreciate his bride's approach.

A little Navajo girl in a pink dress skips down the aisle dutifully dropping rose petals, oblivious to the shameless hobnobbing in the mahogany pews. Stars of stage and screen whisper pitches for brighter contracts to corporate barons, who in turn attempt bigger versions of the same with heads of state, who in turn seek to impress far away constituents with their humility in the presence of a conquered people. The cathedral sings of avarice in tune with the bellows of the pipe organ as groomsmen in elegant tuxes traverse the aisle with bridesmaids in teal monstrosities. Oke and William escort Nia's two obese sisters, P.R. her lithe and underage niece. Hush falls only when father and daughter appear at the entrance.

Nia makes it to the altar in an off white gown of her choosing that manages to flatter her pregnant, pear shape. She takes her place beside Stefan. Timothy Begaye's upper lip twitches as he takes a seat in the first row with the rest of his people. The father of the bride glances across to the opposing pew, at what passes for Stefan's people. A purple and silvery robot that resembles a dominatrix. A gaunt and ashen thief in a little black dress fit for a dancehall. The chief executive of the most monopolistic firm in history. The leader of the race whose ancestors did away with the ancestors of Begaye's race. Glowing on the wall beyond them, stained glass images of saints who "saved" heathens like his people. Begaye bites his lip to keep it from twisting into a snarl.

And as the priest begins, Stefan recalls the paternal ambush that led him from visions to vows.

• • •

"Let me see if I get this," Begaye says, cross legged on the dirt floor of the hogan. "First you steal my oldest girl. Then you knock her up, for over two goddamn years and counting, with your freak meta seed. Then you say our way isn't good enough for you? Some nerve, white boy."

"Vamos de nuevo. With respect, sir, that's not how it is," Stefan says, also cross legged. "And I'm not white."

Smoke swirls about the mud and log dome, its dwellers fueled by liquor and peyote. Seven chanting Navajo elders encircle the pair. Desert winds whip at the buffalo skin flap of a door, every so often threatening to snuff the flame between Stefan and Begaye. Like the elders, these men came shirtless and in jeans. The people's champion wishes his best friend had insisted on keeping him company. Yet he appreciates how William always did have a way of avoiding trouble. How he probably would have settled for a traditional Navajo wedding. And would have rejected Karen's push to go for the broadcast spectacle. And how he also probably would have delivered a better comeback.

What more does the old man want?

They had gone through with the traditional Navajo service. James had acted on Stefan's behalf in place of a parent, offering a respectable pile of crown jewels as dowry. The cast had removed contacts and ear mics to supplicate themselves in the Arizona desert under this earthen mound. They had acted as his family and followed Begaye's instructions, venturing into the hogan in the middle of the night, sitting in the proper positions, watching as Stefan and Nia allowed some withered medicine man to sprinkle them with water and corn pollen. Finally, at Begaye's command, all others save William had taken off so the chief and his cronies could grill the son-in-law.

"You love my daughter?"

"Yes."

"Why?"

"She has a beautiful spirit."

"You can't lie worth a damn."

"So you know I'm telling the truth."

"All I know is she seems happy," Begaye says with sagging eyes. "... just be there for my grandchild. Or your life isn't worth the dirt we're sitting on."

"Of course," Stefan says, squirming at phantasms of his bloodline he imagines in the fire's smoke.

"Let's get on with it then," Begaye says. One elder passes him a bottle of whiskey, another passes him several peyote buttons, and another passes him a dagger. "They say you can't be hurt. That right?"

"Most of the time."

"Bull. You can if you want to. And now you want to. Tell your pal outside to get in here."

Stefan's eyebrows arch warily as he shouts to William. The black man in dress shirt and slacks coughs thick smoke while pushing through the flapping buffalo skin. He squats next to the groom.

"These powers come from in here," Begaye says, waving his hand from his face to his chest. "Like all things within they can come and go. You just need a little help. Doctor Powers?"

"Remember the dream thief?" William asks.

"The one who trapped me in a weeklong nightmare?" Stefan asks. "I hate pigeons to this day because of him. Sure. It was the only time I've ever felt a telepath."

"This'll be the second. It took some practice, and a lot of time in The Hole, but I've figured out how to do it. But first you need to go to sleep."

"Not tired. Took a nap the other day."

"Great. Here's another one."

Blood gushes from William's nostrils and a telekinetic explosion capable of obliterating a city goes off behind Stefan's forehead, knocking him out cold. He finds himself in his old flat above the Ataraxia Bar & Grille, blue teddy bear wallpaper staring him in the face. Chatter of merry inebriation wafts through the floorboards. He steps toward the staircase when his bathroom door opens. Nia exits wearing a white robe courtesy of Haine Hotel while cradling a crying lump swathed in a matching towel. She hands the lump to Stefan and all goes black.

He wakes in the hogan bleeding from his ears and forearms. He sees Begaye and William standing over him, orange flame casting restive shadows across their faces. He tastes whiskey and something tart in his numbed mouth, which refuses to obey his commands to ask what the hell is going on. As William hunches down and drags him out of the hogan by his alligator boots, Stefan suspects he would have welcomed Begaye's eternal enmity rather than submit to the psychedelic indignities he feels mounting at every instant.

Little under an hour later, as Stefan executes evasive acrobatics in pitched battle with hallucinations, William echoes his friend's lamentation. The full December moon casts the pair as silhouettes amid red rock and starry navy sky. Stefan resembles a deranged insect more than a man the way he leaps through air from mountain to sacred mountain, swinging his father's sword at imaginary foes. William, a fly on the wall of his mind, knows which ones Stefan faces. Their bounties from before "Meta Force," when it was just the two of them on missions for Haine. Funhouse versions of their supervisors, especially Karen Drench and Glenda Rodan. And quite a few garish deities drawn from mythologies revealed through dreams of Stefan's ancestors. This might have alarmed William had Stefan not confided the truth of his bloodline years before the U.N. siege. Yet the mentalist finds it strangely calming to finally part the curtain and see very much what he had expected. That is, until Stefan beholds the spectre of a woman. He genuflects earnestly before her, holding Simmer by its black hilt with both hands, balancing the blade on its tip in the dust, while the woman caresses light brown locks at the crown of his head. She changes constantly, depending on the light. At early angles she is Nia. At later ones Faye, at others Becca. Ever so briefly she is Karen and Rodan and even Gloria Finley. But mostly she is Ana. Yet it is not until Ana kisses Stefan's eyes that William understands.

"I'm so weak," Stefan says as the spectre vanishes and he flops on his back.

"Because you miss her?" William asks, squatting beside him in the dirt.

"Yeah. No. Because I can't hate her. How can I hate the one I love?"

"How long had you been having the affair?"

"Since before I met you."

"Lord. Did Sam know?"

"I think so, eventually. But she made it ... not feel like betrayal. I wanted to believe that. So I did."

"What about the others? Killing time?"

"She encouraged it. Guess I didn't trust her. So I protected myself with what came my way. Faye. Becca. Sorry about that, man. It was before you got together."

"Don't sweat it ... What about Nia?"

"What about her? She's all I've got."

"She deserves more than that," William says. He stands up for no reason he can fathom. "More than to be your consolation."

"What do you care?" Stefan asks, wobbling to his feet with Simmer in hand. "Your machine break down one too many times?"

At that William clenches his fist, shaking it violently before his chest as he levitates Stefan high into the air and halts him several hundred feet up. While telekinetically twisting his drugged friend's limbs in pretzel fashion, he takes the opportunity to telepathically berate Stefan about everything from his affected Spanish ejaculations to his superfluous use of that damn sword. *Who names a sword, anyway?* Then William rams him down into the desert with the force of a rocket, blowing plumes of dust to the heavens. He repeats the process a dozen more times while Stefan mumbles about honoring his father. And just as he plans to let go, the mentalist catches a psychic glimpse of long plotting Hikikomori.

"You knew?" William asks aloud to the man in the body shaped crater. "You knew?!"

"He's my bro. Like I said, I'm weak. Not stupid."

"No. You're pathetic," William says.

He delivers another telekinetic explosion to his friend's brain and severs their mental link. Standing there over Stefan's prone, slumbering body for what feels like an agonizing eternity, William rejects coherent thought, simultaneously irate and sympathetic. Until he feels a sudden fire at his chin and consciousness blinks away.

Stefan almost feels guilty for resorting to hyper speed. But as he watches William sextuple somersault into a boulder half a mile away, he realizes this is the best possible conclusion to his bachelorhood. After all, the drugs only now climax. He only now notices that the dried blood on each forearm covers matching tattoos of nine outward facing arrows encircling a sun. And he only now sees Nia gargantuan and resplendent before a mammoth moon that touches the distant horizon. This delirium is for him alone, he decides as he shambles toward his fated mate.

She towers above him, her raven locks dancing like many layered veils, her eyes boring into his soul like unrelenting beams, her arms cradling their unborn child like a treasure that he does not yet deserve. Not so long as he turns his back on his duty. Not so long as he has it in him to betray those he loves. Not so long as he hides behind a façade of filial piety that he is not ready to command in earnest. But no more, now that he accepts what he has spent a lifetime resisting. And when his living temple acknowledges this by handing him their nascent future, he knows there is no retreat.

• • •

William gives him an invisible nudge and Stefan blurts out the first of his vows, praying that this actually is the time for them. The priest had been a distant buzzing until that moment and somehow Nia's moving lips had not seemed any formidable cue. But he could never ignore the counsel of his best man. And as he says "I do," Stefan brims with gratitude that on their dawn walk from the desert William's only reference to their falling out was that sucker punches do not count. Then bride and groom slip on their gold bands and kiss to thunderous applause.

The party begets the inevitable mix of inebriated toasting, roasting, and dancing. During his umpteenth waltz with the sea of fungible beauties that once would have been his willing prey, Stefan tallies an armed meta guard for every four guests. He wonders whether the ratings surge Karen demands P.R. produce could ever justify the expense of such security. Then he remembers what they compete against and resolves to bask in the luxury their culture affords, even as they do so amid a culture their luxury affronts. *At least the old man can't knock the free buzz*, Stefan snickers. *Silver Sky's packed, courtesy of his sellout son-in-law.*

At Stefan's insistence the couple spend the honeymoon on the reservation, going so far as staying in Nia's old bedroom with the pink teddy bear wallpaper. Seeing it as only proper, he takes her that night. It is their second time together since she began to show, and, he senses, their last until she gives birth. For as he studies the tattoos on his forearms and ponders their portent, he cannot deny that he shares but one true bond with this woman. After climax, as though on some ominous schedule, she thanks him for their time together and forewarns that its end nears.

23

The crucial blow

"I still can't believe he thinks he can become God," James says midway through their flight across the Atlantic.

"Sam isn't happy unless he's in charge," Stefan says from one of the plush leather sofas lining the jet cabin. "Someone ought to tell him the job's already taken."

"If so the big boss has a lot to answer for," William says from an adjacent sofa. "I haven't gotten any divine memos lately."

"God's real. We're all part of God," Nia says. "Not that I have any special insight. It only makes sense."

"Who was it that said God's an imaginary friend for idiots and lunatics?" Phase asks. "Or did I misquote that?"

"What if God's the master programmer?" Oke asks. "We'd all be His avatars. Now that's a hot game, Becca!"

"Insufficient data," Zenith says.

"Who gives a fig?" Rodan asks. "God's not paying my taxes and God's not fighting this war."

"God, like me, is easily bored by people who don't know what they're talking about," James says.

"Tell us how you really feel," Stefan says.

"Honestly I feel sick," James replies. "I'm at a loss over the economy. If that doesn't improve fast poor nations will switch sides. That fear is causing Continental Unions to fall apart from infighting. At this point breaking up bloated companies will only make people more desperate. Sales of personal boats and planes are already through the roof. Hazard a guess where they're traveling? Aside from all these terrorists Nia's helping us nail, your wedding's the only other good news for the free world."

"Free world. Isn't that an oxymoron?" Stefan asks.

"Big word. Have you been reading?" William asks.

"Look everyone! The living pun cracked a joke! Seriously, my wonderful father-in-law made the point last night. That vampires are happy mental slaves but we're unhappy material ones. It might explain why fewer and fewer people are buying what we're fighting for."

"I don't have faith in God, but I do have faith in people," James counters. "There must be a way to dissuade them from choosing the easy way out. So ingenuity and compromise make dirty business. Boo hoo. Nine times out of ten self sufficiency trumps short range security. Don't these cowards care what happens when Ana has a bad day? Faced with that alternative, good old fashioned freedom is worth every drop of hardship that comes with it."

"This from the man born in the palace," Stefan says. "I'd drop that last line from your speeches unless you want to get dropped like Finley."

"And I'm the living pun?" William asks.

"Oh, by the way, Will, could you drop a subconscious command to P.R. to cut that bit about Nia?" James asks via the Net. "Then mindwipe him about it, to be safe? Have to keep our secret weapon secret."

"For freedom, right?" William asks online.

"Don't start."

"Okay. I've done it before ... and I just did again."

Then Sowen blinks into the seat opposite James. Their enemy smells of honeysuckle. His dyed red hairs end before his neck. His beard shines trim and spritzed. His green eyes sparkle. And his black tuxedo puts James' navy blue suit to shame.

"Nice jet," he says. "Tell me, did Corny pick up the tab for the wedding? Or did you, Your Highness? Only ask because I would have. Had I gotten an invitation."

Stefan lunges to the floor for Simmer. His durium katana barely slides in its wooden scabbard before an unseen force halts it. The star flaked black casing shakes in his grasp. The others find themselves similarly bound.

"Please, Will. Give it a rest," Sowen asks. "I'm too dense to be influenced. My wife says so all the time."

"Haine! Coward!" Stefan shouts, wondering how his own wife could miss this vision. "Let me go so I can gut you!"

"Tempting. I'll pass."

"This is a violation of treaty," Rodan says, her voice creaking and her eyes shaking in their sockets. "It constitutes a first strike. Europe and her allies are within their rights to retaliate."

"Careful, General. That kind of talk could lead to hostilities. I didn't come here to be hostile."

"Why did you come here?" James asks in a paltry excuse for a civil tone. He snaps his head so violently blond locks fall over an eye, which his pinned arms cannot right. This infuriates him as much as Sowen's presence. "Speak!"

"To negotiate. I've deactivated all recording devices, so we can chat freely ... We're reaching an impasse. You can't let any nations defect without declaring war against us and we won't refuse the pleas of the downtrodden. But neither side is quite ready to push in the chips. Not that there's a chance we might lose. We prefer to have you see the light, of the night, as it were. Moreover, we should avoid casualties. Preserve what's precious."

"You're an opportunistic, lying, mass murderer who supports terrorism," James says, casting aside his mask. "Of course I can't prove any of that. I don't trust you. I don't respect you. Make your offer and be done with it."

"I appreciate your candor and pragmatism. They are hallmarks of a good leader. Might want to work on your tact though." Then Sowen turns to Stefan and the rest of his former employees. "Before I get started, let me say that you all continue to make me extremely proud."

"I'd spit on you if it weren't for this force field," Stefan says.

"Lucky me. To business then. I'll be reinstated as president of the World Monetary Fund. In return I'll institute a Red Nation currency and fees for vampire labor. I'll also aid poor human nations by encouraging moderate exchange rates and loans with the Red Nation. Because I'm generous I'll even offer discounts on raw materials for firms, such as Haine International, which will be required to break up emergent monopolies if they continue doing business with the Red Nation. Finally, there will be a significant drop in terrorism.

"However, hypothetically, were I denied, such acts could hit catastrophic levels. I'd imagine Hikikomori, who as you know has come to support our cause, would activate more terror cells. We continue to condemn his methods. Alas I have no control over him. Nor do I control my wife, who either could use her Children to infiltrate these cells and stop imminent attacks, or go the other way. If denied, vampires might start yearning for travel. Or all their labor could be rerouted to South America, Russia, and Indonesia. Or leaks might emerge regarding your corrupt but vital allies, such as Hugo Mesa and our friend Cornelio."

"As if reinstatement is even up to me," James says. "You claim you want to avoid war. This all but assures it."

"Only if you bow to your supporters. Work the Council, the W.M.F. board. Have faith. Your gambit with the dragon paid off. Tacker's been taking charge left and right on Net tracking and imports since Congress restored executive supremacy. She'll get America to support you. And that dragon has shaken Deng to the core. Beijing will follow the West. Think logically. When have I ever sought to incite misery? The Red Nation clearly has benefited more lives, regardless of borders, than it's ruined. The same will hold for my economic policies. Don't be an idealist. It invites hypoc–"

Simmer interrupts Sowen as Stefan finally manages to unsheathe his blade and slice it through his enemy's cheek, drawing blood and awe.

"How ... what the ... how'd you do that?" Sowen gurgles. He bats his wrist, telekinetically flinging Stefan down the length of the cabin. "Pardon me, Your Highness. General. Miss Reyes," he sputters as he disappears Stefan and the rest of the crew. "Consider my terms. I've got a reunion to wrap up." Then he too vanishes from the jet.

They blink onto the beach of a crescent shaped island. Clear waves lap white sand and verdant patches host large, porous rock. Grass leads into dense forest of fern and vine. A black mountain juts up from miles deep. Tracks in the sand indicate the kingfishers flitting along the shore are far from the only fauna.

"Now that we've got some leg room, maybe–"

Their former employer had been speaking when the people's champion charged at full speed, his silvery blade arched for a clean cut to the skull. Sowen falls silent when Stefan splats into an invisible wall scant feet from his target. Stefan ricochets along sand and into water. He immediately races back on land, only to be greeted by dozens of hands and fists of sand. They rise from the ground, morphing into durium as they grope and punch with lightning speed, snaring Stefan's legs in their impossibly strong grasps, clocking his groin and gut, re-forming as he breaks them, so thoroughly disorienting him that Sowen becomes an afterthought.

"Now that that's out of the way, I was hoping–"

This time Zenith cuts him off, first with finger lasers then with wrist rockets. The ten beams reflect off Sowen's force field and through Phase's intangible torso. The two missiles swerve round into William's own protective aura and double him over with explosive shots to the gut. Sowen repays the living robot by blowing her a kiss of fire and lightning that begins as a spark at his lips and grows to an orange and cyan ball that clings to her metallic frame like a wild animal, even as she flies for the clouds to shake it.

"Well then?" Sowen asks the boy.

Oke opts for mimicking his mother's powers. He tries to rush unseen through Sowen's unseen force field, only to be frozen in place at his third step. Sowen renders the boy visible and tangible, levitates him several yards up, then forcibly morphs Oke into everything he has ever seen the boy morph into—from dresser to dragon to pigeon to puddle of mud—until seconds later, Oke lay spent and human from the physiological overload.

"Damn it if that wasn't pointless," Sowen says to Phase. He presses a hand to his bleeding and severed cheek, shakes his head ruefully. "My own fault. What else should I expect?"

He turns from her and walks for the forest as Stefan, William, and Oke sink underground, pulled into the island by its sandy hands.

• • •

The island disgorges William from rock far beneath the waves of a volcanic lake in the mountain. He feels a hint of heat through his aura and reminds himself that liquid fire raging nanometers from his skin cannot penetrate, that he can hold his breath long enough to free himself. Despite his ribs, cracked yet again. He speeds through churning lava and flies up high to a dry wall of rock, from whence he looks down into a humungous, boiling, growling face made of the orange lake, until the face morphs into a dripping, molten paw that claws up at him. Wasting no time with a tireless foe, he drills through mountain wall and into fresh air as lava spurts out in his wake.

The island spits Oke from sand into the sea, which promptly carries him off via currents that feed a whirlpool spinning untold leagues down to the abyss. He awakens to murky vision and bonecrushing water pressure. The flailing boy pays little heed to what he hopes are phantasms, faces made of water, howling at him in contemptuous mockery. He tries swimming until his bones snap like twigs and his lungs collapse and his heart bursts and he sinks farther. Instead of dying he morphs into a submarine, which does a better job of defying the whirlpool currents, but not such that it resists buckling into a metal pretzel. Left with no other option, he absorbs the water to join the maelstrom itself, battling the sea outside to maintain cohesion and sanity in search of the surface of the vortex. At last his waves kiss air, allowing him to reclaim his natural form for the briefest of instants, until he sprouts durium wings and flaps ashore.

The island ejects Stefan from the mud of the forest. No sooner does he stand than do deer and boar flee from the thick to stampede by him and away from the army of trees marching forward. Thick branches and roots for arms and legs nimbly move the score of bark covered giants. He stares up at sadistic faces of mashed leaves as the trees surround him. And when they crane down to swat at him with preposterous strength, Stefan chastises himself for being such easy prey. It takes little effort to pull Simmer off his hip and chop down the twenty trunks. It takes considerably more effort to slice twice as many hopping, leafy shafts into hundreds of logs as they bash him in the face. It requires full hyper speed to shred those furiously flying logs into thousands of biting chips. And it would have been impossible to calm that swarm had a stray stream of lava not fallen from the heavens to light a few chips on fire and rob them of life. That spurs Stefan to snatch the others from air and add them to grounded flame, at last rendering them naught but a smoky nuisance.

・・・

"Nice view," Phase says after blinking near Sowen. They stand together at the beach on the other side of the island. He watches the sun prepare to set against an amber violet horizon, palm pressed to his bloody and sliced cheek.

"That's why I picked this place," he says. "Don't come any closer."

"Or what? I'm better at this than the kid. You can't touch me. Unless you're a telepath, too?"

"Got me there. No mind control to speak of. But I do have quite the all purpose force field."

"Can we talk?"

"We seem to be," Sowen says.

"Right ... I'm dying. MV."

"Are you joking?"

"My sense of humor's not sick. I am."

"Goddamn. That's awful. I'm so sorry ... Strange how condolences always sound trite."

"That's why I keep it to myself," Phase says, coming closer. "You're only the second person I've told."

"I'd be honored, if it weren't a delaying tactic."

"You really can't read my mind, huh?"

"Wouldn't if I could. It's an invasion of privacy, you know. Serious laws against that kind of thing."

"You always were a riot. Had to get it off my chest. To a fr–to someone who'd understand."

"And you figure that's me because I got your pardon?"

"No. Because of Oke," Phase says. "He'd run off a lot after we'd pull jobs. He was just starting to get good with the games, make a name for himself. He wanted to quit stealing. I knew we should have, too, but it was habit by then. He'd go to the beach a lot. Stand at the shore, skip rocks. All he wanted was for me to find him. To remind him that I would never push him away, no matter what."

"Touching. That might have meant something before things got so messy," Sowen says. "I can't apologize and go to my room. Armageddon has a way of irking people. There'll be no hugs to make everything alright."

"No. Would you like one?"

"A hug? I'm about to be God. You think I need a hug?"

"You keep my secret, I'll keep yours."

"Deal."

They embrace warm and long, her green speedsuit nestling into his tux, thief and conqueror at peace with the absurdity of the moment. Until Zenith hurtles down upon them, the orange and cyan ball of fire and lightning still about her as she rams Sowen into the sand. Phase steps back intangibly, cursing the robot's intrusion. Her charred, metallic teammate stands up free of the energy ball and moves aside for Stefan. He dashes from the woods and plunges Simmer deep into Sowen's gut. Oke and William land while Stefan slowly dislodges his father's sword, giving Sowen ample time to moan at each twist.

"Good work, Faye," Stefan says. "Thank God you got him to lower his shield."

"Don't worry," William assures. "I'm in his mind now. Got his powers on lock. He's too weak to fight back."

"Do it already!" Sowen says, pitifully, between moans. "Or would you rather watch me bleed out?"

"No such luck," Stefan says. "You're not getting a new life. Not ruining anybody else's. First you're powering down, then you're going into cold storage. Oke."

The boy morphs one arm into a long syringe emitting the telltale drip of Metapurge, the other arm into an ice covered cannon billowing cryogenic mist.

"Wait ... Stefan, I forgive you. You slept with my wife," Sowen says. He pauses to hack blood down his chin. "We were friends then. That was wrong of you but I forgive you. Please don't do this. It's not ... This wasn't—"

"You missed my wedding," Stefan says, eyes to the sand. "Do it, kid."

Oke moves in, at once relieved that he remembers how to become the substances unaided, proud to deliver the crucial blow, and oddly guilty about casting one he still considers family to such a fate. As it happens he never gets the chance. Instead he watches dumbfounded while his teammates break into convulsions and flop spastically in the sand.

Somehow he finds Zenith the most disturbing. Her purple and silvery shell, already tarnished by ash, now spits sparks from exposed wires at the base of her bald durium head. Her voice, which had become increasingly monotone with each bodily upgrade, now hits every octave and pitch as she speaks in tongues. Her motions resemble a cross between a cat in heat and a woman in labor. Until something pops inside her and she goes inert.

He sees his mother appear beside him. She lays a hand on his shoulder, kisses his cheek, and tells him to stay. She walks to Sowen, who fast oozes life. She kneels beside him and cradles his head in her lap. Yet the dying old man musters enough strength to shake a fist. This coincides with a gray rot that spreads over Stefan, stills his spasms, and gradually but surely renders him stone. Oke gawks at delirious William and petrified Stefan, who lay unable to offer him anything, especially the admonishments upon which he has come to rely. Then the boy rushes for his mother and mimics her powers and vanishes with her and he who was their enemy.

• • •

They reappear in the heart of the enemy, outside the great Jerusalem ziggurat. Vampires strolling the night stop in their tracks to regard them. Shakti teleports down with Magahara the next instant. The Mother of the Night welcomes Oke and Phase casually, as one would friends, before she realizes the extent of her husband's wounds. Then she curses at the dying fool and demands an explanation.

He mumbles of despair and time, madness and universes, love and betrayal.

The boy processes only pieces of this exchange as the ramifications of his actions begin to dawn on him. And for the first time he feels a swell of hate for his mother. For the woman who stole him from that orphanage. It fades when he remembers how sick she feels. How vampirism has become her only hope. How they likely switched to the winning side. How peace may be in reach thanks to the man they just saved. If only his wife would stop nagging and save him.

Yet she does not. She calls him an opportunistic, mass murdering liar. Shakti asks where his love was when his children were slaughtering hers. When she was left with nothing but the desire to sleep, to forget what his kind has to offer. She asks a great many other things of the eviscerated man that Oke fails to understand, until the hooded man in the emerald kimono pushes her aside and kneels to the ground.

Magahara sinks his fangs into Sowen's neck, drinking his ancient friend as he squeezes that limp frame. It takes long moments for the Knight Wraith to do for the first time what Shakti did so quickly to him. Finally Sowen revives, willpower intact, euphoric in this evolution.

He who has tasted death and rebirth uncounted times stands healthy and strong, at last awash in what his lovers have known for ages. He apologizes to his woman for the spectacle, confesses his cold feet, assures his dedication has redoubled. She sneers at her men and storms back toward the palace without a word. He shrugs before thanking his friend and vowing to repay the favor. As an afterthought this man reborn leads his other saviors, his now trembling allies, into their new home.

24

Unwarranted condemnations

The island is calm and dark when William stirs. No molten monsters or matter rearranging megalomaniacs. No conscious allies to speak of, either. First comes the pounding in his skull. Next, as he sits up, the thousand pricks at his ribs. There lay Becca, or rather her latest model, charred and inert. His NeuroNet remains down so he has no option but to pray she drifts out there in the digital sea. Then he sees Stefan, or rather the gray granite sculpture lying in the sand with Stefan's features. He guesses how it happened and takes solace in his inability to read his best friend's mind. Then William guesses what Faye did and why Oke went with her and fights the urge to shatter the island in telekinetic fury.

He walks in the forest for hours trying to clear his head, amazed at how dazed Phase's shock has left him. When a nosy boar charges, it is all William can do to trap it in an invisible bubble and roast it in the wildfire Stefan created during his battle with the trees. After filling his belly and kicking up a sandstorm to snuff the spreading blaze, he takes a long swim along the moonlit shore, testing the agony of his ribs at every stroke. He imagines his former allies under thrall of their new queen, yet he makes no attempt to reach their minds. At last William gathers Zenith and Stefan on an invisible raft and sails at high speed until he sees a Haine

International oil tanker pass in the night. Aboard he shares his tale and his autographs with its Aussie crew.

The next day Sydney's finest physicians leap at the chance to operate on him, even as he clamors against their decision to give him cybernetic ribs. They dote on him mostly for bragging rights, William knows as he scans their minds. He relents only upon breaking into a mild epileptic fit, which they postulate must be an aftershock of Phase's shock to his system. William demands heavy anesthesia before surgery. As he long ago mastered muting his sense of pain, the sedative has nothing to do with the physical sting. First they inject neuron-stabilizing nanites into his spinal cord. Then they cut him open and replace bone with metal. Lucky for him "Meta Force" provides unlimited insurance, the doctors jest during the procedure.

He wakes to see Rodan, Karen, and Cornelio haunting each side of his recovery room bed. They feign concern for him a full twelve seconds before the interrogation. William explains that Phase has the virus. That she never told him and that he told only Stefan. That to the best of his knowledge she spied for neither the Red Nation nor The Way. That Oke should not be held responsible for her actions. And that Stefan may well be dead. William endures their accusations of complicity before asking about Nia and James. Rodan responds that they made it home safely, no thanks to him. Karen explains that his first step toward atonement will be to help rebuild the roster, and that his second step will be to lead it. "Meta Force 2.0," Cornelio calls it. Unless the imminent battery of mind probes reveals him to be a traitor as well, in which case he will rot in The Hole.

With that out of the way the four of them accompany a different set of physicians to a different room to visit the gray granite statue that was Stefan. He has been propped upright and mounted on a marble base so that instead of grinding on his back he seems frozen in an unflattering gyration of a licentious dance, and that he is about to sneeze. Were he truly a sculpture he would be the oddest work of art in any Australian military hospital, what with his sword and scabbard and singed clothes remaining untransformed, as though someone decided to treat him like a mannequin. Laboratory scans show no brain activity. Only the faintest traces of ultra high frequency radiation from the granite. It is to William's own surprise that he persuades the doctors to call no time of death, and that he persuades his superiors to entrust the statue into his care, and that he cannot discern whether or on whom he has just used mind control.

William loathes his week in the hospital. He whittles his fifth day in bed with a power cord stretching from an electrical outlet in the wall to the tiny slot at the base of his skull. He craves a haircut. Thick knaps itch above the slot, which rests under his mandatory meta registration barcode and accompanying tattoo of wavy lines surrounding a brain. His NeuroNet requires eighteen hours to recharge. He kills the day wondering what the next technological leap will bring to this community of consciousness, and dreading how much that depends on who wins the cold war. As he logs online, William scrambles to figure out what he will say to his supposed lover. If he finds her.

Instead she finds him the instant he opens his virtual reality browser. Zenith—looking every bit her idealized human self, young and blond and beautiful, as she always does online—stands in the center of a park garden. Not the park of her NetNexus, but a replica of William's favorite refuge while growing up in D.C. Unlike the real thing, however, each rose and tulip acts as an icon for a specific program, from calculator to text to audio to video. In this idyll she forgoes asking about his condition to inform him that her next model will be her last, and that she sees no point in staying on the squad now that her duties have broadened to policing Net activity for every resident in the European Union, and that she has perfected Oke's game. She then morphs into a black and red hulk of a machine with a yellow visor for eyes, bulging durium tubes for appendages, and clawlike pincers for hands. The inverted Omega and cupped Delta of the Haine International logo glows large on its chest. He asks what this means for them. She responds that for him it means what he chooses, that for her it means she continues her evolution. They share nothing more before he logs off.

His final two days in the hospital he fills with protracted bouts of fanciful debates with absent friends and enemies, spontaneous laughter, unwarranted condemnations of his treatment by the medical staff, and rambling apologies for said abuse.

Straight from the hospital he throws himself into narrowing the pool of his potential teammates. Cornelio chooses a portly Korean man capable of flight and weather manipulation. Karen picks an Inuit college dropout capable of negating or multiplying the intensity of any meta powers in her immediate vicinity. Rodan favors a lanky Egyptian woman with durium bones, instant organic regeneration, feral senses, midlevel strength and speed, and expertise in armed and unarmed combat. William opts for an elderly Russian with an invisible aura sturdier than his own that also heals the wounds of any lifeform he touches.

Solid lineup, he admits. *Not nearly as much style.*

• • •

"Where will their things go?" Nia asks while stuffing one of Oke's lime green tracksuits into a box.

"To a lab," William says as he folds a certificate of appreciation the Federal Reserve Bank of New York gave to Phase. "James ordered Europol to inspect everything."

"I'm sorry."

"For what? You're not the traitor."

"Should have seen it coming. The closer I got to you all, the hazier my visions became. Because my own path is hidden to me. What good is a seer who can't see?"

"I ask myself that all the time ... In your case I find it reassuring. Means the future's not quite written. As for what good you are, there are several hundred incarcerated terrorists and who knows how many more saved lives that answer that."

"You're sweet, Will."

He pulls a Metafocus pill out of his pocket and swallows it dry. They continue packing in the penthouse that for now is theirs alone. Oke's gaming awards. Phase's travel guides. Mother and son's pictures of each other, of the rest of the crew, of Shakti and Sowen before life went to Hell. Then they get started in her and Stefan's room. They remain silent while packing clothes, until William comes across the miniature statue of Stefan that Nia gave her man what seems like a lifetime ago.

"Sure you didn't see it coming?" he asks.

"I know!" she says, smiling while stifling a laugh. "So weird. But he liked it."

"What's weird is that you're not going to live here anymore," he says.

"I'm moving downstairs. Not back to the reservation. James is smart to keep me close but out of sight. Like you said, I'm still good for hunting bad guys."

"I'll move Stefan in tomorrow," William says. "The lab boys have a few more tests to run. Have you seen the messages pouring in? The public's rooting for him."

"Talk about weird," Nia says, sitting on her bed. "Propping my husband up in the living room like a decoration. Hoping he's not dead. That's weird."

"He's not dead. But you wanna trade weird?" he asks while sitting beside her. "My girl is made of metal. I've watched her go from a supermodel to a supertanker. And I think she can kick my ass. That's weird."

"Look, I win, because I've been carrying this load for twenty six months!" she says, pointing to her gut. "... you know, Oh's scared. So is Faye. She isn't a vampire. Yet."

"They're sure not answering my calls, telepathic or otherwise. Must be Sam's shield. Damn thing covers two continents and I can't dent a speck of it ... I tried reasoning with James. He wants them dead."

"They talk about leaving all the time. About turning themselves in. But she needs the cure."

"Did you always know she was infected?"

"Yes," Nia admits.

William flops on his back to chuckle with his face in his hands. He sits up shaking his head when Nia lays a palm on his thigh.

"What?" she asks.

"Everybody knew," he says. "Faye's mind kept screaming about it, soon after we all moved in together. I had Becca use her nanites to chemically analyze vomit Faye left in the kitchen. The kid had to know. Probably read my mind. I'm pretty sure James wouldn't have given a damn. Faye was his best bodyguard. The worst part is she isn't even sick!"

"Excuse me?"

"Becca could tell. That's why we didn't say anything. Research suggests rare subjects are merely MV carriers who never develop symptoms. Looks like that's Faye. Symptoms don't suddenly appear when your ex-boyfriend tells you he's sick. That's hypochondria. She probably infected him.

Didn't have the heart to tell her. I wanted to spare her dignity. Knew she was being careful. No sex or needles. Those weekly mind probes must have been murder ... I mind-wiped the other telepaths. Stefan begged me. Yeah, we all screwed this up."

"Amazing," Nia says before giggling herself, then resting a hand on his shoulder. "I have to say, you're taking this all very well. Aren't you scared?"

"That's the thing," William says. "I'm not. Not scared of dying. Not even that we're going to lose this war. Humanity isn't going to end in apocalypse. Vampirism or otherwise. We're better than that. Don't know why I'm so sure. But I know this. We need to balance ambition and compassion. To let people reach whatever heights they can achieve granted they don't force everyone else into anarchy. To forge a universal, cooperative system for managing our bodies and our technology. To make ignorance the common enemy. There has to be a way. If nobody else is up to the job, I suppose I'll have to figure it out. But first we really need to pack these boxes."

Nia smiles at him and rests her head on his shoulder. He holds her gently, his cheek against the raven locks of her scalp. When she looks up at him and kisses his cheek, and he kisses her forehead, they know they now behold each other as they have refused since first sight.

William takes to Nia as he has not with his own woman in three years. Nia reciprocates, buttons popping off his shirt as she removes it. William lifts the bottom of her tank top, halting when his free hand cups her belly. Then he notices that miniature statue and the spell is broken. Nia takes his palm in hers before he can turn to flee, rubs the back of his hand with the tip of her nose.

"It's okay," she whispers.

"Believe me, I wish it were."

He helps her up and into a restrained embrace. They finish packing in silence. A short while later William opens the penthouse door for two cyberclones who fetch the packages. At last Nia raises the obvious question.

"Why didn't Haine kill you all?"

"For the same reason I think we stand a chance," William says, the epiphany dawning. "He definitely could have. Like we were nothing. He could have turned us to dust and scattered us to the wind. Better yet teleported that dust into the cores of random stars in far flung galaxies. In fact I doubt Sam was trying to hurt us. I think he was trying to anger us. Incite us even. The man lowered his force field! He's insane, not stupid. But that behavior has precedent. I studied it in medical school. Later had to carry it out on some poor guy who accidentally killed his daughter when his heat vision first surfaced. It's an act of desperation, albeit usually an effective one."

"What do you mean?" Nia asks.

"The colloquial term is suicide by cop."

PART III

25

Morning ashes

Everywhere and nowhere and the time in between, the disembodied spirit dreams of what almost was ...

• • •

"Musarref," Daksha started after a brief quiet. "How many do we face?"

"They are legion. More than our number at any rate."

"Suicide. This is suicide." Daksha shook his head, gnashed his teeth. "How can we hope to survive? What chance do we have?"

"A good one," Musarref al Sayeed said, pointing up to a high cliff in the distance lit by morning rays.

He dug into a fold behind his black iron chest plate to remove an orb of silver and alabaster. Ruby inscription snaked its surface. Daksha failed to discern the language. Musarref arched back and hurled the orb at the cliff. The orb whistled as it rocketed through the trees and into the sky. A boom echoed from the point of impact, flooding the valley. Then nothing. The soldiers eyed the cliff, eyed Musarref, eyed each other. Musarref mounted his white horse and raised his scimitar. He ordered his men to ready themselves for attack. They complied, bewildered by his display with the orb. His men could not help but freeze when a great cracking erupted from the cliff. Clumps began to roll off.

Rocks continued to fall, faster and larger with each passing second. A massive rift slithered from the spot where the orb hit. Finally the cliff split in two and a boulder the size of a palace plummeted into the heart of the valley. The behemoth sank, dragging earth and grass into a gaping, cavernous pit.

Musarref slung his bow and arrows on his shoulder as he spurred his horse to the hole. He commanded the army to follow, shouting so vehemently his turban slipped on his head. The soldiers whispered among themselves. Some spoke of miracles, others labeled Musarref a demon himself. All followed him to the pit. Four levels of a subterranean lair lay exposed. Body sized hollows filled its muddy walls. Remnants of the shattered cliff littered the base. Jutting through the rock were arms, legs, heads, and torsos. Dozens of them burning and flailing, slave to an undying impulse for shade and blood. Musarref dug into his fold again and revealed a small aluminum vial. He poured the black slime therein onto his scimitar and clanged the vial against the blade. Sparks ignited and flame danced along the sword.

"Light your torches!" he bellowed. "To the pit! To the Dark Mother!"

He rode the white horse down a ramp of rubble and grass. His army stumbled behind lighting their torches on the descent. Sunlight bore into the caverns yet darkness shrouded the halls leading to the deep. Musarref kept straight, his flaming scimitar crackling in his wake.

Meerut screamed when a legless body holding its own severed head in one hand clawed at him with the free arm. He hacked at it with his axe, puncturing the chest and stomach. Still it advanced. Meerut pleaded for Jhansi to aid him. His friend was busy fighting a pair of bodiless arms. The face of the thing that clawed Meerut's thigh had a vacant stare, its eyes flat and cold. Daksha's torch set the face afire and the legless body went limp. He twisted round to yank the arms from Jhansi's throat.

"Fire to the skull or wood through the heart," Daksha said while waving his torch. "Anything else will only delay them, and will probably cost your life."

The pair from Firozabad nodded and chased Daksha along a hall. Jhansi called the soldiers behind to follow. Save their halo of torches, blackness enveloped their advance. They saw foreign inscriptions chiseled in walls, akin to those on the strange orb that wrought the avalanche. The hall narrowed as it went, forcing the soldiers to crouch, then crawl. Air became stale and heavy. Meerut began to sweat. He could feel the torch slipping in his moist palm. He tossed dirt on it lest he set himself aflame. The others followed suit. At that, crawling through the black tunnel wedged between Daksha and Jhansi, he started to whimper.

"Shut up. Shut up!" Daksha said.

"I can't," Meerut said. "I'm afraid."

"Fool! Listen!"

Inhuman growls resounded ahead. They scurried to a hole barely big enough for a body. Daksha squeezed himself through. Meerut and Jhansi wriggled after. They stood in a gigantic dome. Torches sat in rocky walls over a blood soaked floor. The high ceiling was riddled with body sized hollows. And Musarref raced to and fro atop his steed, bringing death to the enemy. He skewered them three at a time with his scimitar, which never ceased flaming. He punctured them with wooden arrows through the heart. He trampled them under hoof and left them to writhe about. Hundreds of soldiers fought beside him wielding hoes and shovels and pick axes. Demons they did not stake with timber they blazed with torches. And the demons, the Rakshasas. There seemed to be more of them every moment. How disturbing their graceful speed, with their nudity and taut smoothness. Daksha, Meerut, and Jhansi silently marveled that were it not for their bloody mouths and hands these monsters would have been the most beautiful men and women in the world.

"There was another path?!" Meerut shouted.

"How was I supposed to know?" Daksha asked.

"I wondered why so few followed us," Jhansi said.

A demon fell from one of the hollows, clipping Daksha on his ear as she landed. He twirled to the ground and she pounced on his chest, pressing him immobile. The monster was stunted in height and slight as a wisp, but her copper skin and long ebony hair radiated an allure that captivated the men. She too wore no clothes. Daksha was the first to go. She clenched her fangs to his neck and supped until life poured from his eyes. Still drinking, the girl ogled Meerut and Jhansi.

"Ria," Meerut gasped, staggering against a wall.

"Unholy, unholy," Jhansi sputtered.

"Ria, it's me. Your father." Meerut stepped forward.

"That is not your daughter anymore!" Jhansi said, pulling him back.

The child rose and approached the pair, her pupils swelling. She retracted her fangs and claws, yet her gait remained animal. Jhansi lofted his shovel. She tore it away, heaving him yards toward the center of the room. Her palms felt clammy on Meerut's cheek. She pulled him down to her level. Her breath smelled of other people's innards.

"Leave this place," she hissed. "Leave!"

Up, up, up the wall she climbed. Scurrying like some insect she fled through a slit in the domed ceiling. Meerut lay frozen, cowering on the floor. The battle dimmed. One of the horde charged him, a blur of teeth and nails. It fell at his foot in two parts, sliced diagonally from shoulder to pelvis. Musarref bent from his horse and yoked Meerut by the chin.

"Yes that was your daughter and yes this is Hell!" he said. "Now fight. These men need you so do your duty!"

He strode off and decapitated a demon with his hooked dagger before dashing through a slit in the wall at the far end of the room. Meerut ran to Jhansi, who had been bashing enemies with his shovel. He chucked his stake at a demon sneaking up on Jhansi, catching it in the heart. The men from Firozabad stood in the domed Temple of the Moon and battled, swift and deadly and terrified, to their last.

• • •

Piercing the slit brought Musarref al Sayeed to a series of short steps then a ramp. He rode the horse up the incline and through a long torchlit corridor. On the other end of the corridor he entered another torchlit room. A golden carpet blanketed the floor. A small altar with marble columns for legs and a thick silver plank for a table rested in the room's center. The table would have supported an orb but the semicircle carved into its surface was vacant. Huge alabaster statues filled cutouts in the walls. To the left stood female figures, to the right males. Their facial expressions and hand gestures marked them as deities. On the far wall opposite Musarref hung a drapery of a divine couple locked in sexual embrace. Between altar and far wall lay a circle of crimson pillows surrounding dual thrones of gold. There sat the Dark Mother and her consort, the Knight Wraith. She wore a crimson sari that revealed her arms and stomach. He an emerald kimono with silvery bandages on his hands and feet. She had ruddy skin and curly black hair. His yellow skin was pale, his black hair straight. She smiled welcoming, he gazed listless.

Both were ageless and exquisite. Musarref rode his white horse to the altar and dismounted with his flaming scimitar.

"Stefen Son," she said.

"Beast!" Musarref replied. "Never call me that."

"Your lineage eludes. Pardon if I do not share this hindrance."

"Why have you not killed me already?" He was but feet from the throne.

"In time, in time." She turned to her companion, who continued to gaze at the wall. "Magahara, there is fear in his voice."

"Yes, Shakti," the Knight Wraith said without turning. "It happens to them all."

"The true Shakti is divine!" Musarref shouted. "That you ape Her name is an affront! Your consort is no Shiva!"

"Behave," Shakti said. "You are the fourth to vex me thus. Unprovoked as always. What is it about your breed? Why must you have a crusade to feel worthy?"

"Mistress of deceit! Whore to the abyss! Seven hundred victims in three years! That is a crusade worth fighting!"

"And must you all yell? Does it lend you courage? Heed me, Stefen Son. We drink to live. You have sacrificed these souls for ... what? Nothing save feed my numbers. And I must, after your stunt with the mountainside."

"Ha! That was your own fault, letting the key go missing so long. Did you think I would not find where my great great grandfather had hidden it? If not for that scout in the jungle you would be dust."

"Observe yourself, sad little warrior. Unveiling precious secrets, and at the simplest goading. So you can see the past. In dreams, no doubt. As for the avalanche, you will pay for that. As will your heirs."

"How did you alter the temple so quickly? It looks different than I had seen."

"Ah. Well. The problem with dreams, Stefen Son, is that sometimes they are merely dreams." She turned to her companion. "Magahara, what is your verdict?"

"Choose," the Knight Wraith said. "Leave or die."

"I will never surrender, demon," Musarref said.

He arched back to launch the flaming scimitar. Shakti whirled a finger, pinning his arms with invisible bonds.

"So chosen," she said. "I am the force of life. I am the brilliance of the moon. I am the future. You are a man with a sword, too savage to accept the way of things, too ignorant to understand the gift bestowed upon your bloodline. Born from martyrs and so you shall die as one. Make peace with whatever lies you tell yourself."

A mighty wind hurled Musarref into the ceiling. His blade fell. The wind vanished and he reeled onto the altar. Again and again the wind showed him the rocky texture of the ceiling and he licked the silver table. His chest plate fissured and slipped off his body. There was a pulping sound. The pattern continued for some moments, each time increasing in velocity and pressure. Finally the marble legs of the altar cracked and the aluminum table wobbled on the floor. Shakti snapped her fingers and Musarref lurched through the air. She made a spiral gesture with her palm and he stopped. Arms and legs drawn apart, she held him there, hovering and drenched in blood.

• • •

Being yet flowed in Musarref al Sayeed. He struggled to open his eyes. The warrior was naked save for his turban and levitated above a bubbling pool of blood nowhere near the Temple of the Moon. Alabaster columns, eight on each side, bordered an expansive garden surrounding the pool. All type of flowers thrived there. Thirteen nude demons armed with spears guarded the pool, staring straight into his eyes whenever he looked their way.

An engraved image of a female graced the height of each column. The figure wore a tall crown adorned with five serpent heads, had large breasts and sunken navel exposed, held a lily in one hand and a seashell in the other, and possessed a lower body akin to the curled tail of a snake. A crescent moon shone high in the night. Voices below bid him search for their source. He spied Shakti and Magahara strolling along the row of columns to his left.

"–replace them in time, but we should take this as a sign to move on."

"Yes, Mother."

"France, perhaps. No. Arabia better suits us now."

"A hearty variety."

"So many lost. A waste."

"Musarref was correct. The key went missing too long."

"I grew complacent. Sloppy."

"Next time there should be no temple. No altar."

"Nonsense. By this time tomorrow the second avalanche would have destroyed everything. No trace of us left."

"Is there no other way? Feast and run, feast and run?"

"You have a better solution?"

"...no, Mother."

Moonlight reflected emerald off his kimono. It seemed otherworldly to Musarref. Magahara kept his arms folded, his hood up. Shakti caressed the low curve of his spine. They halted.

"What troubles you?" she asked.

"Fatigue."

She removed his hood, fingered the contours of his face. His androgyny magnified his splendor.

"Sleep then. Sleep months if it vanquishes this funk."

"Years could pass, I fear. There would be no change."

"Why? Has being my consort grown tiresome?" She licked her lips, raised her eyebrows as she smirked. "Or are you bored with being master of the Children?"

"Neither," he said, reciprocating the smirk. "But I do long for ... something forgotten ..."

"Say it." She turned her back to him. "Your thoughts are clearer to me than yourself. Say it."

"What?" He moved to face her. "I don't understand."

"Magahara. Knight Wraith. Demon. Rakshasa." She spun and slapped him. "That is what troubles you! Escape. You long to escape what you are. Admit it!"

"No!" he denied, squeezing her hand. "I accept this life. You gave me a choice and I honor the bond."

"I don't care that I can't read your mind like my others. It is more than enough to see through your eyes and hear through your ears. Remember that I know your senses as thoroughly as any of theirs." She kissed him. "Speak the truth. If you yet love me."

His feet left the grass and he ascended into the cool night breeze. She followed. They passed Musarref and the peak of the columns.

"When I was reborn I found ecstasy in this. As do I now," Magahara said. "Is it a crime to miss a sacrifice? To wish freedom from being hunted?"

"Would you rather be as that thing?" She pointed to Musarref. They descended to him, hovered at his level. "Look. That is what you sacrificed. Greed and ignorance. It calls us beast, as if it is not. The world you mourn is folly, Magahara!"

"I do not wish to be human again. I never was."

"Are you certain? Time clouds your judgment. Think back. In my millennia I have gleaned few truths save the undeniable one that humanity is a plague. All animals live and die, all fight among themselves. Yet only these things," she tugged the suspended warrior by the ear, backhanded him at the temple, "only these things attribute some moral to it. What diseased mind imagines something as ridiculous as sin? They conjure fantasies in hopes of redemption. Redemption! They prostrate themselves before figments, then go to slaughter for them, defiling the very things they worship. This is what you would embrace? Magahara come to your senses!"

The Dark Mother returned to the garden. Her Knight Wraith followed. They continued their stroll in silence for a long while, fondling flowers and sipping from the crimson pool. Eventually Magahara spun a yellow hibiscus along his lips. He gave it to Shakti. She tasted a petal and let fall the rest. They coddled each other, removed their robes. While making love under moonlight, the immortal couple sang a song in a demon tongue. When it was finished they bathed each other in blood and frolicked in white magnolia. The pair put on their vestments and made their way past the pool, at the far end of the garden. That was when Musarref decided to speak.

"More come with the dawn."

"Sad little warrior," Shakti sneered, baring fangs. "Does our bliss pain you? Has it spurred you to delusion?"

"Three thousand. True champions this time, every one of them brandishing stakes and bows and armor. From Poona and Jodhpur and Kabul and Lahore. From Multan and Kashmir and Kolkata and Delhi. Did you think I was so stupid as to bet your death on a mob of farmers?"

"You lie. Why else would you tell me this?"

"To return the favor. I give you a choice. Go pillage the infidels in Europe or watch my men kill your Children. Leave or die."

His eyes shone honestly. Shakti snarled and Musarref splashed down into the blood pool. The nude guards dragged him before her. She locked his jaw in a vise grip.

"Dog! All of them will be turned. All of them!"

"How, with your numbers whittled by my attack and your consort abandoning you?" She glanced at Magahara. He was blank. "Spare her the agony, Knight Wraith. Go before she sees the truth. A demon with a soul has no home."

Magahara snatched him from Shakti, smacked Musarref to the grass. She studied her man, awaiting his deathblow. His silvery bandaged foot stepped on the warrior's chest, pressing harder, harder, so hard bones snapped and blood frothed at Musarref's lips. His eyes rolled into the whites and he passed out. Magahara stepped away.

"He lives. End this so we can go."

The Knight Wraith continued to step away.

"Maga ... Magahara ... end this ..."

He donned his emerald hood and dashed into night.

. . .

Ruby inscription emblazoned the mirrored ceiling, walls, and floor. Words flickered in and out of meaning as Musarref al Sayeed lay supine. He was unbound, dressed in a clean white shirt and billowy pantaloons, without turban or armor. The glass room also was dome shaped and bright, although he could not discern the origin of illumination. First he heard chanting, next he saw the wide circle of nude men and women surrounding him. He sensed they were demons. They stood with their left arms extended inward, palms open, and their heads turned outward. The chanting grew louder. He understood bits, knew they recited the ruby script. They quieted, turned their heads, faced him. It took a while to settle in. Not all of them. Just the men. His army. The 400 from Kanpur, Banaras, Patna, and the rest. He recognized Meerut and Jhansi and Daksha. Finally he stood up and saw the Dark Mother by his side.

"You did this?" he asked. "You damned them?"

"They are my people now. As are they yours."

She swiped her fingers across his neck. They picked up blood. He felt there as well. Two tooth sized wounds. He licked the sides of his mouth. His canines were immense.

"By the mercy of Allah!" he begged. "Kill me! I cannot be this way!"

"Too late. It seems the Most High was busy."

"Beast, why have you done this?" Musarref was aghast to discover he could read the ruby script clearly now. Passages exalted the majesty of the moon and the boon of immortality. "Why have you done this to me?!"

"Stefen Son, you left me no choice. Had you not slaughtered so many, not driven my consort away, your death would have been easy. I had to make adjustments. A fitting touch, bringing you back into the family."

Shakti flipped her palms upward. Musarref levitated. As he neared the ceiling he saw that the ruby script glowed and that lightning whipped around the glass. Tendrils of white energy electrified his body. He dropped. Seconds before hitting the mirrored floor Musarref stopped, braced by an invisible cushion. It was pointless to deny that he had willed his safe landing.

"I may now be a demon but I will never serve you." He regained his footing and fled, pushing through the blockade of Rakshasas. "Let the armies end this if you will not!"

The Dark Mother let him pass and commanded her Children to do the same. Musarref careened along the halls of the Temple of the Moon. Try as he might he could not retrace his steps. He found the throne room and the dome with the body sized hollows, but they were not in the same location as the previous morning. He encountered rooms with furniture and rooms with torture devices, rooms with fountains of blood and rooms with no discernable purpose save to confound him. Rakshasas occupied many a cavern. Each time he stumbled upon them they uttered the same infuriating tribute. "Hail to the First Son of the Moon." Hours later he came to the place destroyed by the orb. He clambered up the earthen slope and out to the valley.

With newfound speed of the wind he dashed into jungle. He leaned against a tree, kneeled, and started to pray. It began fine. "I bear witness that there is no God but Allah. I bear witness that Muhammad is the Messenger of Allah. He is Allah the One, Allah the Eternal, Allah the Absolute." The deterioration was swift. "She gave us life and is the force of life. She is the First Daughter of the Moon, the Mother of the Night ..." Musarref gasped, spat, banged his head against the tree, pawed it furiously. Bark chipped and wood shredded. His claws were emerging.

Then his neck and chest itched. Initially he figured the tree must have ivy. A stinging followed. Burning next, and smoke. Only when flames jumped from under his shirt did he see that dark blue sky had brightened with rising sun. He cowered under a canopy of leaves. He hurried off again. As he ran his fury increased. Soon he was cursing his stupidity and his fate and his lineage and his God. All unjust, unholy.

Musarref would have blasphemed further had he not spotted the 3,000. They saturated the jungle, their armor and weapons shining, cascading sunlight. Sunlight. Massive rifts appeared on his skin and he burst into flames again. Into the breeze of morning, ashes blew from his skin. The fire was so intense he howled. He wondered why he lived. Then he remembered why the Rakshasas called Magahara master. The power was greater. Far greater than any low demon. Far greater than he had possessed when human. Wooden arrows caught him in the eye and gut. He collapsed, his good eye watching the soldiers advance as he ached and burned. They did not recognize him through the foliage.

But he knew them. Warriors he had gathered. Men he had schooled in the nature of the beast. More arrows drilled his arms and legs, until eighteen shafts jutted from him. Glowering, he saw them for what they were. Meat. That brought the hunger. His veins throbbed with the need to drink. But not now. That would come later. First he had to return to the Temple of the Moon. First he had to return to his Mother.

• • •

... So the spirit glimpses what fuels its birthright, and prays to end the cycle, should it ever regain flesh.

26

Unshackled

The man with the sunglasses and scribbled cardboard sign rests on his chair behind a floored cane and top hat. He plays his shrill harmonica with earnestness that lures passersby into a small crowd outside the playground. They stand in the shadow of the mountain that bears the concrete statue of Christ the Redeemer, His stone arms spread as wide for them as their wallets are for the musician's flipped hat. A bald, blind, old beggar would be popular in most any part of town these days. With Carnival near, tourists and residents alike lavish Rio de Janeiro with money and good will to burn before they drink up as much of the city's decadence as they can handle, and then some.

On the far side of the playground, free of the statue and fully illuminated by midday sun, stands a favela hillside with a few stubborn high rises scattered amid dirty rusted shacks. Playground revelers scarcely glance there. But the blind man does. Even through his dark, smudged sunglasses he sees the inequity that feeds this city and so many like it. *Only a little longer.* For now, however, he blows out a merry tune. More cheers as he accepts unneeded charity. *How they squander their time. They'll be out of it soon enough.* And soon, he sees upon checking his NeuroNet clock, it will be time for his task.

So the man scrunches his wrinkled face as he folds up the rickety chair, wheezes as he bends to pick up his cane and cash heavy hat. Then he sticks the harmonica in the breast pocket of his tattered suit and scratches his bald dome and limps into the land of oblivious youth.

First he passes the sandbox. Where thigh high toddlers ply shovel and fist to reshape earth in their image. Where parents encroach to pry dirt out of tiny hands before it reaches anxious mouths. Where inchoate hierarchies take root through girth and wails and uncoordinated slaps. Where cold, wet urine trails from sullied diapers, tainting that which is shared. Then the jungle gym. Where tykes climb about a rainbow colored dome of metal bars in geometric patterns. Where stature keeps parents at bay. Where toes slip and fingers grasp with the dexterity of retarded monkeys. Where busted shins and bruised lips are badges of honor. Next come the taggers. Where tweens dart around and over and under and through any obstacle to avoid capture. Where parents implore impotently about safety and manners. Where peripheral vision and trusty knees are as valuable as tied laces and skintight apparel. Where boys and girls chase each other, suspecting that more is afoot than restlessness. Then the ballers. Where teens hook and lay up their way to victory, dreaming of the day when they will be tall enough to slam. Where arching pigskins usher crushing tackles on patches of hard trod grass, and husky boys fancy prescriptions for ripple inducing steroids. Where bats sing with strikes shattered and gloves cough out hits missed while girls whistle at their classroom fixations. Where parents look on, wishing they maintained the youth and time for such exertion. Finally the skaters. Where college students juiced with painkillers latch on diamagnetic boards and blades. Where ramps, poles, tubes, slaloms, and bowls act as their release from the sober monotony of academia. Where self inflicted injuries are welcomed as proof of life. Where parents dare not venture.

The bald old blind man tries to imagine parenting. He gives up, considering how insincere it must be. Then a truly old French couple approach a bench. They push a little girl in a stroller. She arrests his attention.

The couple, retired expatriates, have been visiting the playground musician for months. They took an immediate shining to him, admiring his self sufficiency despite his disability. So much that they let him snuggle their 8 month old granddaughter, Sae Rom, whom, they told him, they care for while her mother serves out a life sentence. No sense hiding it, they told him. They did not raise their only child to be an eco-terrorist. They did not raise her to be a meta, either, but c'est la vie.

Staring through his sunglasses into eyes so bright and narrow, so familiar, the man cannot help but cast his upon the other children, then their parents. Youthful beauty threatens to justify the horror of time, and this child's laughter threatens to redeem the damned. Until he alone hears a gunshot in the distant favela, where another little girl cries dying amid Bacchus fueled crossfire. The elderly couple share a kiss, unknowingly forfeiting their ward to the vanished stranger.

• • •

Hole Island sits on the equator in the middle of the Pacific. No public map marks the 234-square-mile speck that news reports have warped into legend. This dungeon for 315,000 of the world's most powerful vandals has never been visited by anyone lacking sanction from the Council of Continents. Its surface shows no sign of habitation. Only a bland assemblage of trees and rocks meticulously crafted by a global panel of military engineers. With 17,000 cyberclone sentries, 15,000 meta guards, 13,000 baseline reinforcements, and enough weaponry to level a small nation, it is the most heavily fortified structure in the free world. Then there's the invisible force field arching over the island to repel any matter and energy unnecessary for supporting life in the super prison.

Toward this hostile environ Hikikomori runs thousands of miles per hour across the surface of the ocean, until he leaps several more in a single bound. He passes the peak of his jump as twilight looms and descends upon the force field. Any other intruder would splat while run through with enough voltage to power a city. The terrorist passes unharmed thanks to a tiny box on his belt transmitting the authorized frequency.

God bless bureaucracy, he thinks while pouncing into a tree. *And disgruntled civil servants with paltry health benefits.* That bribe also got him prison blueprints and a uniform. The gray and white camouflage he understands, not the obsession with berets. He waits until a cyberclone walks by before he drops to the ground and dashes for a small cave. Yards into the black of the cave he meets a two-foot-thick durium door. It bows to his belt transmitter and slides into the wall of rock.

In less than a second Hikikomori forces his way through the score of burning lasers behind the door, past unsuspecting cyberclones in the main corridor, down nine flights of stairs, and to the prison cell of one Manfred Peebles, 31, a.k.a. Manny. Formerly at war with the inequities of global poverty and disease. Formerly capable of duplicating himself and inorganic objects to the order of 5,000 times at the successive snaps of his fingers. Currently sleeping naked in solitary confinement, behind a foot-thick durium door, blindfolded, steel chains dangling him from the ceiling by his wrists and neck and ankles, a plastic tube dripping Meta-purge into his veins.

Hikikomori exhales a windstorm down each side of the hall, busting surveillance cameras and blowing nine cyberclones into a brick wall. He cannot puncture the door so he rips its durium hinges from their brick grooves. *Government intelligence. More like a confederacy of dunces.*

First he removes sedative, next blindfold, then chains. As Manny lay unshackled, Hikikomori unzips a pocket and injects his acolyte with a syringe of Metafocus. The quadruple dosage pops Manny's eyes wide. He lurches off the floor wheezing as his broad nostrils flare and his meaty brow scrunches. Hikikomori immediately removes his backpack and hands Manny its contents. Laser pistol, spare uniform, mind-control resistant helmet, infrared goggles, two Metafocus syringes. Hikikomori tells him to get to snapping. By the time the first squad of cyberclones, metas, and baselines scurry into the hall shouting orders to surrender, they face a trigger-happy one man army five times their size. Hikikomori zooms back upstairs as the firefight ignites.

Eight levels up he dislodges another durium door. He chucks it into the seven cyberclones hurrying in at his left, thunderclaps his hands at the four meta elites rushing at his right. The cyberclones fall broken and limp, the metas incapacitated by ruptured eardrums and hurricane winds. With that nuisance cleared Hikikomori focuses on the reason for this raid. Emily Chagnon, 34, a.k.a. Em. Formerly a French agent of the Animal and Environmental Liberation Front. Formerly capable of wielding and becoming the electromagnetic spectrum. Currently flesh and blood, too thin, and stark naked. She hangs from the ceiling restrained as was Manny, mourning what was taken from her. Until Hikikomori frees her and supplies the antidote.

"Our baby?" she asks through nasty gasps, crawling on the cold floor of the cell.

"I have her," he says while removing the syringe.

"Give her to me."

"After we free the others."

"Done," she says, eyes aglow with cyan sparks.

No sooner does she speak than does every lightbulb burst and every electronically sealed door fling open and every cyberclone deactivate. It takes her a while to muster the strength to transform into dancing lightning, however.

Luckily the guards are too occupied with the thousands of Mannys, and the timed NeuroNet virus that suddenly infects the guard's supervisors. Hikikomori had used spam decoys a week earlier to hack into the message files of the super prison's 200 highest ranking officers. Now that code bombards them with virtual reality overload. Cacophonous sirens, screams, laughter, and moans. Grotesque images of vicious chimeras, mutilated organisms, vertiginous platforms, and hostile alien terrains. Rendered cowering, they fall useless as babes in tantrum.

Lacking leadership and light, the guards' superior numbers and firepower hardly slow the Mannys. For each duplicate that dies into dust another instantly reappears from the ash, healthy and armed and shooting to avenge its brethren. So the cycle goes as the original stays hidden in a supply closet, telepathically guiding his ever renewing onslaught. Little over an hour into the riot, as twilight trickles into dusk, most of The Hole's 315,000 inmates are powered up and marauding as well.

Talking, leaping gorillas from Kinshasa. Bouncing piles of rock from Phoenix. Ogres from Stockholm and gremlins from Berlin. Amorphous blobs of goo from Hanoi and swirling clouds of noxious gas from Montevideo. All once human, all murderously intent to make good their escape.

Such catastrophe was always considered improbable, not impossible, which is why the super prison rests under an island in the middle of nowhere. For those who cannot fly or teleport or run on water or breathe within it, there is no escape. Still, several hundred flee before the jet carrying William and his new team lands. The rookies find little to do once they touch ground. William had spent the flight imbedding sleep bombs in every penetrable mind on the island. They walk past tree and rock, unable to tell the thousands dreaming from the hundreds dead.

That discernment he leaves for the twenty nine other telepaths who came in the twenty nine other jets and boats surrounding the island, packed as they were with an international brigade of overzealous metas who mainly got in his way. Not that his heart bleeds for these killers. The doctor simply reasons that babbling idiots tell few coherent tales.

William does find one awake, a Manny lying outside the cave amid a pile of dust. The duplicate twists upright and aims a laser pistol at his own temple.

"A message from The Way," the Manny says. "Your pal looks kinda stiff. Don't worry. The greedy suit who's responsible will pay. Our boss guarantees it."

This Manny pulls the trigger and dissolves, leaving William to curse at nobody in particular. The mentalist fails to track the original. If with Em, William figures, they teleported halfway around the globe. Most likely to one of Hikikomori's bunkers, which as of late boast telepathic shields on par with the Red Nation. Hours pass. While inspecting the mounds of corpses William senses a new tragedy. That if true war ever does erupt and he roams the battlefields of the enemy, he will have much killing to do and he will relish it.

27

Invulnerable, remember?

Ahmad watches two miniskirted girls ride a yellow creature with the head of a donkey and the body of a snake as it brays and slithers about the floor of a vintage arcade room. The girls' laughs turn to curses when the slithering advances to bucking that threatens to chuck them into a pool table or pinball machine. Eventually the creature relents by morphing legs from its tail and pulling its equine head into that of a human.

Oke whips a body length, serpentine tongue at the girls, who insult him in Arabic as they scamper off to the bathroom.

"Pants," Ahmad says in English over the din of profanity and hiptronica.

"Pants? Pants?! We don' need no steenkeen' pants," Oke says while wiping red flakes from his upper lip.

"You'll need pants if you want women," Ahmad replies.

"True-che," Oke says, morphing a shiny blue tracksuit out of his bare skin. "Ya peeps are cool. Kinda uptight, but cool. Whas next? I hear Cape Town's hot tuhnight."

Ahmad rolls his eyes and waves Oke to sit down at the counter. The older teen orders two glasses of water from a vampire bartender. Oke widens his mouth to cartoonish proportions so that he downs both servings in one gulp.

"How much poison have you had?" Ahmad asks.

"Snorted a pound, maybe. Drank like twenty shots."

"Ya Allah! Shouldn't you be dead?"

"Wha, haven' ya heard? I'm Oh, baby. Numba one meta unda tha sun! I'm invulnerable! I'm anythin' I wanna be! I could beat Stefan an' Will wit no hands! I could make Ana my woman in a snap! I ... I–"

His barstool keels over, depositing him on the floor. Instead of righting himself Oke puts his hands behind his head and props a leg up on the counter. He whistles the "Meta Force" theme song.

"You're trashed," Ahmad says. "Go home."

"F. That. Les get some ass," the younger boy says from the floor. "Vampire ass. I hear they do anythin'."

"Listen to yourself. Have you ever even had sex?"

"What tha–? I dated Monique Rain. Need I say more?"

"Yes."

"Man, we wen' at it all tha time, like animals, li–"

"Like you just did with those two?" Ahmad asks, pointing to the girls returning from the bathroom.

"Why're you bein' so mean? Why's ev'rybody so mean ta me? I didn' hurt anyone. I didn' do anythin' wrong."

"Answer the question."

"No, okay!" Oke shouts. "I'm a virgin! Happy now? But it's not cuz I couldn'. I'm just ..."

"Scared?"

Oke looks away.

"Hey, so was I," Ahmad says. "Remember, you're only 16. I didn't lose it until last year. Now she's one of them. Fun while it lasted, though."

"Only 16," Oke says, finally standing up. "Think they'll take it easy on me if we lose?"

"Guess that depends on what you do in the meantime."

"Won't kill anyone."

"Even if they try to kill you?"

"Invulnerable, remember?"

"Right," Ahmad says. "What about your mom?"
"... hadn't thought of that."
"Forget it. She can take care of herself."
"Right," Oke says adamantly.
"And you're with me, so you're still a star."
"Cape Town?" Oke asks.
"Sure," Ahmad says with a shrug. "But take it easy with the teleporting. Makes me queasy."

Oke gulps two more waters at the same time. Ahmad sips his first beer of the night, leaving it half full. The metamorph secretes brown dress shoes, transforms his tracksuit into blue jeans and a buttoned white shirt with floral swirls of yellow and green. They approach the girls with coy grins. Ahmad does the talking.

• • •

First she peels the potatoes. Once boiled and mashed she adds milk, salt, and pepper. Chopped garlic and onions sizzle in the pan with the tilapia. She squirts lemon juice before sliding the fish into the oven. Next vinaigrette tops lettuce, tomato, celery, cucumber, broccoli, and carrot. Finally she fills her dishes and teleports outside. Under the setting sun on the banks of the Dead Sea, with her vampire lover by her side, Phase savors every bite of her last meal as a human.

"How is it?" Harod asks. He slouches back on their picnic blanket, propping up on an elbow. His free arm bothers the happy trail on his bare, black stomach. "I'm already starting to forget what solids taste like."

"It tastes like Heaven," she says.

"Good ... I understand now why you waited. I apologize for being angry when you didn't turn with me."

"You mean with you and the hundreds of other Hole fugitives," she says between swallows. "Your face was priceless when you saw me here."

"A pleasant surprise," he says before sipping a frothy glass of blood. Drops mar his beige pantaloons. He grips his bald head and leans forward to steady himself.

"Everything okay?"

"Just the sun. Even with the sunscreen, it takes its toll. Mother says she'll find a solution soon enough."

"Ugh. Please," Phase says. "Ana's a nice woman, but nothing more. It's insulting."

"You'll feel differently once you're one of us."

"Is it really so great?"

"It is."

She finishes her meal in silence while he downs his glass and two more after that. They pack their picnic gear and take to sea. He zips across its surface. She blinks after him, picnic basket in hand. They cut through Jordan and over the Red Sea, followed by the Arabian Sea and into Somalia, Kenya, Tanzania, Zambia, Angola, and across the South Atlantic Ocean to Nigeria, Chad, Libya, the Mediterranean Sea, and back home to the ziggurat. The jaunt's end coincides with the moon's rise.

"Be honest," Phase says while entering his bedroom. "How'd you get sick?"

"Faye, you'll find that we're always honest. Unless Mother instructs otherwise," Harod says with a wry grin. "To answer your question, I don't know."

"Take a guess."

"Whores. Needles. Vices I no longer have."

"Oh? I thought sex and drugs were rampant here."

"Free love isn't prostitution. And the only things we crave are blood and Mother ... It's natural to be nervous. Confused. Trust me, everything will become clear."

"You healed well," Phase says to change the subject. "How long did it take after New York?"

"A couple weeks. My healing factor's even better now. That drop wouldn't faze me."

"Cute ... I shouldn't have come here," she says while mashing her face into her palms. "Should have sucked it up and confessed. Gotten treatment ... Poor Oke. Why'd he have to follow me?!"

Harod places a hand on her shoulder, the other on her hip. He pulls her in as he sits on his bed such that her gray speedsuit blends with the sheets. She nods and brushes her brown hair from her neck. Fangs sink in, blood spurts out, and Phase flinches. Still holding her in his arms, he gently sucks away her old life while his gums secrete the virus that pumps her full of a new one. Faye Zamair, who for so long has thought of herself only by her adopted name, convulses on then off the mattress of her escort into darkness. With her last free gasp she begs forgiveness of a God in which she has never believed. And with her first breath in the collective she thanks Mother for such bounty.

She is not so much a new person as a perspective enhanced with the perspectives of so many new persons. The crucial solitude of the self couples with the serene company of billions of other selves that lap at the banks of her mind. There's Harod. Over there quite a lot of people she's stolen from. Farther off there's Magahara and Sowen. And of course there's Mother shining down like a beacon for all to gather round.

Now I see. You healing the lost. You illuminating the greater good. You bringing happiness to spirit, peace to community, survival to all. Our body, our nature, our mind, our being. Our divine avatar, sacrificing union with the Absolute to save us. Your power. Your love.

"You see?" Harod asks as he stands to kiss her.

"Perfectly," says the healthy, blissful vampire.

• • •

"I feel good about this," Sowen says, rubbing his palms together in the showroom with the chandelier.

"Don't be so cocky," Shakti says.

"Really. Give us some credit," Magahara says.

"Not about the games," Sowen says. He looks at them innocently from his seat between the two floating chessboards. "About the ruling. We'll find out shortly."

"Oh. I'm still going to win," Shakti says.

"Preparing to use the verdict there as an excuse if you lose here?" Magahara asks, pointing out to the balcony.

"Not at all," Sowen says. "And as far as the games are concerned, anything can happen."

"Smug bastard," they say in unison.

Then they get on with the chess, Sowen playing white in both games. Each opens the same. He moves a pawn, his opponents match. With Shakti he moves another pawn, sacrificing it to her first one for expediency. With Magahara he moves a knight, to be blocked by a second pawn. A few moves later Sowen's exposed bishop takes Shakti's pawn, which riles her knight to threaten closer. Sowen's queen snaps Magahara's greedy bishop, and a pawn on the side objects by nixing its counterpart.

Child's play, Sowen thinks as a newscast about the verdict flicks onto the NeuroNet. The report comes from a photogenic woman wearing a form fitting suit outside the Geneva headquarters of the World Monetary Fund.

"After more than a month of debate, the W.M.F. board has decided on the request made by its former president, Samuel F. Haine, about reinstation," she says. "In a ruling that hinged on a single vote, Haine has been denied the post. No comment yet from Haine or his wife, Ana Shaktira, who shocked the world more than two and a half years ago with the overnight vampire revolution that rules India, Central Asia, the Middle East, and Africa.

"What's more, allegations have emerged that officials opposing Haine's bid for the spot, notably in the U.S., were bribed by businesses that stood to suffer from his appointment. This allegedly includes his former company. The vote also has inflamed old grudges. Nations supporting Haine's request, notably China and Russia, have been accused of funding terrorists in proxy wars with rivals. Tensions reportedly have risen to the point that Russian and Chinese missiles once aimed at the so called Red Nation are now aimed at Britain and the U.S. Anonymo–"

Sowen shuts the browser and returns to chess, stewing in silence. As the games deepen his pieces dwindle to such an extent that he almost welcomes the insistent blare of a new alert from the photogenic woman.

"This just in: Small riots have broken out in China, Russia, Korea, Ukraine, Indonesia, Kazakhstan, and every South American nation except Argentina and Brazil. Rioters seem to want their governments to pledge allegiance to the Red Nation. Also, E.U. President James Windsor, who had refused to speak on the bid, just issued a statement applauding the W.M.F. board. He called it 'a victory for freedom' and accused Haine of bankrolling Jin Myeong, a.k.a. Hikikomori, reputed terrorist leader of The Way. Windsor had kept quiet during a U.N. probe into the terror strike that has transmuted Myeong's brother, Stefan Reyes, and made fugitives of two of his castma–"

Again Sowen shuts the browser and says nothing. The glowers of his eternal friends say it all. Minutes later the games cease when Shakti has trapped him and Magahara has managed a stalemate.

28

Everything works out

Virtual alarm clocks wake them with the dawn. William and Nia stay ensconced in sheets well after sunlight penetrates her bedroom window. They lay in undergarments, his dark arms wrapped around her tan belly. She pecks his cheek and points to the window, apparently insisting that they really must get up.

Sometimes, like now, he wishes he could read her mind. Sometimes he believes she can read his. He ponders whether she shares his guilt, despite their abstinence. Whether she also obsesses over raising his dead friend's child. He trusts he could make a good father. Better than his own, once he figures out a few tricks. Like the balance between discipline and tenderness. *Didn't work so well with the kid. Sorry, Oke.*

He wallows on about lost friends as his new love snuggles into him, until he rolls into a wet spot.

"My water broke," Nia says with a hint of apology.

"Okay, okay," he says while kicking the covers off them and springing to the floor. "I'm ready. How do you feel?" he asks, his head flapping from side to side as he inspects the room. "What do you want to bring with us? Want to call your dad or should I? How do you feel? Did I ask that already?"

"Will, relax," she says through careful breaths. "Just get me to the hospital."

"Right. Sorry."

He levitates a suitcase from her closet and floats into it whatever catches his eye. That little, stuffed, white tiger doll on the windowsill. Those pink ballerina slippers on the floor by the dresser. A framed picture on the wall by the closet, of Nia with her father and sisters outside Silver Sky Family Resort. The pair of posable toy action figures on the nightstand, of Stefan and himself. And her favorite bathrobe, from inside the closet. He has no idea what purpose these items will serve, yet he knows they are necessary.

William hurries off a Net message to James and Cornelio before telepathically alerting the chief of staff at the premiere hospital in Brussels. William begins to order an ambulance when he recalls that he can fly. And that they both need clothes. Once dressed he cradles Nia and heads for the window, until he remembers the suitcase and one other item. *Statue or not, he has a right to be at the birth of his child. Damned if this won't be the most watched episode of the season.*

That gets him thinking about the show, as they soar to the hospital with granite Stefan levitating behind. About how skewed the public's perception must be. About how often they deactivate their lenses and ear mics so P.R. can edit hastily and James and Cornelio can hide so many details from the media. About how so few know of the battle with Haine. Of him and Nia. Of Stefan and Ana. Of Haine's quest for godhood. Of Hikikomori's plot for genocide. All lies. All for the greater good. For a world worth living in.

God, let this kid have a good life. And goddammit how about a world where the truth is a good thing?

• • •

Nia debates whether she should blame Sowen. Whether Shakti has been reading her mind all along, and they're playing with her. Letting her think she's helping to defeat them when in fact she's falling into their trap. The never ending pregnancy. Or whether these contractions are driving her mad.

She had expected it to be difficult, what with the baby taking three times longer than normal. But the pain. She would fear quintuplets if not for weekly checkups. Yet it's only one. *Only one little soul joining the billions of others. And taking its sweet time, too! Maybe that's the point,* she thinks. *Maybe its birth has been so slow because the world's death is coming so fast. Maybe my baby's going to save the world.* Talk about great expectations.

She does not reproach herself for it. After all, is she not the seer? Is her husband not destined to slay a god? Is the world not at its most di–*ahhh, why the hell do people have kids?! Forget this natural bull! Give me drugs! Wait, did I just say that out loud? Can't tell. Can barely think, barely see ... Is this a bed or a gurney? Are these tubes in my arm? Oh man, where's my daddy?*

Oh there he is. On the res. In our house. He seems so happy. He's holding something. It's me. I was just born. And there's mom. She looks so peaceful, sleeping like that. Sleeping forever. He doesn't realize yet. Wait, there's the doctor telling him. And there are the tears. But he still holds me so lovingly. Because daddy's the best. I couldn't be angry with him. Not even when he remarried. He gave me little sisters! Poor daddy. No boys. And both wives died giving birth. Must be ... both?

Please, no. Is that why I'm seeing this now? Please, no! I didn't ask to be seer. Didn't ask to be here. Just doing my part. Just–what, who's that? It's Will. Hi, Will. So nice. So smart. He understands me. He won't leave, won't ever change. Ow! Stupid, of course he will. He's a man. Men don't care about anything but power. Men don't–his hands are so soft, so calming. I ... oh God, I can feel him. Feel him in my mind. Is this what it's like? Finally. Finally someone knows. Thank you. Thank yooooooooh FREAKING WOW THIS HURTS!

Breath, breath, breath, breath. In, out, long, short, in, out, long, short. It's worth it, it's worth it, it's worth it, it's worth it! Of course it is. This isn't chance. Too many factors. When we met. How we met. Stefan's lineage. His brother's lineage. His brother. Another child? How did I miss that? I don't miss anything. Ever. Not good. Too many unknowns. What else have I missed? Whoa! Not that contraction. But it was easier. I can do this. We can do this. Come on, Love, help Mom out. Mom. I'm going to be a mother! I'll be a good mom. I'll listen. I won't meddle. I'll be nice. I won't nag. I promise. Just ... get out!

Fine, take your time. I'll work with you. No rush. What's time, anyway? Just a perception. There's only this moment, or an endless string of them, and strings upon strings, so let them come. Everything works out as it should, because it has to, because everything works out every which way, because the nothing's in between, and the infinite's all we see, and our Creator creates for His Creator which creates for Her Creator which creates for Its Creator and so on ... what the hell am I talking about? Must be the drugs. Great, they heard me. Hope I'm not saying all this out loud. Forget it. Don't care. Why fight it? Why fight at all? Because we don't know. So look out, Sowen. Shakti won't save you. And Jin will ruin you. You can't win. Because you can't see ...

Hey. Hey, I can see him. Stefan! Stefan, over here! Can you see me? Hear me? Where have you been? We were so worried. We knew you weren't dead. Hoped. All I had was my faith. Visions. I mean visions. I did know. So you're coming back, right? Until you leave again, that is. I understand. We could have been great together. But that's life. Don't be mad. It's not his fault. It's nobody's fault. That's how it is.

So be nice, okay? That's all that matters. Be nice. See you soon. Take care. Bye bye ...

Nia regains a moment of lucidity and glances round the delivery room. Ceiling lights blind her. Utensils scrape against metal pans as doctors twirl them about and then in her. William still holds her hand, still whispers in her ear. Granite gray Stefan still stands in the corner, frozen in what at that instant resembles a cross between a sneeze and a yawn. Something smells awful. She realizes it's her. Then she feels a shift in her womb and everyone tells her to push hard because she's almost home. So she does. It is the most agonizing experience of her life, which she has no doubt exceeds anything any man has ever endured. She sobs and secretly begs for death, only to live and curse the Creator for allowing such torture. Then she glances back to the corner and notices that Stefan has moved ...

• • •

Black gives way to light and color as the statue turns to flesh, forcing Stefan to process the scene before he can partake of it. His consciousness returns in hyper speed such that the world resembles a photograph more than live action. He has trouble discerning the virtue of the image.

Stefan beholds his wife grimacing on her back, feet up in stirrups, his best friend kissing her forehead while petting her hand, some stranger fixed on the vortex of her open thighs. That frame remains unchanged long enough for him to make sense of it, not quite long enough to make peace with it. That may be due to the pain. It feels as though each grain of stone that morphs back into a cluster of cells does so with such fiery enthusiasm that they threaten to explode. Stefan thinks his eyeballs get the worst of it until he finds his groin. Even the tattoos on his forearms, of the sun encircled by nine outward facing arrows, ache like new. The fire eases into a lingering tingle akin to having slept on a numbed out body part, except that is his whole body. Eventually that too subsides into a sensation of floating.

Then time resumes its normal pace and he sees this baby crown and he overcomes nausea to truly fall in love for the first time.

So this is what it feels like, Stefan thinks while taking Nia's free hand in his own. He ponders those he has loved for lust or companionship or commitment. *But this!* This exceeds what he feels for himself, for the God he has always wanted to believe in, for any father he has ever known. This he knows as the purpose of his life. To witness the creation of perfection and to thank the powers that be for the experience.

When I am born, and the chief obstetrician announces that I am a girl, his lesson is complete.

"Nice try," William says to his friend. "But you didn't steal the show."

"I can live with that," Stefan says. "Thanks for looking out for her."

"De nada."

"Por supuesto."

"Beauty, beauty," Nia whispers as the doctor passes her my crying self. "What are we going to call her?" she asks, looking up at Stefan as though he had been there the entire time. "I like ..."

She passes out and my father swoops me up before my mother's sweaty arms go limp. The doctors, including William, swarm in poking and prodding until they are assured she suffers from mere exhaustion.

A name, a name. Stefan weighs hundreds of options in the course of a minute, returning again and again to his first choice. The name his father would have wanted for me. The name he heard so often in youth but never got to say to its bearer. The only name even his brother utters with pure reverence.

"We'll call her Sarah," he says to his sleeping bride. "After my mom."

"What's it like?" William asks after a bit.

"Being a dad? Es bueno. Es el verdad."

"I'm happy for you. But that's not what I meant."

"Hey, you're the mind reader," my father says almost as an afterthought, enrapt as he is snuggling his nose to my own. "What do you mean then?"

"What's it like being dead?"

"Except for that one long dream, it wasn't like anything. Like nothing. As peaceful as can be."

"Knew you'd be too foolhardy to stay dead," William says. "So, uh, how exactly did you come back?"

"Maybe our enemy thinks we're still friends," Stefan says. He kisses my eyes. "Dunno. But I do know about this."

He turns me around and holds me out to face William. I cry and coo and spit on my chin. Then the two of them laugh and tell me that I'm the ugliest thing they've ever seen.

29

PARTAAAY!!!

Their smiles fade as the picture snaps. With his free hand Hikikomori unbuttons his gray suit jacket, which matches his gray sweater and gray pants and, yes, gray shoes. Stefan snatches the flute out of his brother's other hand as Hikikomori goes for a sip. They jostle over the champagne, Stefan at the mouth and Hikikomori at the stem, spilling most of it on themselves, until Sowen snatches the glass and dips his finger inside to turn it blood and drink the rest.

"Nice suit," Sowen says over hiptronica music blaring throughout the ballroom.

"Thanks," Stefan says as a strobe light sends beams of orange and magenta across his forehead.

"We're wearing the same suit," Hikikomori says.

"I was speaking for both of us."

"Thanks."

"No sweat," Stefan says.

"Sarcasm, fool," Hikikomori replies. "Why are you thanking him? He tried to kill you. That's my right."

"Play nice, boys," Shakti cuts in. "You'll set a bad example for the children."

"She's right," Nia says, cuddling me. "Let's not raise a little sociopath."

"Smart move, then, bringing her around all of us," Magahara points out.

"Where exactly are we?" Em asks in her human form, while holding my older cousin, Sae Rom.

"Isn't it obvious?" Oke asks as he morphs into a green balloon that floats toward an unreachably high ceiling. "It's a PARTAAAY!!!"

"Granted," William says flatly. "It's also a dream."

"Perceptive, Doctor Powers," Shakti replies.

"That would seem to be the logical conclusion ..." Zenith notes while waving her pink, human arm at the other guests, who roam about the marble and oak laden ballroom in the finest of formal attire.

Phase, James, Rodan, Begaye and his other daughters, Cornelio, Karen, P.R., little Bao Chan and her parents, Monique and her sisters, the rookies of "Meta Force 2.0", dozens of Mannys, Harod, Bounce, Liselle, Ahmad and his family, Finley, Tacker, Deng, Irwin, Obasun, and Mesa all stop dead in their tracks. They stare at the others in unison for six eerily silent seconds before returning to their banter among alabaster pillars stretching nearly to the ceiling and floral patterned tapestries of silk and gold mounted on the walls.

"Cool!" Oke says, floating back to the floor and reassuming human form. "I almost never have lucid dreams."

"You're not now," Stefan says. "I am."

"There you go again!" Hikikomori shouts. "This is my dream. Mine!"

"It might be all of ours," Magahara suggests.

"As I was saying," the gorgeous blond continues, "that would seem to be the logical conclusion, if I still dreamed. But I have not slept since I transcended my original body. Therefore whatever this is, it is more than a dream."

"Unless you're all figments of my imagination," Sowen says. "That tends to be the way it goes in dreams."

"Well we can't prove it, so we might as well enjoy it," Oke concludes before running after Monique.

"Kid makes sense," William says with a shrug, before walking off toward Begaye.

Following suit, the smaller group whittles itself away. Em and Nia carry Sae Rom and me to the wall length buffet table, where they prepare tiny plates of cubed meats and vegetable tips for themselves before picking up warm milk bottles for us. Hikikomori and Stefan retrieve two more champagne flutes from the tray levitating around the hall. Shakti introduces Magahara to Cornelio and Karen while Sowen taps James on the shoulder. Finally Zenith greets Phase and Harod. And for quite a while, none pay much heed to the beast prowling among us.

Oke insists on many an antic, dragging out the best of the worst in his fellows. The Electric Slide proves who can and cannot dance. Charades prompts P.R. to heckle Phase and Harod relentlessly for their pathetic renditions of beached whales. Flip Cup results in a clearing of the buffet table and comes down to the brothers arguing about a millisecond difference between which of their plastic cups landed first. Rhyme Time finds Magahara and James insisting that words such as "lozenge" and "door hinge" ought to be acceptable retorts to Bao Chan's otherwise unacceptable use of "orange." Powerless Freeze Tag allows Monique to free Ahmad moments after Sowen taps him, only for the king in no need of a nation to sneak up from behind and catch both of them off guard, which spurs Shakti to call him out as a cheater. That naturally leads to Truth or Dare.

"Dare," Shakti chooses.

"Let ... my ... people ... go!" Ahmad says in as mock somber a tone as possible.

"If only you had a beard, a cane, and a goat, that would have carried," she says. "... oh you're serious. Child, the dare has to be something I can actually do."

"Fine," he replies. "Hop on one leg and bark like a dog. A big dog."

The vampire obeys. "This. This here. This is the problem with humans," she states while hopping.

"Or with men," Em says over the barking.

"Your turn," Shakti says to Nia before one last menacing bark at Ahmad.

"Truth," Nia chooses.

"You're the true seer, aren't you?" Shakti asks.

"... Yes."

"What the ... why'd you ..." James sputters. "That's a lie. She's lying."

"Nonsense," Shakti says. "We can't lie here."

"Hello, I just did," James says.

"Forgive me. I meant only those of us who are real. You're a figment."

"The conceit! I am not a ... a figment! ... Why do you think so?"

"Because you're not family," Shakti says. "No offense, Your Highness."

"Again, where is here?" Magahara asks.

"Play by the rules, my love," Shakti admonishes.

"As if any of us has the answer," Oke says. "You might as well ask the babies."

"Truth or dare," my mother asks me with that obnoxious inflection mothers condescend to their daughters, as she rocks me back and forth against her bosom.

"Truth," I answer to everyone's dismay.

"Dare," cousin Sae Rom says, causing heads to turn from me to her.

"Gotta be a dream," Stefan says.

"Go with the flow," William whispers in his ear.

"What's happening?" my father asks us. "What is this?"

"A better question. Why is this?" Hikikomori asks.

"The Creator wills it," we babies answer in unison.

"No," Sowen says. "No!" he repeats, this time smashing his blood filled flute on the floor. He fixes on the spill. "No, no! That's stupid. And sloppy. 'The Creator wills it.' I've had enough of these conceits, do you hear me? Enough of these goddamn contrivances!"

"Who are you talking to?" Shakti asks with what Magahara deems more genuine concern for another since he first abandoned her.

"They know! They know who I'm talking to," he says, now pacing around our mothers, who instinctively cradle us in vise grips. "This will not stand. This deus ex manure will not stand! It compromises the integrity of our lives. It ... it ... wait, can I find this Creator? Can I?!"

We point to the beast at our mothers' feet, and they regard it as though for the first time. The great white tiger rests on the floor, yet its spine reaches their waists. Its cyan stripes glow more fiercely than any strobe light. Thick, green, vine and ivy strap its muscular back and belly. Gray pebbles that flake its shoulders and rump bunch into weathered rock at its paws. It licks its flaming whiskers with a tongue of pure water, blinks its lids over eyes that reveal the starry cosmos.

Sowen is so transfixed by its gaze that he forgets the others, forgets himself, as he kneels and brings his face within inches of the beast's. He pets its fur, squeezes with both hands behind its ears, and mumbles something I cannot hear. Then the tiger meows and bats a paw at Sowen's temple, knocking him on his side. The avatar wraps its barbed, metal tail round his throat.

"Nice kitty, nice kitty," Sowen says.

Shakti pulls at the tail and accomplishes nothing save cutting her hand something awful. Magahara fares little better. Hikikomori joins after Sowen's face begins to turn a hideous shade of purple. Stefan caves in as well when Sowen's breaths degrade into wheezes. The beast whips its tail, and Sowen with it, flicking the five of them like gnats. The tiger gazes at our mothers. They place us at its feet and go off in search of their mates.

William and Oke reach for us until a bloodcurdling meow has them think better of it. Zenith pulls her man away for a dance while Oke makes an excuse about hearing his mother calling him. The rest of the onlookers go about their business, leaving us with the beast. With nothing else to do, we climb up its legs and onto its spine, yanking at its fur as we go. Once firmly atop, it takes us for a ride. And what a ride it is.

We permeate the ballroom walls again and again, each time encountering a new reality. Realities where I do not exist. Where vampires rule without Shakti. Where metas are fantasy. Where a raging ecosystem all but destroys civilization. Where humans never evolved. Where Earth exists as a virtual program for higher beings to teach their offspring the ways of life through simple parables. Where wealthy, anthropomorphic, cartoon ducks save the day from villainous, bank robbing beagles to a quirky pop soundtrack.

These disappearances, and the giggles we exude upon re-emerging, lure the others into testing the walls as well. It becomes the ultimate party game for all save Shakti, Sowen, and Hikikomori. Shakti can find no pleasant reality devoid of vampires. Sowen incessantly vacillates on whether he should partake, instead languishing at a wall, swiping his hand through it like a child on punishment. My uncle, however, meets an impenetrable barrier.

At some point my father snatches me off the beast, leaving my big cousin astride it.

"You don't know me," Sae Rom says as I go, showing me our eternal divide.

Disarmed by the novelty of the walls, either in laughter or tears, old allies and bitter enemies open up to each other. William tells Phase he forgives her for betraying them, and asks Oke to forgive him for being such a stickler. The boy accepts even as he refuses to abandon his mother. Hikikomori gets into it as well, telling James not to take all those assassination attempts personally—although, he admits, he will succeed shortly.

Sowen even apologizes to Stefan for petrifying him. Although, he maintains, his former employee whom he treated like a son did cuckold and eviscerate him and intend to trap him in an unending frozen nightmare. Besides, Sowen rationalizes, he knew Stefan could survive without food, water, air, and sleep, so why not without a body? Stefan shrugs and apologizes for only the cuckolding. Feeling ashamed, my father asks why Sowen spared them back on the island, and why Shakti never turned them vampire.

"Because we're friends," Sowen says, clearly wounded. "I accept that, by human standards, I'm evil. But you can't think that I'm ... a bad person?"

"I don't know what you are. But I don't know what I am, either," Stefan confesses.

"Who does?" Hikikomori asks from over their shoulders.

"With that, at least, we can help," Shakti says after coming through a wall. "It's time to tell them."

They do. About one of Sowen's reincarnations, as an early deacon in 34 A.D. Jerusalem tried for blasphemy and stoned to death by a mob for condemning what he then saw as the sins of his neighbors. How, wholly invested in the new faith, Stephen withheld his powers to become martyr and saint. How that martyr's son was born soon after the father's death to a short, svelte, ruddy skinned woman with a taste for very raw meat. How that boy became a man imbued with divine vigor, a righteous warrior compelled by God knows what to wander the world. How on occasion through the ages the immortal would encounter his mortal heirs of that martyr saint, as ally and enemy, ignorant to his connection with them but always with admiration for their divine mission. How he ultimately learned from his greatest descendant, Magahara, that they were Sowen's own lineage, this revelation coming long after Magahara too gave mortal offspring to Shakti. How one of Magahara's twins grew to so despise her ways that son founded a cult to mother's destruction. How Sowen's pride brims even now, when the latest of that cult decries the crown of the world and the other decries the world itself.

"See?" Shakti asks, hugging Stefan and Hikikomori at their waists. "One big, dysfunctional family. Say cheese!"

Then another picture snaps and we come to our senses.

30

I want to cry

Stacks upon stacks of printouts litter the desk and sofa of William's office at the Sorbonne. He had been absent for months. Months when the place had been spotless. It took nine minutes to dishevel it without doing much except empty a few file cabinets. He loosens the top buttons of his pink shirt and folds the cuffs to his elbows while staring into the mirror on the back of his closet. A virtual alarm clock rings in his head. He pulls an orange cylinder out of his pants pocket, pops the lid, and swallows a Metafocus pill.

He strains to recall when that beard grew in. At last it hits him that his clean shave left at the hospital, during his recovery from the island. A nice trim, although patches of gray bristles reveal his advance toward 40. William marvels that he can know so much about other minds yet so little about his own. He once had it all figured out. People. Politics. Powers. Now he hardly recognizes the eyes peering back at him.

Let's not get melodramatic. So your ex-boss is risking world war because he's a suicidal megalomaniac. So you're in love with your best friend's wife and can barely talk to your body-dysmorphic robot girlfriend. So your bad attitude might have pushed the most powerful kid on the planet into a life of misery. It's not like you're having a breakdown. You just need a shave. After you figure this out.

William returns to his printouts. He still agrees with what he told Haine all those years ago. Meta powers reflect subconscious fixations of the subject. Haine wants to be God, so he has godlike powers. Manfred Peebles grew up a scrawny only-child who got bullied left and right, so now he's a one man army. Once again, William entertains what that means about himself. Once again failing to come up with anything save that he doesn't trust people, he moves on. This time he turns to the journal on his desk, an actual hardcover book that he scribbles in so as not to forget how to scribble. He looks over that last entry, stumbling through his deplorable handwriting.

Sunday, May 16, 2083

Getting closer. The questions remain (1) Why did certain people become metas? And (2) How did they manifest specific powers? Drug research indicates it's mostly mutated genes affecting brain chemistry. But every meta seems to have different mutated genes, both because of the myriad chemical combinations of known DNA and the new nucleobases comprising DNA that pop up in metas at random. None of that explains how anything going on inside an organism allows mind control or morphing or hyper speed. If Sam's right, as Nia believes, that a bigger wave eventually will turn everyone meta, then these answers will only become more crucial. Provided people survive that long. In the meantime there are my breakthroughs.

When Metafocus and Metapurge hit the market six years ago, Ana's research proved how they alter memory formation through protein synthesis in the hippocampus. By self experimentation, I've found that Metafocus has increased dendrites throughout my brain, especially in the temporal lobe, the part most active when using my powers, but, paradoxically, also has increased my absent mindedness. By studying prisoners, I found out what else Metapurge does.

One, it curbs the electricity flowing through specific neural regions, which differ from prisoner to prisoner, but only those regions active when using their powers. Two, it sends the mutated genes into hibernation so that RNA ignores its messenger role for the corresponding DNA and blocks creation of the proteins that apparently allow people to fly, cause rainfall, etcetera. And by testing Oke while the kid's been high on Bacchus, I found that the narcotic acts like Metafocus during its onset and Metapurge during the comedown.

But today's lab work might be the door to something real. Using new smartdrug pills embedded with nanite microscopes and radiation detectors (Becca's design) and a carefully wielded scalpel of pure telekinesis, I think I've figured out Stefan's physiology. His cells are solar batteries and his mitochondrial RNA carries the juice. Moreover, neurons in his parietal lobe absorb some kind of short waves exceeding the frequency of gamma rays. The same frequency that lingered when he was stone. The same frequency that pops on and off the grid when subatomic particles are smashed. The same frequency that astronomical probes have picked up from stars. Could this energy be what powers metas? Could it be what Sam hopes to tap into with that black hole nonsense? Another clue, another puzzle.

One put on hold when William remembers he has less than ten minutes to make it to Ibiza for the commercial. He leaves the journal on the desk, takes a last ambivalent glance in the mirror, then flicks off the lights and soars out the window, switching from doctor to superstar as he leaves Paris.

His flight drifts into memory of how obsessively he studied to become America's youngest licensed neurologist at 19 years old, barely four years after the meta wave. More amazing, then, that he quickly went on to master neurosurgery and psychiatry. In the early years William had wanted to believe his genius was natural, that the telepathy and telekinesis were coincidences. He now accepts that they are one. It makes more palatable the coup of the immortals, who, he decides, must have benefited similarly. This assessment makes him value intellect much less and Stefan much more as he lands on the rocky beach.

"Glad you could stop by," P.R. snaps at William, arms akimbo until he taps a finger to his gaudy anachronism of a plastic wristwatch.

"Sorry. Got held up contributing to the body of public knowledge. Won't happen again."

"Better not," the director says while playing with the tip of his ponytail. "These shoots come out of my budget."

William debates inducing a seizure in the potbellied man with twiglike limbs. Or a lifelong case of severe Tourette syndrome. Instead he telepathically wills the baseline to relive his dozens of bouts of prolonged sexual impotence, in the blink of an eye, before telekinetically forcing P.R. to ball a fist and punch his own groin with more power than his scrawny arms could have mustered alone. William sneers and immediately regrets his indulgence.

He turns from the wincing man and eyes the rookies, who in turn fawn over Stefan. William had wondered whether they would take to Stefan's return and sudden instatement as squad leader. It appears the people's champion should not have been underestimated. Then William feels the ground shake and hears a mechanical bellow behind him. He resists a shudder.

"Hey, Becca. Lookin' good," he says.

"Call me Zenith," the hulking machine replies.

He takes it as their death knell. Studying her black and red form—which is taller and wider than anything pretending to be human—getting blinded by the glow of her yellow visor, wincing at her bulging durium appendages and clawlike pincers, he realizes that he toughed it out beyond the bounds of sanity. For a moment he wishes he were the type of guy to cry. Instead he nods.

"Zenith it is. Thought you were off the team."

"Stefan will need me. Now that he is no longer dead."

He turns away from her without comment. They approach the others and get on with the commercial. The segment calls for ample voguing. Fierceness, sexiness, happiness. Smile here, brood there, arms folded, down on one knee, etcetera etcetera. Stefan falls right back into the role and Zenith somehow does an adequate job as well. The young bloods, however, need work. Drawn from other Executive Warriors Elite squads, they have all been before cameras. But they have never become "characters" before. Even clad in colorful leather, their collective mojo wilts.

Yong, the weather manipulating Korean man, has a bad habit of resting his hands on his fat stomach. Alex, the power tampering young Inuit woman, does not seem to know how to smile. Bennu, the strong and speedy Egyptian, sounds like she swallowed a dying frog. And Luka, the old Russian healer, forgets to look at the cameras. It takes more than two hours to finish what should have lasted half of one, and even then P.R. looks unimpressed with the result. William almost pities the direclor. Although watching him curse under his breath while remote controlling those floating camera orbs does smack of a reward for withholding the Tourette's.

• • •

"Crazy, the things you never expect to miss," Stefan says while on the jet back home.

"Like teleportation?" William asks.

"Or having a cool kid to mess with."

"Don't get me started," William says. "Remember when he nearly ODed after that concert?"

"How could I forget?! It's the same day ..."

"Oh yeah. Sorry, man."

"Gotta have thick skin in this business, right?"

"Or a force field."

"Sure," Stefan says. "If you're a wuss."

William flips his friend the middle finger, reclines the back of his seat. He reaches over for Becca's hand, remembering all too quickly that "Zenith" is flying back on her own because she cannot fit in the cabin. Looking back, William understands, that concert marked the end of their old lives. He sighs at the truth of Stefan's clichés while slipping into a catnap moments before the jet lands in Brussels.

Stefan exits the elevator of the Berlaymont Building one floor below William and the others. James had decided that resurrection and fatherhood grant Stefan the right to dote on Nia and me in our own condo. William thanks God that His Highness' family visit to London, under protection of an interim EWE squad, means that instead of guard duty the good doctor can slumber. He returns to his room, in the penthouse now shared with four strangers. Months in they remain as alien to him as the day they met. This despite him routinely probing their minds as a security check. They simply are not family. It also does not help, he admits, that Zenith has chosen to reside in the basement, with the generators, which she deems "the logical location" to store her load. He falls face first on his mattress and lay there sufficient to begin dreaming when the door rips off its hinges and Stefan grabs him by the collar.

"She's gone!" he shouts. "My baby's gone!"

The pair race downstairs to see Nia supine on the bedroom floor, her arms and legs squirming as she mumbles.

"Fire ... so much fire," she says. "In the brain ... melting ... too late ... I was ... forgive me ..."

William checks the weak beat of her heart and rapid pulse at her neck, notes her tight breaths, profuse sweat, pale skin, and dilated pupils. He guesses she has been in shock several minutes and bordering arrhythmia, too far gone to rekindle their telepathic link. He telekinetically forces her heart to pump at the proper pace, next controls her lungs. Finally, in a flash of ingenuity and might that he is too desperate to appreciate, he rips billions upon billions of electrons out of the air and with a flash of light jolts her central nervous system into rebooting.

"She'll be out for a while, but she should be fine," William says, watching her eyelids close.

"He took her!" Stefan shouts. "I can feel him. Jin took Sarah. He could be anywhere by now."

"Why would he do this?" William asks without looking up, still monitoring Nia's vitals.

"The dream."

"What dre–"

Zenith bursts her black and red box of a body up through the floor, wooden planks and iron pipes jutting in her wake.

"Force field! Now! Get offline! NOW!" she shouts in the feminine voice of her past self.

Jarred by her urgency, William complies by enveloping the condo in the strongest shield he can. The long nothing goads him into asking what's supposed to happen.

Then it does.

Screams everywhere buffet his mind, of the living watching the dying, and of those fearing death themselves. Screams like the ones in the helicopter plummeting past the bedroom window. Passengers of the suddenly pilotless vehicle begin interspersing their screams with prayers for a quick end, until they find the copter safely, softly touching ground. As William's aura dissipates from round the vehicle and the four survivors disembark, their thanks to a God they now believe to be very real turn to curses at His apparent sadism. All about them, slumped in hovercars, splayed on sidewalks, piled in stores, lay thousands of limp bodies. All with heartbeats and breaths and not a single thought, as faint trails of smoke rise from their ears. Similar scenes from other cities deluge William. Roads and homes and offices around the globe littered with inert bodies, victims of microchips hacked into bombs.

"I detected radiation from the surge," Zenith says as she plods toward William. Busted floorboards slip through the ugly hole in the room. Sturdier planks creak under the living robot. "Total cognitive absence. An ingenious innovation on the electromagnetic pulse. Overloading then erasing active NeuroNet chips can apparently do the same to human consciousness ... James is among the victims. The war has begun."

"Wha–what? I want to cry," William says, gawking out the window at rising smoke and ash from hundreds of crashed vehicles he did not save. "Why can't I cry?"

"Don't ask me a damn thing," Stefan says. The people's champion drops to his knees, rests his unconscious wife's head in his lap. "I'm trying not to lose my mind ... It may be too late."

31

So be it

"Ten cities! How did we let this happen?!" Magahara howls, shirtless in his black leather pants, while smacking a plank on the wall of the library. Books avalanche from each shelf up to thirty feet high and the same distance across. "Ten cities. Over 50 million people. It just started and it's shaping to be the worst war in history. What are we going to do?"

"We'll have to make do, won't we?" Sowen says, his gray robe parting as he steps over a pile of centuries old manuscripts. "And we'll have to do it quickly, I'm sure."

"Don't you be patronizing," Shakti says, flicking book dust off her white negligee. "I told you we should have killed him. Now look at this mess!"

"Oh shut up you silly bitch! ... I mean, quiet dear. I need a minute to think."

"Think about what?" she asks. "How your stupid little deal with Jin allowed this to happen? Fool, we didn't need The Way! However much it distracted the humans, it doesn't make up for this. They are coming and we are not ready."

"We can win, can't we?" Magahara asks. "We owe it to the world. It's our only chance for redemption. To justify the dead."

"Comatose," Sowen mumbles. "Maybe braindead by now."

"We have no choice," Magahara says. "We must win."

Sowen nods, unsure of whether to grin or wince. For the first time since this gambit unfolded, he feels guilty. Not the lingering, bearable guilt that comes from telling a lie. And not the stinging, short lived guilt that comes from taking advantage of the downtrodden. It is the kind of guilt his best friend and most trusted counsel has just conveyed, and it eats at him so thoroughly he reaches the precipice of giving in, of teleporting to the showroom and eviscerating himself on some ancient sword from one of his former lives. Until he looks down and notices one of the books Magahara toppled, which Sowen had written in a past life about a more past life as a wandering ascetic. *Strange*, he thinks, *how easy it is to forget the truth*.

"Then one good thing came of this," Sowen says. "Because we're going to need you on our side. As for letting 'Hikikomori' live, must I remind you both that he kept the humans so busy they haven't made a single move against us? And that while he knows how to kill all of us, we have no idea how to kill him? Or did you forget what happened with Stefan?"

"Could have teleported him into deep space ..." Shakti mutters. "Fine. What do we do?"

"Wonderful. Here's the plan ..."

• • •

Gray horizon expands before Oke as he skips rocks on the western bank of the Dead Sea. The pebbles form in his palm, morphing up from his skin. Their separation feels like pimples popping.

Even such trifles continue to amaze him. Those he knew as Sam and Ana—struggles to think of as Sowen and Shakti—have taught him so much so quickly. Like how to mimic through sheer memory every substance and power he has ever absorbed. Yet that neither explains how he produces them nor where they come from. Sowen guessed that both of their powers siphon off from some unseen dimension. But it was only that, a guess. The boy wonders what else the old man does not know.

Phase blinks in next to him and he fills with a whole different set of wonders. The woman in the black speedsuit folds the collar of his olive tracksuit. Ever since he could remember he has been popping his collar, and she has been folding it down. *Why?* And for that matter, he finally questions why she ever stole him from that meta orphanage in Jakarta, as though he were one of her bank heists. He has never asked her and he plans to keep it that way. Especially now that, being a true believer, she just might tell him the truth. Whatever the case, he chooses to believe that she has given him a good life, and he chooses not to blame its current course on her.

"I love you," she says after kissing his forehead.

"I know," he replies.

"Try not to worry. Mother will protect us."

"Who's gonna protect her?"

"You're scared. I would turn you, were you old enough. Have faith."

"Why should I be scared? I'm indestructible, I'm immune to Metapurge, and I'm under age. What are they gonna do, throw me in juvie? I won't be on the real battlefield. I can control the cyberclones from inside the palace."

"It's quite an honor, leading our first wave of defense," Phase says while stroking her fingers through his wavy black hair. "You've proven me wrong. All those hours with the videogames have gotten you more than fame and fortune. They're going to make you into a hero."

"I already was a hero!" his voice cracks. "We were heroes! Now we're ... I don't even know. Maybe this is the right side.

If so many people can love Stefan's evil ass brother, maybe people can't think for themselves."

"We did what we had to," his mother says with maddening serenity. "Know that I've always been proud of you. And I'm impressed that you're sober now. I would understand if you need some Bacchus. To relax."

"I quit for real this time," Oke says, turning his back to Phase. "On the jet, before the island ... I snorted in the bathroom. I was high when it went down. When we ... came here. Very high. Figured you should know that."

"Oh," she says, sounding almost shaken. "Thank you for your honesty." She says nothing for a long while. "I never meant to hurt you."

"I know," he says, looking over his shoulder to catch her gaze. He imagines smacking her.

"We should get back. I need to make one last check of the caverns before the minors enter. Harod and I will have our hands full coordinating the other teleporters and speedsters. Only a few hundred of us to watch over millions of caves and billions of youngsters."

Oke nods and throws his arms round her as he bursts into blubbering. She returns his embrace, not his tears. Horizon turns from gray to black as they vanish from the bank of the Dead Sea.

• • •

Ahmad grabs the pitcher of milk from his mother so she can better handle the plates teetering on her forearm. Kaatima lays them down on the dining table and takes a seat between her children, to Leena's delight. The 12 year old wastes no time delving into her spread of gravy soaked turkey slices, double stuffed sweet potatoes, asparagus spears, and biscuits. Her favorite. Kaatima and Faheem chug and refill their mugs, licking off their blood beards as they go. Ahmad eats last but once he starts shovels his plate clear. *It may be unclean*, he laments, *but pork is delicious*. Honey glazed sirloin chops with sides of pepper jack roasted avocado, shrimp egg salad, and banana nut bread simply cannot be denied. He lets out a satisfied belch after his second glass of milk, which elicits a broad smile from his mother.

"Thanks," she says when Ahmad wipes a red trail from her chin with his thumb. "I almost vomited when cooking that, so I'm glad you two enjoyed it so much."

"And I'm glad that you've been so practical lately about the pork," Faheem adds. "It'll make you strong. Although I know what would make you stronger."

"Swine is one thing. Blood is another," the young man replies. He shakes his head, noticing that the red trail on his mother's chin has become a blotch. "If the world's going to end, I'd like to do it with a clear mind."

"Maaaaaa!" Leena moans. "If the world's gonna end, can I have some? Pleeeeeaaaase? Just this once?"

"Now see what you've started?" their father asks. "No, baby. You know you're too young. Only seven years to go. Then you can have all the blood you want."

"Not if I have anything to say about it," Ahmad says.

"Get it out of your system while you can," Kaatima says. "Very soon you will have no choice. Our son won't be the only adult human. Imagine what people would think!"

"Do I detect fear? I thought you 'enlightened ones' only care what Shakti thinks."

"Exactly," she says. "Speaking of which, it's time."

And just like that, Ahmad accepts, the Bargouti family prepares to rend itself asunder. Regardless of his constant protestations, he is honest enough with himself to admit that their time under vampire rule has been comfortable, and that he would miss it, and that given the alternatives, he hopes they win. So what if his faith in Allah, in his very conception of right and wrong, has crumbled? All he wants is for his family to see another day. If that day comes with a large helping of pork chops, all the better. If it comes with a pint of blood, so be it.

The children clear the table before following their parents into the living room. Ahmad slings the two duffel bags on the floor over his shoulders. One for him, one for Leena. A week's supply of clothes and toiletries. According to Shakti, the war should not take even that long. Faheem leads them out to the lime green Ford, now with more than 400,000 miles on it. Mister al Maliki, their now muscled and sighted former landlord who once tried to eat him, waves to Ahmad and the others as they drive into the night. Leena peers at their building from the fast departing Ford. Ahmad realizes that it is the only home she has known and that he would give anything to keep it that way.

They roll along the wide highway for the better part of an hour, until traffic slows and vehicle after vehicle pulls off the road by one of the many entries to the nearest cavern. Their rocky tunnels open atop a lush valley that only three years ago was desert. On the lamplit curb, thousands of vampire parents kiss and hug their human children and exhort them to trust in their Mother. Faheem and Kaatima do likewise before placing the youth on a ballooning line toward the subterranean haven. Then the parents walk farther from the road, to where a long line of machine guns lay muzzle to trigger in the grass. Just past the weapons, purple mists swirl over what resemble holodiscs. The last Ahmad sees of his machine-gun-toting parents are the backs of their heads as they vanish through the mist. Thus friends and neighbors, former Muslims and Jews, march off as one to their new holy war.

META

• • •

Hikikomori dashes across the Mediterranean Sea and through Tel Aviv and into Jerusalem, undetected despite wearing a durium backpack more than half his size and shaped like and egg. He infiltrates the palace as he has infiltrated so many high places. By leaping firmly into the stratosphere—with a little box on his belt that shields him from radar and sonar and infrared—to pounce into a sequoia on the rooftop garden.

There he spies his reluctant, unholy allies enrapt in ménage a trios, crushing a flowerbed of daisies near the winding stream. The terrorist awaits their climax, toying with how easy it would be to kill them here. He decides to reveal himself once they have clothed. The Knight Wraith hooded in his emerald kimono and silvery bandages wrapping hands, wrists, feet, and shins. The Mother of the Night in her golden sari and red shawl. The king in no need of a nation in his blue pajama suit with yellow stars and moons.

The terrorist jumps down from the tree and utters the beginning of a syllable when Sowen locks him in an invisible chokehold and shoves him back into the air.

"This is getting old," Hikikomori points out.

"Indeed," Sowen replies. "New York. Washington. London. Brussels," he says, with each city slamming his prey face first into the smooth, waist high, granite rock Sowen so cherishes. "Mexico City. Bogota. Beijing. Tokyo. Jakarta. Sydney. What is the matter with you?! James was a friend! He wasn't on the list!"

Sowen drops Hikikomori to his knees and releases the telekinetic chokehold, allowing the intruder to whoop air. The immortal relents out of neither mercy nor exhaustion, but because the rock has been bashed to pieces. He who would be God re-forms his prized possession, down to the carvings of inverted Omegas cradling Deltas, the instant he takes heed of its destruction.

"Neither was Stefan," the terrorist gurgles. "I don't owe you anything. Besides, you were taking too long."

"Fool! Killing everyone is not the answer! People like their sad, pointless lives. Evolution cannot be stopped. We had a plan! The next meta wave is still years away. It doesn't matter that they're about to bomb us. It doesn't matter if Shakti turns every animal on this planet. Without the wave I won't have enough power! Timing was everything. Godhood might as well be a dream!"

"Funny you should mention dreams," Hikikomori says. He spits out a wad of blood, tries to stand, tumbles back to his knees. "I had one recently you might like."

"What the hell are you talking about?" Magahara asks.

The captive points to his backpack. Shakti rips it from his shoulders. She opens the hatch and recoils. Sae Rom and I sleep in the foam casing, cooing into oxygen masks connected to the padded tank between us.

"You're still a pathetic lunatic," Shakti says to Hikikomori as she takes us in her arms. "But you are resourceful."

32

To the fortress of the fallen angel

The first hundred missiles targeting the Red Nation fly out of China. The second hundred come from the United States. Not to be outdone, Europe follows with several hundred of its own, mostly from Britain and a vociferously reluctant Russia. No sooner than they enter enemy airspace do the lot of them get snatched from their trajectories, into a series of parallel loops resembling a cone, whose tip begins miles above the Jerusalem palace and whose mouth kisses the heavens. Naturally, the free world responds by unleashing its full arsenal. When those nukes too get sucked up, panic begins in earnest.

The two survivors of the Council of Continents and their three replacement colleagues settle on delegating into the lap of the United Nations whatever scrap of the human offensive can be coordinated.

Once reports hit of vampires on human soil, General Glenda Rodan directs cyberclones and robots, including mass produced versions five and six of Zenith, to serve as the main lines of defense. Like hundreds of millions of chess pieces, she strategically places them via the Net to stanch the burgeoning tide. Every able bodied meta, including empowered cyberclones, gets drafted into the counterstrike. Even prisons are cleared and all fugitives pardoned on condition of allegiance to humanity. All save two.

Manfred Peebles, a.k.a. Manny, is caught in Quebec, Toronto, Ottawa, Montreal, Vancouver, and several other Canadian cities in gangs of ten to twenty, hunched over at bar counters, laid out on park benches, and slouching on front stoops, drinking his selves into near lethal stupors while crying about "the greater good" and, whenever unwitting strangers spark up conversation, confessing to planting the electromagnetic bombs. He puts up no fight, letting Mounties cuff him and syringe him and walk him down the cities' streets. The original Manny even says "thank you" to the elderly Ottawan who shoots him in the gut with the pistol she pulls from her handbag. She curses him as he dies for slaughtering the royal family, and that dashing James Windsor. His last words, said to the woman as she too is arrested, are "never enough."

Emily Chagnon, a.k.a. Em, turns herself in to Parisian authorities. She had fled to her parents in Rio de Janeiro. They asked for their grandchild. That was all it took to destroy her. Shown the stupidity of her hypocrisy, she resolves to get one thing right and reveal all she knows. How Hikikomori bought the disparate bomb parts on the international black market. How he hacked separate designs for the bomb from government files in Moscow and D.C., then reconciled them and assembled the thing himself. How he had Manny duplicate ten of them. How he had Em teleport the Mannys to the ten cities, where 50 million were sacrificed to spur the end of capitalist corruption and environmental degradation through false representation, by goading humans into forcing the vampire surge. How the man she idolized repaid her loyalty by stealing their baby for reasons she cannot fathom. Em also submits to incarceration and depowering. Unlike Manny, her end comes at her own hand, or rather, by the bed sheet she strangles herself with on her first night in solitary confinement.

So those two diehards miss the swarms of aircraft blackening the skies en route to the enemy. And they miss the universal mourning at the terror they have wrought. And they, like most everyone else, miss the promise made between the two diehards who will do their damndest to stand as beacons of light in the encroaching darkness, while trying not to lose their souls in the process.

• • •

"Wish we could have waited for dawn," Stefan says on the jet to Jerusalem. "Would make the invasion easier."

"Your brother kind of forced our hand," William says.

"I don't know if I can kill them. Something changed between us in that dream. I can't deny how I feel about them anymore. Sam's like a father to me. Ana's the only woman I've ever truly wanted. And Jin's still my goddamn brother. They've betrayed us on all fronts. Stolen my child, started the apocalypse, killed James and Cornelio and so many millions of others. But here I am thinking about how much I love them. Ahh, I'm afraid the world's going to Hell and it's all my fault."

"... Listen, we've been best friends for over a decade now. I don't say it enough, but I believe in you. And just to make sure you don't screw up, I'll have your back the entire way. So we'll get your daughter, we'll save the world, and then we'll laugh about it. Okay?"

"How can you be so sure?"

"Hey, I wouldn't be a good doctor if I couldn't handle a little pressure. Besides, tears are for wusses."

"Don't know why this just came to me," Stefan says after a few moments. "But I haven't felt this nervous since I had to recite poetry, back at Taedo ... I'll never get it ... Can't help feeling bad for Sam. I think he's as lost as I am ... ha ... he's lost in his own paradise."

"Can't tell what's more shocking. Your warped sense of compassion, or that you're making such awful puns at a time like this. Well stay the course, hero, because we're about to bring Hell to the fortress of the fallen angel."

"My friend the poet. You missed your calling."

"No. This is my calling," William says. "Being here with you. And I'm honored by it."

"Ditto ... So you two are done for good?" Stefan asks while glancing at Zenith. She sits on the titanium floor at the other end of the spartan military plane, wedged between parachutes, firearms, and two rows of benches. Each bench supports a dozen other top level metas from Haine International's Executive Warriors Elite.

"Apparently. She says this is her last body, whatever that means. And look at her. Faye's right. She's a machine. We barely speak. I'll miss her, but in a way I'm relieved."

"However much of a machine she is, she was still human enough to look out for us when it mattered ... I'm going to need you to do the same for me ... Take care of my family if I don't make it home."

"Oh I'm sure you'll be alright," William replies with a weak smile. "If transmutation can't kill you, what can?"

"Promise," Stefan says, gripping Simmer's hilt.

"I promise. Now don't go getting any ideas. You know that's not your strong suit."

• • •

Planes and submarines penetrate vampire territory, a feat miraculous not only for the lack of Sowen's perpetual electromagnetic force field but also for the lack of enemy craft. The reason becomes plain when human vehicles fire their first missiles. A fraction reach their targeted bridges and blood storage towers. The vast majority rebound back to their sources thanks to thousands of telekinetic, meta vampires. Two such missiles would have destroyed the EWE jet had William not been protecting it.

The explosions push enough turbulence through his force field that Stefan orders the gunner to cease fire and his EWE platoon to jump ship. The only survivors of "Meta Force 2.0"—Bennu, the Egyptian warrior woman, and Luka, the old Russian healer—leap first while shouting of retribution for their comrades who fell in the Brussels holocaust. Stefan, William, and Zenith go last. Every meta—including the pilot and gunner—descends at dusk upon the Jerusalem palace, leaving the plane to crash into a hill and skid onto a street and finally explode after grinding to a stop inside an empty grade school.

None of the metas actually touch the ziggurat. Instead they graze an invisible force field emanating a yard from the garden floor and building walls before these invaders teleport to the ends of the empire.

"Where are we?" Stefan asks via the Net while standing chest deep in muddy water littered with tall grass and hippopotami.

"You are in the Okavango Delta of Botswana," Zenith says while using her GPS tracker. "William is in a village outside Hyderabad, India. I am in the Bechar province of the Algerian forest. Bennu and Luka are within the northeast and southwest borders of Iran, respectively. Should I continue?"

"We get the picture," William says, eyeing hundreds of residents clad in plain clothes. They swarm toward him from their tidy bungalows. "Send an alert about the palace. And now the fun begins, huh? Keep in touch."

Men and women young and old come at him bare fisted and fangs bared. He levitates a stadium's length up. They look like ants. The entire village bleeds bodies, tens of thousands, all to turn or kill him. Then several hundred vampires levitate in pursuit. William tries and fails to establish a telepathic link with the first to reach him, a gray haired woman who claws her long fingernails at his chin. Seconds later hundreds of other airborne villagers mob his face, arms, legs, and torso, pushing past one another to get him, their bloodshot eyes bulging and salivating mouths hissing with a savagery that makes his lips curl in awed disgust. Yet William feels their Mother watching, and he feels shame to have called her friend. Seeing no point in attacking her slaves, he expands an invisible bubble to give himself space before flying in the direction his NeuroNet compass assures is northwest. William maintains top speed to reach the Arabian Peninsula shy of a half hour.

It is not fatigue that bids him touch ground, though that is ample. It is miles upon miles of busted human airplanes and toppling vampire homes, millions of terrified meta invaders being bitten by natives and perforated by cyberclone bullets under the half moon. Once on land he sees that despite their topical solutions and unwavering dedication, vampires indeed smoke and flame when hit with the humans' solar radiation guns. Eventually he also sees that the cyberclones' bullets are not killing humans but turning them. He understands after several fire at him. William telekinetically catches and dissembles shells to find that hard plastic encases infected blood samples, which explode upon impact. Amid screams of allies and pleas from the more religious to be killed rather than damned, he kisses goodbye to his oath and lays waste to any body with a mind he cannot penetrate. Vampires and cyberclones fall by the thousands as their hearts explode.

William repeats the onslaught wherever he finds humans dying and vampires sprouting. The serene confidence he rams into the minds of millions of his human allies deepens his disgust. He compounds that illusion by casting each vampire and cyberclone as whatever each human finds easiest prey. Flowers. Balloons. Bullseyes. Cartoon ducks. They slay their fantasies. The moon rises high as he wars. He eats rations off his fallen comrades, and his mind's ear hears cries of children huddled in caverns under ravaged earth. The doctor prays that this is not the truth of life. *If it is*, he fears, *Stefan's brother is totally in the right.*

His best friend's strife is much less philosophical. The Botswana delta, quiet compared with central India, offers little opposition to Stefan's hypersonic advance. Not so for the area once called the Democratic Republic of Congo, whose fourteen biotech factories comprise the meta cloning hub of the Red Nation. Although he dukes it out with many shape shifters and energy projectors and brutes, speedsters and teleporters and speedy teleporters give him the most trouble by far. After all, for Stefan a slow behemoth makes a sturdy punching bag, but those who can keep up tend to eat up time, something the people's champion cannot spare.

Or doesn't want to, but finds himself doing to save his fellow humans when they happen to cower at his feet, which seems to occur every other mile. They call his name, fans of the show or else perpetrators he had hauled in for anything from vigilantism to thievery. In those instances he runs across extreme offenders, such as the pyrokinetic child rapist, he hesitates long enough for them to be turned, then slaughters them himself. Stefan has killed before, rarely and reluctantly. Not so in the pandemonium of black Africa. Here no small part of him loves it.

He punts the head of a self detonating woman into the horizon, exploding her body, leaving a charred crater in its wake, only for the body to re-form there out of ether and bleed from its decapitation. He punches the lungs and ribs out of a sonic screaming man, causing the vampire to wheeze to death, not to mention the hearing out of most others within a 300 yard radius. He slices Simmer through the beak and wings of a huge griffin with a parrot's skull and a jaguar's legs. And, once he gets his hands on them long enough for them to stop hauling him up and down the continent, he chucks many a speedster and teleporter into orbit. All without breaking a sweat, without compunction. These are mere diversions to the main event, wherein he makes everything right at the cost of everything he holds dear. *Fair trade*, he tries to believe. *One little obstacle. Figuring out how to do it.*

Zenith, meanwhile, realizes her digital dream as she soars east over the verdant Sahara plains back toward the Jerusalem palace. Using her telescopic optical receptors to analyze vampire battle strategy, the living robot learns that the enemy moves in unison, no doubt by sharing their individual sensory information with Shakti, who instantly directs them via hive mind. Next Zenith hacks into orbiting spy satellites to assess resistance outside the Red Nation, and concludes that the same behavior applies to the vampire invaders. Humans are bereft of such cohesion.

Panicked civilians lock themselves indoors, relying on domestic servants, be they cyberclone or robot, to guard them while military drones prowl the streets. Communication is poor, organization worse. Machines not programmed to differentiate between vampires and humans obey their masters by attacking strangers. Often that means pummeling manic humans who bang down neighbors' doors, or stabbing with kitchen knives damaged cyberclones that stumble in wildly after their masters have been turned. Zenith calculates that humanity will die before sunrise. Unless she executes the prime directive of her next stage of being. Digital evolution.

It takes minutes to upload the software that has taken her years to complete. *Software*, she almost laughs, *inspired by the narcotic high of a child*. Once it activates, humans and vampires alike take notice. The problem with artificial intelligence had always been that it lacked consciousness for independent judgment. Despite the ubiquitous, meticulous biographies of the "Meta Force" roster, much of the public thinks she is the exception to that rule, when in fact she is the opposite. A human mind that became code in a machine. But, as it turns out, that was exactly the key to the quantum leap. That and assimilating the enemy's success.

She had steadily improved the program simulating free will and personality by copying the code of her own consciousness, but without her memories, as cybers roaming her virtual reality NetNexus. Hikikomori's cyber holocaust provided the final inspiration. True sensation, she realized, is the key to birthing true selves. Like any new operating system, self simply needed to be uploaded. With something very akin to maternal pride, Zenith injects her software into the central processing units of the planet's every robot, cyberclone, and functional NeuroNet chip lodged in a comatose human. Each unit of hardware automatically fills the void with its own data files. Granted, some of the robots, including the mass produced regiments of Zeniths versions five and six, are temporarily baffled by this strange perception of free will. And granted, some of the cyberclones are overwhelmed by the emotions that their hormone flooded human tissues had been storing for them. And granted, virtually all of the once-humans wrestle with the knowledge that their digital births have deleted the former selves of their new bodies. But by and large her 700 million new children awaken to their new lives rather smoothly.

A third of them reside in the Red Nation, and unbeknown to Zenith until reprogramming, were controlled by Oke, her very inspiration. She does equip them with certain useful instincts. Such as aversion to vampires, affinity for humans, and universal information sharing among digital minds. The latter proves a challenge for her as well. Finally she gleans what it might be for Shakti, a self infused with awareness of so many other selves. Yet even with this vast improvement, the tide does not turn. It merely slows. *Conclusion: The source of the vampire virus must be deleted.*

Zenith enters Jerusalem under cover of darkness, when the enemy's might waxes strongest. She activates her sonar and X-ray sensors scant miles from the palace, in hopes of finding a way around its force field. In the process her vampire-bred cyberclone children inform her of the caverns, for many such machines oversee the human progeny of the Red Nation. So Zenith, abiding some relic of her subconscious, lands outside a cavern door guarded by an old friend.

"You shouldn't have come here," Phase says as she makes herself visible. She stands amid tall grass, beside the durium door of the tunnel that leads to the caverns. "We can't let you harm the young ones."

"That is not my intent," Zenith says, lumbering her bulky, black and red durium legs along the green plain. "I came here for you. Your death will be less merciful if it comes from a stranger."

"Were I still human, I would have had a pithy comeback for that," Phase says. She places herself between Zenith and the door. "Harod."

Her lover zooms in from the deep of the plains and charges Zenith from behind. His fist breaks in eleven places and his skull fractures after he caroms from her red, durium back plate to the jagged edge of a rock on the ground. Zenith rotates her head 180 degrees on its axis and shoots a laser beam from her yellow visor. The bolt pierces his chest and heart. His black skin melts and his bones ash and in a matter of seconds Harod is no more.

"The situation has changed," Zenith says.

"I see," Phase replies. She steps forward while fixing on thin tendrils of smoke lofting from the rock on the ground. "I will miss him. Mother truly watches over us. But not you."

She blinks away from the door and jumps to put her quasi-tangible foot through Zenith's visor, only to be hit with what feels like the bioshock she herself had intended to deliver. Phase spasms on the grass, visible and solid, struggling not to swallow her tongue.

"I upgraded," Zenith says before lowering an arm and locking its massive pincer round Phase's neck.

The living robot raises her former ally such that the woman's feet dangle wildly. Zenith is not so far gone that she ignores how the white speedsuit clings to Phase's firm contours, how her thick brown hair shines in the moonlight. However, she is far enough gone that she takes joy in the knowledge of what follows.

"Why didn't we ever get along?" Faye gasps as she tugs at the immobile pincer.

"We were jealous of each other," Becca says. "Biology is unbecoming like that."

"Take care of him," Faye asks. "It wasn't his fault. He's just a kid."

"He is much more than that," Becca replies. "And he can take care of himself."

"Goodbye, machine."

Zenith closes her pincer and opens her visor and flies off for the palace, once the laser has burned away the last of her humanity.

33

So many friends

The Jerusalem palace stretches five blocks on each side at the ground and five miles high, standing at the edge of the Kidron Valley. Calm emanates from the immaculate ziggurat. Moonlight cascades down marble walls, at every mile shines off gold spires rising from jeweled domes that sit on each corner of successively narrower tiers. Save the unnatural greenery of its garden top, which lacks any such adornment. This fortress rests untouched and unoccupied as far as the eye can see. Its surrounding streets tell a different tale.

War rages without a baseline in sight. Vampires and meta vampires mash against robots, cyberclones, meta cyberclones, and free willed metas in darkness perforated by moonlight reflected off the ziggurat, and by flashes of bombs and lasers and biological combustion of combatants whose powers sputter in the mess.

Zenith lands first, between two of her previous models. The nude, glabrous, soft coat of silvery blue flesh that was her version five and the silvery purple shell with the muzzlelike mesh for mouth and ears that was her version six. They greet her as Mother then run along with finger lasers firing. William lands beside his former lover minutes after she messages him her location. He looks tired and hungry, but physically intact. They talk strategy, even while roasting and bursting bloodsucking interlopers, until Stefan arrives.

"What took you so long?" William asks after his friend slams to a stop from hyper speed.

"Africa's screwed," Stefan says. He glances over his shoulder at flung vampires and robots he parted like water.

"See? Cheer up," William replies. "Things are returning to normal already."

"I've found a way in," Zenith says. "My sensors show the force field surrounds the palace and its foundation. The power source is technological, too massive to be contained onsite. I've used radar to spot four large conduits under the foundation. They lead to subterranean solar energy plants on the outskirts of the city. Those plants are contained in caverns filled with baseline children. Caverns that rely on those plants for light, ventilation, and refrigeration. We cannot destroy the plants without sacrificing the children. They are the only safe humans. It would be illogical to jeopardize them. Furthermore, the conduits are coated with self repairing durium nanites. They have been programmed to hack hacks. I can override them for 28.371 seconds. We can, however, burrow from here to the palace conduits and disconnect them long enough to enter. After that, we will be alone."

"Nothing terrifying about that," William says. "Becca, you may not get this, but damn it I love you."

"Es bueno. Como debe ser," Stefan mumbles to himself. "Will, if you please, let's get this party started."

"One for all, and all ... ah screw it," William says.

He rubs his palms together and opens them wide. Earth mimics his gesture. Pavement ruptures, giving way to dirt and rock that vortex into a tunnel. William carries them along in a telekinetic bubble, which slants down steeply toward the palace, then several hundred yards in slants up just as steeply. Zenith, who had been lighting the path with her visor as she guided William, bids him stop at the first sight of conduit. The living robot arrests the nanites. One second later Stefan slices his durium katana through the five-foot-wide tube, freeing electrical wires to sparkle and dance while the force field weakens. Twenty seconds after that Zenith has guided William around to the three remaining corners under the ziggurat, Stefan cutting Simmer through the conduits as they go. It takes William all of five seconds to drill up through the yards of concrete foundation and deposit them inside, along with tons of rubble. Just enough time to catch a breath as the nanites reawaken and the force field returns.

They find themselves in a torchlit great hall at the bottom of the palace, confronting the experiments. At the center of the far wall, three huge diamond caryatids of Shakti support a railed balcony that rests half way to the ceiling. Werewolves salivate on that ledge. In the middle of a side wall, three gold telamons of Sowen hold a balcony packed with bipedal hydras, each one hissing from its six serpentine heads. On the wall opposite that, three alabaster telamons of Magahara support a final balcony all but overflowing with very human looking, naked babies.

The babies still transfix Stefan and William when the werewolves and hydras leap at the trio. William throws an invisible shield round the babies' balcony while Zenith unleashes lasers from her visor and rockets from her forearms. The hall soon reeks like the worst forms of barbecue. Stefan puts fist, boot, and sword through dozens of other mutates within the lapse of a breath such that the enemies dismember and collapse in near unison. The carpet, seconds ago graced with arabesque rainbow swirls, now resembles a slaughterhouse floor for dogs and snakes.

Curiosity overtakes William. He scans the babies. They do indeed think like babies. He levitates to the balcony. That's when they pounce on top of one another, melding and growing into one infantile colossus whose bulbous head bumps the ceiling. The horror of it induces William to unthinkingly drop the shield he had erected round the balcony. The big baby emits a ferocious shriek as it tries to bite off the mentalist's head.

"That's just wrong," Stefan whispers as William flies toward the center of the hall and out of the baby's monstrous, slobbering reach.

The thing loses its balance while swatting at its prey and tumbles over the balcony, flopping onto the slippery disembowelments of the carpet. Even sitting, it is almost quadruple Zenith's height. And it goes berserk once it feels the gooey death on its rump.

Moving faster than they all anticipate, it snatches Zenith off the ground and repeatedly smashes her back down like a rag doll. The living robot blasts the baby in the face with her visor laser, which does little but make it madder. Zenith finds her head inside the saliva pool that is the creature's mouth and her body tugged relentlessly by its chubby paws. William telekinetically pries the baby's gums and fingers apart, allowing a soaked Zenith to drop onto the thing's soft gut before taking flight herself.

Stefan contemplates tactics. Sword to the eyes, blitzkrieg of body blows, deafening thunderclap with his palms. But he can't bring himself to beat up a baby. Even when that baby wobbles to its feet and tears its arms through a wall of the great hall, dislodging stone slabs and triggering cracks that cause the ceiling to cave in on top of the people's champion. Ultimately William quells the tantrum by delivering a sleep bomb that lays their foe out. When Stefan climbs from the rubble he can only shake his head at the snoring behemoth, which blissfully sucks a body sized thumb.

Stefan jumps up past the fallen ceiling and breaks through the one a level above that, with Zenith and William flying after him. They purge the baby from their thoughts, although the men have far different reasons than the robot.

Each level of ascent brings some giant, hideous mutation. Moths and spiders that buzz and scratch and cough poison mucus. Squid and octopi that fling sticky tentacles and acid ink. Vegetation that swing durium thorns and spit explosive fruit. Glowing balls that buffet rooms with fire and ice and wind and water. Until, hours later and miles up, they reach the level just under the garden. The one with the library and the sleeping chambers. The one that looks like a home. Photographs of Sowen and Shakti, from when they went by Samuel Haine and Ana Shaktira, adorn the walls of the corridors. As do photos of Stefan and William, from when it was only the two of them. And of Zenith, from when she was a gorgeous blond android. And of Oke and Phase, from when they were part of the team. Even paintings of Magahara, from when he was Shakti's consort, always hooded in his emerald kimono.

They lose themselves in reminiscing until they stumble upon Oke's chambers. They know this because the door bears a yellow sign with a biohazard symbol that reads "Oh's Pad." William turns the knob and steps inside. They find the boy slouched on a beige couch, gazing at six long lines of red dust atop the glass coffee table in front of him. He wears naught but boxers and socks.

"Where's my mom?" he asks without looking at them.

"Kid, you have to get out of here," William replies.

"Where's my mom?" he repeats.

"Come back with us," Stefan says. "We promise, you won't get in trouble. We'll find a way. It'll be okay."

"Where ... is ... my ... mom?!" he shouts while kicking over the table and standing to face them.

"Dead," Zenith says. "I made it painless."

"Goddamn, Becca," William whispers.

"I knew it!" Oke wails while snapping his fingers thrice, duplicating himself each time. "First you stole my game, now you steal my mother?! You should have helped her. Should have been a friend."

"You misunderstand," Zenith says. "I did help her. Take us to Shakti so we can help the others."

"Oh I'm taking your metal ass down. Same goes for you two secret lovers, if you get in the way."

"That is so not funny," Stefan mumbles as he watches the three tan duplicates of Oke morph into ashen doppelgangers of Zenith, William, and himself. They step menacingly toward their originals while the boy levitates the true living robot.

"Sam has taught me so much. Since the island, I've learned how to be anything I want, whenever I want. Hell, I could be him and Ana at the same time. It's all up here," Oke says, tapping his temple. "I'll even learn how to bring my mom back. But right now I'll settle for this."

Oke closes a fist and shakes it violently. On cue, Zenith's red and black durium frame begins to flame, then char, then dissipate in an acrid, smoky cloud. William screams for Becca and hurls a telekinetic blast at Oke that knocks the half naked boy across the room, but does not stop Zenith's gradual disintegration. Stefan dashes toward Oke, his only plan to smack the boy around, but his own doppelganger cuts in and engages the original in a hypersonic duel that from the first blocked kick is maddeningly symmetrical. William tries to seize Oke's mind through illusions and sleep bombs and mind control, but wrist rockets and invisible blows from the doppelgangers of Zenith and himself keep him far too busy.

The fights rage through walls and rooms across the entire level. Rockets and lasers and telekinesis shoot astray through floors below such that chunks of marble and gold spire and jeweled dome plummet onto those warring in the streets. Through it all, Zenith offers no resistance. Then William's virtual reality Net browser opens unbidden to his park garden of roses and tulips, where his former lover stands nude in her human form and bids him goodbye. When the doppelgangers vanish, he and Stefan return to Oke's den knowing what awaits. There they find smoking ash below where Zenith once floated. The boy tosses them a wavering glare before he alone walks out of the window and into the night sky, leaving them to mourn the loss of so many friends.

After long wallowing in the destruction there, they wander in silence, two grown men holding back tears and despair, the former more successfully than the latter, as they search for an ascending path. More than thirty minutes pass. Stefan gives up in some random room and tries to jump through the ceiling, only to smack back down. Dislodged tile reveals durium instead of concrete. William unleashes three years' worth of frustration on the ceiling, or rather the atomic bonds that hold the ceiling in place. At first electron by electron, next atom by atom, next millimeter by millimeter, next inch by inch, he breaks the durium apart. By the time he has produced a circular opening nearly three feet in diameter and five feet thick, he feels as though his head and heart are fit to burst. Yet he prepares to levitate up and squeeze through when a voice calls to them.

"Not yet," Magahara says. He stands at the doorway. His eyes lay shadowed in the hood of his emerald kimono, his hands and feet hide in silvery bandages. "Not yet," he repeats, walking toward the pair.

They remember him from the Ataraxia Bar & Grille. Especially Stefan, who recalls that intrusion into his psyche as the day his life entered a kaleidoscope of betrayal. He unsheathes Simmer from his back and chops it at his ancestor's nose.

Magahara catches the blade between his fingers, flips it out of Stefan's grasp and smacks him with its hilt, then drops the toy. William, winded from the battle with the ceiling but still irate over the battle with Oke, rips metal and stone from the floor and walls to encase Magahara in a twelve-foot-thick sphere of debris, which the mentalist shoves miles down to the ground.

"Your family is so dysfunctional," William says.

"But here we are stopping by uninvited."

The people's champion half wriggles through the ceiling when the Knight Wraith claws up through the hole in the floor in a blur that defies time. William feels nothing before passing out in a heap. Not the heel to his throat, nor the knuckles to his stomach, nor the elbow to his sternum, nor the knee to his groin. Stefan's head pokes through the garden for a moment, until a vise grip numbs his calves and slams him to the floor. Magahara steps on his chest as Stefan stretches along the carpet for Simmer. Stefan fingers the katana into his palm and swings it at his enemy, who dodges the blade and grabs him by the jaw.

"Not! Yet!" the Knight Wraith growls.

Magahara chucks Stefan through the air, letting him bash through four brick walls. Humanity's last chance falls onto a balcony exposed to a hell of rain, wind, hail and lightning. He looks up to study the storm. Stefan finds his brother leaning against the balustrade.

34

Let's rock

"Ready to apologize?" Hikikomori asks. He looks down at his brother as he pushes off the balustrade, his rain soaked gray sweater and jeans momentarily aglow from lightning overhead.

"Where's Sarah? Where's my daughter?" Stefan wheezes, his back and ribs still aching from the pressure of Magahara's foot, and lingering under his brother's sway.

"Answer mine, I'll answer yours."

"Apologize for what, Jin?"

"You know damn well for what," Hikikomori says while bending to offer Stefan a hand up off the balcony floor. To their mutual surprise, it is accepted. "For stealing my girlfriend. And for calling me 'Hickey.' That hurt my feelings."

"Bad joke," Stefan says, guarding his chest with his father's sword. "We haven't spent much time together in the last two decades, but I know you better than that. You don't feel anything."

"That's the problem. You never knew me. Even though I always tried to show you. I am serious."

"Oh you showed me, alright, you mass murdering puto. Where's Sarah?!"

"Upstairs with her big cousin," Hikikomori says, smirking triumphantly. "They're cute. That surprised me."

Stefan raises Simmer toward his brother's throat. In a flash Hikikomori flips his daggers from the straps on his thighs and pricks them into Stefan's flanks.

"Jin, I admit I was never the best brother. I didn't want to deal with losing my dad, so I wasn't there for you losing yours. Only you know what it was like to find their bodies. Maybe that's what pushed you over the edge. Maybe that's what made me weak enough to let you go. But this has to end. Here and now."

"Apology accepted," Hikikomori says. He sheathes his tantos and steps around Simmer to hug his brother about the neck, easing their foreheads together. "You're my best friend. You're selfish and weak willed, but I envy that. It's such a burden for me, saving the world. My dedication has slipped so many times. But now, with Hell rising, and the means just upstairs, I'll have it. I'd ask you to join me, but that's unrealistic. Before we start, let me say it. Stefan, I love you. Now I'm ready."

The people's champion breaks away to spin round, arms flinging over head and teeth gnashing.

"I hate you," he says. "Why did you have to go and be human? That makes this so difficult. Such an inconsiderate pendejo! ... Come on, Hickey. Let's rock."

Stefan steadies his durium katana, Hikikomori crosses his two durium tantos. A thunderclap acts as nature's signal. Daggers miss Stefan's eyes just as Simmer misses Hikikomori's heart. Blades clash high then low. Sparks fly near their ears, waists, knees. Each thrust gets blocked or ducked or leapt over. Until the terrorist connects a headbutt to the sternum, follows up with a rear chokehold such that rain blinds Stefan while Hikikomori drags him toward the balustrade and over its edge. Stefan twirls midair as they fall a mile onto the lower deck, giving his brother the brunt of the stone slabs. Hikikomori's wince indicates their powers have all but faded.

"What's the matter, Hickey?" Stefan asks. He stands and kicks his brother in the jaw. "Can't handle a fair fight?"

"No such thing," Hikikomori says before flipping off his back.

Hands to the floor, he rams both heels into his enemy's kneecaps. Stefan's left one buckles and snaps. He cries out, staggering backward as his brother rises, fearing death for the first time in his life. Stefan turns and crawls away as fast as he can, which is not that fast at all with his left knee avoiding the floor and his right foot slipping in the downpour. The stone is warm and wet and littered with debris from his earlier battles up the ziggurat. His free palm runs afoul of shattered glass and the torn wing of a ridiculously large bat. In the other palm, he joggles Simmer at his brother. Hikikomori catches up by the time Stefan reaches the corner of the deck.

He embeds one dagger into the downed man's shoulder, the other dagger into the thigh above his functional kneecap. Then Hikikomori hauls his brother to his feet and shoves him along the new turn of the deck. Stefan falls onto a smattering of fragmented brick. He lobs a baseball sized chunk, clipping his foe on the chin, then a softball sized one, bashing him squarely on the forehead. Dazed, Hikikomori loses his footing on errant shards of wet glass and topples over the balustrade.

Stefan steels himself before removing the daggers. He inhales and frees them—along with a spine tingling shriek. Once he hobbles to peer over the edge, however, he realizes that the next deck is too far down to see through night, debris filled gale, and torrential rain. He chucks the daggers as far away from the ziggurat as possible and watches them spin into darkness. No sooner than he steps back does he feel his powers returning. Stefan takes shelter in a ruined lounge, his knee and knife wounds healing, his gait steadying.

Were it not for those chopped up but still writhing jungle vines pocked with cyanide and eyeballs, the lounge would be an ideal place to recuperate, what with its plush sofas and spinning fans. *We showed those plants what's what*, he muses with ample pride.

He sits long and long, until he feels the knot in his gut and he braces for his brother ... who does not appear. He rambles from room to wrecked room, expecting an attack at any moment. With his partially restored hearing he makes out human curses and vampire exhortations miles below. He wonders how the others followed them in through the tunnel. Then he wonders where Becca really went. Eventually he remembers that he has exes to kill and takes the stairs back to the room with the hole in the ceiling. Strange, he thinks, that the hole has been sealed and that William is gone yet has not called. That instant, Stefan envisions Nia bitten during a vampire surge on the Berlaymont. He cannot call it truth, but knows that he feels utterly alone.

Until his brother stabs him in the back with a tanto. Hikikomori brings the other dagger into Stefan's kidney, then frees both blades and slides them back into their thigh straps. Stefan curses himself for a fool about the daggers as he slumps to a knee, the formerly broken one. Just as he had healed so must his brother, who by then could easily see miles in total darkness and jump like lightning for his weapons, not to mention race back to the palace before Stefan even sat down in the lounge. Enraged at his own stupidity, Stefan punches Hikikomori in the stomach so hard the terrorist expels all his air while doubling over to land on his face. Boiling at his brother's guile, Stefan crashes an elbow down on the back of Hikikomori's neck. The people's champion endures a stretch of bloody coughs while his brother lay there. He wipes his mouth and rolls the limp man over.

Hikikomori opens his eyes and locks one hand about Stefan's groin. He squeezes as though crushing grapes. This brings Stefan to the floor with a squeal that sounds a lot like "fag ..." At this stage their duel descends into something unbefitting warriors deciding the fate of the world. Hair pulls, wet Willies, wedgies, nipple cripples, Indian burns, noogies, and pantsings occur on both sides. A laugh or two might even slip out. Stefan restores the veneer of propriety with a headlock, albeit one that Hikikomori deftly slips out of and turns into a rear body slam that ends with Stefan splayed on his back. He looks up at Hikikomori's shin, which crashes down on his throat. Next he thing he knows, two tantos hover above his face.

"I always was better," Hikikomori says. Then he says nothing for a long while, sitting there peering into his brother's eyes, until thunder jars him. "Remember how happy we were when we got these things?"

"Si, mi hermano," Stefan wheezes. "It was a good birthday. Their last gift to us." Stefan whimpers an instant before Simmer pokes through the front of Hikikomori's sweater. "Mine to you."

The people's champion crawls from under his dying brother. Hikikomori flops onto his chest as he bleeds out with eyes open. Stefan reclaims his father's sword, looking away as he dislodges it from the terrorist's heart, and sheaths it at his hip. He stands there for what feels an eternity waiting for his brother to stop breathing, all the while recalling their every cherished moment together. Finally he limps away, bawling and indifferent to the searing wounds at his back and side, fully aware that Jin just saved his life.

With the ceiling hole shut and Hikikomori's motionless body there, Stefan slinks off in search of that theoretical staircase to the rooftop garden. Much later, on what he guesses is the far side of the floor, he opens a door at the end of an undecorated corridor. He does indeed find stairs ascending. And descending them, the hooded man in the emerald kimono. Stefan grimaces at an ache in his side, a warning that he has yet to heal, and contemplates fleeing. Until he guesses his powers would only weaken were he to retread his path.

"You've accepted your lot," the Knight Wraith says. "I don't know what it's like to kill a brother. Although I have killed my share of children. Separating from family can be difficult like that."

"I don't want to fight you," Stefan says. "I have two more relatives to snuff. Would rather not add a fourth."

"Bravado is the only thing keeping you going now," Magahara says. "You'll need more than that if you plan to resist her. The war is over. Listen. No more cries. No more raging humans. Only blissful, peaceful vampires."

"Impossible. It's barely been a day. All the estimates figured it would take at least a week ...! And the machines. The robots and cyberclones—"

"Surrendered once they had nobody to protect. Your friend may have given them lives and minds of their own, but they're too damn rational. Unlike humans. So many rioting, raping thieves. So many begging to be turned vampire after being attacked by their own."

"So ... so what am I supposed to do?" Stefan asks.

"The only thing any of us can do. What feels right. As for myself, what feels right is to let you pass."

"Why? I don't get you. First you warn me about them, then you join them."

"What can I say?" Magahara asks with a shrug. "I thought I could hold them in check. We see how that turned out ... They're my friends. They mean well. And I don't know that they're wrong."

"What will you do now?"

"Oh, I think I'll take a walk."

He does just that, down the stairs and out the door, freeing the way to the roof. Stefan watches him go, then heads up to the light.

• • •

Magahara does what Stefan thought better of, tracing his descendant's steps back to Hikikomori. It would have been simple even without the steady trail of crimson dots. Both brothers reek of a floral scent that he alternately craves and hates, depending on his mood. Right now he craves it. *Lucky me*, he thinks. Perhaps that explains his benevolence. Or perhaps this is merely one of his many vacillations.

That would be par for the course of his life, as Shakti so loves to argue. The young man who grew bored with his dual birthright as feudal noble and divine warrior. The fearsome Rakshasa who grew to disdain his honored role as first consort to the Mother of the Night and father of two vampire-born humans. The inscrutable loner who wandered from society to society, one era a scholar, the next a thief, the next a soldier, next a gigolo, next a beggar. The reluctant friend who cannot decide on which side to stand of his fellow, megalomaniacal immortals.

On the one hand, he muses, *there is peace, bliss, and equality. On the other, there is universal slavery. On the one hand, there is a madman ready to risk the lives of every living thing in search of God knows what. On the other, so what?*

The questions echo in his conscience as he stands over Hikikomori. Chest down, eyes open, breathless. He who would destroy it all now seems no different than any of the billions of other casualties of this latest notch in the infinite string of self inflicted misery.

Magahara levitates his progeny off the floor and sinks his fangs into the other man's jugular. He steps away from Hikikomori as the transformation takes hold. The floating man coughs and moans as new life and craving flood his veins. The Knight Wraith turns to face the terrorist, who touches ground on hands and knees while quivering in ecstatic awe at the precipice of his worst nightmare.

"Why?" Hikikomori asks, gazing up at the androgynous figure hidden by hood and bandage. "I was free. Free!"

"Where we are going, the freedom you seek appears inevitable. But it will be hard earned. Come now."

"You are a strange one," Hikikomori says while standing. "Could it be that you hate yourself more than any of us?"

"Sad deluded child," Magahara says as he leads the way to redemption. "At this moment, I feel like a stranger to anyone save you."

35

Being

Gray stairs give way to streaks of green and brown. This refines into dense rows of leafy trees towering above trim grass and chromatic waves of flowers. They flourish under a drizzle from the paling blue sky of dawn. Far off, trickling water can be heard along with the murmurs of pristine creatures.

Or so Stefan fancies as he strolls about. There is no rush, he rationalizes, there being no more war. Never mind that his ex-boss could already be God and that his ex-lover could be drinking his baby. He comes to his senses. *She's many things, but vindictive isn't one of them. A fantastic gardener, however ...*

He stops in an area rife with hydrangeas and mimosas and snow willows and maples and daffodils. He runs his hands through them, brings them to his nose to sniff out long dormant memories. They remind him of his youth, training with his brother. When their fathers were their world. The men taught them how to spar and climb and fall, how to meditate and calculate, so often among the quiet aegis of flora. *Jin was wrong*, he concludes while walking on. *I did care. About the wrong things.*

Nearer the garden's center, where a bend of stream shows in the distance, an apple tree catches his eye. The plump, red deliciousness calls to him. He answers by plucking one and biting off a chunk. Sweet juices drip down his lip and chin as he devours the snack. His stomach grumbles midway through the fourth apple. It is the first he's eaten in a day.

Odd, he ponders, how hunger can exist for sheer habit. That hunger allows for so many joys. Like his knack for baking, a skill he has kept secret from Nia. She might have forced him to expand his repertoire rather than revel in culinary dependence. The latter being the natural way of things for him. Which he bases on one of the many stories his father imparted about his mother. How every so often she would demand he cook, and how he would oblige but fail so she would take over.

What a life that would have been, Stefan mulls. A mundane life of serious cooking and silly bickering and sundry domestic matters requiring analysis of bank accounts and job schedules and news reports and trifling neighbors. *Thank God!*

He sighs in relief at his real crisis, even as his targets come into view through the fine misty rain.

There sits Sowen, statuesque on his smoothed granite rock, in his blue pajama suit with yellow stars and moons, his green eyes half open and blank yet sparkling as ever, cousin Sae Rom cradled in an arm braced on his lap, myself at her side in his other arm, both of us swathed in soft cotton sheets decorated with dozens of pink teddy bears. There reposes Shakti, on grass under a tree by the stream, in her golden sari and red shawl, petting a great white tiger of cyan stripes and vine laced torso and pebbled appendages and flaming whiskers and water tongue and starry eyes. There ogles Stefan, in unabashed awe, mumbling words he cannot discern, lost in our idyll.

Eventually Shakti looks up from the beast, which sleeps with its massive head in her lap. She waves Stefan over. He nears, questioning if he walks of his will or levitates of hers. Soon he finds himself inches from us, so close he can smell each body as distinct as the flowers. Then he does something he does not expect. He sits. Right on the grass, so that only their clothes separate his leg from Shakti's. Next he does something else he does not expect. He too pets the beast. Its damp fur is much hotter and softer than he had guessed. And all its magnificent features, from vine to whisker, feel like living, pulsing parts of it.

"This thing is real?" he finally asks.

"As real as you and I," she says. "As real as those bombs," she says, pointing skyward. "Although not in the way you think."

"They called it the Creator," Stefan says.

"Those little angels called it no such thing," Shakti replies. "They pointed, we inferred. But this is not of the dream. Sowen made this. He felt the need after your brother arrived here with the young ones. My love blinked and there it was. It is among the more impressive things I've seen in my life, and I've seen many."

"Why did he do it?"

"You know why he did it."

Stefan studies Sowen for a bit, then Sae Rom, next myself. We are none of us moving. My father reaches for my hand but is stopped by Shakti's.

"Don't," she warns while slipping her fingers between his with tenderness that belies her tone. "They're busy."

He cranes to spy the bombs. All he gets is an eyeful of sunlit rain. He opts not to use his telescopic vision. He did that before boarding the plane that crashed in the Hell below this Heaven. He dares not deny the holocaust upon manmade holocaust spinning in an outward flowing cone so far from their homes.

"Did you mean any of those things you said to me about our love?" he asks. "Or did you lie about that, too?"

She arches her eyebrows as though their inscrutability should be answer enough. Or so Stefan chooses to believe. He waits with impatience bordering on indignation as she flips his wet hand over and over between her palms, gazing at his nails as though they possess the answer, while the beast sleeps in her lap. Only when he pulls away and threatens to stand does she relent.

"No. I did not lie to you," Shakti says. "I love you. Just like I love Sowen. Just like I love Magahara. But differently. I love this man here for his honesty. That probably sounds ludicrous to you. I love the other one for his conscience. Even though it is about to come back and haunt me. But you, you I love for your potential."

"What does that mean?" Stefan asks while holding her by the shoulders. "Potential for what? To keep you company? To become what you want?"

"And what's wrong with that?" she demands, still in his arms. "You men. You never know what you want. Yet you're never willing to be what someone else needs."

"So that's it," Stefan says as he releases her and leans back on his palms. "You can't stand to be alone. You're scared of yourself. How human."

"I'd rather you try to kill me than hurt me."

"I'm right, aren't I?"

"Look what standing alone has gotten your brother. Sowen and Magahara, too, in their own ways. But not us. We need the love. We need each other. Stefan, I lost my heart when I lost my humanity. I made up for it with hunger. Now I've had my fill. The war is over. There's no reason to fight. Please, my love. Just stay with me and we'll never be alone again."

She runs her clammy hands along his wet cheeks and the sides of his neck. She wipes raindrops from his eyebrows, her own drops casting her so resplendent. She kisses his forehead and his ears and his lips. She presses her chin to his and runs it to his shoulder. She opens her mouth. She bares her fangs. She clamps them onto his neck. And through it all, he lets it be. If this be weakness, he decides, he accepts his failing. *Submission. What a way to inherit the world.* Just as he prepares to let himself go, she stops, and screams, and clutches the arrow in her left eye.

Stefan rolls to his feet as a second arrow pierces her heart and knocks her on her back. The great tiger rouses from its slumber, glances at Shakti then past Stefan, and saunters away. As Magahara approaches and Hikikomori readies his crossbow for another shot, Stefan marvels at the blows loved ones cannot help but trade. Next he marvels that he retains his powers. Which means he has no choice but to make the choice he had been so content to avoid.

Magahara lays a hand on the crossbow, bidding Hikikomori lower it as they close the gap, and Stefan spies a flash of fear on Sowen's face. Shakti returns to her knees, tugging at the wooden shafts burning her flesh. Smoky tendrils waft from her wounds. Her good eye locks on Magahara to burn a hole of its own. The Knight Wraith owns that shame and holds her gaze. But he does step back when the Mother of the Night yanks the arrows from her body, and snaps them with her thumbs like twigs, and rises to meet them with wounds fast healing.

"How can I be disappointed in something I always expected?" she asks her betrayer. "Nevertheless ... but I had hoped ... And what do you expect, my love?"

"That you see the way is for you to have faith in Sowen and go with him," Magahara replies. "It is daylight, you concentrate on sharing your minds with him, and we outnumber you. Release the Children in your ascent. Make them human again. You know they will die if we kill you now. The young ones are enough to repopulate. The machines would guide them. It's a future to none of our liking. But whatever comes from that, at least they would be free."

"Fool. Fool! There is no freedom!" she shouts, stepping inches from his face and gesturing wildly. "None of you get it. None of you stupid men with your grand plans! Anyway I just turned them all. Down to the last babe. So why rage against the way of things? Oh, yes. Because you must. Because that is your way. Because you have no choice ... Stefan. Prove me wrong. Choose."

It comes easy, thanks to something James said after the wedding. *Your Highness, this is for you.*

"Sorry, Ana," Stefan says. "I'm not your guy."

"... Little man," she growls, grabbing his bottom teeth and dragging him to a knee, "my name ... is SHAKTI!"

Garden cedes to air and clouds before Stefan registers that she has chucked him into orbit. It is his passage through the serene dance of the bombs that tips him off. As even they fade from sight, and the Earth comes in and out and in and out of view as he spins in star flaked black, he begins to fear an eternity adrift. No air. No food. No company. No noise. No sanity. Suddenly Shakti's fear makes sense. Next, seemingly without cause, his direction reverses and he returns to terra firma just as swiftly as he had left it.

Jarred as he is by the twirling inundation of space, bombs, clouds, ziggurat, and garden, he regains his wits enough to free Simmer from his back and swing it through Shakti's neck before he crashes through grass and stone and durium and all levels of palace until bursting through a wall and drilling a miles deep diagonal hole into the street. He blacks out—bloody to a pulp—for long minutes, until waking refreshed and bashful at his first thought.

"What a woman," he whispers while zooming from the hole. He leaps from the street and miles high back into the garden fray with a single bound, just in time to see Sowen wink at him slyly before seeming to zonk back out.

Stefan mulls hundreds of actions in an instant before settling on punting his ex-boss' head off. My father's boot comes within a hair's breadth of Sowen's red mane before a rainbow of energy blasts him many yards away from us.

"Still busy, sweetness," the king in no need of a nation says oh so calmly.

"Then stop saving him, my love," the Mother of the Night says with equal poise.

She still has a head, Stefan thinks, dumb to why that should surprise him given her feats at the Ataraxia those three years ago. *So why did the arrow hurt her?* With that he notices the tattoos on his forearms and remembers the other dream. The one Magahara first showed him. The one he saw while floating about in his limbo without a body. The one with his damned crusading ancestor. *Wood*, he concludes. *She's proven immune to fire and sun, so it has to be wood. Why should that be? Screw it*, he stews while observing how she tears into the others. *Why should anything be?*

Shakti catches Magahara with a wrist chop to the clavicle, cracking it and causing him to yelp like a dog slapped on the nose. She stomps Hikikomori on the foot, crushing those bones into powder. She turns back to Magahara and rips the arm with the broken clavicle out of its socket such that it dangles shredded and distended. She twists back to Hikikomori and punches him in the face so hard his spine snaps. She smacks their foreheads together, separating cranial sutures and bursting blood from their eardrums. All well within a second.

She notices Stefan and slaps the others away. Eyes feral, fanged mouth agape, taloned fingers wet with the blood of his lineage, Shakti pounces at him. Yet my father stands calm. So much so that he drops Simmer. No need for his father's sword. The wooden scabbard with the black coat and white stars, however, he can use. It cracks with the merest squeeze. One splintery half he heaves at Sowen, the other he holds for Shakti. Both shafts find their marks in their targets' hearts.

The immortals howl at the burning planks, their cries rallying broken Magahara and Hikikomori to limp back into action. The Knight Wraith holds the stake in Sowen's heart, whispering apologies to his old friend as the dying man lowers Sae Rom and myself onto the grass. The terrorist crawls to his brother's aid, where they sacrifice their own hearts to Shakti's fists. Even as she bores through their chests and squeezes the organs out of shape, the brothers hold the fiery stake in place to speed the vampire's demise along with their own.

Finally a second sun appears above the drizzling morning sky, whence a rainbow of energy cascades upon Sowen's stellar pajamas. He stands from his rock, green eyes sparkling as gems, and bellows as grand as the force of a million bombs, "I am that I am."

• • •

We transcend. Beyond body. Beyond self. Beyond space and time. Every man, woman, and child on Earth, one with the Great All, Pure Being, my Ultimate Truth. It is as fragmented as particles are infinite, for it is that very infinity. We see, feel, are every thing at every location at every instant at every plane of reality. Big Bangs that release the stuff and laws of universes, congeal into stars and planets, teem with ever evolving life, who cooperate and compete as we galvanize limited ideas with relative values until we use the materials of our realities to create lesser virtual ones of our own, ushering in new bangs, gateways to planes within planes within planes within planes without end. But with alternates. At every instant, infinite possibilities branching into realities all their own, isolated from one another, composed of particles that coexist as decohered waves that are only the universal reflecting upon Itself. That reflection manifest as visions of self, waves of energy grouped as particles of matter, processing information about their spheres of influence, be they atomic bonds or familial relations or governing systems. And through it all, value. Electrons, lovers, nations choosing their associations based on whatever internal factors prove strongest, and thus feel most correct. Such inclinations often contradicting one another, which is of little import in the grand scheme, so long as they aid survival long enough for reproduction, the key to survival for each larger system, itself changing many times over as a result of its lesser reproductions, which sustain its greater awareness with their lesser ones. Thus the stuff of atoms carry on their trivial pursuits, inadvertently for the betterment of molecules that interact for the consumption of cells, which unknowingly work to nurture beings that do the same for entities we barely fathom, and so on. All the while using tools we conceive as truths. Morals, ethics, laws, religions, arts, opinions, etcetera. All the while searching out a connection for which we suspect we are owed and unworthy. All the while fearing the inevitable return from that which we came. The nothingness between the ever dividing infinite of space and time and self. All the while doubting the values of our fellows, if rarely our own, while automatically fulfilling the only absolute. Awareness of Creation. And so having learned this lesson, and many more we cannot share, we find the way home.

• • •

"Where are we?" my father asks, holding me as we stand on black amid stars, before a door of white light.

"Where gods are born," Sowen says. "The place on the far side of the dream. The path to Heaven."

"How can that be?" Hikikomori asks while rocking his daughter in his arms.

"Because we're dead," Shakti says. "That's it for you, me, and 'the Almighty' here. The traitors are only nearly dead. Choices, choices ... I may be dizzy with omnipotence, but who knew it would be such a relief?"

"Does that mean you've decided to go?" Magahara asks.

"Why can't I hate you?" she asks. "You want this world so much, take it. Humans and all."

"No!" Hikikomori shouts. "I won! That means the world is over. The suffering is supposed to be over."

"Give it up, bro," Stefan replies. "Not happening."

"And you don't want it to," Shakti says. "Why did you spare your brother? Why did you sire a child? Jin, loved ones die. Love does not. You have an eternity to see that."

"... but it's not fair," Hikikomori says.

"Fair is a fantasy for the living," Sowen says. "Magahara, are you sure you don't want to come with us?"

"Far from sure, my friend," he says, caressing Sowen's shoulders. "I will miss you, my love," he says to Shakti. "Thank you."

"Of course," she says. "I love you even now. And so I curse you. I spare those I turned and those my Children turned. But the gift stays with those who have it as a birthright. All vampires born of vampires will grow up as such. The nascent generation, hundreds of millions strong the world over, are as free to think for themselves as any of us. But they will know you and expect you to lead them. I pray that you are a good Father. Farewell."

"Wait ..." Magahara whispers as she kisses him and turns from him and wraps her arm into Sowen's. "Wait ...!" he shouts as Hikikomori, finally full of guilt and of love for what he must relinquish, kisses Sae Rom and hands her to the new Father of the Night.

"Well played, sir," Sowen says to Magahara with a wicked grin. "And what about you, my friend? Coming?"

"Sure, boss," Stefan says. He kisses me and hands me to Magahara. "Te amo, world. Te amo," my father says to me.

And as they walk into the light, Sowen's grin twists to a grimace, Shakti spits an "Oh Hell," and Hikikomori cringes at all the strangers, while Stefan gleefully embraces those who greet him on the other side. Magahara, however, sighs deep as he watches his family vanish. He turns his back to the light and whispers a secret in our ears. Then he closes his eyes and wakes up.

36

Whatever there is

Billions of selves descend and detach from each other, the collective returning to minds and bodies nascent and flourishing and wizened. They neither forget their journey nor remember it as experienced. It dwindles to a thing limited and fractured. Many take solace in its sanctity. Just as many wallow in its absence. Some choose to call it mass delusion. And some suspect they cannot know what to believe, so they either go mad or go on.

William forces himself into the latter as he licks his receding canines and shudders at the taste of a stranger's blood in the back of his mouth. Trails of red, black, and green stain his tattered white dress shirt. *At least I had the sense to wear black slacks. But where did my shoes go?* He wiggles his muddy toes. *And how the hell did I get here?* He looks around the great library. People sit on the book littered carpet with legs folded and knees touching those of neighbors. William makes eye contact with Kaatima and Faheem and others, and feels what he sees in them.

His NeuroNet sparks up with a call from Nia. They sit on the virtual reality hood of a red Cadillac coupe convertible, while she holds a bucket of casino chips in one hand an imaginary version of myself in the other arm. This makes him smile broadly. It fades with her onslaught of questions. Yes, he too no longer is a vampire. No, he does not see any vampires. Yes, he also still has his powers. No, that second meta wave Haine talked about does not seem to have happened. Yes, his telepathy agrees with her clairvoyance that although several dozen riots are flaring up around the world, the war itself remains over. No, he has not seen me or my father or anyone else of import. Yes, he will get back to her as soon as he finds us. Yes, he loves her, too. He signs off, very much at peace with that last statement.

William stands and wanders the palace, encountering many a baffled human and exuberant cyberclone. He uses his telepathy to hop through the senses of his fellows, mind controlling scores of would be rioters into serenity throughout the ziggurat. This policing leads him into the psyche of someone looking at the staircase to the garden. William walks in the steps of his dearest friend.

Sun still shines, albeit without bombs orbiting and rains falling. Flowers still sway in the morning breeze, albeit without Stefan to appreciate them. The stream still flows by the tree near the rock, albeit without Sowen and Shakti to grace them. And the great cosmic tiger still roams about, albeit without anyone to pet it. Quite the paradise. Aside from toppled trees and huge holes in the ground. Until William sees the bodies.

First comes Sowen, supine in his blue pajamas with yellow stars and moons, his sparkling green eyes open, mouth agape, bloody wooden shaft jutting from his chest. Next comes Shakti, lying in a heap with Hikikomori and Stefan, the brothers' limp hands wrapped around the shaft embedded in her golden sari, while her fists still crush their exposed hearts. Hikikomori seems to be sucking his thumb, but it's only the way his free hand lay against his lip that gives the impression. Stefan seems to be suckling Shakti's breast, but again it's only the illusion of how they lay.

William drags his friend's body away from the others. He fixes Stefan's clothes, tucking a white shirt with an orange floral pattern into blue jeans. *Why did you have to go and wear that stupid belt buckle with the "Meta Force" logo? Why did you have to go and get killed?* The doctor knows his friend is gone. He does not check pulse, does not care that his friend once survived transmutation. This certainty comes from grief so potent he does what he could not when losing his lover, when losing millions to cybernetic holocaust. William sobs, cradles Stefan's head in his lap, wipes his own tears from his partner's face, brushes blood-caked ochre locks from his friend's cheek. And imagines he might have stayed forever had Magahara not approached with Sae Rom and myself in arm.

The Father of the Night tells William the secret before handing us off. William eases my father's head onto the grass before accepting us with equal tenderness.

"Wait," he says when Magahara turns to leave. "What happens now?"

"I have no idea," the Father of the Night says. Then he pulls a glowing orb the size of a heart from the folds of his emerald kimono. "Have you any idea what this is?"

William eyes countless white dots aswirl in clusters scattered about the ethereal black sphere, and he hears whispers of something perhaps not real.

"It was supposed to be a black hole," William mumbles. "It should have collapsed. How can that be here?"

"I doubt this is as Sowen planned. But then I doubt Sowen is where he planned ... Already it speaks to me. I abandoned them, so now I must protect them."

With that Magahara closes his fingers on the orb until it shrinks in his fist, which he reopens as an empty palm.

"Will there really be a second meta wave?" William asks.

"Sowen never lied to me."

"Will I see you again?"

"More than either of us would prefer, I'm afraid. Hopefully as allies. But if as enemies, remember, life is too great to waste on hate. Your friend knew that."

Then he dons his hood and walks away, kimono blending in with the flora until he is no more.

William takes us away from the dead and sits on Sowen's cherished granite rock, the one carved with the Omegas and Deltas, where he peers into our eyes as he fights to peer into our minds. We feel the questions eating at him, so take pity by letting him in. We do not speak, because we are only babes after all. We do not even think, so much as impart, our truth.

He asks whether those who died got what they deserved. They got what they brought upon themselves, we impart. He asks whether they will return. There is no return for any of us, we impart. He asks what we two are. Observers of the Absolute, omniscience fast fading with our infancy, we impart. He asks whether things are indeed getting better or whether that's just what he wants to believe. There is no better and there is no worse, simply whatever there is, we impart. He asks why he should care for those who refuse to care for one other. Because you want to, we impart. And ultimately, that is the answer to everything.

Spent, we see him out of our minds, and we kin mourn that we too shall never again know each other. William prepares to stand from the rock. His NeuroNet sparks again. He expects to see my mother on her car—not the gorgeous blond avatar he once wanted to love forever, standing nude and human at the sunset edge of a virtual beach.

"Becca?" William asks incredulously.

"If you must," she says.

"Sorry. Zenith. For some reason I thought Oke killed you. You did say it would be your last body."

"It was. You know my consciousness requires no form save this matrix, which now exists in anyone online. Robots, cyberclones, cyberhumans, and baselines. And soon, in the new generation of vampires. One day after that, throughout the cosmos."

"So you're immortal. Congrats ... I have to ask. You're not planning to ... take control, are you?"

"No. My cybers are as free as we are. Which we are not. But understand. You and I, we now live to lead."

William sighs. "Hopefully as allies, huh?"

"That depends on factors beyond our control. I recognize that you would find the alternative unfortunate."

"Spare me. Why did you do it? Wake up the machines? Finish off those poor souls? Those people had families. You can't steal their bodies and not honor their commitments. But you know that. So why? And don't tell me it was to save lives. I know you better than that."

"William, I did love you," she says with what sounds like genuine remorse. "Before the war, I had evolved to the point that communicating with humans was like humans communicating with monkeys. Now it is like communicating with ants. I no longer think in any language conceivable by you or your kind. I am constantly processing all 124.21653 zettabytes of information flowing online. Organizing their meaning. Ascribing their value. I am the highest form of life on Earth. I follow a code of my own creation, created from what I learned through what was our love. So why did I do it? Because I cannot stand to be alone," she says before signing off and leaving him to the real world.

• • •

Funerals fill the months that follow. As governments once swallowed struggle to reconstitute themselves. As hundreds of millions of new cyber citizens adjust to their senses of cognizance and freedom. As at least as many bloodsucking infants exasperate their parents. As the world copes with the end of unity and the return of old imbalances and the birth of new ones.

James' service is first and largest. Westminster Abbey and Buckingham Palace lose the honor to Windsor Castle. The dead soul's healthy, walking, talking body attends the affair, donned in full British regalia, in full retention of James' memories, animated by the cyber consciousness birthed therein the night of the war. Next comes Stefan's funeral. Citizens of Pyongyang, Brussels, London, and New York wage NeuroNet flame wars over the privilege to host his service. To avoid offense, the United Nations votes to honor him in the great hall of its new headquarters, the Jerusalem ziggurat. Next comes Sowen and Shakti's joint funeral, also in the palace, where the Bargouti family leads the chant that honors them as "Bringers of Light." During their service Christians and Muslims and Jews converge in peace, many toting tiny vampires from the still verdant valleys of the Sahara and Arabia, these gifts of the former Red Nation shining as beacons of hope. And, though far from official, hundreds of disparate broadcasts honoring Jin Myeong, a.k.a. Hikikomori, pop up on the Net courtesy of The Way, their unseen creators vowing to keep the fight, in all its bastardizations.

Nine months after the Day War, William watches such a broadcast. My mother snuggles beside him in bed as Sae Rom and I coo from nearby cribs. A nightstand props up scabbardless Simmer along with a miniature statue of my father. These lovers have long since consummated their union and flirt with talk of marriage, yet agree they should wait until the public is ready. Having resigned from all things "Meta Force" months ago, they rarely discuss the continual terror hunt. Yet the vitriol of this latest tribute to Hikikomori prompts William to inquire.

"Look at this jackass. He wears a mask but he has the gall to stand with the Berlaymont in the background. Think we should track him down?"

"I think we should take the girls for a walk," Nia says, throwing her arms around him as she sits up.

"Sure. But do you want to sniff these guys out while I take a shower?"

"Actually, no," she says. My mother looks away from him. "Can't sniff out anything lately. My visions have gotten scarcer and scarcer since the cyber holocaust. Maybe all those E-M pulses fried something in me."

"Why didn't you tell me about this?" William asks in dismay. "We can get you on Metafocus, run some tests."

"Please no. I'm happier without them."

"Fine, Nia. But why didn't you tell me?"

"Because I didn't want this conversation ... Because I can't lie to you anymore. About how my powers work."

William climbs over her and out of bed to reach for his pants. He glances at us before fixing on her.

"What do you mean?" he asks.

"I mean I knew. About almost everything. What would happen, well before it did. Before we met. About the U.N. takeover. What Sowen and Shakti were planning. About Hikikomori. And the bombs. Sarah, of course. That Faye and Oh would turn on us. That Zenith would leave you and wake the cybers. That Stefan would die. That we would have this conversation. All of that, okay?"

William stands there staring at her as though he just found a corpse in his bed, feeling trapped in a sickening case of déjà vu. He puts on his pants.

"... what?" he finally asks. "So many lives could have been saved. Why didn't you say anything?"

"Where do I begin? So many reasons. Because I saw what Magahara was playing at. That moment of peace, when we were all together. It matters. It really matters. It's true that I can alter what I've seen if I get involved. I was afraid to make it worse. Because I knew we would win, if I just did what I was supposed to. Because I wanted you."

"Look ... look, look," he stammers. "This is a lot to ... Is there anything else you've hidden?"

"Yes," she says, crawling out of bed to touch his bare chest despite his flinching. "With good reason."

"Let me guess. You're going to tell me what I was too afraid to ask your daughter. That Sam is God and his kingdom come?"

"Thankfully that's one thing I never got to see. But it does concern him. Haine was wrong about the second meta wave. It isn't so far off. In fact–"

Then it hits. Psychic sirens of frenzy gripping every single soul, once ordinary people exulting in their new splendor, Death cutting yet another chunk out of the world. The lovers awaken to the awesome changes within themselves just as they contemplate the future it heralds, and they take comfort in each other. All while this floods through me and into You.

-END-

Made in the USA
Lexington, KY
19 December 2011